DATE

AMERICA'S
LONGEST WAR

AMERICA'S LONGEST WAR

Rethinking Our Tragic Crusade Against Drugs

STEVEN B. DUKE AND ALBERT C. GROSS

Foreword by The Honorable Kurt L. Schmoke,
Mayor of Baltimore

A JEREMY P. TARCHER / PUTNAM BOOK
Published by G. P. Putnam's Sons / New York

A Jeremy P. Tarcher/Putnam Book
Published by G. P. Putnam's Sons
Publishers Since 1838
200 Madison Avenue
New York, NY 10016

    Jeremy P. Tarcher, Inc.
    5858 Wilshire Blvd., Suite 200
    Los Angeles, CA 90036
Published simultaneously in Canada

Library of Congress Cataloging-in-Publication Data

Duke, Steven B.
    America's longest war : rethinking our tragic crusade against drugs /
Steven B. Duke and Albert C. Gross.
      p.   cm.
    "A Jeremy P. Tarcher/Putnam book."
    Includes bibliographical references and index.
    ISBN 0-87477-541-8 (hc : acid-free paper)
    1. Narcotics, Control of—United States. 2. Drug abuse—United
States. 3. Drug legalization—United States. I. Gross, Albert C.
II. Title.
HV5825.D93   1994
363.4'5'0973—dc20   93-17357 CIP

Design by Irv Perkins Associates, Inc.

Printed in the United States of America
  2 3 4 5 6 7 8 9 10

This book is printed on acid-free paper.
    ∞

To our children, and to the memory of Paul Reynolds

Contents

ACKNOWLEDGMENTS

WE WISH to express our appreciation to the many people who helped us write this book. Without their generous contributions, much would be missing, although the opinions and all the shortcomings of the book are of course our own responsibility.

We are grateful for the helpful comments on various excerpts by professors Charles Reich and Harlon Dalton of Yale Law School, and by Professors Joanne Conaghan, Charles Wiggins and Chris Wonnell, of the University of San Diego School of Law, by Professor Samuel Fetters of Syracuse Law School, by Yale Law School students Michele Anderson and Adrian LeBlanc, and by attorney Bruce Abbott. Publisher William F. Buckley, Jr., Princeton University professor Ethan Nadelmann and Rand Corporation economist Peter Reuter provided useful insights in telephone interviews. Corporate drug program consultant Robert Arganbright not only shared his extensive knowledge of the drug-abuse field and commented on parts of the manuscript, but also located many valuable newspaper and magazine articles.

Publications consultant Michael Johnson, judicial attorney Charles McKain, school psychologist John Pappas, educator Stephen Tadlock and administrator Peggy Whan helped us clarify ideas for the book by discussing or debating the issues. So did artist-author Bert Dodson and environmentalist Bonnie Dodson, advertising executive Ira Ginsburg, sociologist Roberta Ginsburg, and countless students and colleagues at the Yale Law School.

Attorneys Charles Andre, Lynn Casey, Christian Paul, Hal Tyvoll, and Herbert Pounder, medical technician Mary Lare, and engineer Paul Reynolds provided crucial insights and important sources of information.

Susanne Bacon, of the Lexis Corporation, provided invaluable assistance by helping us locate essential research sources from her company's computer data base. Gene Coakley of the Yale Law School Library was especially generous and resourceful in finding for us primary and secondary sources. We could not have written the book without his help.

We are indebted for the contributions of researchers Hank Garfield, Pamela MacKinnon, and Gloria Tierney, historian David Ritchie, attorneys Emily Shieh and Kevin Skehan, and journalists Allan Bock and Dean Latimer.

Dr. H. Wayne Carver II, Chief Medical Examiner of Connecticut, taught us much about drugs, toxicology, and causes of death.

Peter Ortego, a student at the University of Colorado School of Law, Luke Ryan of the University of San Diego School of Law, Curtis Mulkey and Gina Nagler of Golden Gate Law School, and Yale Law School students Roger Citron, Diana Jarvis, Carla Jones, Miriam Longchamp, Richard Manaloff, and Renee McDonald provided invaluable research assistance. The assistance of some went well beyond research.

Dave Fratello, Assistant Director of Public Information, Drug Policy Foundation, and Eric E. Sterling, Coordinator, National Drug Strategy Network, read a draft and made many valuable suggestions.

We thank Eunice Heidman, who word-processed parts of the manuscript and also called on her skills as a librarian to create a computer data base from thousands of newspaper and magazine clippings on drug topics. We also wish to express our appreciation to Sarah Nord, Susan Gonzales and, especially, Jill Tobey, for their superb secretarial assistance.

Richard St. John, a Stanford undergraduate, helped us with both research and editing.

Literary agent Richard Curtis helped bring this project to fruition by remaining supportive during its more difficult moments. We are also grateful to editors Rick Benzel and Hank Stine and publisher Jeremy Tarcher, who took an active interest in the book from start to finish.

Dean Guido Calabresi and the Yale Law School provided generous financial support of research.

FOREWORD

ON APRIL 25, 1988, I addressed the U.S. Conference of Mayors, in Washington, D.C. Although my speech that day was about anticrime measures in Baltimore, in a few brief paragraphs at the end I spoke about one of the most important issues facing America—the failure of our national drug policy. In doing so, I set out to accomplish three goals: First, to call attention to the fact that the prosecution and incarceration of substance abusers will not stop either drug abuse or drug-related crime. (I learned that first hand as Baltimore State's Attorney, where in spite of prosecuting thousands of drug offenders, drug trafficking and violent crime simply grew worse.) Second, to urge the American people in general, and my fellow mayors in particular (whose cities suffer the brunt of drug addiction and crime) to enter into a constructive debate about viable alternatives to the wasteful war on drugs. And third, to spark a change from our current policy of using the criminal law to fight drugs to a policy that emphasizes public health strategies.

I achieved my first objective almost as soon as I spoke to the U.S. Conference of Mayors. The speech received immediate attention from the press and public. Since 1988, I have addressed numerous organizations, including law-enforcement agencies, with the simple message that the criminal law is not an effective tool against addiction and drug-related crime. On the contrary, tough laws against possession, along with mandatory minimum sentences, serve only to keep jails filled beyond capacity and the profits from illegal drugs high. And it is those profits that create the crime that is plaguing communities across our country.

My second objective—promoting a national debate on drug policy—is being achieved. In September 1988, Congress conducted hearings on the question of national drug policy. The media began taking a second look at the efficacy of the war on drugs. And over the last five years, I've received hundreds of letters from ordinary citizens who want to add their voice to the debate.

I recognize that the national weight of opinion favors our current policy. Nevertheless, the debate that has gone on since 1988 has been useful. It has also changed some minds. Respected jurists, including federal judges, have come out in favor of changing national drug policy. A resolution calling for a new national commission to study drug policy has been signed by leaders in medicine, law, economics, and criminal justice. Thus the debate, of which this book is a part, continues and must continue, because we are not winning the war on drugs.

A December 1991 National Institute of Drug Abuse survey showed that the number of weekly cocaine users increased 29 percent in 1991. Moreover, there is every reason to believe that the total number of cocaine and heroin users is much higher than the NIDA survey indicates since the survey is based on volunteered information. In Baltimore, the number of drug addicts has remained stable at around 40,000. Another sign that the war on drugs is being lost is the increase in violent crime. Nationally, 1991 and 1992 were the most violent years ever. And 1993 is likely to be worse. Many cities had record numbers of murders, a large proportion of which were drug related. Many of the victims of these murders were simply innocent bystanders who happened to get caught in the middle of a violent battle over drug turf or money.

Where will the national drug policy debate go from here? What is needed is objective analyses of our current strategy and sensible proposals to support or refute that strategy. I, for example, strongly support a national commission to determine how all drugs—legal and illegal—should be regulated. I have also formed a drug-policy working group in Baltimore to recommend harm-reduction policies. Others, including the authors of this book, are analyzing the flaws in the current system and looking for alternatives. All of this work, much of which is going on in universities and think tanks, constitutes an important contribution to the debate on national drug policy and must continue.

My third objective for my speech at the U.S. Conference of Mayors—changing national policy to a public health strategy—has not yet been achieved. This may in part be due to the fact that many people still do not understand what advocates of a public-health strategy want. A public-health strategy is an effort to treat drug abuse as a medical problem rather than a crime problem. This strategy is not legalization, that is, the sale of drugs in the private market as now occurs with alcohol and cigarettes. The term I use is "medicalization." It is a policy that treats drug abuse as a disease to be handled by competent medical professionals. The government, *not* the criminal traffickers, would control the price, distribution, purity, and access to addictive substances. This would take most of the profits out of drug trafficking. A public-health strategy would also give drug abusers the opportunity to receive the treatment they need and would make it easier to keep drugs *out* of the hands of children.

Although the majority of Americans probably oppose dropping criminal sanctions against drug users, I believe there has been a gradual shift toward accepting the need for more treatment and alternatives to incarceration. This strategy is already being tried with considerable success in the Netherlands, and should be adopted in the United States as well.

In sum, even though a national public-health strategy is a long way from being adopted, the philosophical underpinnings for such an approach are gaining currency. Those underpinnings—that addiction is a disease to be treated and that criminal sanctions create far more crime than they stop—are further explored in this book. I commend this book to you, as a clear and complete analysis of all the important issues in the debate. Reading it provoked my thought; I hope it will provoke yours too. Out of the debate, facilitated by this book and others, we should find a safer and more humane way to treat the devastating disease of substance abuse.

—KURT L. SCHMOKE
Mayor of Baltimore

PREFACE

AMERICA HAS been using the force of criminal law against its citizens to punish them for consuming disfavored drugs for nearly eighty years. The intensity of those efforts has frequently been described as a "war." As such, it is America's longest and most self-destructive war.

One of the casualties of war is truth. A prime example of that occurred on September 5, 1989. On that day, in his first television speech to the nation as President, George Bush stared into the cameras, held up a clear plastic package marked "evidence," and solemnly intoned that he was drastically escalating the "war."[1] The President was not speaking of war against another nation or against an evil leader; he was talking about a war against a class of inanimate objects—illicit drugs.

Inside the package that the President held aloft was rock cocaine, harvested earlier that day from Keith Jackson, a nineteen-year-old dope peddler enticed by law-enforcement officials to a drug sting in Lafayette Park, across the street from the White House. Far from being a regular trader at that venue, Jackson needed travel directions from his sham "customers" to enable him to find the White House. The purpose of the staged drug deal was to permit the President to suggest that drugs were being dealt virtually on the steps of the White House, and thus that the country was in grave peril. Such theatrics are reminiscent of the "unprovoked attack" on American ships in the Gulf of Tonkin that triggered our war against North Vietnam.[2]

Since Keith Jackson invaded Lafayette Park, the federal government's annual spending in the war against drugs has doubled. Civil liberties have been curtailed at almost every turn in the interest of the drug-war effort. As with the Vietnam war, moreover, our leaders have repeatedly seen the light at the end of the tunnel.

As in most wars, numbers emerge that suggest that victory may be on its way. Casual use of illegal drugs appears to have taken a downturn, not since President Bush escalated the war against drugs, but since 1980. However, the number of people who use cocaine weekly, "the addicts," virtually doubled since 1985. Thus, we are told, the war seems to be "working" with the casual user—the middle-class experimenter. However, it seems to be having little impact on hard-core addicts who may be willing to steal or kill to feed their cravings.

Crime rates have been in a general uptrend in this country for three decades despite a strong force in the opposite direction: the aging of the population. Teenagers, who commit a disproportionate share of our violent crimes, are a smaller and smaller proportion of the population. Still, in many of our cities, murder rates are at record highs, reflecting turf wars between rival drug dealers, and other drug-related violence. The drug war has made these problems worse, not better.

George Bush was not the first president to invoke the imagery of war in an effort to induce the nation to support his antidrug efforts. President Reagan declared a war against drugs in October 1982, in a radio address to the nation. President Nixon, almost a decade before that, had labeled drugs "public enemy number one" and declared "all-out global war on the drug menace." Victory has never been in sight. On the contrary, except for minor setbacks and lulls, the enemy has steadily advanced during that period. The drug problem, broadly understood, has never been worse in this country than it is today.

We are spending more than $12 billion a year on the drug problem at the federal level and far more at the state, city, corporate, and private levels. Fifty billion dollars in annual expenditures to curb our national consumption of illegal drugs is a reasonable estimate.

We are losing perhaps $100 billion per year more in drug-related crime, medical costs, and lost productivity. Another $60 to $100 billion is spent every year by consumers to purchase the illicit drugs themselves. The total annual cost of the "drug problem" in dollars, therefore, may be as much as $200 billion, more than the entire annual deficit only a few years ago.

That estimate does not take account of what we spend on the two major licit drugs, alcohol and tobacco, the true costs of which may exceed those of the illegal drugs.

Nor does it include another figure that, if measurable, would make the others appear microscopic in comparison. Throughout our nation, in city after city, drug dealing and the violence and intimidation that accompany it have converted family neighborhoods into war zones and fear-ridden, rat-infested slums. Gangs of hoodlums fire automatic weapons at each other, killing innocent bystanders. Life in many inner cities has become unbearable; and the schools, filthy fiefdoms of the drug gangs. The destruction of property values attributable to the commerce in illegal drugs is staggering. Block after block of the once-stately residential buildings in our inner cities is simply being abandoned to crack dealers or other criminals.

At the same time, health and welfare expenditures are being drastically reduced, cities are literally going bankrupt, needed schools and libraries are closing, police and fire department staffing and budgets are being reduced, our doors are closed to the homeless, and taxes and deficits are soaring.

Many of our most serious social problems are directly related to the intensity of the war against drug distribution and use. Most drug overdoses, including poisonings from contaminated drugs, are attributable to the illegality of the market. The possibility of a family life is eliminated for thousands of children because one or both parents are jailed for a drug-related offense. Our prison population has doubled in seven years, and one in four black males in his twenties is either in jail, on probation or on parole, mostly for drug-related offenses. As much as half our violent and property crime may be related to drug prohibition: either committed as part of a drug-distribution scheme or to get money with which to buy and consume illegal drugs. Both the human and the economic costs of the drug war are staggering.

Our aim is to examine the effects of intense criminalization of drug commerce on both the consumption of drugs and the health of our basic institutions. The victims of wars are never limited to the enemy; innocent people and precious institutions are also damaged and die. This is as true of a "war on drugs" as it is of a real war. We also explore and applaud alternatives: drug education and treatment for drug abuse.

People are induced to change their behavior by education—increasing their knowledge of the behavior itself, by threats or inducements, or a combination of both, together with appeals to morality. The war on drugs utilizes all these methods, but the emphasis is on the punitive. Nearly two-thirds of the federal drug budget is earmarked for law enforcement. Drug dealers receive savage sentences, even life without possibility of parole. There is talk about imposing the death penalty on them or even shooting them on sight. Drug consumers are also being punished, most noticeably by forfeiture of their homes, cars, boats and other valuables merely because they were used to consume or store small quantities of marijuana or other drugs. For the first time in our nation's history, the federal government now claims the right to compel schools and colleges to punish students who use or possess illicit drugs. Judges are now authorized to suspend licenses and welfare and other benefits of those convicted of drug offenses. Efforts to ferret out and punish drug criminals have intensified, and courts increasingly approve deprivations of civil liberties in the name of drug-war necessity. These efforts threaten to destroy much that is fundamental and unique about America and its Constitution. The costs of conducting the war might be justified were a Hitler invading our shores, but are they warranted when the enemy is a chemical that is harmless unless ingested by human beings?

Our conclusion, like that of a growing and articulate chorus, is that the costs are not remotely justified; that much of the drug-war artillery is worthless and in many cases is counterproductive. The casualty rates among those who have nothing to do with illegal drugs is unacceptable. We also assess the arguments in favor of "legalization" and conclude that regulated legalization—though not unfettered availability—should be pursued.

We do not lightly arrive at the pro-legalization conclusion, nor did it originate with us. Once an unthinkable—or at least unmentionable—solution to major aspects of the drug problem, legalization is now an option seriously proposed by prestigious publications such as *The Economist,* statesmen such as George Shultz, jurists such as Robert Sweet, academicians such as Milton Friedman and Ethan Nadelmann, social commentators such as William F. Buckley, Jr., and Ernest van Den Haag, law-enforcement officers such as former San Jose police chief Joseph McNamara, and politicians such as Mayor Kurt Schmoke of Baltimore. Those advocates have made some convincing arguments for legalization, and in the pages that follow we will present them, as well as our own, for this drastic though sensible remedy for an intolerable status quo.

We concede that the issue is debatable; that reasonable policymakers can differ on whether heroin and cocaine, like tobacco and alcohol, should be freely available, at low cost, to any adult desiring to purchase them. A rational case cannot be made, however, for the garrison state that we are in the process of creating. Long after the appetite for currently illicit drugs has subsided or been transferred to lawful drugs or other substitutes—or we have decided to permit our people to make their own decisions about chemical use—we will need our institutions and our civil liberties. The battles to recapture our liberty and our integrity may be fiercer and even more formidable than the drug wars in which they were lost.

Chapter 1

An Overview: The Greater Evil

"The chief cause of problems is solutions."

ERIC SEVAREID[1]

IF THERE is a single key to understanding America's "drug problem," it is recognizing the difference between the costs of drug use per se and the costs of efforts to prevent drug consumption. Most of the current rhetoric obscures the difference. Those who want to step up the drug "war" typically attribute all the killings, bribery, corruption, and drug-related crime to the "drugs" themselves and the commerce in them. Those who believe in de-escalating the war, or even legalizing drugs, on the other hand, often declare that the problem is not drug consumption itself, but rather the *criminalization* of drugs. The true problem, they assert, is not drugs but contemporary "solutions" to the "drug problem."

Neither position is completely correct. There are two components of the "drug problem," both of which are "but for" causes of our dreadful drug disease. The first is the human appetite for drugs and the costs of feeding that appetite. This is the baseline "drug problem" that would exist in a free market where the government took a neutral stance on consumption of and commerce in drugs. The second component is the effect or consequence of efforts to prevent commerce in drugs; the costs and casualties of the war itself, to revisit the military

1

metaphor. Both components in combination are the cause of our current malaise. Neither alone accounts for anything, because neither exists alone. The claimants are right, however, in emphasizing the need, analytically, to separate the two parts of the problem. Understanding is otherwise literally impossible.

THE EVILS OF DRUG CONSUMPTION PER SE

Although we will return to most of these matters in detail later, a brief sketch of the evils of drug usage in a hypothetical free market is needed here, to clarify the issues to be discussed hereafter.

Adverse Effects on Physical Health

The specific health effects of particular recreational drugs are often hotly debated scientific questions, and we attempt to analyze the data and draw whatever conclusions are possible later in the book. At this point we simply note that some of the recreational drugs, such as tobacco and alcohol, commonly cause major long-term illnesses or life-threatening acute health crises for habitual users. Prolonged tobacco use causes cancer and cardiovascular illness, alcohol abuse causes cirrhosis of the liver and other illnesses, and cocaine, if snorted, can cause damage to nostrils and nasal membranes. If smoked, cocaine may cause lung damage. However consumed, cocaine can occasionally kill its user. Marijuana, if smoked, might cause lung cancer, although that has not been established. Marijuana is often blamed for genetic damage and suppression of the immune response, but the evidence warranting these concerns is weak.

The risks of psychoactive drug use are substantial but no greater than those accompanying many other recreational activities. The task for policymakers is to assess the relative risks of illegal drugs and compare those risks to others we take—or permit others to take—with hardly any qualms—hang-gliding, motorcycle riding, hunting, bicycle riding, boating, boxing, mountain climbing and so forth. Having made such comparisons, policymakers should then decide what we are willing to pay for efforts to reduce or control the risks of taking drugs. The risks are not nearly as great as is commonly supposed, nor can they be eliminated by prohibition. (In fact, the risks are increased by prohibition.)

Criminogenics

Promotion of public health is not the only basis on which drug prohibitionists attempt to justify the current distinctions between legal and illegal drugs. Prohibitionists also claim that certain drugs are "criminogenic"; that is, the use of those drugs directly causes the user to commit crimes. Our drug history is replete with fears and phobias on that subject. Cocaine, for example, was said to make African-American men bulletproof and inordinately dangerous. Opium was said to make the Chinese users sex fiends, and marijuana made murderers and rapists of Hispanic Americans. The facts are far more prosaic. There is no evidence that heroin or marijuana are at all criminogenic in this sense. If anyone ever "went crazy" on any of these substances and committed a violent crime, it has never been reliably recorded. Alcohol is another matter. There is evidence, albeit not as compelling as is popularly supposed, that alcohol contributes importantly to violent crimes such as murder, robbery and rape. It is clearly a causal factor in reckless and negligent homicide, especially when automobiles are involved.

The criminogenics of cocaine are unclear. It seems likely, however, that the depression, anxiety, and emotional instability often experienced by cocaine abusers is positively associated, in a causal sense, with crimes of violence. There is, however, a further complicating question: whether the criminogenic effects are directly attributable to cocaine intoxication, as in the case of alcohol, or are attributable instead to cocaine withdrawal. To the extent that violent crimes are traceable to cocaine withdrawal, they should be discounted if not disregarded, for in our hypothetical free market, involuntary withdrawal from cocaine would be uncommon. To consider the criminogenics of withdrawal as a cost of drug usage rather than of drug prohibition would make little more sense than to count the criminal consequences of tobacco withdrawal as part of the criminogenics of tobacco.

Accidents

One can hardly be unaware of the danger posed by abusers of alcohol and other drugs who drive cars, command oil tankers or operate other machinery. About 12,000 people are killed every year *because* an automobile driver was intoxicated.

The strongest case exists against alcohol, but some accidents are attributable to other drugs, including even tobacco.

Effects on Work and Incentives to Work

The conventional belief is that drug users—particularly users of illicit drugs—are an irresponsible, unproductive lot. There are, however, many difficulties in drawing inferences about cause and effect. Abusers of psychoactive drugs, whether legal or illegal, are also an unhappy lot. Some are mentally ill. The abuse of drugs may be a symptom of their depression and hopelessness, or a poorly managed self-medication.

The irresponsibility and apparent laziness of many drug abusers is due in some measure to the illegality of their drug use. Drug users who are paying $200 per day for their drugs can hardly be expected to work happily at a fast-food outlet for minimum wage. It is also impossible for many drug users to hold many of today's jobs, for their drug use would soon be discovered by testing. In addition, abusers of illegal drugs inevitably associate with others who condone their habits, and the subculture that does so largely rejects the values of Horatio Alger, Jr.

The anti-motivational effects of illegal drug use are, in any event, greatly exaggerated. Many, perhaps most, parents of teenagers who use illegal drugs are unaware that their children use such drugs. This is also commonly the case in marriages where one spouse secretly uses drugs. One can argue, of course, that family members do "know" at some level but are engaged in "denial." Even so, "denial" could hardly be such a common experience if the antimotivational effects of drug use were palpably obvious.

Effects on Quality of Life

When any substance is used excessively, the quality of life is diminished both for the users and those around them. No doubt many of the 10 million or so Americans classified as alcoholics would consider themselves better off if they did not drink to excess. The lives of many are wrecked by alcoholism and the families of alcoholics are miserable. But 90 percent or so of the consumers of alcohol, who are not obsessed with it and who could give it up if strongly motivated, believe that alcohol makes a positive contribution to their happiness and even the happiness of their friends and families. Consumption of alcohol is deeply ingrained in the American culture, is part of many religious ceremonies, and accompanies—and lubricates—most celebrations, whether a national holiday, a wedding, or a dinner party.

Drugs that America regards as illicit provide equivalent pleasures to many, far greater pleasures to some, and this has been true for centuries, in most cultures. In fact, use of both opiates and cocaine was common among upright citizens in America and elsewhere in the latter half of the nineteenth century. Freud used cocaine and advocated it as a cure for fatigue, foggy thinking and many other conditions. Several of our presidents,[2] including perhaps even the abstemious Abraham Lincoln,[3] also used cocaine. Ulysses S. Grant was apparently a user of both morphine and cocaine, as well as alcohol and tobacco.[4]

We do not produce these examples to besmirch historical figures, but to show that it is the modern stigma attached to drugs—not any inherent quality of the chemicals—that makes their use shocking. As reported by Edward Brecher, when these drugs were legal and were as widely, if not more widely, used as they are today, few serious problems with their use were noted.[5] Few users found such drugs to interfere seriously with the quality of their lives.

If the reader finds this difficult to accept, it may be because we have for so long associated the use of drugs with secretiveness, dishonesty, stealing and irresponsibility. But much of that is the result of criminalization. It is necessary to cover up what one is consuming, and to lie about it, if the consumption is criminal (and if one must associate with drug dealers in order to acquire it). It may also be necessary to steal in order to buy the drug if, as is the case with cocaine and heroin, it is very expensive.

Although the evidence is inconclusive, we think that the use of heroin and cocaine in a free market system would adversely affect the quality of the lives of the users and those around them in a way not appreciably different than does alcohol use. Roughly the same proportions of users would become abusers, and their abuse would be approximately as crippling to life's other enterprises as abuse of alcohol.[6] But the total *number* of drug abusers in a free market system would not be essentially different than is the case in our hybrid system of legalization. In a free market system hardly anyone would be a drug abuser who does not already abuse at least one psychoactive drug. The negative contributions of marijuana would be far less than heroin, cocaine, *or* alcohol.

THE EVILS OF EFFORTS TO PREVENT THE USE OF DRUGS

Weighing against the evils of recreational-drug consumption are a multitude of evils caused by efforts to prevent drug use. Our drug-war approach relies heavily on criminalizing both sale and use of illicit drugs.

Global Evils

We now consider as a violator of American criminal law anyone who knowingly participates in any phase of the process whereby drugs are introduced into this country. Tens of thousands of Peruvians, Bolivians, Colombians, Burmese, Thais, Pakistanis, and Jamaicans are therefore technically guilty of American criminal offenses even though they have never come near our borders and would be surprised to learn that they are American criminals. This includes peasant farmers eking out a meager existence for their families as well as smugglers.

Our government has also become a kidnapper. Our drug agents have actually gone to South America, kidnapped suspected drug kingpins and forcefully brought them to the United States for trial.[7] In the case of Manuel Noriega, we did it on a grand scale, sending our army to invade Panama, in part for the unprecedented purpose of kidnapping the leader of another sovereign nation and bringing him to the United States for trial.

We engage in extensive and costly efforts to persuade foreign authorities to arrest and extradite their citizens who have violated our drug laws. Sometimes we succeed. We even urge the governments of these countries to prosecute their drug producers under their own laws, and to eradicate their crops, destroy their labs, and otherwise to make it costly for drug producers or exporters to operate. The result of these activities is to force the major drug producers to create their own armies and to terrorize the officials of their countries into permitting their continued operation. The governments in country after country in South and Central America are perpetually destabilized.

Interdiction Evils

Drugs produced elsewhere for our markets have to clear our border. That is not difficult. Most authorities estimate that at least 90 percent of the illicit drugs destined for the United States are successfully smuggled into the country. But the smuggling process, involving high-tech boats and airplanes, sophisticated secretion of the drugs and counterintelligence that often involves bribery of our officials, is also very costly. Once the drug actually crosses our border, its caretakers, consignees and purchasers on this side of the border are under much greater risk of being caught, convicted and imprisoned. As a result, the free market price of cocaine and heroin is increased between 70 and 140 times![8] Imported commodities that would cost *in toto* perhaps a hundred million dollars in a free market cost $60 to $100 *billion* under prohibition.

The money spent by Americans on imported drugs is hard for the smugglers to get out of the United States. Moreover, America is still a pretty good place in which to invest and a wonderful place in which to spend and enjoy wealth. Consequently, the drug importers try to keep a substantial portion of their funds in the United States. They need banks to cooperate, either to get the money out of this country or to convert it into usable forms if left here. Hence, the money launderers who help smugglers disguise their funds as legitimate. Since money laundering is a crime, recruiting and maintaining money launderers is expensive. Getting the money out of the country without having it confiscated is also costly and often involves bribery. The entire process corrupts and burdens domestic and international financial systems.

To make the smuggling of drugs more costly and less attractive, we punish money launderers, but to the extent we are successful, we help to push the money out of our banks and out of our industries. The money is either stashed away or physically exported in trucks, planes, ships and cars to other countries. We thus deprive ourselves of billions of dollars of potential investments.

Corruption Costs

What is the result of all this money flowing in illegal, clandestine channels among armies of criminals whose lives are under constant threats from within or without? Corruption of policemen by the hundreds. Prosecutors, judges, legislators, lawyers, bail bondsmen, witnesses, jailers, are all under great corrupting influences, and many succumb. Our federal judges are among the least corruptible in the world; scandal rarely touches them, yet U.S. district judge Robert Collins was recently convicted of accepting bribes in a drug case,[9] and

U.S. district judge Walter Nixon was convicted of perjury in a drug-case investigation.[10]

Only one time before in our history was corruption of our law-enforcement officials arguably a more serious problem, and that was during our efforts to enforce alcohol prohibition. The corruption during Prohibition may have been greater than it is now, but there are reasons to fear that we will eventually exceed that level if we continue on our present course. Illegal-whiskey merchants during Prohibition were not under constant threat of death from their competitors—except in Chicago and a few other places—and the threat of long prison terms was not nearly as great either. Nor was the money nearly as plentiful. Both the utility of and the opportunity for bribery were therefore more limited than is the case today.

Crippling Our Criminal Justice System

This comprehensive process of intensive criminalization, our "war on drugs," undermines our criminal-justice process. It diverts resources needed by police, prosecutors and courts for dealing with other crime, thus exacerbating our crime problems. It generates billions in cash that makes murderers out of otherwise petty criminals. Those who are not moved by money to murder are motivated to commit it to silence witnesses and otherwise to defeat the efforts of law enforcement. The indirect cause is, ironically, the very same force that ostensibly wants to protect witnesses: the law enforcement enterprise.

Treating illicit-drug distribution as tantamount to treason, the attitude embraced by the most ardent drug warriors, undermines the rule of law and the freedom of nonusers in myriad ways. Shortcuts and circumventions of the Constitution are overlooked in the name of drug-war necessity, and criminal convictions in drug cases are subjected to little scrutiny. Rights of individuals to privacy of their homes, effects and persons are routinely subordinated to the interests of the government in carrying out the drug war.

Seduction of Our Children

The multibillion-dollar drug business seduces our young away from more mundane, longer-term efforts to achieve material and social success in an increasingly competitive economic system. Educational efforts are hampered by the presence of the dandies in fancy clothes and costly cars who are so conspicuous in America's lower-income neighborhoods. A decade ago many of us were worried that the existence of the millionaire basketball player was sending an unrealistic, seductive message to our young people that diverted them from serious education. The major rival of that image is now the corner drug dealer. The huge salaries of professional athletes are no longer perceived as a major problem but rather as part of the solution: persuade our youngsters that they can get rich playing basketball or football or prizefighting, and they may spend their free time in gyms rather than running dope. Unfortunately, the gyms are not available because our frenzied preoccupation with the drug war has led us to misappropriate the funds needed to build recreational and even educational facilities in our cities.

Health Evils

Much of the damage to health inflicted by drugs is the result of criminalization. Drugs are taken by contaminated needles because unauthorized needles are illegal. Drugs are injected rather than taken some safer way because they are so costly and injection gives better "bang for the buck." The illegal black market is unregulated, so that consumers have no assurance that the drugs they buy have the purity represented, or even that they are drugs: sometimes they are poison, or they are cut with chemicals that are more harmful to health than the drugs for which they were surreptitiously substituted. One who is cheated in the drug business cannot resort to the legal system for redress, but must look to extralegal systems.

There are manifold other evils generated by the war on drugs. We consider most of them at length later. It is sufficient here to note that what most of us think of as manifestations of the drug problem are usefully thought of as by-products of criminalization. While there would be no problem if there were no drugs, or if there were no appetite for drugs; neither would most of these problems exist if drugs were legal.

These enormous costs of criminalization might still be a bargain if, after a few years of intensive enforcement efforts, the illicit-drug problem were eliminated, once and for all. If we can be certain of anything related to this subject, however, it is that no such happy ending is possible.

We may reduce the number of consumers of illicit drugs by our drug war, but it is unlikely that we can have any considerable impact on the hard-core users, the users we commonly refer to as "addicts." Hard-core addicts have little to lose by threats of forfeiture or imprisonment. They have already lost, or soon will lose, family, job, status, property (or never had them to begin with). The threat of punishment has a hollow ring. Since addicts—daily or at least weekly users—may consume 80 percent or more of our illegal heroin and cocaine, we may greatly reduce the numbers of occasional "users" without substantially diminishing the overall demand levels for the drugs. If the demand levels remain fairly constant, virtually all of the drug-enforcement evils will remain in place.

Unless we relent, our intensive criminalization of drug commerce will be so stressful that our society will disintegrate from the strain, as it has already begun to do in our inner cities and as some areas did during alcohol prohibition. Gangs will kill for fun, as well as for drug turf. Our cities will seem like purgatory. Our suburbs will also be plagued with crime.

We will eventually retreat from an unwinnable war, just as we did in Vietnam. But in the drug war, as in Vietnam, the dead will be gone forever, and wounded will remain so for a very long time. We should de-escalate now, and at least selectively and provisionally, legalize.*

Clearly, however, government has a productive role to play in reducing drug abuse. The government has engaged in laudable efforts to persuade people to reduce their intake of alcohol and tobacco, and with considerable success. Therapeutic assistance to abusers of both legal and illegal drugs has also been too successful to justify its limited availability. All users or abusers of any psychoactive drug, whether tobacco, alcohol, heroin, cocaine, marijuana or any other, who seek help to curb or discontinue their use should receive such help at public expense. (The savings in health costs and crime alone more than justify the expenditure. Compassion need not enter into the matter.) Hardly anyone could seemingly disagree, yet help is often denied even the chronic addict on hard drugs. Both education and treatment work, and if we devoted the resources we now spend on criminalization to education and treatment, our cost of drug use would be drastically diminished, whether or not drugs are legalized.

---

*We use the terms "legalize" and "decriminalize" as synonyms in this book. Some analysts draw a distinction, proposing "decriminalization" as a compromise between prohibition and legalization. Such proponents often mean by "decriminalization" punishing the sale but not the consumption of drugs. We think that makes little sense. It was, in fact, the system we suffered under during alcohol prohibition.

Under prohibition, the innocent suffer at every turn. The users of illegal drugs do not bear even a fraction of the economic and social costs of their drug use; the nonuser bears a large portion: in unsafe streets, overcrowded, expensive prisons, diluted law-enforcement resources, hospital emergency rooms filled beyond capacity and inner cities becoming unlivable. In a system in which recreational drugs were legal, virtually all of these social costs would disappear overnight. We would still have some health problems associated with drugs. We would still have deaths by overdose, perhaps more than we have today, but we would have freed tens of billions of dollars to attack the problem of drug abuse in constructive ways, including treatment, education and meaningful vocational opportunities to those involved in, or tempted by, drugs. We would still have heroin and cocaine abusers, just as we have alcoholics and heavy smokers, who would pose serious social and medical challenges. But for the most part, under such a system, the drug abusers would pay the penalty for their abuse, and the penalty would be greater than it now is because the alternatives or choices available to them—which they would be giving up to be or remain an abuser—would be far more attractive than they are today.

CHAPTER 2

Identifying the Enemy: "Drugs," "Drug Abuse" and Other Concepts

"In terms of drug use the rarest or most abnormal form of behavior is not to take any mind-altering drugs at all. Most adult Americans are users of drugs, many are frequent users of a wide variety of them."

PRESIDENTIAL COMMISSION'S TASK FORCE ON NARCOTICS AND DRUG ABUSE[1]

FEW IMPORTANT concepts are fuzzier than the meaning of "drug." The *Random House Dictionary of the English Language*, Second Edition, lists nine definitions. However, no conception of "drug" comes close to describing what we as a society commonly think of as drugs. The reason, as SUNY professor Erich Goode says in *Drugs in American Society,* is that the concept of "drug" is a "cultural artifact, a social fabrication."[2] The *only* characteristic that all drugs share and non-drugs lack is the societal label "drug." Among the many aspects or dimensions of a substance that contribute to the likelihood of its being called a "drug" by Americans are its medical utility, its psychoactivity—the extent to which it affects mental processes, its utility as a recreational substance, its illegality for general consumption; and finally, how many people think of it when asked to give examples of a drug.[3]

A few generations ago, not many Americans thought of tobacco or alcohol as "drugs," yet today virtually all who have professional interests in drugs do so. These substances are rarely taken as food and have little utility other than mind or mood alteration. Were they not specifically exempted by federal law, they would both be controlled as dangerous drugs. They are examples of substances that meet almost any definition of "drug" but are still not generally considered by the law or by some people as drugs.

There is, in any event, little basis for disagreement about the proper classification of the "drugs" we consider in this book. With the exception of tobacco and alcohol, which are behaviorally and pharmacologically but, only to some extent legally, classified as "drugs," the other major drugs we are concerned with—heroin, cocaine and marijuana—are drugs in *every* sense of word. They are legally classified not only as "drugs" but as a special kind: "controlled drugs"—drugs that are mind- or mood-altering and involve some hazards.

Although our primary focus in this book is on only five psychoactive drugs—alcohol, tobacco, marijuana, heroin and cocaine—the numbers of psychoactive drugs on the planet is almost infinite. Literally hundreds are known to exist in the continental United States. The rain forests of the Amazon contain perhaps thousands more. Psychoactive effects are a common result of ingesting plant substances. According to Professor Ronald Siegel, we may have discovered less than 10 percent of the world's plant drugs.[4] Moreover, new laboratory-produced, synthetic "designer" drugs are being discovered every day. There is literally no limit to the number of mood-altering drugs that can be brought to market.

We largely confine our analysis to these five drugs because they constitute the main subject matter of today's "drug problem." These are our five psychoactive drugs most commonly consumed for nonmedical purposes. Heroin, cocaine and marijuana are the drugs that most consumers use illicitly, the prohibition of which has produced our gigantic, catastrophic black markets. How we as a society regulate less popular drugs is interesting and even important, but it does not present a public-policy issue of great magnitude or urgency.

Virtually every conceivable legal approach to the "drug problem" is now in place with respect to one or more of these five drugs. The relative dangers of the five, both to society and to the user, stretch across a broad spectrum, from astonishing safety to dire dangerousness. Yet the disparate legal approaches we have in place for each of the five do not match up with the broad spectrum of drug dangers. America's approach to psychoactive drugs is incoherent, contradictory and hypocritical.

In considering the role of law in drug control, it is still useful to have at least a superficial sense of the alternative recreational drugs awaiting their place on center stage in America's drug follies, for, as history demonstrates, the identities of the drug enemy are in a constant state of flux. Yesterday's panacea is tomorrow's poison. Recreational drugs come in and out of fashion like clothing styles.*

Apart from the vagaries of taste, changes in a drug's availability and in perceptions of its dangerousness affect the direction of drug consumption and cause the rediscovery of a currently unpopular drug. For example, the discovery of amphetamines in the 1930s all but destroyed the meager market for cocaine for thirty years or so. Our experience with "speed freaks," in Haight-Ashbury and elsewhere during the 1960s, then suppressed the appetite for amphetamines and contributed to the stampede into cocaine in the 1970s. Now, as evidence of the debilitating power of cocaine mounts, drug users are beginning a search for alternatives. The hallucinogen LSD, which lost popularity since the 1960s, is said to be staging a comeback.[5]

The discovery of new drugs and new applications of old drugs (including vaccines) during the twentieth century has accomplished wonders in extending the human life span and the quality of life. Drugs are virtually the foundation of modern medicine. Psychoactive drugs are central to the practice of modern psychiatry. Little but warehousing was done for psychotic patients until the discovery, mostly since World War II, of modern psychotropic drugs. Such drugs permit millions to lead normal lives today. In American society, moreover, depression, anxiety, insomnia and other mood disturbances are almost as common as headaches. The suffering associated with these disturbances is drastically relieved by antidepressants, tranquilizers, sedatives and other psychoactives. The drugs that accomplish so much good for the millions with mood disturbances are also at least poten-

---

*A short-lived fad arose in South Florida in 1990. Someone allegedly discovered that the slime secreted by the Florida cane toad causes hallucinations, and "toad-licking" was added to the language to describe a new means of getting high. See James A. Inciardi, *The War on Drugs II* (Mountain View, California: Mayfield Publishing Company, 1992), 283.

tially available for today's illegal-drug users. Not only are the drugs they use often the same ones prescribed by doctors, there is no clear difference between the function of medication by many psychotropic pharmaceuticals and the function of "recreational" drug use. In both cases, the user may be seeking relief from misery with the help of drugs.

CLASSIFYING DRUGS

Psychoactive drugs that are used recreationally (and also, in many cases, medically) are generally subdivided into several groups depending on their principal or usual effects when taken by human beings:

1. *Stimulants.* Drugs which directly affect the central nervous system and tend to produce arousal, alertness or even excitation and which remove or inhibit lethargy and fatigue are stimulants. They include amphetamines (known in recreational-drug circles as speed), cocaine, caffeine, nicotine and Ritalin.

2. *Depressants.* Drugs which retard the flow of signals through the central nervous system and tend to produce sleep, relaxation or lethargy are *depressants.* These are further divided into *narcotics* and non-narcotics or *general depressants.* Narcotics inhibit a main function of the central nervous system, the perception of pain. These are the opiates—morphine, heroin, codeine and various synthetics such as Percodan, methadone and Demerol. General depressants inhibit bodily functions more broadly, producing relaxation or drowsiness. They include alcohol, sedatives and tranquilizers.

3. *Hallucinogens.* These drugs tend to produce hallucinations, hence their name. They include LSD, mescaline, peyote, psilocybin and many others.

4. *Marijuana.* Some classify marijuana as an hallucinogen, some as a stimulant, some as a depressant. Some feel that it deserves it own category, since it does not closely resemble any of the other types of drugs.

5. *Inhalants.* These drugs are classified by their usual means of use, rather than their consequences. They have stimulating effects of a very short-lived, intense kind. They include amyl nitrite ("poppers"), butyl nitrite and nitrous oxide ("laughing gas"). Many ordinary household chemicals are used as inhalants but are not legally considered "drugs" at all.

Other drugs are used in psychiatry but rarely, if ever, recreationally.

They do not fit under any of the above classifications. Examples are Lithium and Prozac.

Legal Classifications of Psychoactive Drugs

Loosely regulated drugs: These include tobacco and alcohol. The regulation consists mainly in tax and tax-related regulations and in limiting the places where and the persons to whom tobacco and alcohol can legitimately be sold. Other regulations of alcohol include times during which it can be sold (nighttime, morning and holiday restrictions are common) and the other activities with which the sale of liquor can be combined, e.g., dancing, entertainment, dining. There are also numerous restrictions on where tobacco can be smoked or liquor can be consumed.

Drugs that have either abuse potential or pose health hazards, such as allergic reactions, are often dispensed by prescription only. The Food and Drug Administration has authority to require that drugs be sold by prescription only or even to prevent their sale entirely, absent proof that they are both safe and effective for a medicinal purpose.

Other drugs that involve hazards that are thought to be acceptable when weighed against their medicinal value, such as aspirin and ibuprofen, are sold over the counter without prescription, virtually the same as food. Even some strongly psychoactive drugs like caffeine are treated like food if contained in beverages such as coffee, tea or sodas.

Controlled drugs: The federal Controlled Substances Act distinguishes five categories of drugs on the basis of their "abuse potential" and their medical utility. Each controlled drug is assigned a place in one of the five categories or "schedules." The schedule in which a drug is listed determines whether it can be used in medical treatment and, if so, what kinds of records must be kept and so forth. The schedule in which a drug appears also affects the severity of the criminal penalties for unlawful possession or distribution of the drug.

Schedule I drugs are those that are thought to have great potential for abuse and *no* accepted medical utility. They include heroin, LSD, mescaline, peyote, PCP, Methedrine, methaqualone (Quaaludes), and, absurdly, marijuana. Schedule I drugs cannot be distributed legally, even by prescription. They may be used only for research, under severe restrictions.

Schedule II drugs are those with great abuse potential but also with accepted medical uses. These can be dispensed by unrefillable prescriptions, careful records must be kept, and they must be stored in a vault. These include morphine, cocaine, methadone, amphetamines, short-acting barbiturates (such as Seconal, Amytal and Nembutal), and the major psychoactive ingredient in marijuana, THC (Marinol).

Schedule III drugs are believed to have lesser abuse potential than Schedule II and some accepted medical utility. These can be dispensed on written or oral prescription, which can be made refillable. They include long-acting barbiturates (like phenobarbital) and diluted narcotics (such as codeine, which is a constituent of opium).

Schedule IV drugs have low potential for abuse and accepted medical use. These include minor tranquilizers such as Valium, Librium, Miltown and Equanil. These can be prescribed in the same manner as Schedule III drugs.

Schedule V drugs are those having very little perceived abuse potential and controls are minimal. They include medicine containing traces of opiates.

Most controlled drugs can be and are used not only for medical purposes but recreationally, to make the user feel good, or at least different. Generally, the distribution of illicit drugs that is the subject of this book occurs outside medical channels. Even such drugs which are lawfully produced and can in theory be prescribed—such as cocaine—are in fact mainly manufactured and distributed in black-market channels rather than through doctors and pharmacies. Most of the sedatives and tranquilizers, on the other hand, are patented or trademarked drugs made by mammoth pharmaceutical companies and are less commonly—though frequently—distributed in black-market channels. When the latter drugs are abused, it is often with the acquiescence of health professionals, but professional regulatory mechanisms in tandem with criminal penalties seem capable of keeping such illicit distribution within tolerable limits. The prescription of drugs like cocaine and morphine is rare in recent years, because there are other substitutes that do not carry the onus and risk of legal sanctions to the health professional that these drugs do. Indeed, as the war on drugs has escalated over the past two decades, the prescription of even Schedule III and IV drugs has been in a downward trend. The legitimate practice of medicine is significantly chilled by drug criminalization.

DRUG-ABUSE TERMINOLOGY

Every serious discussion of pleasure drugs involves the use of such terms as "addiction," "dependence," "tolerance" and "withdrawal."

Others frequently encountered are "physically addicting," "psychologically addicting" and "drug abuse." Since we will use most of these terms ourselves, we should try to explain what we mean when we do use them.

The term "addiction" has undergone many changes during its lengthy life. In Shakespeare's *Othello* it meant a strong inclination ("Each man to what sport and revel his addiction leads him"). Before the twentieth century, it was common to talk of addiction to work or sports or theater without any sense of exaggeration or incongruity. Gradually, the term became medicalized and encrusted with the idea of disease. It has also become loosely linked to criminality. One meaning of drug addiction is virtual enslavement. One who is addicted to a drug, it was often said, lacks the power to choose between taking the drug or refraining from doing so.

Closely allied with the idea of chemical enslavement is the process of withdrawal from drugs. One who is addicted to a drug demonstrates an addiction by suffering withdrawal symptoms when deprived of it. If the withdrawal symptoms are extreme, as they often are with barbiturate or heroin addicts or severe, long-term alcoholics, the person is addicted. If powerful physical symptoms of withdrawal are not present, neither is addiction. Such was a common view of addiction a few decades ago. However, our recent experiences with cocaine and other non-opiates produced, or at least coincided with, another change in the meaning of addiction. Although the craving for cocaine can be as powerful as the desire to use any other drug, abstinence rarely produces any perceptible physical symptoms. The term "psychological addiction" sprang into use to describe dependence upon a drug like cocaine that was not "physically addictive." Once unhinged from withdrawal symptoms, the concept of addiction was free to revert to its older meaning—a habit with at least some undesirable attributes. We now talk of addiction to food, sex, work, television and so forth. We are said by some to be an "addicted society."

It was inevitable that the "physical" view of addiction would give way to broader meaning. For one thing, the difference between "physical" and "psychological" addictions is hard to reconcile with our knowledge of the interdependent interconnectedness of mind and body. The opiate-linked view of addiction suffered from another affliction as well: it was a carrier of the idea that addicts are helpless to refrain from feeding their addictions and thus were not morally responsible for their plight. It was therefore larded with debatable assumptions about free will and the power to choose. To describe persons as addicted was to label them sick and not therefore responsible.

The term "dependence" has now been substituted by many health professionals for both physical and psychological addiction. There are many reasons for doing so. A relatively new term like "dependence" can be employed without the extensive historical, medical and cultural baggage of "addiction." "Dependence" is also less value laden or judgmental than "addiction." It does not conjure up the image of crazed killers running wild through the streets in search of a "fix." It also invites qualifying adjectives suggesting the relative strength of the dependence, such as "strong," "weak," "mild," "extreme."

In this book, when we use the terms "addict," "addicted" or "addictive" we usually employ them in the narrow sense in which they were used to describe dependence upon opiates or barbiturates and the accompanying withdrawal symptoms (but divorced from any related assumptions about free will or moral irresponsibility). There is still a useful distinction to be made between drug dependence that has physical manifestations—"addictions"—and drug dependence that is not dominated by the urge to avoid such withdrawal symptoms. We will generally adhere to current custom, however, when speaking of the broader relationship of the drug to its user. We will call that relationship "dependence," to include both "physical" and "psychological" "addiction," thus eliminating the need to distinguish between them.

What is drug "dependence"? The World Health Organization's Expert Committee on Drug Dependence defined it as "A state, psychic and sometimes also physical, resulting from the interaction between a living organism and a drug, characterized by behavioral and other responses that always include a compulsion to take the drug on a continuous or periodic basis in order to experience its psychic effects, and sometimes to avoid the discomfort of its absence. Tolerance may or may not be present."[6] Although vague, this definition is useful, provided "compulsion" is interpreted to mean nothing more than a powerful urge. As with "addiction," we reject the idea that drug dependence is the equivalent of surrendering at the point of a gun. We agree with many others who repudiate the idea that drug-dependent persons are not responsible for their drug taking.[7] That is a moral judgment best left out of terminology used to describe the relationship between drug consumers and their preferred drugs.

But if we assume that all drug taking involves choice, the idea of "dependence" may need further definition. If people take a drug because they enjoy its effects, they are not necessarily drug-dependent. Persons are dependent on a drug only if taking the drug occupies a major space in their lives and only if their relationship to the drug causes harm to themselves or others in a way that is inconsistent with their professed values. A person whose drinking costs him job after job, or divorce after divorce, or conviction after conviction, is dependent upon alcohol. It occupies a position in his life that is inconsistent with his professed, conscious, value system. Whatever may be the case, he *feels* compelled to drink. That is what we mean by a powerful urge.

Another common term is "drug abuse." By that, we simply mean the consumption of a drug, usually but not necessarily by a drug-dependent person, in a manner that causes substantial harm to the user or to others. A teenager who rarely drinks but gets drunk on prom night and crashes his parents' car is a drug abuser, at least on that occasion.

"Tolerance" and "withdrawal" are two closely related terms whose meanings are not value laden and hence are fairly clear. Tolerance is an adaptation of the nervous system to the effects of a drug. A given amount of the drug has lesser effects as tolerance develops. Users must increase their dosages to maintain a constant pharmacological effect. Tolerance can develop to most psychoactive drugs, although the speed and extent of tolerance varies widely from drug to drug, and from user to user. Tolerance to some of a drug's effects may develop more quickly than to other effects. With barbiturates, for example, tolerance to sedation, the desired effect of the drug, develops faster than does tolerance to toxicity. This is a major reason why some habitual users of barbiturates accidentally overdose.[8]

Not much is known about why tolerance develops. A general theory, however, is that some psychoactive drugs are regarded by the body as alien invaders, somewhat like hostile bacteria. The body opposes the alien effects by setting up defenses which tend to reestablish the body's equilibrium. More drug is then required to overcome the enhanced ability of the body to maintain its natural state. The increased amounts of the drug produce new opposition forces, even more drug is required, and so on. In some cases, the body's adaptations are known to occur at the cellular level. When morphine is ingested, the nuclear DNA manufactures more of various proteins which appear to weaken the effects of morphine.[9]

"Withdrawal" is the subsidence or disappearance of the intoxicating or other direct or desired influence of a drug. Withdrawal symptoms (sometimes loosely referred to simply as "withdrawal") are the manifestations of that subsidence in the use of an addicting drug. Withdrawal symptoms can range from vague discomfort, typical of nicotine withdrawal, to increased blood pressure, nausea, cramps, chills and diarrhea, in opiate withdrawal, to weakness, cramps, nausea, anxiety and hallucinations, with alcohol withdrawal. Little is known about why withdrawal symptoms occur and why they vary from drug to drug. One suggestive theory is that the body's oppositional forces—those that produce tolerance—are like a taut spring that remains in place only so long as the drug is regularly ingested. When the drug is no longer present, the spring is released and attacks whatever is in its way. Although withdrawal seldom produces any permanent ill effects, it can be fatal if the drug withdrawn from the addict is alcohol or barbiturates.[10]

CHAPTER 3

Our Most Harmful Legal Drugs

"If the rationale for [drug prohibition] is to prevent persons from killing themselves, it seems apparent that the state has made the wrong recreational drugs illegal."

RUTGERS UNIVERSITY PROFESSOR DOUGLAS HUSAK[1]

TOBACCO: OUR WORST DRUG

BY FAR the most serious drug problem in the United States—and in the world—is the tobacco problem. The principal drug in tobacco is nicotine, the substance that causes addiction and accounts for some of the damage smoking inflicts on the human body.

The worldwide tobacco plague began in the New World. Columbus and other early explorers saw natives carrying rolls of dried leaves, setting them afire, and inhaling the smoke. The explorers tried it and were promptly hooked. They made sure to take tobacco with them when they left and even carried seeds, to assure a ready supply wherever they traveled. Soon, everywhere the mariners went, in Europe, Africa or Asia, tobacco was planted and produced. The natives who tended the plants also became addicted.[2]

The consumption of tobacco did not become commonplace in Western Europe, however, until the early seventeenth century, when it was thought to be a newfound panacea for all kinds of illnesses, from toothaches to labor pains, corns, gangrene, paralysis, halitosis, flatulence, even, ironically, heavy coughs and cancer. Tobacco also was touted as a treatment for tetanus, gonorrhea, epilepsy and plague fever. As Jerome Brooks reported in *The Mighty Leaf,* there were "fifty-nine separate maladies (and some malignant or incurable diseases among them) for which tobacco was advised as the unfailing specific. This collection was in addition to the listings of minor ailments, such as warts, insect bites, poor eyesight, falling fingernails."[3] Physicians of the day advised against regular use of tobacco, just as today's warn against unnecessary use of antibiotics. A popular suspicion was that doctors opposed smoking because the general use of the "holy herb" would make their services unnecessary.[4] The doctors began to pamphleteer against the habit, and while reaffirming the medicinal value of tobacco, warned that its regular use would produce sterility, melancholy and blackened brains. No one listened, and the doctors took up the habit themselves. Seventeenth-century beliefs in the curative power of tobacco lingered, in muted form, into the twentieth century, when tobacco companies were still making mild medicinal claims in their advertising ("Throat hot? Smoke Kools").

The rest of the seventeenth-century world was spared the knowledge of tobacco's magical curative powers, and Eastern Europe and Asia regarded the infidel weed as unhealthy and unwholesome. The Sultan of Constantinople ordered the death penalty for smoking tobacco in 1633.[5] Japan prohibited tobacco in 1603, Russia in 1634, Saxony in 1653, Bavaria in 1652.[6] The first of the Romanoff czars invoked a range of penalties. Ordinary offenders were usually sentenced to "slitting of the nostrils, the bastinado, or the knout"[7] and persistent offenders were executed.[8] The Emperor of Japan imprisoned both buyers and sellers and awarded the property of any possessor of tobacco to the accuser.[9] Nowhere did these draconian provisions succeed in reducing or even controlling the stampede into tobacco addiction. In Japan, for example, prohibition began in 1603, and the penalties escalated repeatedly thereafter, but before two decades had passed, the habit had become commonplace among the elite who had prohibited it.[10] Turkey repealed prohibition in 1655 and went on to become a major exporter of tobacco.[11]

Smoking was mostly a male habit in America until World War I. By then, American cigarette makers had begun using milder tobacco and mass producing cigarettes by the billions. Mild, inexpensive cigarettes ("tailor-mades") replaced cumbersome hot and irritating pipes, cigars, chewing tobacco, snuff and "roll-your-owns." Women and children joined the stampede.[12]

The Temperance movement was not confined to alcohol, however. The seventeenth-century effort in Europe and Asia to prohibit smoking was renewed in America three centuries later. By 1921, fourteen states had enacted tobacco prohibition. Men, women and children continued to puff, and tobacco prohibition was completely over in six short years. In Idaho, both prohibition and repeal occurred in the same legislative session.[13]

Physical and Psychological Effects of Tobacco

That tobacco is a powerful drug cannot be doubted. Its nicotine taken straight in tiny doses is fatal. A 60-milligram dose—the nicotine in three cigarettes—will kill an adult.[14] It is even used in pesticides. Fledgling smokers invariably cough violently and, if they succeed in inhaling, usually become dizzy and are often nauseated; they sometimes vomit or lose consciousness. Only smokers who have developed tolerance can smoke with little apparent physical consequences. Yet even they can get high if they want to. If deep, frequent puffs are taken and retained in the lungs for several seconds, even a heavy smoker can achieve profound psychoactive effects, similar to those experienced by the beginner. That was apparently the usual method of smoking in seventeenth-century Russia.[15] Smoking also curbs the appetite. This accounts in part for the popularity of smoking among young women, some of whom are more weight- than health-conscious.

Although the physical effects of nicotine are fairly standard, the psychic effects are far less consistent. Some find smoking a tranquilizer, others a depressant, still others a stimulant. The psychoactive effects of smoking seem to be heavily dependent upon the expectations of the user and the setting in which the smoking occurs.

Whatever the effects, they are barely noticeable to the typical smoker, whose blood/brain levels of nicotine are regularly replenished every half hour or so and whose tolerance levels are very high. Smoking cigarettes is the only drug addiction that is also truly habitual in the sense that its practice is in many cases virtually unconscious. Some heavy smokers often light up a cigarette without realizing that they are already smoking one or two others.

Tobacco Withdrawal and Addictiveness

Nicotine withdrawal symptoms are also far from uniform. Some smokers will experience little more than a craving, a vague though strong feeling of discomfort coupled with the sensation that it can be relieved only by a smoke. A study by the American Institutes of Research showed that a majority of smokers deprived of the drug experienced nervousness, drowsiness and anxiety. A large minority suffered light-headedness, headaches, fatigue, constipation, diarrhea and/or insomnia.[16]

While these symptoms seem much milder than withdrawal symptoms experienced by heroin addicts, something is lost in the descriptions, for nicotine is more addictive than heroin. Neither in the pleasure reported by its addicts—hardly any—nor in the pain reported in withdrawal, does nicotine seem to compare with heroin, yet until recently at least, most people who smoked four or five cigarettes in their lifetime didn't stop until they smoked 400,000, that is, until they smoked daily for forty years or so.[17]

The ratio of addicts to users is higher with cigarettes than with any other commonly used drug. Probably a minority of users of heroin are hooked,[18] and only about one in six users of crack cocaine become dependent.[19] Yet virtually all smokers of tobacco are addicted. As reported by the Surgeon General, "chipping" or occasional use of heroin is common; it is rarely seen in smokers. Only about 10 percent of people who smoke are occasional or intermittent smokers.[20]

Although nicotine is the chemical responsible for addiction to smoking tobacco, it is still meaningful to speak of tobacco as the problem drug and the smoking of tobacco as the process to which smokers are addicted. Nicotine is only one of about ninety carcinogens in tobacco smoke. Nicotine that is ingested by means other than tobacco smoke causes far less damage to the body than does tobacco smoke containing an equal amount of nicotine.[21] That is why the Food and Drug Administration has approved nicotine-laced chewing gum and nicotine patches to help smokers quit.

Tobacco smoking is not only far more harmful than other means of ingesting nicotine, it is far more addicting. The smell and taste of the smoke from the 4,000 chemicals in tobacco are pleasant to most smokers and even to some nonsmokers. Thus, some of the pleasure in smoking is not attributable to nicotine. Still, there are virtually no smokers of denicotinized tobacco. The mess, cost and risks of smoking such tobacco clearly exceed the minor pleasures derived from it. What is addicting about tobacco smoking is a combination of the nicotine in the smoke and the method of delivering the nicotine to the brain. When any drug is smoked, the drug is delivered to the brain, via the bloodstream, in a few seconds. The speed of delivery is an aspect of the reinforcement process, adding leverage to the addictive power of the drug itself.

In a study completed in 1988, the Surgeon General concluded that tobacco use met all the criteria of drug addiction and that, in fact, the "processes that determine tobacco addiction are similar to those that determine addiction to other drugs, including illegal drugs."[22] In comparing one index of addiction, relapse rates, the report observed that the relapse rates of persons addicted to heroin and tobacco are similar. Of those who achieved abstinence, approximately 80 percent relapsed within five years, whether the drug involved was tobacco or heroin.[23]

Many smokers who have quit using both tobacco and illegal drugs, such as heroin, contend that kicking tobacco was more difficult than kicking heroin.[24]

Smokers who are deprived of tobacco behave "remarkably like heroin addicts."[25] There was both a food and a cigarette shortage in Germany following World War II, and tobacco rations for German civilians were cut to two packs a month for men and one pack for women. A German researcher questioned hundreds of Germans and found that "the majority of habitual smokers preferred to do without food even under extreme conditions of nutrition rather than to forgo tobacco."[26] Tobacco shortages were even a factor in the disintegration of the Soviet Union. Demonstrations, which in some cases rose to the level of riot, occurred in 1990 as a result of tobacco deprivation, and the economically hard-pressed Soviet government was forced to spend several billion dollars of its hard currency purchasing American cigarettes to quell the disorder.[27]

In the summer of 1992, the State of Vermont decided to prohibit smoking in its prisons. A black market emerged and the price of a pack of cigarettes jumped nearly 2000 percent to a price of about $40. A single cigarette sold for $3, more than the price of a pack on the legitimate market. Threats and violence were used to get cigarettes. Some prisoners traded other drugs and sex for tobacco. In November 1992, Vermont wisely rescinded its tobacco-in-prison prohibition.[28]

In Italy, where tobacco is distributed through a state-owned monopoly, tobacco workers struck in early November 1992. Italian smokers, who rank only 15th in the world in their per capita consumption of cigarettes (well behind America, which ranks 6th), panicked. Within three weeks, the price of a pack of cigarettes rose as high as $35; prostitutes were pricing their services in cigarettes; a man was mugged in Florence with the threat, "Your cigarettes or your life."

Smokers created miles of stalled traffic while driving to Switzerland and France to buy tobacco. Police began warning smokers about buying "doctored" cigarettes.[29] An Italian reporter who had a three-pack-a-day habit ended up at a crime-ridden train station trying to score. "I was offered heroin, cocaine, grass, amphetamines, Ecstasy, but not one pack of cigarettes," he wrote. Eventually, he was told that a smuggler was en route from Naples with a supply. When the train arrived, the smuggler was overrun by deranged smokers, yelling, clutching at him, thrusting money, begging. He was able to buy a carton of Marlboros for $36. He then ran off. "Like a thief. Like a drug addict."[30]

Criminogenic Effects of Tobacco

Given the powerfully addicting nature of tobacco smoke, it is worth contemplating what our society would resemble if tobacco, like heroin, were included in the legal concept of "controlled drug" and its consumption were prohibited. Professor Ethan Nadelmann of Princeton has vividly, and correctly, drawn the portrait:

[M]illions of Americans . . . would no doubt defy the law, generating a massive underground market and billions in profits for organized criminals. . . . Throughout Latin America, farmers and gangsters would rejoice at the opportunity to earn untold sums of "gringo greenbacks," even as U.S. diplomats pressured foreign governments to cooperate with U.S. laws. Within the United States, government helicopters would spray herbicides on illicit tobacco fields; people would be rewarded by the government for informing on their tobacco-growing, -selling, and -smoking neighbors; urine tests would be employed to identify violators of the anti-tobacco laws; and a Tobacco Enforcement Administration (the TEA) would employ undercover agents, informants, and wiretaps to uncover tobacco-law violators. Municipal, state, and federal judicial systems would be clogged with tobacco traffickers and "abusers." "Tobacco-related murders" would increase dramatically as criminal organizations competed with one another for turf and markets. . . . Tobacco-related corruption would infect all levels of government, and respect for the law would decline noticeably. Government expenditures on tobacco-law enforcement would climb rapidly into the billions of dollars, even as budget balancers longingly recalled the almost $10 billion per year in tobacco taxes earned by the federal and state governments prior to

prohibition. Finally, the State of North Carolina might even secede
again from the Union.[31]

Such calamitous consequences would be the result of prohibition, not
of tobacco addiction itself.

Hundreds of property crimes involving tobacco are committed simply because tobacco is a valuable commodity. A truckload of cigarettes can be worth $100,000, and the cargo is therefore an attractive
target for hijackers. Since taxes on cigarettes vary greatly from state
to state, tax evasion or bootlegging of cigarettes also occurs. International smuggling happens, too; lower-taxed Mexican cigarettes are
brought into California, and northern smugglers earn an estimated
$435 million a year bringing two-dollar-per-pack American cigarettes
into Canada, where the tax makes a pack worth seven dollars.[32] Such
crimes, however, have little to do with the qualities of the product
itself but rather reflect prices or price differentials.

The only way in which it may be useful to speak of a drug as
"criminogenic" is if the drug directly affects the propensities of its user
to engage in criminal activity for some reason related to the pharmacology of the drug, as when the drug removes inhibitions toward
violence. In this sense, tobacco is probably innocent. History contains
allegations that tobacco use leads to criminality, but little proof.
Withdrawal from tobacco may be another matter. An addict who is
denied access to cigarettes is likely to lash out, sometimes violently,
especially if the behavior has a prospect of producing access. If we ever
had a serious shortage of cigarettes (or partial success in prohibiting
them) a breakout of nicotine-related violence would hardly be a surprise. For American planning purposes, however, a severe, unan-
ticipated shortage of supply seems very unlikely, and no one can
seriously suggest the prohibition of cigarettes. Our society would
crumble from the strain. The only point to be made in speculating that
tobacco prohibition could be criminogenic is to underscore the difference between the criminogenic nature of the drug itself and the possible criminogenics of prohibiting the drug.

For later comparisons with illegal drugs it is also noteworthy that
most violent criminals are probably "under the influence of" nicotine
when they commit their crimes. There is therefore a "positive correlation" between tobacco use and violent crime. While no one could
argue that tobacco use therefore predisposes smokers to commit violent crimes, precisely the same putative causal connection is commonly seen between violent crime and illegal-drug use.

Is there any connection between tobacco use and offenses of negligence or recklessness? Yes, but how much or why is unclear. A study some years ago, headed by Dr. Joseph Di Franza, of the University of Massachusetts, found that smokers had 50 percent more auto accidents and got 46 percent more traffic tickets than nonsmokers.[33] Such gross disparities could not be entirely explained by the fact that the smokers were younger and were heavier drinkers than the nonsmokers. Dr. Di Franza opined that smokers are greater risk-takers than nonsmokers and thus smoking is a means of identifying persons who are less careful than others. Other factors included the likelihood, borne out by interviews, that smokers were often distracted from their driving by problems with cigarettes: they were dropped and were burning clothing, car seats or skin, and so forth. Only in the latter sense is it meaningful to infer a causal link between smoking and crimes of carelessness. Even then, the causal link is not a criminogenic one. That smokers are greater risk-takers than nonsmokers is obvious, but no one has established smoking as the cause of that attribute. Smoking probably is a symptom of carelessness rather than its cause.

Virtually every marijuana smoker, every cocaine user, and every heroin addict first smoked cigarettes before graduating to any of the other drugs. Cigarettes are therefore "gateway" drugs, to use the current prohibitionist jargon. It would be silly to suppose, however, that if we could wave a wand and eliminate tobacco, and thus an early step or "gateway" to hard drugs, we could eliminate or even significantly deter experimentation in illegal drugs. More likely, in removing the "gateway," we would simply have lowered a hurdle and our youths would even more readily—and at a younger age—commence their experimentation with illegal drugs. In any event, it does not seem useful to speculate that tobacco use, although a precursor to other drugs, may be criminogenic in the sense that it may predispose cigarette smokers to try a different drug, for, as we shall see, even that drug is not likely criminogenic.

Adverse Health Consequences

If cigarette smoking is innocent of the charge of inducing criminal behavior, it is a major culprit in human sickness, misery and death, easily dwarfing all other drugs combined.

There is hardly a part of the human body that is not damaged by cigarette smoke. Smoking accounts for 30 percent of all cancer mortality[34] and is the major cause of lung cancer and a cause of throat, lip and mouth cancer, of emphysema and cardiovascular disease. It contributes to stomach and intestinal cancer and other damage to the gastrointestinal tract and injures the reproductive organs of both sexes. Smoking cigarettes even prematurely ages both facial skin and the brain. There is evidence that smoking increases the risk of getting leukemia by 30 percent.[35] Smoking has even been found to accelerate AIDS. A recent British study concluded that smokers who are infected with HIV develop AIDS twice as quickly as those with the virus who do not smoke.[36]

In addition to the risks common to both men and women who use tobacco, female smokers using oral contraceptives are especially likely candidates for cardiovascular diseases.[37] Research has also shown that smoking by pregnant women injures the fetus, reduces the birth weight of the newborn and may cause long-term neurological deficits in children.[38]

Neonates are not the only "passive smokers" whose health suffers from tobacco use by others. According to a 1986 report by the United States Surgeon General, involuntary inhalation of secondhand tobacco smoke causes cancer and other health problems for nonsmokers.[39] One study by Stanton A. Glantz and Dr. William Parmley of the University of California at San Francisco concluded that secondhand smoke kills more than 50,000 Americans per year, about 15,000 by cancer and 37,000 by cardiovascular disease. Studies of rats showed that those exposed to secondhand cigarette smoke nearly doubled the accumulation of fat in their arteries and increased the tendency of their blood to clot. This is the major explanation for the large death rates among secondhand smokers from cardiovascular disease.[40]

According to the Surgeon General, 390,000 Americans were killed by cigarettes in 1985,[41] and that number grows every year. A more recent estimate is 434,000 deaths per year.[42] And many of the deaths are agonizingly painful. Cancer is one of the worst ways to die, yet cigarettes claim more than 100,000 American lives by cancer every year.[43]

Estimated losses of productive capacity due to tobacco-caused employee illness run into the tens of billions of dollars. None of this litany of nicotine hazards includes the very considerable fire damage, injuries and accidental fatalities caused by use of this drug.

The damage caused by smoking is international, not just a uniquely American problem. Oxford University epidemiologist Richard Peto has projected for the World Health Organization that the planet's current population will be decimated by smoking; that is, 500 million people—roughly one person in ten worldwide—will die from smoking-caused ailments.[44] According to *Smoking and Health, A National Status Report, Second Edition,* 1990, "[s]moking is the chief preventable cause of death in our society. It is directly responsible for . . . more than one of every six deaths in our country. The number of Americans who die each year from diseases caused by smoking exceeds the number of Americans who died in all of World War II, and this toll is repeated year after year."[45] The same report estimates the annual economic costs of smoking (not including the cigarettes themselves) at over 52 billion dollars. This sum represents health-care costs, lost income, and lost productivity due to premature deaths.[46] If you add the costs of the cigarettes themselves, approximately 55 billion dollars, it brings the total economic cost of tobacco smoking to about 107 billion dollars per year!

America is also the major exporter of tobacco to the rest of the world. While the proportion of smokers in the population has been decreasing in the United States since 1973, it has been increasing elsewhere in the world. Since 1960, it has increased in India 400 percent and in Papua, New Guinea, 300 percent.[47] According to the World Health Organization, increases in cigarette consumption between 1971 and 1981 outpaced population growth in all developing regions.[48] Smoking has increased 500 percent in China since 1965.[49] China holds mass executions of "drug dealers," as many as sixty-two in one day recently,[50] but it has the highest rate of smoking by males in the world. At least 62 percent of males are smokers (only 8 percent of women smoke).[51] The notion that nonsmokers have rights to clean air has not yet penetrated China.[52]

While some agencies of the federal government—along with many states and cities—have been actively discouraging our citizens from smoking, there has been no such American effort regarding citizens of other countries. On the contrary, our government continues to assist our tobacco companies in expanding their markets abroad. As a result, any income lost by American tobacco companies from red׳ ɔed domestic sales has been more than made up in exports.

The American tobacco companies hardly need the government assistance. Because of effective advertising, in Japan, where more than 60 percent of males smoke, the populace considers American tobacco products far more stylish than the domestic competitors.[53] Our cigarette manufacturers bear no resemblance to other American enterprises that have failed to penetrate the Japanese market. By 1991, United States market share had grown from less than 2 percent in 1985 to a respectable 15.2 percent of Japanese tobacco sales.[54]

The good news is that Americans are kicking cigarettes. The per capita consumption of cigarettes has been on a steady downtrend since 1973.[55] Half of the Americans now living who once smoked have quit. Still, there are 50 million cigarette smokers left in American society, with a life expectancy far lower than that of nonsmokers.

To summarize: considering the current 50 million American smokers as the relevant population "at risk," the evidence shows that they are risking approximately 400,000 deaths per year, at a financial cost of $107 billion, for an annual cigarette-caused death rate of almost seven per thousand smokers and an annual financial cost of more than $2,000 per smoker.

ALCOHOL

Alcohol is a natural, spontaneous product of the fermentation of sugar in overripe fruit, in honey, or in the sap of trees. Starch in grain also readily converts to sugar and thence to alcohol. What we customarily refer to as alcohol is technically ethanol or ethyl alcohol. Other members of the alcohol family, such as wood alcohol (methyl alcohol) or rubbing alcohol (isopropyl alcohol) are deadly poisons. In keeping with custom, however, we will refer hereafter to ethanol as alcohol.

Alcohol was an early human discovery. It has been consumed as a pleasure drug virtually from the dawn of civilization. Favorable references appear in both the New and Old Testaments and many other ancient texts. After Noah emerged from the Ark, according to the Hebrew story, he saw a goat eat grapes, which caused it to frolic about. Noah ate them too, and thus discovered wine. A Greek legend credits apes rather than goats with leading man to fermented grapes.[56] The ancient Egyptians excelled in the art of making both wine and beer; a divinity ruled over the use of each.[57] Distillation seems to have first appeared in ninth-century Arabia, after which distilled spirits spread throughout the world. Public drunkenness has been a feature of virtually every society since the early Egyptian dynasties.[58]

Man is not the only animal that enjoys alcohol or its effects. According to psychopharmacologist Ronald Siegel, the appetite is virtually universal among animals, even insects.[59]

Alcohol is the most commonly used recreational drug in America. According to the National Institute on Drug Abuse's 1991 Household Survey, 69.7 percent of American males between the ages of eighteen and twenty-five used alcohol during the month preceding the survey, and 50.9 percent of the entire population over the age of eleven did so as well.[60] Nearly 85 percent had used alcohol sometime in their lives and 68 percent did so in the last year. That translates to about 130 million occasional or more frequent users of alcohol, more than twice as many as smoke cigarettes.

Psychoactive Effects of Alcohol

The psychoactive effects of alcohol are even less uniform than those of tobacco. Although classified as a depressant, alcohol has a wide spectrum of apparently contradictory effects. At various dose levels, and in various settings, it may depress or stimulate, tranquilize or agitate. Some drinkers have predictable reactions, almost regardless of dosage. A mild euphoria is commonly associated with moderate dosages, followed frequently by a tranquilizing effect. Alcohol intoxication often temporarily elevates the drinker's self-esteem and his or her sense of power, wit and mastery. While doing this, it also deadens the brain's critical, cognitive functioning and motor skills, and actually reduces the intelligence, perceptual power and physical competence of the drinker. The double-barreled power of alcohol to reduce competence while appearing to have increased it is probably unequaled by any other drug.

Most people can consume alcohol in moderation, regularly or intermittently, without serious health or social consequences. A minority, however, roughly 10 percent, are addicted or dependent. Some of these feel a strong need to remain under the influence virtually every waking moment. Others alternate between dry periods and binges, where they get rip-roaring drunk and then swear off until the next binge. Still others, including perhaps a majority of teenage drinkers, get dangerously drunk from time to time but are not alcohol-dependent.

Some tolerance is developed in most regular drinkers, so that a larger quantity of alcohol can be consumed while producing similar effects. There is uncertainty about the extent to which this tolerance is learned or psychological and to what extent it is physiological. Most drinkers do not become physically addicted to alcohol, even if they are alcohol dependent, but some who engage in heavy drinking on a regular basis for many years do become physically addicted. In such drinkers, the withdrawal symptoms can be both more painful and more dramatic than the symptoms of heroin withdrawal. Hallucinations are common. Death is occasionally the final stage.

Health Effects of Alcoholism

The adverse health consequences of chronic heavy drinking are staggering. When taken in large quantities—perhaps three or four ounces per day—alcohol is a poison that rivals nicotine in its pernicious effects on the human body. As stated in *Alcohol and Health, the Seventh Special Report to Congress, 1990,* "Alcohol affects almost every organ system in the body directly or indirectly."[61] It causes three types of liver damage: fatty deposits, hepatitis, and cirrhosis, the ninth-leading cause of death in 1986.[62] Regular alcohol use can precipitate esophagitis, exacerbate peptic ulcers and increase the risk of gastrointestinal cancer and pancreatitis. Chronic alcohol abuse contributes to cardiac dysfunction and other cardiovascular disorders, including hypertension. Alcohol also adversely affects immune, endocrine and reproductive functions.[63]

Heavy, prolonged alcohol consumption also takes a terrible toll on the human brain, causing dementia, blackouts, seizures, hallucinations and peripheral neuropathy.[64] Alcohol-related dementia accounts for nearly 20 percent of all admissions to state mental hospitals.[65] Brain cells are destroyed and atrophy is produced, with loss of memory and impaired learning capacities.[66]

There are more than 1 million short-term hospitalizations every year that involve alcohol-related conditions.[67] In a 1990 report, the Centers for Disease Control analyzed alcohol-related deaths for 1987 and estimated the annual death tolls "causally linked" to alcohol at 105,095. Excluding intentional and accidental deaths, the mortality attributed to alcohol-related illness was nearly 50,000.[68]

When alcohol does not directly cause death, it may act synergistically with other drugs to bring about that result. Alcohol is commonly used in combination with other drugs. The majority of cocaine-related deaths probably involve use of alcohol.[69] Many readers will remember that in 1986 basketball star Len Bias died in his early twenties of a heart attack publicly attributed to cocaine use. However, in *The Great Drug War,* Arnold Trebach points out what most of the press failed to report at the time: Len Bias probably died not from cocaine alone, but from heroic doses of alcohol and cocaine in combination.[70]

The Public Health Service also estimates the annual economic cost of alcohol abuse and dependence at about $130 billion, about 60 percent of which is attributable to lost employment and productivity and 13 percent to health care costs.[71]

Although difficult to quantify, alcohol abuse also contributes importantly to family disruptions, spousal abuse, child abuse and neglect.[72] According to a 1989 Gallup Report, "drinking" has "been a cause of trouble" in about 1 family in 5.[73]

Alcohol is also a factor in suicide, the number-one cause of intentional deaths in this country. Studies show that suicides are considerably less predictable if alcohol is involved than if it is not, suggesting that alcohol is "but-for" cause of a significant number of suicides.[74]

Given all these hideous health consequences as well as a notorious association with crime and violence that we will discuss shortly, why has no major non-Islamic society succeeded in getting rid of alcohol or even tightly controlling it? Our lengthy traditions, including religious rituals, have deeply embedded alcohol into the fabric of our culture. It is difficult to imagine what America would be like without its beer, wine and liquor. We tried prohibiting alcohol between 1920 and 1933 and it was a colossal failure. The only societies that have ever succeeded in virtually eliminating alcohol consumption once it was introduced have been homogeneous religious communities like the Muslims and the Mormons.

Our deeply ingrained patterns of alcohol consumption largely predated our discoveries of the terrible toll that heavy drinking takes on the human body. But even if that knowledge had preceded general use, the attractiveness of alcohol would probably have won out over its dangers. The fact that it can be consumed orally in tasty drinks that are highly compatible with food gives it a great advantage over many competing drugs.

The pleasures of alcohol are hard to measure but, unlike those of smoking cigarettes, not impossible to describe. Most people find that a drink or two relaxes them and is an antidote for stress. It often produces a sense of well-being and is a social lubricant of immense utility. To the chagrin, possibly, of the members of the temperance movement, alcohol also seems to have very significant, albeit mysterious, health *benefits*. Study after study has found that drinking moderately is associated with reduced cardiovascular disease, for both men and women. A three-year study published in *The Lancet* in 1991 confirms these results for a group of more than 44,000 male health workers.[75]

That alcohol might be good for one's heart seems counterintuitive. Given what we know about the damage alcohol can do to health in general and to hearts in particular, it would seem almost certain that teetotalers as a group would be less susceptible to heart disease than drinkers. If nothing else, the drinkers should be less health conscious than the nondrinkers. Drinkers are more likely than nondrinkers, for example, to smoke cigarettes, which clearly causes cardiovascular disease, but the study published in *The Lancet* found that the negative correlation between cardiovascular disease and alcohol consumption is essentially the same for smokers and nonsmokers.[76] The drinkers in the *Lancet* study also consumed more fat and cholesterol than the nondrinkers, but that did not eliminate the cardiovascular health advantage, either.[77] Drinkers also are less likely to engage in regular exercise, which denies them another cardiovascular benefit.

What about drinking could possibly counterbalance these disparities? One explanation that has been offered is that drinking might raise levels of high-density lipoprotein (HDL), a blood chemical that is thought to provide protection against cardiovascular disease.[78] Another is that regular drinking flushes the cardiovascular system, much as acid cleans out a clogged plumbing system.

Another possible explanation for the findings relates to the connection of drinking and stress. Animal studies show that those that are subjected to stress resort to alcohol, if available, to relieve their stress.[79] If this is also true of human beings—which it surely is—then one would suppose that drinking would be a *symptom* of stress and thus that drinkers as a group are subjected to more stress than nondrinkers. If inability to handle stress effectively is a cause of cardiovascular problems, as some researchers claim,[80] the stressed-out drinkers should have more heart attacks, not fewer. But the animal studies also show that when stressed animals resort to alcohol to relieve stress, it works. Moderate use of alcohol may be such an effective tranquilizer that it more than compensates for the tension of those who consume it and that it actually reverses the order of things and makes the nondrinkers, who don't need alcohol to deal with stress, less able to cope with stress than the drinkers, who needed its help.

We cannot yet determine what causes the cardiovascular protections that moderate drinking seems to afford. It is sufficient here to note that the research on alcohol and heart disease illustrates how even the most harmful of drugs may have beneficial as well as injurious effects. A drug policy that prohibits drugs runs the risk of denying humanity the benefits and therapeutic uses of the prohibited drugs.

Is Alcohol Criminogenic?

There were more than 3 million arrests for "alcohol-related" offenses in 1988.[81] Most are offenses that involve alcohol by definition, such as driving under the influence, drunkenness, liquor law violations. The system costs of processing 3 million arrests, even relatively minor ones, is huge. The costs to the arrestees, in lost work time, legal fees, bail bonds, and similar expenses is also great. The humiliation and degradation of jail is also a matter of magnitude when it happens on such a grand scale.

Most of the so-called alcohol-related offenses are not very serious crimes; they are crimes at all because they either offend the sensibilities and esthetics of influential segments of the community or they are thought to have the potential to ripen into more serious crimes, such as assault or homicide. They are, in a sense, inchoate offenses. In attempting to assess the criminogenics of the drug, therefore, it is perhaps best to disregard those inchoate offenses and try to determine the more serious harms actually attributable to the intoxicated conditions. Even with our inquiry thus constrained, there are many such harms.

If one considers reckless and negligent homicides to be serious crimes—and the law does so in every American jurisdiction—it is clear that alcohol is criminogenic.

Alcohol not only impairs one's ability to drive a car or operate other machinery safely, it often subdues the inclination to do so. Most drinkers also overestimate their abilities when under the influence, whatever the ability being tested. There are numerous other ways in which alcohol intoxication contributes to accidental fatalities. For example, drivers involved in fatal crashes who have been drinking are three times as likely as other drivers involved in such accidents not to be using seat belts. This failure itself accounts for hundreds of deaths annually.

How many of the 45,000 annual traffic fatalities are the result of alcohol? About half were "alcohol-related"[82] but this tells us little. An accident is "alcohol-related" if any of the participants had a blood-alcohol-content (BAC) of .01 percent or more.[83] Such a level is a mere one-tenth of the BAC generally regarded as constituting legally impaired driving.[84] In California and some other states the legally-impaired-driving level has been reduced from .1 percent to .08 percent, but that is still 8 times greater than the "alcohol-related" measurement threshold of .01 percent. There is no evidence that a BAC of .01 percent or even .03 percent causes significant impairment in driving performance.

However, it appears that when the driver in a fatal crash has *any* alcohol in his blood, he is legally intoxicated in roughly two-thirds of the cases. (That is, in two-thirds of the cases involving alcohol, the driver has a BAC of more than .1 percent rather than merely the .01 percent level that would make the accident alcohol-related.) If we multiply one half (the proportion of accidents that are alcohol related) by two thirds (the proportion of legally intoxicated drivers found among the alcohol-related accidents), we obtain an estimate that a drunk driver is involved in about one third of all traffic fatalities. David S. Reed, in a sophisticated analysis of the data on drinking and driving, concluded that approximately 12,000, slightly less than one fourth, of all annual driving deaths are actually caused by drinking, i.e., would not have occurred had none of the participants recently been drinking.[85] According to the Centers for Disease Control, alcohol was also causally linked in 1987 to 190 boating deaths, 202 aircraft deaths, 4,052 deaths by accidental falls, 2,119 deaths by fire, and 1,657 deaths by drowning.[86]

Alcohol and Violence

The causal relationship of drinking and intentional, violent crimes is less clear. Virtually any policeman will tell you that domestic violence, including assaults and killings, is caused by drinking. Such crimes do seem to be disproportionately associated with drinking, at least in America. Some 50 percent to 60 percent of homicides, for example, are accompanied by drinking, i.e., either the perpetrator or the victim, or both, were drinking at or shortly before the crimes.

Many facts cast doubt, however, on the relevance of the raw data that connect drinking with violent crime. As noted earlier, probably as many perpetrators of violent crime are under the influence of nicotine when they commit their crimes as are carrying alcohol in their systems. Few would suggest that nicotine causes violent crime. Moreover, *young* males commit a highly disproportionate share of violent crime, and about 75 percent of them drink alcohol frequently and they get drunker, oftener, than virtually any other segment of the population. Rather than alcohol explaining their crime, being young and male may account for both their crime *and* their drinking. The crime and the drinking could be independent.

Another factor is intensified social relations. Many violent crimes occur during social interactions, either at home or in public gathering places, and this is where and when most drinking occurs as well. The social interactions themselves could be a more significant causal factor than the drinking that accompanies them. Possibly, social interactions without the lubricant of alcohol could be even more stressful, more conflictual, and more criminogenic than those gladdened by booze. Despite all these reservations, it still seems probable that drunkenness causes violence, even if light drinking does not. But where is the evidence?

Scientific assessment of the relationship of drinking to violence is difficult to obtain because experimental models are nearly impossible to construct. However, some studies provide rough approximations of experimental situations, and they strongly suggest a causal relationship between drinking and violence. Due to general food shortages between 1917 and 1918, Scandinavians were allotted alcohol rations of approximately one third the pre–World War I level; *the assault rate declined,* while the general crime rate more than doubled.[87] More recently, state monopolies on alcohol distribution were interrupted by a 1963 Swedish strike, a 1972 Finnish strike and a 1978 Norwegian strike; in all cases, significant reductions in violent crimes accompanied reduced availability of alcohol.[88] Similar results were achieved in Poland during the Gdansk shipyard strike of 1980, during which the workers voluntarily imposed prohibition on themselves. Experimental closing of Swedish liquor stores on the Saturdays during the summer of 1981 was accompanied by weekend rates of violence lower than those of weekdays.[89]

During the 1991 Gulf War and the preparation for that battle, American soldiers, who were deprived of alcohol in deference to their Saudi Arabian hosts, committed far fewer violent crimes and fewer infractions of military discipline than their peers have committed in either peacetime duty or comparable deployments for the Panama invasion and the Vietnam war.[90]

In all these cases, reduced consumption of alcohol correlated with reductions in violent crimes. On balance, then, the data seem to support the common understanding or folklore that intoxication leads to violence. This does not mean, of course, that heavy drinking usually leads to violence. Some people who drink become more inhibited, not less; some become happy, loving, agreeable; some become hostile, nasty, aggressive; some, all of those things, depending on their moods at the time, and other circumstances. That alcohol begets many moods, some not remotely connected with violence, does not negate the fact that among the moods sometimes begotten by booze are hostility, aggressiveness, intolerance, hypersensitivity, and a desire to hurt others. Such moods often translate into violent acts.

There are other questions to be asked, however, before concluding that alcohol is criminogenic for violence. It is possible that persons who would otherwise drink alcohol excessively and become violent as a result, if they abstained or were denied access to alcohol, would resort to some other drug that is even more criminogenic than alcohol. Fortunately, as we will explain later, there may be no such drug. Even if there were, it is not clear that most violent drunks would switch to it rather than a less dangerous drug or even—sobriety.

A final question remains. If alcohol intoxication leads to violence, is this due to a pharmacological effect on the drinker or to something else? Is there something inherent in an alcohol high that triggers aggressiveness, meanness, violence? A common view among experts is that alcohol intoxication triggers expectations in the drinkers and that the mood that emerges depends on a combination of what the user expects (the "set") and what the surrounding society or culture (the "setting") expects. In short, intoxication is more a catalyst to violence than a deep cause. The causal link between alcohol and violence is more sociocultural than it is pharmacological.

In an anthropological study of many societies throughout the world, Craig MacAndrew and Robert Edgerton reported in *Drunken Comportment* that there are no uniform or generalizable behavioral effects of drinking.[91] The comportment of the inebriate varies dramatically from one society to the next. A Yurana Indian from a tropical rain forest typically becomes withdrawn and acts as if no one else exists.[92] Mestizo villagers in Colombia, no matter how drunk they get, retain a "rigid mask of seriousness," whereas in another mestizo village in Bolivia, mild intoxication produces conviviality, playfulness, garrulousness, but drunkenness results in stupefaction. Verbal or physical aggression never emerges at any stage. Numerous tribes and villages throughout the world do not experience anger or violence as a by-product of intoxication. Many deny that they are capable of such feelings while drunk.

In some societies, the effects of alcohol differ markedly depending on the setting. The Papago Indians of Arizona traditionally got drunk on cactus wine to celebrate the arrival of the rainy season. They would drink enough to vomit and pass out, but were virtually never hostile or unruly. When white men arrived and liquor was introduced for nonceremonial use, getting drunk acquired a deviant quality and violence appeared. Thus, in the same society, two different settings produced markedly different behavior patterns.

MacAndrew and Edgerton conclude from their study that "the presence of alcohol in the body does not necessarily conduce to disinhibition, much less inevitably produce such effect."[93] The fact that disinhibition of violence does not always or even usually follow drinking, however, is not inconsistent with its following in a significant segment of drinkers, at least some of the time. Everything cannot be attributed to the influence of setting or culture. In experiments with elephants, for example, some elephants when drunk become solitary, aloof, quiet; others frolicsome, others amorous, and still others mean and nasty, like people.[94] Elephants are unlikely to have developed deep cultural expectations about the effects of drunkenness.

Even to the extent that a proclivity to violence in human drinkers is a cultural product, the linkage between alcohol and violence is no less real, especially in the United States. Our culture has constructed patterns of expected drunken comportment, to which most of us try to conform. Unfortunately, aggressiveness and machismo are part of those patterns. For at least a century, Americans have believed that inebriation leads to violence and, in part because we believe that, it does.

These cultural constructs are not cast in marble, however. Part of their durability rests on the assumption that persons are not wholly responsible for their drunken behavior. We have recently seen marked changes in that attitude where drunk driving and spousal abuse are concerned, and there is reason to hope that liquor will continue to lose its stature as a near license to commit crimes against others.

There is another way in which drinking leads importantly to crimes against the person, which has been distinguished from criminogenics by the term "victimogenic." Data show that if a victim is drinking, he or she is much more likely to be a victim of a crime of violence than if not drinking. This is most obviously the case with robbery victims who are or appear to be helplessly drunk or "passed out" and with rape victims, who are or appear to be especially vulnerable when intoxicated. Inebriates also often precipitate or initiate violence and end up dead or seriously injured when their victims retaliate. The perpetrator of the ultimate, charged crime of violence could have been sober, yet the drinking and criminal behavior of the victim could have been a "but-for" cause of the perpetrator's crime. In such a case, alcohol would be both criminogenic and victimogenic. Up to this point, we have considered only the possible relationship of a single drinking event to a single episode of violence. There are, however, almost limitless ways in which chronic, heavy consumption of alcohol may lead to criminal violence. Chronic inebriation tends to make inebriates unemployable and to push them into a lifestyle and a sub-culture that is itself criminogenic. Unemployed alcohol abusers tend to associate with others; with drug addicts, drug pushers, prostitutes, thieves and robbers who condone violence and for whom violence sometimes seems necessary for survival. Prolonged excessive alcohol consumption also produces brain damage which may manifest itself in aggressive, violent behavior. The poor nutrition and sleep deprivation associated with the alcohol-abusing lifestyle may also produce acute personality changes that predispose the drinker to violence.

CHAPTER 4

Our Most Popular Illegal Drugs

"In wise hands, poison is medicine; in foolish hands, medicine is poison."

CASANOVA DE SEINGALT (1725–1798)[1]

MARIJUANA

MARIJUANA (also spelled marihuana) is the flowering tops, leaves and small stems of the cannabis plant, a genus of plants in the hemp family. A group of chemicals found in cannabis and in no other plant are called cannabinoids. One of sixty-one cannabinoids is believed to be the major mood-altering substance in cannabis. It is called delta-9 tetrahydrocannabinol or THC.

When users speak of marijuana, they are usually referring to the chopped flowers, leaves or stems of the plant. More concentrated sources of cannabinoids are also usually included in discussions and legal treatment of marijuana: hashish and hashish oil. Hashish is the resin of the cannabis plant, which is removed by crushing and boiling the leaves and stems in water. The resulting residue when dried is semisolid and can be smoked, chewed or mixed with food, as can any other form of marijuana. Hashish oil is obtained by extracting it from the plants with organic solvents. It has a very high THC content, up to 30 percent. It too can be eaten in food or sprinkled on tobacco or marijuana leaves and smoked.

43

At least a thousand years before Christ, the Chinese cultivated cannabis for making rope, fabric and paper from its fibers. Thereafter, in much of Europe, indeed throughout the world, cannabis became an important source of rope, fabric and paper. The demand for hemp was so great in the sixteenth century that Henry VIII commanded farmers to devote part of their land to its cultivation.[2] It was planted in Jamestown, Virginia, in 1611, by order of the King. By 1630, most of the clothing worn by the American colonists contained hemp fiber. Both George Washington and Thomas Jefferson grew hemp on their plantations. By 1850, it was the third-largest American crop, exceeded only by cotton and tobacco.[3]

As sailboats were replaced by steamboats, there was less demand for rope. Other countries, such as Russia and Italy, grew a better quality of the fiber for clothing. The industry slowly dwindled. It was reactivated during World War II, when interruption of world trade created a shortage of rope and clothing materials. The government actively promoted the growing of cannabis by American farmers.[4] As a result, America is littered with wild cannabis plants, originally cultivated during the war effort. The commercial value of cannabis fiber has since been largely destroyed by synthetic fibers, such as nylon.

The use of marijuana as a drug may be as old as its other uses. It seems to have been employed as such in ancient China and India. Herodotus in the fifth century B.C. wrote of the Scythians burning marijuana on hot rocks and producing a vapor that made them shout aloud.[5] Romans in the second century made a dessert out of cannabis seed and were aware of warm and pleasurable sensations that could result from eating it.[6] Ancient literature suggests that marijuana was used as an aid in childbirth because it both increased the strength of uterine contractions and alleviated pain. Archaeologists recently discovered physical evidence confirming such uses in a 1,600-year-old Roman tomb near Jerusalem. They found the skeletons of a teenager and her full-term fetus. They also found the ashes of marijuana and concluded that it had been administered in an attempt to facilitate the childbirth.[7]

The intoxicating properties of the plant were known to the Arab world at least by the twelfth century. *A Thousand and One Nights,* a collection of Arab stories written around that period, contains "The Tale of the Hashish Eater."

Europeans knew of the intoxicating qualities not later than the sixteenth century, when it was written about and compared with alcohol. However, it seems not to have been used as an intoxicant in Europe before the nineteenth century. It then became popular among French and English writers. Baudelaire, Oscar Wilde and Havelock Ellis all wrote about their experiences with hashish. A few American writers of the period also experienced the drug and wrote about it, but most Americans remained ignorant of the intoxicating potential of cannabis until the twentieth century. Contrary to the hopeful suggestions of some proponents of marijuana legalization, there is no evidence that Washington or Jefferson ever smoked marijuana or even knew that others had done so.

Marijuana as a recreational drug was not discovered by a significant number of Americans until around 1915, when California enacted the first laws prohibiting it. The states began to fall in line and, ultimately, in 1937, federal law also prohibited it. Even during this period, however, the use of marijuana was largely confined to Mexican farm laborers, sailors, musicians and young writers. Marijuana was never popular in the general population until the late 1960s.

One reason for the long delay in general experience with marijuana in America was the effectiveness of the sensationalist propaganda against it. Typical is a 1928 book entitled *Dope,* which asserted that "the man under the influence of hasheesh catches up his knife and runs through the streets hacking and killing everyone he meets."[8]

In testimony before Congress in support of the Marijuana Tax Act, Harry Anslinger, head of the Bureau of Narcotics and Dangerous Drugs, compared it unfavorably to opium: "[H]ere we have a drug that is not like opium. Opium has all of the good of Dr. Jekyll and all of the evil of Mr. Hyde. This drug [marijuana] is entirely the monster Hyde."[9] *Scientific American* called it "more dangerous than cocaine or heroin,"[10] and *Newsweek* labeled it a "dangerous and devastating narcotic."[11] Virtually all magazine and newspaper articles during the 1930s that discussed marijuana proclaimed it the creator of maniacal frenzies in which the user was likely to commit all sorts of unspeakable crimes.[12] This baseless nonsense has been thoroughly repudiated since the 1960s by virtually everyone with any knowledge of the drug. No one now claims that marijuana leads to violence.

For whatever reason Americans were slow to focus their recreational-drug appetites on marijuana, they more than made up for their tardiness in the 1960s, and the popularity of the drug has persisted for more than a generation. NIDA's National Household Survey for 1991 estimates that nearly 68 million Americans over the age of twelve who are living today have used marijuana. That number continues to grow as the population ages and marijuana retains its popularity. About 20 million Americans are estimated to have used the drug during 1991, and 10 million of those used it in the previous month.[13]

More people use marijuana than use all other illicit drugs combined.

Psychoactive Effects of Marijuana

As with other drugs, the set and setting in which marijuana is consumed strongly influences the effects experienced by the user. Persons who smoke marijuana for a specific health reason, such as to inhibit nausea, rarely note a significant "high" from the drug. Practiced recreational users, on the other hand, usually experience a high from a placebo, i.e., marijuana from which the active ingredients have been secretly removed. The psychoactive properties of marijuana, however, are far from imaginary. Virtually everyone who smokes anything but the weakest marijuana experiences alteration of mood or consciousness which they attribute to the drug. Marijuana is often consumed in social situations as part of group behavior. But, like alcohol, it can and sometimes is used in solitude. The expected effects are different depending on such changes in setting.

As noted by Erich Goode, long lists of supposed marijuana effects were circulated in the late 1960s and early 1970s that "were completely fraudulent and based on no knowledge of what the user actually felt under the influence of the drug. Nausea, vomiting, diarrhea, and psychotic episodes appeared frequently on these lists, and yet [interviews of users show such effects] to be virtually nonexistent."[14]

Goode himself interviewed 200 marijuana smokers and—without providing them suggestions or lists of possibilities—asked them to describe the effects of marijuana on them. The most common response, obtained from 46 percent of the subjects, was that marijuana made them more relaxed, peaceful, calmer. The next most common response was that it made them more sensitive or perceptive. Other effects mentioned by more than one fifth of the interviewees was thinking deeper or more profoundly, a sense of merriment or easy amusement, exaggeration of mood, slowing down or stretching out of time, introversion, feeling happy or pleasant, mind wandering or free association.[15]

Other studies have ranked importantly a number of effects that

Goode's respondents apparently thought less significant, such as feeling hungry (the "munchies"), greater appreciation or enjoyment of music and sex, and feelings of paranoia.[16]

While there are minor variations among the studies, they converge on several points. First, the marijuana experience is almost uniformly described as pleasant and relaxing. And although claims were made from the 1930s until the 1960s that marijuana led to violence, all of the studies show otherwise. Marijuana as a trigger to violence seems never to have been reported by any user to any researcher. The relationship is almost certainly in the other direction: one who is high on marijuana is extremely unlikely to engage in violence.

It would be a mistake to infer from such reports that pleasurable effects are uniform among *all* persons who try marijuana. Many people who try marijuana once or twice do not find the experience a pleasurable one and discontinue use. Of the 68 million Americans estimated to have used marijuana at least once, according to the 1991 Household Survey, fewer than a third used it during 1991 and fewer than one sixth used it during the previous month.[17] Thus, the majority of marijuana users do not find it pleasurable enough or worth the money or risk to continue to use it.

This does not necessarily mean that the effects on regular users are substantially different from the effects on others who do not find the experience pleasurable, but it does suggest that there is at least wide divergence in *evaluations* of the effects. A substantial alteration in consciousness, involving altered perceptions of time, memory distortions and abnormal patterns of concentration are experiences that appeal to some people and not to others. Many novice users of marijuana are frightened by the experience. Feelings akin to paranoia are commonly associated with marijuana use, and hardly anyone enjoys such feelings. Hallucinations are also occasionally experienced, and such effects are not always desired by the user. One reason why marijuana is regularly used only by a fraction of those who try it may be that the psychoactive effects are less predictable than with most other pleasure drugs.

Much of the unpredictability of effects is probably due to the illegality of the drug: there is no standardization of the purity or potency of the drug and no labeling or disclosure requirements. Large initial variations in strength, due to such things as the variety or strain of the plant and the proportion of leaf to stem, are compounded by the fact that the major active ingredient, THC, seems to deteriorate with exposure to air and thus with the age of the material.

Long-Term Psychological Effects

Unlike tobacco and heroin, marijuana is not generally addictive. Very few habitual marijuana users feel any strong need to use it on a daily basis. In the most recent NIDA Household Survey, only about half the people who used marijuana in the previous year also used it in the previous month and only about one-fourth used it weekly. When marijuana supplies temporarily dry up in a neighborhood or town, there is no frantic scurrying or traveling to fill the void. Most marijuana users lie back and wait out the hiatus. Such an attitude would be unimaginable among a group of tobacco smokers deprived of tobacco.

Proponents of marijuana prohibition had to abandon their claims linking the drug to violence. Resiliently, they have now reversed field and complain that marijuana is too effective a tranquilizer: it produces an "amotivational syndrome," which is a pompous way of saying it makes people lazy. To the extent that this observation is applied to one who is "high" on marijuana, there is undoubted—but misleading—truth in it. One who doses on most cold remedies, who drinks a beer or two, or even eats a hearty meal is likely during and shortly after that experience to be disinclined to work or study. Indeed, this is true of virtually any activity, including work and study themselves!

The issue deserves to be taken seriously only if the claim is that marijuana use actually interferes with the desire to work or study in a significant way, either because the user is unwilling to defer using the drug until a more appropriate recreational period or because habitual marijuana use produces something akin to an alteration of character. There is no cogent evidence to support either proposition. While the common psychoactive effects of marijuana are inconsistent with most work and virtually all study, it is because the drug interferes with such activities that it is not commonly used during them. Marijuana is employed to enhance or improve *recreational* activities, not to impair or impede work. Among 200 users interviewed by Erich Goode, only a third had so much as read anything while high, and two thirds of them said the experience was worsened by the drug.[18]

About the only means of objectively determining the existence of the so-called amotivational syndrome that anyone has suggested is a comparison of performances in school. Most of the studies show little or no difference in the grades of marijuana users and the grades of nonusers, thus providing no support for the amotivational claims.[19] One study showed that in comparison to nonusers, grade averages were higher among those who used marijuana occasionally and lower among those who used it daily.[20] It is unlikely that *any* causal relationship is suggested by these findings. More likely, the use of marijuana is a marker or symptom of something else. It is plausible that occasional users of marijuana are better adjusted socially and academically than abstainers while heavy users are less well adjusted than either of the other groups. To the chagrin of marijuana prohibitionists, a recent study of adolescents reached precisely those conclusions.[21] One who engages in any activity that is inconsistent with achievement has demonstrated lack of motivation, but one would not think of the alternative activity as the cause of the weak motivation. One who consumes drugs, exercises, eats, or watches television to excess is likely to suffer lower achievement in work or school. But if we do not attribute the lower achievement in such cases to the exercise, the food or the television, neither should we attribute it to marijuana.

Marijuana and Machinery

Marijuana intoxication appears to have no adverse effects on the performance of simple tasks or on reaction time, but it does impair the performance of complex tasks.[22] Whether driving an automobile or operating other equipment is a complex task is unclear.[23] Some laboratory studies of driving skills using simulators have suggested that subjects experiencing a normal social high are not impaired by it.[24] Several comparisons of the driving records of comparable samples of users and nonusers of marijuana have found that the users have a greater number of traffic violations but not a significantly larger number of accidents.[25] This may suggest that although marijuana users may be impaired as drivers, their altered perception of time and/or their awareness of their marijuana-induced impairment causes them to drive more slowly than they otherwise would and thus minimizes the accidents resulting from their impairment.[26]

Such comparisons assume that marijuana users are under the influence *while* driving. This is probably not often the case.[27] Alcohol drinkers are different. It may take a few hours after the last drink for a drinker to become completely sober. Frequently, drinkers will achieve their maximum level of intoxication a quarter of an hour or more after their last drink (the "one for the road") and may continue to be intoxicated for another two or three hours, during which they can drive a hundred or more miles. Marijuana smokers get high almost immediately when they smoke and the high recedes quickly, disappearing in an hour or so. Marijuana consumption patterns are also different. In an evening of socializing, during which they smoke marijuana, the typical users get high, relax, eat and drink, may nod off, return to normal, and then go home. The escalating pattern of consumption so often observed in social drinking is unusual among marijuana users because too much marijuana produces unpleasant effects (such as hallucinations or anxiety) and experienced users control their intake to avoid these effects. Drinkers, on the other hand, are often unable to appreciate that they are intoxicated when they are obviously so to others. They continue to drink. Those who are seriously impaired by alcohol also commonly overestimate their driving and other abilities drastically. They also tend to speed. None of these effects of alcohol seems to have counterparts in marijuana. Marijuana consumption is not—and is not likely to be—nearly as serious a highway safety problem as is the drinking of alcohol.

Nonetheless, the possibility that marijuana use contributes to deaths and injuries from accidents cannot be dismissed. Some marijuana smokers actually smoke *while* driving. Given the unpredictability of marijuana's effects, this is surely an unsafe practice. Moreover, persons who eat marijuana in brownies or other food may find themselves unwittingly impaired while driving, for two important differences exist when marijuana is eaten rather than smoked. Once the marijuana is eaten, the ingestion of the drug is out of the user's control. Also, the rate at which the drug reaches the brain is severely slowed when intake is through the digestive system rather than through the lungs. These differences can contribute to an undesired, unexpected and impairing level of intoxication. Driving cars or operating other equipment under the influence of marijuana clearly should be discouraged.

Acute Physical Effects

The acute effects of marijuana on bodily functions are minimal. The heartbeat rises measurably (increasing 20 to 25 beats per minute) but not enough to make the user conscious of a rapid pulse. Blood circulation and temperature in the extremities are increased significantly. The eyes tend to redden. A dryness in the mouth is commonly experienced. And that is about it. Until recently, it was commonly believed, and repeated in police manuals and learned literature, that marijuana also caused dilation of the pupils. As late as 1971, a California court relied upon the appearance of enlarged pupils as a major factor supporting arrest for marijuana use.[28] Laboratory studies have shown, however, that no such dilation occurs.[29]

Given such mild, almost insignificant physical manifestations of marijuana intoxication, it should not be surprising that no death from a marijuana overdose has ever been established.

Adverse Effects on Health

Approximately 100 million Americans over the past three decades have smoked (or eaten) marijuana. Millions of these have used marijuana on a regular, almost daily basis for decades. Despite these massive numbers of long-term users, no reliable evidence has appeared that such use has *any* adverse effects on their physical health. Drug policy analyst Mark Kleiman aptly notes, "if there were important medium-term effects of moderate levels of marijuana smoking, they ought to be apparent by now."[30] Long-term adverse effects—such as cancer—can theoretically still appear, but time is beginning to run out on them as well.

Other societies have used marijuana for centuries. Yet in no society has any official or respected study found serious adverse physical effects on humans from smoking marijuana. Indeed, in no less than nine official investigations of the problem, in both the United States and elsewhere, none have found any significant adverse effects on human health, even mental health. Here are a few.

• From 1916 to 1929 in the Panama Canal Zone, the U.S. Army conducted a medical investigation of marijuana, which it reported in *The Military Surgeon* in 1933.[31] The Army found that it was "not possible to demonstrate any evidence of mental or physical deterioration in the users."[32]

• In 1972, the Canadian government's Le Dain Commission published a report suggesting that marijuana is a relatively harmless drug. According to the commission, the short-term physiological effects of smoking marijuana are "slight" and have "little clinical significance."

The Le Dain Commission concluded that the characteristic deep inhalation of marijuana smokers puts them at some risk for "respiratory complications."[33] However, the commission pointed out that even heavy cannabis smokers consume much less marijuana than the average cigarette smoker consumes tobacco leaf, and that fact decreases lung-cancer risk relative to tobacco use.

• The 1972 report on the National Commission on Marijuana and Drug Abuse—nine of whose thirteen members were personally selected by then-president Nixon—found that the only damage proved is bronchitis, in heavy, chronic smokers.[34]

• The privately funded, Washington-based Drug Abuse Council, in 1980 issued a 291-page report titled "The Facts About Drug Abuse."[35] The Council found that "marijuana use in moderate amounts over a short term poses far less of a threat to an individual's health than does indiscriminate use of alcohol and tobacco."[36]

This and other evidence led the DEA's own administrative law judge Francis L. Young to conclude in 1988 that marijuana is among the safest therapeutic substances known and is less hazardous than many common foods.[37]

In spite of the foregoing findings, marijuana retains its DEA classification as a Schedule I narcotic, which cannot even be prescribed for its therapeutic uses. And Bob Martinez, former Director of the Office of National Drug Control Policy ("the drug czar") under George Bush, wrote in a 1991 letter to Paul Reynolds, an advocate of marijuana decriminalization:

A growing body of medical research is evidence that marijuana is far from a harmless substance. This research links chronic marijuana use to a litany of physical and mental ills. Among these are memory deficits, decreased infant birth weight, immunosuppression, a contributory role in schizophrenia, certain forms of cancer, and infant lukemia [misspelling in original text]. Fact being [sic] marijuana is a very harmful drug in and of itself.

Additionally, marijuana has proven to be a gateway to the use of harder drugs such as heroin and cocaine—of which the debilitating consequences I am sure you are aware. The question becomes why would we want to abandon a strategy that is working for a prescribed National [sic] disaster?[38]

Is Marijuana Criminogenic?

Reasonable people can differ over whether the proof of marijuana's psychological and physiological safety is sufficiently solid and long-term to preclude any possibility of negative health effects, but no one can seriously argue that marijuana per se is criminogenic. As noted, it has no positive correlation with violence. It is not addictive. Even if it were addictive, its cost of production is minuscule—comparable to the cost of producing lettuce or watermelons—so that the need for money to buy the drug could never be a serious motivation for predatory crime in a legalized system. Indeed, even though prohibition increases the cost of marijuana to the consumer by a factor of more than 100, there is no evidence even under the current prohibitory regime that people rob or steal in order to get the money to buy marijuana.

Given the fact that a minority of respondents in several studies report that marijuana increases their enjoyment of sex, it is remotely possible that marijuana use might lead to sex crimes or to at least undesirable sexual practices. But there isn't a sliver of evidence that marijuana leads to violent crimes having a sexual element, such as rape. Nor is there evidence that marijuana contributes to sexual promiscuity or "unsafe sex." Many legal things increase the enjoyment of sex: perfume, dinner, candlelight, music, a glass or two of wine, privacy, to name a few. Such stimulators of romance surely contribute more, singly or in combination, to the enjoyment of sex than does marijuana, yet there is no rational support for prohibiting any of them.

Marijuana *prohibition,* on the other hand, is clearly criminogenic. We discuss this in detail in later chapters, in connection with drug prohibition generally, but we at least note here that the criminogenics of prohibition apply not only to "hard" drugs that are addictive, such as heroin, but to marijuana even though it is neither addictive nor expensive. If marijuana is illegal to buy, then users are forced to seek out illegal sources for the drug. This often brings them into contact with criminal elements. Marijuana is "victimogenic" in that the buyers are vulnerable to predatory crime when they go about the process of "scoring," because of the neighborhoods and the persons with whom they come into contact. Also, since it is often obvious both to predators and to police that an intended illegal purchase brought the victims to the places where they were victimized, they are not likely to complain to the police about routine robberies or rip-offs. Beyond that, the process of participating in the distribution of illicit drugs—even as a pure consumer—brings the user into social contact with sellers and users of hard drugs (and other criminals) and encourages the marijuana user to forge social bonds with such persons. As "outlaws," all users of illicit drugs have common interests and common experiences that provide mutual emotional and even logistic support, inviting the marijuana user's entry into the "drug culture." Marijuana users who are arrested are branded criminals and may even spend time in jail. The adverse effects on self-esteem that inevitably accompany such experiences are decidedly criminogenic. These are just a few of the ways in which criminalization of marijuana is criminogenic. Similar effects would likely be experienced were we to criminalize the sale and use of chewing gum.

HEROIN

When the seed capsule of the unripe opium poppy is lanced, a resin is exuded. When the resin is dried, the brown gum that forms is called opium. It has been an important medicinal and recreational drug for several thousand years. The usual method of ingestion for a millennium or more was as a liquid, drunk in various potions. With the discovery of the New World and tobacco, the opium pipe was invented, and smoking rapidly became a common method of taking the drug.

The major active ingredient of opium, a white crystalline powder, was first isolated in 1803. It was named morphine after Morpheus, the god of dreams.[39] Morphine soon became one of the most valuable pain relievers in medicine, and it still is highly valued in pain management.[40]

In 1874, the English chemist C. R. Wright discovered that heating morphine in acetic acid would produce a new compound, diacetyl morphine. In 1898, a German company, Bayer Pharmaceuticals, introduced the chemical Wright had synthesized as a cough suppressant. Bayer gave its new product the trade name "heroin" and marketed it with Bayer's other recently introduced "wonder drug," aspirin. Heroin differs from morphine primarily in one respect: it is about two and one half times more potent, on a per weight basis. Because it is more concentrated, it is more suitable for smuggling and illegal distribution. That is why we have a heroin problem in America rather than a morphine problem. Most medical patients cannot tell the difference when they receive equivalent doses. Intravenous users, on the other hand, slightly prefer heroin because injecting of morphine causes unpleasant tingling sensations that are absent when heroin is injected.[41]

Taken by syringe, heroin can be injected into the muscle (as it commonly is when used medically), under the skin or into the veins. The latter method is much preferred by most addicts, since it produces a quick, powerful "rush" which is an important pleasure of taking the drug. Heroin can also be inserted into any body cavity, where it is absorbed by the bloodstream. It can also be eaten, smoked or snorted, as cocaine typically is. Most methods of use are not only less pleasurable than "mainlining," they are less efficient. When the drug is eaten, the liver neutralizes most of it before it reaches the general circulation. Smoking also wastes a good deal of the drug.

Heroin and morphine are only two of many members of the opiate family, drugs derived from opium. The opiates also include codeine (a valuable cough suppressant), dilaudid and paregoric. Chemists have also synthesized many opiate-like drugs which are not derived from opium. They include the painkiller Demerol and the common synthetic used to "maintain" heroin addicts, methadone. Other synthetics, some of which are far more powerful and dangerous than heroin, include fentanyl. The entire family of natural and synthetic opiates is chemically classified as "narcotics."

The opium poppy will grow almost anywhere.[42] It is grown extensively in India, Pakistan, Afghanistan, Laos, Thailand, Burma, Mexico, Iran, and Turkey. It is also cultivated in Africa and South America, mainly Colombia. During the nineteenth century, opium poppies were grown throughout New England and in the midwest and far west of the United States. During the Civil War the Confederacy grew opium poppies in order to counteract battlefield shortages of morphine caused by the Union blockade. Growing such poppies was not illegal in America until 1942.[43]

Opiates were entirely legal and commonly used in the United States during the nineteenth century. A liquid potion called laudanum (tincture of opium) was used to quiet crying babies.[44] Another potion called Godfrey's Cordial, consisting of opium, molasses and sassafras, was especially popular in England during this period for administration to infants under the age of two![45]

Morphine was originally heralded as a cure for alcoholism, and there was some evidence that it worked. Heroin had an even stranger introduction. Bayer and other companies sold it solely as a cough suppressant. It worked dramatically well for that purpose.[46]

Most regular users of opiates during the nineteenth century, at least in America, were women. Opiates were widely sold—and effective—for menstrual discomfort and other "female troubles." Sexist attitudes also contributed to its popularity. Women generally were excluded from the saloons, where men imbibed alcohol, and smoking by women was socially disapproved—even illegal. So opiates were among the few pleasure drugs approved for women.[47]

The Harrison Act of 1914 and the effects of alcohol prohibition and its repeal together altered the gender ratios drastically. During the 1960s, it was estimated that male heroin users outnumbered females by at least 5 to 1. Now that heroin is unpopular among middle and upper classes and is common among female prostitutes, the ratio is still about 2 male users per female user.[48]

The Extent of Heroin Use in America

A federal agency, the National Institute of Drug Abuse (NIDA), regularly interviews Americans in their homes regarding drug use. They call their study the Household Survey. But because many regular heroin users are homeless, a Household Survey is likely to miss many. Estimates of the extent of heroin use are notoriously unreliable and speculative. For most of the last forty years, the estimates of heroin users ranged from about 300,000 to 1,500,000, with most hovering around 500,000. The DEA currently estimates the number of users at about 750,000. NIDA's 1991 Household Survey contains no estimate of the number of current users; merely estimates of those now living who have "ever used" heroin: 2,886,000, and "used past year": 701,000.[49]

There is some evidence that heroin use is on the increase. Among the probable contributors to this trend: more and more people are becoming homeless and permanently unemployed; more are becoming derelicts or castoffs from society. Heroin has an extremely strong attraction to the hopeless. Heroin is cheaper and purer than it has been for decades. It is thus not only more available, it is safer to use because there is less need to mainline it. Finally, a major competitor, cocaine, is rapidly losing its popularity, since it is no longer regarded as the nonaddictive, entirely safe drug it was once commonly believed to be. Although addictive and hardly safe on the black market, heroin is no longer viewed as the lone monster drug.

Psychoactive Effects of Heroin

Street users of heroin distinguish between the "rush" and the "high." Injection immediately produces a rush that lasts only a minute or two. Other methods of administration produce no rush at all. The focus of the rush is in the abdominal area and it is often compared to a sexual orgasm. Norman Zinberg interviewed a number of heroin users while they were under the influence. He summarized their collective descriptions of the rush as a feeling "of great relief. Tension runs out of the body, the bones and muscles feel fluid and relaxed."[50]

After the rush comes the high, which can last four or five hours, and which can be produced with a sufficiently strong dose by any method of intake. The high is a warm, drowsy, tranquil state involving great relaxation. There may be a slight but pleasant dizziness. Users who are high distance themselves from both external and internal stimuli. As with other drugs, however, the experience of a high will vary greatly with differences in set and setting. According to Professor John Kaplan, "what is true about one user may not be true about another, and what was true about most users a few years ago may not be true today."[51]

Full-fledged heroin addicts typically describe the "high" as simply "feeling normal." Since they are in perpetual flight from the discomfort of withdrawal, they concentrate on eliminating the anxiety felt on the edge of withdrawal. Succeeding produces a feeling of normality. Avoiding withdrawal appears to be too serious to produce strong feelings of pleasure. Relief is a more accurate term for the experience. Some street users term this "getting straight" or "getting right."

Because most regular heroin users in America are deeply embedded in the drug and crime cultures, it is difficult to speculate about the effects of the drug per se on the user's motivations to participate meaningfully and productively in mainstream activities. Given the stigmatization of heroin use, the correlation between heroin use and detachment from society is almost definitional. Most regular heroin users are parasites on the larger American community. However, much of this parasitism is due to three factors: (1) the illegality of heroin, (2) the deep disapprobation of heroin users and (3) the costliness of the drug. Since addicts must remain under the influence of the drug virtually all their waking hours, they cannot work unless they are high, yet they cannot remain high on less than $100 per day. They typically are unskilled and cannot earn that kind of money legitimately. Thus, few conclusions about the compatibility of work and heroin use can be drawn from the general behavior patterns observed in America.

Nonetheless, we should not write off American street addicts as hopelessly incompetent. If they are under the influence of any drug at all, the derelicts we see passed out in an alley or on a park bench are likely loaded with cheap booze. Street junkies are apparently energetic hustlers who are not only capable of working, they are employed, seven days a week, in a very demanding occupation—finding affordable, safe, quality drugs; stealing and burglarizing, selling booty, conning, conniving, avoiding the police. Street addicts have in heroin "a purpose in an otherwise purposeless life. The activities of the addict become a full-time job."[52] Edward Preble, an anthropologist, and John Casey, an economist, studied New York street addicts and reported that they are

> actively engaged in meaningful activities and relationships. . . . [T]hey are aggressively pursuing a career that is exacting, challenging, adventurous, and rewarding. They are always on the move and must be alert, flexible and resourceful. The surest way to identify heroin users in a slum neighborhood is to observe the way people walk. The heroin user walks with a fast, purposeful stride, as if he is late for an important appointment—indeed, he is. He is hustling . . . *taking care of business.*"[53]

History provides a number of examples of opiate addicts who led normal, productive, even creative lives, including doctors, lawyers and politicians. Among the more famous were Dr. William Halsted, a brilliant surgeon and a founder of Johns Hopkins medical school, and Senator Joseph McCarthy, the infamous red-baiter.[54] That at least suggests that it would be possible for most addicts to do so, provided their use of heroin were not criminal. Our experience with methadone maintenance programs corroborates this. Heroin addicts can avoid withdrawal and substantially eliminate their craving by using the synthetic opiate methadone. Many of them are also able to engage in productive employment despite being under the influence of methadone, yet the psychoactive effects of methadone and heroin are similar.

Our experiences with heroin in Vietnam also suggest that heavy heroin users are capable of productive work. Thousands of American soldiers used large quantities of the extremely cheap heroin available in Vietnam, on a daily basis. By conventional standards, they were addicts, fully feeding their heroin appetites. Yet virtually all of them performed their military duties satisfactorily, some with distinction. In fact, their heroin use went largely undetected by their superiors. The Army found it necessary to institute urine tests to identify its heroin users.[55]

Dr. Jerome Jaffe, an eminent drug expert who was President Nixon's director of the Office of Drug Abuse Prevention, described the rare addict who can avoid the street:

> The addict who is able to obtain an adequate supply of drugs through legitimate channels and has adequate funds usually dresses properly, maintains his nutrition, and is able to discharge his social and occupational obligations with reasonable efficiency. He usually remains in good health, suffers little inconvenience, and is, in general, difficult to distinguish from other persons.[56]

It would still seem plausible that, all other things being equal, a heroin addict, even in a state of free availability, would be less motivated to work effectively and productively than a nonuser. But much work—even in America—is physically or psychically painful. If heroin, or any other drug, alleviates the pain—or even the tedium—of such work, it might in such instances actually promote rather than diminish productiveness. Ironically, it was just this argument that helped get opium declared illegal in the first place. Giving vent to a racist sentiment shared by many white workers of the time, labor leader Samuel Gompers complained that their opium use gave Chinese immigrant workers an unfair advantage in the labor market. The Chinese were said to be able to work longer and harder because of the drug.[57]

The tendency of heroin users to turn inward and to distance themselves from the concerns of others suggests that heroin would be a handicap in any activity requiring extensive social interaction. Test subjects under the influence of heroin also show some reductions in performance on a variety of mental tests, mainly exhibiting a slowing down of mental function rather than inability to produce accurate or valid responses. There is, therefore, a *partial* similarity to alcohol, which adversely affects both speed and accuracy on mental tests.

On the whole, heroin usage would probably produce some impairment of productive capacities among workers engaged in anything but mundane, simple tasks. It also would impair driving or operation of other machinery. It is doubtful, however, that the impairments from normal heroin usage would equal those of alcohol intoxication.

Nonmedical use of heroin is undesirable, and it should be discouraged. But a system of prohibition that relegates the drug to the black market makes heroin use even more debilitating and dangerous. The black market is unregulated. Users have little basis for determining the purity or potency of the heroin they are getting and thus cannot control their highs. The unpredictability of the effects of the drug, therefore, makes it more difficult for the user either to function productively or to avoid accidents. The black market arbitrarily imposes a death penalty on unlucky users.

Acute Physical Effects of Heroin

The most significant physical consequence of a normal dose of heroin may be primarily a psychological effect that passes as a physical one: the altered perception of pain. Morphine and heroin do not remove pain entirely. Rather, the opiates leave untouched the awareness or feeling of pain, but they make it bearable, even insignificant.[58] A major advantage of opiates as painkillers is that sensitivity to touch, sights and sounds is maintained. This leads some to posit that the major analgesic effects of opiates reside in their tranquilizing effects: they remove the anxiety over the pain so effectively that the perception of pain—as pain—virtually disappears (this phenomenon is similar to the analgesic effect of hypnosis, which can permit major surgery without drugs).[59]

The opiates effectively suppress the coughing reflex. They also cause the smooth muscle of the gastrointestinal tract to contract, resulting in constipation in normal users and making the opiates very effective treatment for dysentery, diarrhea and other digestive ailments. Blood pressure is lowered, sexual potency or libido is suppressed, menstrual irregularity is produced and the pupils of the eyes are constricted. Some users experience warmth and excessive perspiration. All of these effects are temporary.

Addiction, Tolerance and Withdrawal

That opiates are physically addicting cannot be doubted. Nor is there any doubt that the human body develops tolerance to them, requiring greater and greater dosages to produce the same effects. When there is addiction and tolerance followed by withdrawal, the withdrawal symptoms can be extremely unpleasant. The symptoms of heroin withdrawal are almost the opposite of a heroin high. Instead of constipation, there is diarrhea; instead of bodily warmth, there are chills; instead of constricted pupils, there is dilation; instead of reduced blood pressure, there is an increase. Nonetheless, while withdrawal from alcohol and barbiturates can be fatal, withdrawal from heroin rarely if ever causes death. The overall symptoms of heroin withdrawal have been compared to a severe case of the flu.[60]

Because tolerance develops from the regular use of opiates, many addicts do not experience a high. Rather, they simply maintain themselves in a "normal" state, perhaps because heroin is so costly that they cannot afford steady increases in dosages, sufficient to maintain highs. The addict must settle for a lesser dose just sufficient to defer withdrawal. The great financial cost of escalating tolerance even inspires some insincere applications to heroin treatment programs: addicts who want to "detox" merely to reduce their tolerance levels so as to cut down their costs and regain some euphoria. Once withdrawal is complete, the addict can resume heroin use at much lower doses and produce the previously unaffordable highs.

Both the power of heroin addiction and its universality are controversial. In the 1950s and early 1960s, there was a common myth that heroin was almost instantly and permanently addictive to any user. Henry Giordano, Commissioner of the Bureau of Narcotics, even testified to Congress in 1968 that, according to the agency's research, anyone who used heroin more than six times would become an addict.[61] This is absurd. There have always been a substantial number of heroin users, called "chippers," who control their use by spacing it out, perhaps by limiting it to weekends, and they never become addicted. By most accounts, chippers outnumber addicts.[62]

Even regular, sustained opiate users do not always become seriously addicted. And hardly any heroin addiction is permanent. It has long been known that addicts over the age of forty are rare. The myth of permanent addiction required the assumption that premature deaths from the ravages of heroin accounted for the rarity of middle-aged former addicts. It is now widely known, however, that people tend to "mature" out of heroin, even if they never undergo successful treatment. It now is also known that even younger addicts "spontaneously remit," to use the jargon of the Surgeon General.[63] They just quit.

This was dramatically demonstrated by our Vietnam veterans. More than 15 percent of our soldiers in Vietnam regularly used heroin and by ordinary measures were addicted. Yet 90 percent of them kicked the habit as soon as they returned home.[64] Some became chippers, and thus made "it quite clear that former heroin addicts can, at least in some circumstances, move to controlled, nonaddictive use."[65]

Serious addiction and withdrawal problems are also rare among medical patients who receive regular doses of morphine. Once they leave the hospital, few such patients feel addicted or are in serious danger of readdiction.

Both the medical and the Vietnam experiences strongly suggest that the power of addiction and the anxiety about withdrawal are mainly situational. They may rest more on the bleak, pathetic environments that surround the typical American addict than on the pharmacology of the drug. The medical patient associates the drug with relief from the pain of a temporary medical problem. When that problem goes away, so, usually, does the need for the drug. The Vietnam soldier used heroin as self-medication to provide psychic escape from the horrors of the war. When removed from those horrors, the soldier no longer needed the drug.

Long-Term Effects on Health

As with marijuana, study after study has failed to find that the regular use of heroin, in conditions of relatively free availability, produces any substantial adverse effects on mental or physical health. As put by Edward Brecher, "There is . . . general agreement throughout the medical and psychiatric literature that the overall effects of opium, morphine, and heroin on the addict's mind and body under conditions of low price and ready availability are on the whole amazingly bland."[66]

The adverse effects on the user's health are either quite indirect or are attributable to prohibition. One who regularly doses on opiates may feel unperturbed by what might otherwise be excruciating pain. Since pain is often a symptom of serious disease, heroin causes the addict to delay seeking needed medical treatment. More important, prohibition leads the addict to avoid seeking medical help out of fear of arrest or otherwise being denied access to the drug. American addicts, moreover, will not have the funds to pay for medical help; their resources will be almost entirely devoted to acquiring drugs. Most addicts are in a state of poverty. If not homeless, they are nearly so and, in any event, live in filthy conditions without proper nourishment. These conditions of poor hygiene cause far more death and disease than does the drug itself. They are largely the products of prohibition.

Deaths by Overdose

Decades of misinformation and media coverage of tragic celebrity deaths, such as those of Lenny Bruce and John Belushi, have created the popular impression that heroin users are commonly dying from overdoses. However, that public perception of overdose risk is exaggerated. Addicts are more likely to die from poor health and disease. Another frequent cause of death is homicide. In the late 1960s, drug researcher Edward Preble studied seventy-eight heroin addicts who resided in the Spanish Harlem neighborhood of New York. In the early 1980s, Preble painstakingly investigated what had happened to the members of this group. Twenty-eight had died during the intervening years. Forty percent of those fatalities were caused by homicide.[67]

Although the overdose phenomenon has long been observed and recorded, it is still mysterious. It has been demonstrated that it takes seven or eight milligrams of pure heroin per kilogram of body weight injected directly into the vein to kill an unaddicted monkey. Assuming the similarity of humans, it would take 500 milligrams—fifty times the usual street dose—to kill an unaddicted adult.[68] Thus, while it would seem possible to kill a novice with a heroin overdose, it is hard to see how such a death could be accidental.

Even more puzzling is the fact that virtually all persons counted as having died from heroin overdose are unmistakably heroin addicts.[69] Addicts who build up tolerance can inject an enormous quantity of heroin without killing themselves. Addicts who have had access to large quantities of heroin have reported using more than 1,600 milligrams a day. In a Philadelphia experiment, 1,800 milligrams were injected into an addict over a two-and-a-half-hour period, and he didn't even get sick. In another Philadelphia study, addicts were given up to nine times their ordinary dosages, by injection. No significant physical or other changes were observed or even measurable; the addicts didn't even get sleepy.[70] There is, therefore, no established dosage of unadulterated heroin that is clearly sufficient to kill an addict, yet addicts die every day from their injections. Some of them are found with the band around their arm and the syringe in hand, suggesting that death was virtually instantaneous. Why does this happen?

Pure heroin almost never reaches the street. It is "cut" a minimum of five times before reaching the customer, by a wide variety of chemicals. Common adulterants include quinine, lactose, sucrose, mannite, procaine and baking soda. Most of these diluents are relatively harmless to most people, but allergic reactions are still possible.

Quinine is different. It is a common adulterant because it tastes like heroin and makes it impossible for the user to determine the purity of the product by tasting it. Quinine also causes vasodilation which mimics the vascular effects of heroin sufficiently to confound users into believing they have a high-quality product. Unfortunately, quinine can also cause cardiac arrest when injected into a susceptible subject. This accounts for many "heroin overdoses."[71]

Persons who have died from "overdose" are also often found to have ingested alcohol or barbiturates, as well as heroin. Both these substances act synergistically with heroin and can produce pronounced respiratory depression. Pulmonary edema (fluid in the lungs), symptomatic of respiratory failure, is frequently present in "overdose" victims.[72]

There are also cases in which heroin has intentionally been adulterated with lethal poisons, either by a competitor who wants to destroy the "reputation" of the dealer or by the dealer himself who wants to dispose of a bothersome customer and simultaneously signal to the market that his drug supply is potent. Some of these poisonings can be erroneously labeled as overdoses.

Criminogenics and Heroin

In America, heroin addicts commit a vastly disproportionate share of property crimes but very few crimes of violence unrelated to the pursuit of property. At one time, it was commonly claimed that the propensity of addicts to commit crimes was directly caused by the drug's effect on the brain, producing moral weakness and a thirst for violence.[73] Such claims have from time to time been made about every recreational drug, even tobacco. But there has never been any evidence to support the theory with respect to heroin, any more than there was any support for identical claims about marijuana. No intelligent person really believes such theories today. On the contrary, the prevailing view is that much, perhaps most, of the addict's criminality is simply and solely the result of the interaction of his addiction and the law's prohibition.

For a combination of reasons, in a state of prohibition, most addicts cannot hold a steady job. Even if they could, they couldn't earn enough to support their addiction. Hence, they must either give up the use of heroin or engage in a parallel pattern of predatory crimes. But if property crimes are committed by the addict because of the high cost of the drug, this is a strong argument for legalizing the drug, for if we make heroin freely available, we remove the motivation to commit the crime. Recognizing the logic, some prohibitionists reverse field. Having abandoned the claim that we must prohibit heroin because it makes its user a crazed murderer or rapist, the prohibitionists deny now that there is any causal connection at all between heroin and crime. They claim, for example, that in many cases the heroin addicts were thieves before becoming addicts. If they didn't spend the proceeds of their crimes on heroin, they would spend them on food, clothing, shelter, wine or horses, but they would keep stealing even if heroin were free, or even if they quit using it. Thus, it is argued, since there is no causal link between heroin addiction and the criminality, prohibition is necessarily innocent of any contribution to the addict's crime. In short, the addict is a criminal for reasons unrelated to his addiction.

The evidence is overwhelming, however, that addicts steal in order to feed their habits, in prodigious numbers. Many studies have shown that when addicts engage in frequent use of heroin, their criminal activities increase proportionately. When they curtail their use, they also curtail their thefts. In a study of Baltimore addicts, 237 members of the sample committed more than 500,000 crimes during their average of eleven years on the street. The addicts' criminality was six times as great when using heroin daily as when abstinent or only occasionally using.[74] Other studies show that when addicts go into treatment or methadone maintenance programs their crimes drop off sharply.[75] Still other studies demonstrate short-run positive correlations between property crime rates and increases in the costs of heroin, as well as positive correlations between property crime rates and addiction rates.[76]

That prohibition accounts for huge amounts of property crime by heroin addicts cannot seriously be doubted. But it is still possible that some criminogenic nexus exists between such crimes and heroin use per se. People who are highly dependent on a drug, the use of which is heavily stigmatized (even though legal), will have difficulty succeeding in employment and other social exchanges. They will be drawn toward a subculture that condones criminality more than the rest of society will countenance. They will be caught up in *milieux* that are conducive to crime, and may well adapt to them. In this sense, at least, heroin may be mildly criminogenic.

Another linkage to crime is that, like many severe alcohol abusers, heroin addicts are also often themselves crime victims, a status facilitated by their addiction. One who is more than moderately high on heroin is passive and ill-equipped to provide resistance to a thief or a rapist. The addict who overdoses may even be unconscious, or nearly so, and completely defenseless. Much of this victimization is also attributable to prohibition, for it forces the addict to buy drugs of unknown variety or potency. Such merchandise will often make them sick or they will overdose on it, and will be lucky if they live. The economics of addiction assure that the addicts are on the street, exposed to predators during most of their lives as addicts. They have no safe place in which to keep their valuables, no real home in which to retreat.

COCAINE

About 7,000 years ago, according to Peruvian legend, some llamas, only recently domesticated, were deprived of their normal forage and sampled the leaf of the coca plant. It seemed to give them energy.[77] The plant was not very palatable to humans as food, but they tried it anyway, chewing and sucking on the leaves. They discovered that what worked for the llama worked for its keeper. Thus began history's longest and most intimate relationship between a society and a shrub.

The mastication of coca leaf has for thousands of years been a daily practice for most adults throughout large regions of Peru, Bolivia, Colombia and Argentina. In some areas, 90 percent of the adults partake daily of the leaf. It not only provides mild stimulation and staves off fatigue, it suppresses hunger and is thought to be invaluable in the daily occupations of the inhabitants of the harsh mountain regions. Coca has also become part of religious ritual for descendants of the Incas, who believed coca was divine.

Coca chewing does not appear to cause addiction or any other serious health or social problems. It is regarded by much of the Andean populace substantially the way many Americans regard coffee or tea, except that it has a second important use: as a household remedy for a wide range of physical complaints. It is the treatment of choice for dysentery, indigestion, cramps, diarrhea, stomach ulcers and pain. It is also commonly used for toothaches, rheumatism, even hangovers, taken internally or applied as a poultice for its anesthetic qualities.[78]

The appetite for coca chewing never spread to Europe or North America. But various drinks made from coca leaf were introduced with much success in nineteenth-century Europe. The most popular was called "Mariani's wine," a mixture of wine and coca manufactured by a Corsican, Signor Angelo Mariani. His wine became popular with Christians who practiced fasting: among other benefits, it was helpful in suppressing their pangs of hunger.[79]

In 1885, a purveyor of patent medicine in Georgia named John Styth Pemberton introduced a product similar to Mariani's in America. It was called *French Wine Coca—Ideal Nerve and Tonic Stimulant.* In 1886, he added another coca product and called it *Coca Cola.* It was originally advertised as a "remarkable therapeutic agent" for a long list of ailments but evolved into a recreational drink. It contained two stimulants: coca and caffeine. In 1905, the company substituted decocainized coca, which remains in the product today.

The main stimulant in coca leaves, the alkaloid cocaine, was isolated in 1844, but little was made of it until around 1883, when a German army physician issued pure cocaine to Bavarian soldiers and reported that it gave them energy and helped them resist fatigue. An impoverished Viennese physician learned of it and tried it on himself. Writing of its wonderful qualities in a "Song of Praise," Sigmund Freud made both it and himself famous. Freud described in nearly ecstatic terms the ability of the drug to increase "vitality and the capacity for work" while providing "exhilaration and lasting euphoria" without "any of the unpleasant after-effects that follow exhilaration brought about by alcohol." Freud also opined that cocaine produces "no craving for further use" and is valuable as a treatment for both depression and morphine addiction.[80] A controversy soon developed over the latter claims and Freud abandoned both the claims and the drug after about three years, even though he never felt addicted to it.[81]

An even more famous, though fictional, user of cocaine in the late nineteenth century also did much to popularize the drug: the eminent detective Sherlock Holmes, who found cocaine "transcendentally stimulating and clarifying to the mind."

Cocaine enjoyed considerable popularity in the United States from about 1890 to 1905. It was believed effective in treating not only fatigue but sinusitis and hay fever, among other maladies. Learned journals also recommended it, as Freud had, for drug and alcohol addiction. It was not only an ingredient of tonics and soft drinks, it could be bought in coca-leaf cigarettes, pre-mixed with wine or liquor, in tablets, ointments, and sprays.[82] Saloons began putting a pinch in a shot of whiskey. The popularity of cocaine subsided several years before it became illegal in 1914, largely due to the perception that it could be addictive.

What residual interest in cocaine remained after it became a black-market product in 1914 was all but extinguished by the discovery in the 1930s of amphetamines ("speed"), synthetic stimulants having very similar psychoactive effects to cocaine, with at least three advantages: (1) they were extremely cheap, since they cost almost nothing to produce and were manufactured by pharmaceutical companies, (2) they were easy to obtain, in quasi-legitimate channels, since doctors often prescribed them for depression, weight loss, even heroin addiction, (3) the high was much longer lasting: about seven hours compared to half an hour or less for cocaine. A generation of experience with amphetamines, however, convinced many users that speed was pregnant with problems. For one thing, its intravenous use, which was common, sometimes produced a profound paranoia with hallucinations.

Cocaine was resurrected in the late 1960s. Freud's claims that cocaine was not only beneficial but nonaddictive were dusted off, endlessly repeated and widely believed. Finally, it was thought, we have discovered the wonder drug that is problem free. The use of cocaine increased faster during the 1970s than did the use of any other illegal drug. Among high school seniors, according to one survey, cocaine use doubled between 1975 and 1979.[83] In all age categories, according to another study, cocaine use doubled between 1972 and 1979, but leveled off between 1979 and 1982. Problems of dependency and side effects were once again experienced and casual use began a downtrend about 1982.[84]

The downtrend in cocaine use was slowed in 1985 by a technological breakthrough. Until this point, most cocaine users snorted it. Intravenous injection was more efficient, but also more dangerous; it was eschewed by the middle and upper class user. Smoking the drug was preferred by many, but its melting point was so high that it could not be smoked in its powdered (hydrochloride) form; it had to be converted to "freebase," a chemical form with a much lower vaporization point. The standard method of converting cocaine hydrochloride into smokable freebase was a dangerous and lengthy process that involved "cooking" the cocaine in an alkaline solution and then extracting the base using volatile solvents such as ether. (The fire from such a procedure nearly killed comedian Richard Pryor.) Someone discovered, however, that you can convert cocaine hydrochloride into a smokable rock form (now called "crack," after the sound it makes when smoked) just by heating it in baking soda and water. That discovery reinvigorated the cocaine market and greatly increased the population of cocaine abusers.

When administered intranasally, cocaine reaches the brain in three to five minutes. But when cocaine is smoked, the brain is bathed in about eight *seconds*. The effects from smoking are also highly concentrated whereas they are more diffuse with other methods. As a result, a very small quantity of cocaine can produce an intense though brief high if smoked. The discovery of crack reduced the cost of a single cocaine high from about $30 to $3 or $4, thus placing a crack high within the financial grasp of virtually everyone. Cocaine, which had been by far the most costly drug—about four times as expensive as heroin—became democratized.

Despite the discovery of crack, the number of cocaine users in America resumed its decline from its highest levels around 1980. Since 1985 alone, the number of persons who used cocaine as often as once a month has been cut in half. According to the 1991 Household Survey, nearly 24 million Americans have used cocaine some time in their lives, but only about one-fourth of those had used it at all in 1991, and only about one in 13 used it during the previous month.[85] The number of *weekly* users, however, has been increasing. Thus, while casual use is down, cocaine *abuse* is probably up.

Physiological and Psychoactive Effects

A local anesthetic that is still valued for that purpose in medical practice, cocaine when snorted constricts the nasal blood vessels and produces sniffles, or a runny nose. Intranasal dosages of 25 or 100 milligrams elevate the heart rate about 10 to 15 beats per minute and also produce slight increases in systolic blood pressure (10 to 20mm).[86] Blood circulation in the skin and viscera is reduced. Appetite is suppressed.

When cocaine is used concurrently with other drugs, heart rate and blood pressure may increase even more. Alcohol, for example, also increases heart rate (but decreases blood pressure). When alcohol and cocaine are taken in combination, heart rate increases are three to five times those produced by either drug alone. These effects are even more pronounced when the user engages in physical activities.[87] Similar synergistic effects on pulse and blood pressure are produced when cocaine is combined with marijuana.[88]

As for psychoactive effects, cocaine acts as a stimulant in the brain. Like other pleasure drugs, the psychoactive effects produced by cocaine are influenced by set and setting. However, the user commonly experiences euphoria. Such feelings include an enhanced sense of self-worth, of mastery and competence, of energy and power. Fatigue is temporarily vanquished. Sociability and sexual arousal are often enhanced. Unlike alcohol, which produces similar psychoactive effects in some drinkers, this sensation of greater energy, alertness and competence induced by cocaine is not spurious; there is no decrement in mental acuity or motor skills. In fact, experiments demonstrate that fatigued subjects actually improve their mental powers temporarily when they take the drug in moderate doses. Along with amphetamines, cocaine is popular among some truck drivers and college students cramming for their exams or writing term papers after lengthy procrastination. Robert Louis Stevenson allegedly wrote the novel *Dr. Jekyll and Mr. Hyde* in three days under the influence of cocaine.[89]

Some users feel a rush when they take the drug intravenously or smoke it, which is analogous to the rush experienced by heroin mainliners. The rush disappears after a minute or so and the high begins its descent almost immediately and vanishes after twenty or thirty minutes (or sooner, if the cocaine is smoked). When the high diminishes, many users feel a strong desire for another dose, a desire sometimes augmented by irritability and dysphoria. If supplies are available, repeated administrations will often continue for several hours, even days, followed by a crash, when the user is exhausted and sleeps for long periods.[90]

Chronic Consequences

There is little or no development of tolerance for cocaine, other than an acute tolerance that arises in the course of a binge and then disappears during the crash.[91] Nor is there clear evidence of withdrawal symptoms. The majority of cocaine users indulge only intermittently; they spend most of their time—a week or two, typically—cocaine sober before returning to the drug.[92] They then spend an evening or so on the drug and another period away from it. This is inconsistent with addiction as we use that term and as it applies to opiates. It is a pattern of drug use usually observed with only two other common recreational drugs: alcohol (among bingers) and amphetamines.

Most users of cocaine suffer no serious physical or social problems from it. That is why even people who should have known better trumpeted it during the seventies as a nonaddictive, harmless drug.

Before the crack era, only a fraction of cocaine users developed dependence upon cocaine. Estimates range from about 2 percent to 20 percent, with 5 to 10 percent being a reasonable approximation.[93] A distinct minority, however, suffer immense social and occupational penalties for their abuse of the drug. It is common knowledge in virtually every community in America that one or another prominent local business or political career has been destroyed by a cocaine preoccupation. Jobs, marriages and fortunes have all "gone up the nose," to use a vernacular description of the tragedy.

Smoking the drug is much more reinforcing than snorting it,[94] and repeated doses are affordable, at least at the outset. Dependence is therefore more frequently found among cocaine smokers than among snorters. With crack, we experienced a revival of the myth that once enveloped heroin: once a user, always a user. Appraisals more removed in time from crack's introduction are less hysterical. There are in fact many occasional crack smokers who function fairly normally, who hold down important, legitimate jobs and handle most of their duties reasonably well. Many would place the former mayor of Washington, D.C., Marion Barry, in that category. More responsible estimates are that only about one in six crack users is seriously dependent on the drug.[95] No doubt that figure is fluid. As more is learned about the patterns of use that lead to dependence, users will tend to avoid such patterns, just as chippers learned to handle heroin, and the percentage of users who are "addicts" may be reduced over time.

For those who abuse cocaine, intoxication prevents sleep and curbs appetite, and can plainly have detrimental effects on physical health. Preoccupation with cocaine can also produce neglect of hygiene and inattentiveness to illness, exacerbating whatever diseases or other health problems the user has. Chronic cocaine intoxication can also put a strain on the cardiovascular system similar to that inflicted by tobacco, with indeterminate ill effects. This seems especially likely if cocaine use is combined with other drugs having similar acute cardiovascular effects, such as alcohol, tobacco and marijuana. Intravenous injections can spread numerous diseases, some of which, like AIDS, are deadly. Smoking crack may also cause serious lung damage, perhaps even cancer, but there will be no way to determine that for some years. Heavy intranasal use over time can do serious damage to the nasal passages, even rupturing the nasal septum.

Cocaine abuse is also causally linked with abuse of alcohol, heroin and other depressives. The heavy cocaine user often takes these drugs to augment, vary, or even to moderate some of the effects of the stimulant and to reduce the unpleasantness of the crash. Polydrug abuse is common.[96]

Many chronic cocaine users also experience disturbing and disagreeable psychological effects. Among the more frequently reported feelings are anxiety, depression and irritability. Other common complaints include cognitive deficits, lack of motivation and absence of sex drive. The most serious chronic effects attributed to the drug are seizures and paranoid psychoses. All of these symptoms of chronic cocaine abuse disappear when the user remains drug free for a few weeks. The possibility that some of them are withdrawal symptoms cannot be completely discounted. As with other drugs, it is also possible that some of the apparent side effects are erroneously attributed to the drug. Since persons with mental disorders are also frequent drug users, the apparent causal connection between the drugs and the psychoses may be spurious. Nonetheless, there is general agreement that in some cases the nexus is real, particularly because these effects parallel those long experienced with amphetamines. The pharmacological and behavioral effects of amphetamines and cocaine are strikingly similar.

Thus, some cocaine abusers experience adverse psychological effects including, in rare cases, temporary psychoses. Casual cocaine users do not consistently experience any negative consequences. There appears to be no adverse effect on work among most casual cocaine users. In fact, a recent study found that cocaine users earn 37 percent more in wages than nonusers,[97] casting doubt on the common assumption that cocaine use routinely leads to poor work performance. The number of star and superstar athletes who have used cocaine while excelling in sports also undermines common assumptions about cocaine.

Fetal Danger

Many heavy cocaine users are young women. They often also use alcohol and tobacco. All three drugs pose a threat to fetal health. Babies born from cocaine-using mothers weigh less and are less healthy than other babies. How much of this is due to the mother's neglect of nutrition and hygiene generally and how much is directly due to the effects of the drug on the fetus is unknown. A correlation is clear, however, and mothers have been criminally prosecuted for delivering cocaine to their fetuses. Such treatment of cocaine-

dependent mothers is controversial. Chronic use of alcohol by pregnant mothers is undeniably harmful to the fetus, as is chronic use of
tobacco and, in many cases, aspirin and other drugs, yet criminal
prosecution is reserved for mothers who use cocaine. This appears to
some as racist, because cocaine abuse is more common among ethnic
minorities than with the majority.[98]

Cocaine Fatalities

Heart attacks and strokes in apparently healthy young people, including athletes, are frequently accompanied by cocaine intoxication, especially when combined with one or more other drugs that have
interactive effects. Acute toxicity can develop and cause seizures, some
of which can be fatal.[99] The toxicity may also account for blood vessel
blockages and abnormalities in heart rhythms. Determination of cocaine's effect is difficult because as both an anesthetic and a stimulant
the drug has multiple influences on cardiac function. According to the
Secretary of Health and Human Services, "despite the lack of concrete
evidence linking cocaine to cardiovascular events in human subjects,
there is a growing body of circumstantial evidence suggesting that
cocaine may lead to myocardial infarcts and strokes."[100]

Cocaine and Criminogenics

What we said about the cost of heroin motivating its addicts to commit
property crimes also applies to cocaine. While the appetite for heroin
among addicts is almost perpetual—they need a fix every four hours or
so—the need for heroin is at least temporarily satiated by a sufficient fix.
In contrast, the more cocaine the users take, at least within limits, the
more they want, so that enormous amounts of cocaine, and money, can
be used up in brief periods. In this respect, some cocaine bingers
resemble the compulsive gamblers who lose their homes in single sprees
of gambling. In a 1983 telephone survey of a sample of callers to
Cocaine Hotline (a number that people can call who need help with
cocaine) the average caller reported spending $637 per week on cocaine
the week before calling the hotline, with a range from $200 to $3,200.
Forty-five percent said they had stolen money from employers, family
or friends to support their habit. Eighty-five percent were white, and
they had completed an average of fourteen years of schooling. Forty
percent had incomes over $25,000 per year.[101]

   The democratization of cocaine by the invention of crack has exacerbated the crime problem. The demographic and ethnic makeup

has shifted to inner-city minorities, the average level of education has drastically diminished and cocaine has deeply penetrated the ranks of the unemployed. These users—even more likely to be drug dependent than the middle-class snorter—must earn their drug money illegally.

Beyond the crimes attributable to prohibition, is cocaine one of the few drugs that is criminogenic in and of itself? The answer is unclear. Hotline users report having both suicidal and homicidal thoughts, but such thoughts are not unconnected to the dreadful social environment that often surrounds cocaine abusers. Nor is it clear how likely such thoughts are to result in action. It does seem probable, however, that if cocaine abuse causes extreme irritability, depression and paranoia, it also sometimes leads to violence against others. That it does so in substantial numbers is doubtful.[102]

THE RELATIVE DANGERS OF THE FIVE DRUGS

There are many subjective benefits and both subjective and objective costs of using each of the five drugs we have analyzed. Unfortunately, it is impossible to quantify many of these costs and benefits. One thing these drugs have in common that is quantifiable is that, with the possible exception of marijuana, they all can kill. Where they rank as chemical killers cannot clearly establish their relative evils, since there are many effects of the drugs that are ignored in such an analysis. A comparison of their lethal potential, however, is a beginning point for ultimate comparisons. Many will find the results astonishing.

Before getting to those comparisons, some difficulties should be acknowledged.

The data are not as complete or as reliable as we would like. A federal agency, the National Institute on Drug Abuse (NIDA), gathers information on the health consequences of (licit and illicit) drug abuse. Since 1972, NIDA has conducted an annual survey of hospitals and medical examiners called the Drug Abuse Warning Network (DAWN). In the DAWN survey, NIDA tabulates the number of patients requiring emergency-room treatment for many drug problems and the number of drug fatalities observed by medical examiners.

There are some serious problems with this survey. Neither the emergency-room data nor the reports from medical examiners are truly representative of the drug problem in the entire nation. For instance, the emergency-room data for 1990 were contributed by only 415 hospitals in 21 major metropolitan areas and 88 facilities from nonurban areas.[103] NIDA does not gather data from all the emergency rooms in the 21 cities, and most Americans live outside the 21 cities encompassed by the survey. However, in 1989, NIDA began using sophisticated statistical sampling procedures to estimate how many drug episodes they might have counted, if they had surveyed every hospital—rural or metropolitan—in all of the continental United States.[104] Thus, in 1990, NIDA directly observed 110,-448 drug episodes at the participating hospitals,[105] and projected it would have counted 371,208 drug episodes[106] if it had surveyed the larger, more inclusive group of all emergency rooms in the coterminous United States.

Nearly 400,000 drug episodes at emergency rooms seems horrible, but NIDA further reports that nearly half of those people took the substances with the intent to kill themselves.[107] If drugs did not exist, presumably most members of that group would have found other means to attempt suicide. In any event, the projected number of episodes involving illicit drugs represents less than one half of 1 percent of the 82,323,486 emergency-room visits[108] that NIDA estimates occurred for all causes in the lower forty-eight states.

What about drug fatalities? This too is difficult to determine, from NIDA's nonrepresentative samples, and in this case NIDA has not attempted to project its fatality data for the rest of the country.

According to NIDA, in 1990, American medical examiners reported 5,830 deaths in which there was at least some indication of drug use by the victim (not counting alcohol alone, or tobacco).[109] In that year 2,162,000 Americans died from all causes.[110] Thus, drug-related deaths represented only about ¼ of 1 percent of reported fatalities. Moreover, for nearly 40 percent of the reported drug fatalities it is possible that the legal drug alcohol actually caused the death.[111] In fact, use of "alcohol-in-combination" with some other drug, at 2,304 mentions by medical examiners, comprised the second-largest category of lethal drug use. (Alcohol-related death alone is not recorded by DAWN.) Cocaine, for which there were 2,483 mentions, was apparently the most lethal drug, in *absolute* terms. Heroin was third, with 1,976 mentions.[112]

Comparisons to fatalities from two legal drugs—alcohol and tobacco—also are important. Ideally, one would divide the number of fatalities for each drug by the number of that drug's users. Thus you would obtain the rate of fatalities per person at risk for each drug, and you could directly compare their dangerousness. Unfortunately, there are difficulties in comparing the fatality statistics on legal and illegal drugs:

First, tobacco and alcohol fatality figures are based on complex statistical analyses of the general population and mostly reflect deaths from chronic diseases, such as lung cancer.[113] Although DAWN attempts to record chronic as well as acute drug-related deaths, most illicit-drug deaths occur suddenly and are tabulated one by one.

Second, under the best of circumstances cause of death is difficult to determine. Even if medical examiners devote substantial resources to determining a cause of death, they often cannot be sure which of several factors—e.g., underlying disease, long-term neglect of an illness, accident or recent drug use—actually caused the death. Regarding its DAWN report, NIDA warns that its tallies of drug-abuse fatalities include cases in which drug usage was merely a contributory factor.[114] NIDA cautions that: "Some medical examiners may include cases involving circumstantial evidence. Other medical examiners may report only drug-abuse deaths confirmed through toxicologic analyses."[115]

Third, multiple-drug use by the victims is typical. In 1990, only 10 percent of the deaths reported by DAWN "were single-drug cases in which the drug was clearly the cause of death."[116] Often the victim has used both legal and illegal drugs—e.g., alcohol and heroin. Drugs are notorious for their synergistic effects. Hence, for 90 percent of the cases, more than one drug was used, and none of the drugs may have possessed the ability to have caused the death by itself.

Fourth, NIDA's DAWN statistics on drug fatalities cover only twenty-one metropolitan areas, which comprise only 31.56 percent of the United States population. In contrast, the Centers for Disease Control's alcohol data and the Surgeon General's tobacco data are truly nationwide. Projecting the DAWN data proportionately in order to estimate the total fatalities for the United States is unsatisfactory because the cities participating are not a representative sample of the nation. Those cities very likely have a higher percentage of drug users than nonurban areas, but from NIDA's survey procedure there is no way to estimate how much more than average the twenty-one metropolitan areas are impacted by drugs.[117]

Despite these difficulties, James Ostrowski, a policy analyst at the Cato Institute, has attempted such comparisons between legal and illegal substances. He published this comparison in the *Hofstra Law Review*.[118] To permit his comparison, Ostrowski argued persuasively for several assumptions. He assumed that the twenty-one metropolitan areas, which contain approximately a third of the United States population, experience disproportionately more illegal-drug fatalities than other areas. To reflect this assumption in an estimate of the national totals, he multiplied the DAWN illegal-drug-fatality data by two, rather than three. He also provided a lengthy analysis which attempts to establish that 80 percent of illegal-drug fatalities are attributable to prohibition itself rather than the pharmacological effects of drugs. Accordingly, he believes that proper comparison requires discounting the estimate of illegal-drug fatalities by 80 percent to account for such phenomena as deaths due to contaminated needles, adulterated drugs and uncertain doses. In summary, Ostrowski first doubled, then discounted by 80 percent the illegal-drug numbers, while he took the numbers for the legal drugs at full strength. The table on this page[119] shows the result of his calculations for two legal and two illegal drugs.

Drug	Users	Deaths per Year	Deaths per 100,000
Tobacco	60M	390,000*	650
Alcohol	100M	150,000**	150
Heroin	500,000	400***	80
Cocaine	5M	200****	4

*United States Surgeon General, *Reducing the Health Consequences of Smoking: 25 Years of Progress* (Rockville, MD: United States Department of Health and Human Services, 1989), 160.

**See Secretary of Health and Human Services, *Sixth Special Report to The U.S. Congress on Alcohol and Health* (Rockville, MD: United States Department of Health and Human Services, Public Health Services, 1989), 11–12. Estimates vary greatly, depending upon whether all health consequences are considered (for example, cancer, heart problems), or only those traditionally associated with alcoholism (for example, cirrhosis of the liver, psychosis due to brain damage). [Remainder of note deleted.]

***[Ostrowski's note summarized for brevity: Ostrowski averaged DAWN's cocaine and heroin fatality statistics for 1984, 1985 and 1986. In addition to doubling for NIDA's nonrepresentative sampling technique and discounting by 80 percent for prohibition-caused fatalities, Ostrowski subtracted suicides and discounted deaths in which both heroin and cocaine played a role.]

****[See note above for explanation of this figure.]

Until we have drug-fatality statistics that are more representative of the entire nation, we must consider the preceding table as little more than suggestive speculation. For what it is worth though, an illegal drug—marijuana—is by far the least dangerous drug; its hazard is so small it is off Ostrowski's chart. Ostrowski observes, "Thus, for every death caused by the intrinsic effects of cocaine, heroin kills 20, alcohol kills 37 and tobacco kills 132."[120] In other words, none of the illegal drugs is remotely as dangerous to its user as alcohol or tobacco. And no drug is as dangerous as tobacco. We can question the numbers but the rankings are difficult to dispute. Other scholars have calculated similar rankings.[121]

CHAPTER 5

Lessons from the Past

"[Americans exist] in a kind of time-vacuum: we have no public memory of anything that happened before last Tuesday."

GORE VIDAL ON DRUG PROHIBITION[1]

MOST AMERICANS operate as though drug prohibition were an immutable law. We proceed on the assumption that we have no need or power to reconsider ancient policies, when in reality we have had drug prohibition for less than eighty years. Soon after its inception, drug prohibition spawned new problems far worse than the evils the policy was designed to remedy, yet we forget how or why our drug-prohibition experiment began.

The story of drug prohibition can be divided into five periods:

- the pre-prohibition epoch (the dawn of history to 1914)
- the pre–Cold War period (1914 to 1945)
- the Pax Luciano (1945 to 1964)
- the Age of Aquarius (1964 to 1978)
- and the Age of Narco Glitz (1978 to the present)

One critical concern here will be to consider how drug commerce was woven into the fabric of society during each of the five periods, so we can acquire some detached perspective on our current problems.

THE PRE-PROHIBITION EPOCH (DAWN OF HISTORY TO 1914): CHEMICAL ANARCHY

During the first period—the pre-prohibition epoch—there were no "illegal" drugs. For most of human history, drug use has been informally controlled by cultural norms, and the criminal law had no role in determining what people ingested. A major exception, which we noted in Chapter 3, involved tobacco, where prohibition was a short-lived failure throughout Asia in the early seventeenth century (as it was again in America in the 1920s). Prior to 1850, drugs (such as marijuana, coca leaf, opium, alcohol, tobacco and caffeine) were all in widespread, legal use in Asia, Europe, Africa and the Americas, and nobody seems to have thought much about it. Virtually no one suggested prohibition.

Every culture develops means to relieve stress and to achieve pleasure—games, dancing, meditation, religious worship, drug use. Two things stand out when considering the long view of recreational drug history:

First, that with each form of release, there were social controls; people who overindulged were censured by their peers or superiors.

Second, that cultures were mostly monotheistic about pharmacological releases. There were alcohol cultures, marijuana cultures, opium cultures and peyote cultures. In Northern Europe people drank beer and whiskey. In Southern Europe they drank wine and absinthe. Natives of North America took peyote. Indochinese peoples smoked opium. The notion of a varied menu of highs is a relatively recent one.

Travel changed this. Beginning at about the time of Columbus, tea, coffee, tobacco and, finally, opium jumped cultures, becoming exotic imports. In each case there were obvious reasons: drug cargoes were light and compact; spoilage was rarely a problem; marketability was certain; profits were high.

Each of the societies involved in the post-Columbian trade already had developed social controls that governed the use of the culture's indigenous drugs of choice. There were "drunks" in each of the cultures, but people with a position to maintain—work, family, warrior status, etc.—could imbibe to excess only occasionally. The first exceptions to this rule were wealthy people. They could afford to purchase imported "foreign" pleasures. Also, in the privacy and security of their own estates, they could be "drunk" as often as they wished. Only when new substances became available to less wealthy people, the powerful and wealthy classes began to perceive drug problems. Existing cultural controls had seemed adequate to regulate the use of familiar domestic drugs by the lower classes and the use of the exotic imports by a few wealthy eccentrics. However, those cultural controls were not easily adaptable to the unfamiliar imported intoxicants. Laws might be needed to lessen the threat to the existing social order posed by large-scale, lower-class use of exotic substances that might interfere with their fitness to work, or make their behavior less predictable.

At first the British made no legal or moral distinctions among the important mind-altering substances. Opium came to England primarily from Persia, Turkey and Egypt, and to a lesser extent from India. Importers, wholesalers and brokers distributed the opium to retailers, who sold it over-the-counter for medicinal and nonmedicinal use. English physicians of the time considered opium an indispensable medicine and what we now call "addiction" had been documented even before the nineteenth century. Drug historians Virginia Berridge and Griffith Edwards observe that "Medical authors, . . . such as George Young in his *Treatise on Opium* published in the 1750s and Dr. Samuel Crumpe in his *Inquiry into the Nature and Properties of Opium* of 1793, stressed the main features of addiction and the possibilities of withdrawal, but with no sign of moral condemnation."[2] Indeed, we are told that Crumpe himself was an opium user.[3] Berridge and Edwards conclude, "Opium was just a commodity like so much tea."[4]

Hence, there was only muted moral outcry over the two wars in 1839 and 1856 in which England, with the assistance of France, forced China to accept opium, the only Western trading commodity for which self-sufficient China had any need. In the eyes of British contemporaries of the opium wars, the economic benefits of the trade were far more important than the drug's damage to Chinese society.[5] In large part the British colony of India was supported by its opium trade with China. Opium overcame China's self-sufficiency to turn the balance of trade in British India's favor.[6]

What are we to conclude about the easy availability of narcotics in England before the 1870s? This was hardly a period of decline and degeneracy in England. While opium use was unrestricted and addiction was widely recognized and well tolerated, England led the West into the industrial revolution and plundered much of the rest of the world. Although local English merchants sold opium without so much as a prescription, and British exporters in India forced China to buy that product, English literature, science and culture flourished.

Opium eating in preindustrial English society was regarded merely as a "bad habit." Few people died as a direct result of drug use and it is not hard to imagine that drug use enabled some people to cope with what otherwise might have been overwhelming circumstances. Between 1840 and 1868, when opium was freely available in England, the death rate from narcotic poisoning was only 5 to 6 per million population.[7]

The Emergence of the Drug-Abuse Concept

During the industrial revolution people moved from communities in which social behaviors had ritual limits, into the freedom (but also the misery) of the new cities. There, they looked for cheap, effective and quick relief from ennui, crowded conditions and alienation. Americans turned to whiskey and wine. The English working class turned to gin.

As industrialization progressed, improved international trade expanded the drug options beyond alcohol. Opium imports rose, and in 1844 it was discovered that a new potent drug could be isolated from the coca leaf, pure cocaine. In the industrial revolution, for the first time, consumers simultaneously faced the availability of a varied menu of imported drugs and the weakening of cultural controls associated with demographic removal from countryside to towns.

Berridge and Edwards argue that "The same process can be seen today in many parts of the Third World, exemplified by breakdown in age-old informal controls over drinking practices in the anomie of the squatter compounds, the shantytowns, the *villas miseras.* Drinking in many primitive cultures has been closely controlled by custom, and the African village where everyone in all his doings is intimately responsive to cultural behest provides a setting where there is no need for laws to regulate drinking."[8]

Disjuncture did not lead to perpetual anarchy; humans have a great capacity for developing new group rules. Though in the years following the industrial revolution, English city dwellers were offered a number of new pleasures (opium, morphine, heroin, cocaine) and the industrial exploitation of a common "medicinal" one (the mixture of sherry and opium called laudanum), there is little evidence that at the end of the nineteenth century abuse was widespread. The numbers show growing use of opium, for example, in the middle and late years of the nineteenth century, but its use declines as the last Victorians grow old. The British generation of the First World War wanted a different drug; they returned to alcohol. In the meantime, both in Britain and America, people trained in medicine and pharmacology were staking out their turf, and this would profoundly change the world's psychopharmacological landscape.

The practitioners of nineteenth-century medicine had little power to cure disease. The main thing the physician could do was to make the patient feel better, and "opiates were preeminent for these functions and were apparently used with great frequency."[9] The physician was in competition with the pharmacist, however, since both could and did dispense opiates and other drugs. In fact, both were in competition with the corner grocery store; anyone could sell drugs to anyone else. The physicians and pharmacists needed to have this changed. The change began in England, with the Pharmacy and Poisons Act of 1868, which forbade the sale of opiates by anyone other than a pharmacist.[10]

Other forces were also working to medicalize the problem. According to Berridge and Edwards, the transition in the perception of opium use from a "bad habit" to an "addiction" marks the way in which "the nineteenth century evolved the treatment of addiction as a method of dealing with the individual who in some way offended society's ideas of what was decent and orderly."[11]

Anglo-American Contrasts

Several things make the history of opium use in nineteenth-century America slightly different from the history in Britain.

First, the industrial revolution came later to America than to Britain, and the workers moved not from the countryside to the towns but from other countries to new cities. This may have ensured some continuing cultural controls among ethnic groups as well as the notion that certain kinds of highs "belonged to" certain ethnic groups. While opium smoking in England was regarded as uncivilized, something the Chinese did in their dens in London's dockland, opium eating was widespread and therefore almost "naturalized." It was the view of some white Americans, in contrast, that cocaine, marijuana and opium were respectively black, Mexican and Chinese drugs. The drugs were "foreign."

Second, America suffered a civil war in which morphine was widely used to alleviate pain. Whether the Civil War boosted the number of Americans who used morphine excessively is a point of contention. Drug consultant David Bellis, in *Heroin and Politicians: The Failure of Public Policy to Control Addiction in America,* says it did.[12] Yale drug historian David Musto, however, says, "The first statistics on the importation of opium date from 1840 and reveal a continual increase in consumption during the rest of the century. . . . The Civil War, far from initiating opiate use on a large scale in the United States, hardly makes a ripple in its constantly expanding consumption."[13]

Third, America's temperance movement, confined for forty or so years after 1785 to a social and political elite, eventually became a mass movement. By the late nineteenth century, the saloon had lost its middle-class legitimacy and had become a den of iniquity. A potent force behind alcohol prohibition was the need of fundamentalist Protestants to establish their cultural and political hegemony over newer immigrants, mainly Roman Catholics. Prohibition had symbolic value in this endeavor.[14] Even though not responsive to the Protestants' needs, some of the stigmatization of alcohol spilled over onto other drugs, so that opiates and cocaine, along with tobacco, became morally suspect as well.

The regulation of drugs did not commence in the United States until the last years of the nineteenth century, when municipalities and states began enacting piecemeal restrictions on drug trade. This early American legislation superficially appears to have been motivated by white communities' fears that use of specific drugs might inspire minority males to act violently or express sexual interest in white women. Thus, after much racist anti-Chinese agitation, California's legislature in 1881 outlawed the opium dens where the San Francisco police claimed they had "found white women and Chinamen side by side under the effects of this drug—a humiliating sight to anyone with anything left of manhood."[15] These local laws provided a legal ground on which to harass ethnic minorities but contributed little to controlling the use of drugs.

The Harrison Act (1914)

Ethnocentrism, though important in the first wave of American drug regulation, probably had a minor influence on passage of America's Harrison Act, which instituted federal drug prohibition. Instead, concerns about international trade, mediated through the developing professionalization of health care and rivalries between physicians and pharmacists over drug revenue, shaped the legislation.[16]

Religion-based moralism and other forces that were converging to produce alcohol prohibition a few years later also contributed to passage of the Harrison Act. According to David Musto, however, few Americans cared much about the drugs controlled by the Harrison Act. The Act was merely "a routine slap at a moral evil."[17]

More significant in bringing about the legislation, according to Musto, was our desire to promote trade and other relations with China.[18] Toward that objective, America supported efforts to suspend the long-standing submission of China to the opium trade enforced upon it by Great Britain. The result was the Hague Opium Convention of 1912, which called for control of opiates and cocaine, with the signatories agreeing to "endeavor" to control their own traffic in these substances. Since America had committed itself to such an "endeavor," something like the Harrison Act was necessary to avoid international embarrassment.

Finally, as enacted, the Harrison Act fell far short of outright prohibition of cocaine and opiate distribution. First, it exempted potions and patent medicines sold over-the-counter and by mail order if the concentrations were below specified limits. Second, pharmacists could sell the drugs on prescription by a physician, and physicians could prescribe them. Physicians could also distribute the drugs themselves, and were not even required to keep records of their distributions on house calls. Drug distribution had become medicalized in America.

THE PRE–COLD WAR PERIOD (1914 TO 1945)

Early in the twentieth century, the notion of controlling drug use by law had emerged, and as America entered World War I, drug history began its second period. It is here that the modern drug problem took on many of its present attributes, such as:

- desperation of addicts who cannot get maintenance doses from physicians;
- selective prohibition that exempts tobacco and alcohol (after 1933) but includes marijuana (after 1937) and hallucinogens such as peyote;

- fears that drug abuse will corrupt and despoil our youth;
- black markets;
- the role of organized crime;
- corruption of officials by drug merchants;
- association of drugs with predatory crimes.

Some drug prohibitionists blame the chemical properties of drugs themselves for our drug problems. However, the aspects of the problem listed above did not exist prior to drug prohibition.

The Harrison Act Becomes a Drug-Prohibition Act

As we noted, the Harrison Act appeared merely to medicalize the distribution of opiates and cocaine. Alcohol was considered to be a far greater evil. Indeed, during the latter part of the nineteenth century and the early part of the twentieth, morphine was widely considered a cure for alcoholism.[19] Opiates were even included in some treatments for *opiate* addiction.[20] The Harrison Act was not designed to overturn these practices. It was, after all, a tax and registration act, which required dispensers of these drugs in concentrated form to be licensed and to pay a small fee—$1 per year. According to Edward Brecher, "Far from appearing to be a prohibition law, the Harrison Narcotic Act on its face was merely a law for the orderly marketing of opium, morphine, heroin, and other drugs."[21] The right of the physician to prescribe was spelled out in seemingly unambiguous terms: "Nothing... in this section shall apply . . . to the dispensing or distribution of any of the aforesaid drugs to a patient by a physician, dentist, or veterinary surgeon registered under this Act in the course of his professional practice only." Says Brecher, "It is unlikely that a single legislator realized in 1914 that the law Congress was passing would later be deemed a prohibition law." Soon, however, law-enforcement officers took the position that a doctor could not prescribe opiates to an addict to maintain his addiction. The argument was that addiction is not a "disease," the addict who seeks a maintenance dose is therefore not a "patient" and maintenance doses are therefore not supplied "in the course of his professional practice."[22]

The courts at first seemed to reject this bizarre interpretation. Indeed, in a 1916 decision, *United States v. Jin Fuey Moy*,[23] the Supreme Court held the Act inapplicable to a doctor who prescribed morphine to a patient, and questioned whether if it had applied, the Act would be constitutional. However, three years later, in *Webb v. United States*,[24] the Court upheld the constitutionality of the Act and the criminal prosecution of a physician who prescribed for addict maintenance and the pharmacist who filled the prescription. The claim that an order for morphine to make an addict comfortable is a "physician's prescription" was, said the Court, "so plain a perversion of meaning that no discussion of the subject is required."

What caused this reversal? Between these two decisions, a marked change in attitude toward drugs had occurred. We had fought World War I, the 18th Amendment requiring Prohibition had been passed, and we fell into a period of intolerant, suspicious nationalism. According to David Musto, drug addiction by 1918 was perceived as a threat to the national war effort.[25] After the war, maintenance of addicts was considered of a piece with "other un-American influences which would dissolve the bonds of society."[26]

In any event, by 1919 we had acquired—almost by accident and contrary to the will of the 1914 Congress—opiate and cocaine prohibition along with alcohol prohibition.

The Prohibition Experiment

Alcohol prohibition went into effect in January 1920. During the thirteen years of Prohibition, the dreaded saloons, where vice was virtue and virtue vice, disappeared. Instead, each saloon was replaced, according to some counts, by three "speakeasies."[27] Women, who had been excluded from the saloons, were invited to the illegal speakeasy and thus became consumers of liquor in unprecedented numbers.

Smuggling became an epidemic. Canada became the principal source of our liquor for a short time, and thus gained eminence in exported whiskey that continues to the present day. Entrepreneurs reacted to the market for illicit alcoholic beverages by increasing domestic production. By the end of Prohibition, the number of domestic distilleries and breweries was at least a hundredfold greater than at the beginning. There were 1,724 distilleries and breweries in the United States in 1917.[28] In 1930, however, nearly 282,000 distilleries were *seized*.[29] The production of wort and malt, used to make beer, increased sixfold.[30]

At least half the alcohol drunk in the 1920s was illegally distilled from denatured industrial alcohol.[31] In 1920, the amount of industrial alcohol domestically manufactured was 28 million gallons. By 1923 it had grown to 81 million gallons, with no comparable increase in industrial production. Official estimates of the amount of industrial alcohol that went to bootleggers annually varied from 6 million gallons to 60 million gallons.[32] The conversion of denatured alcohol to drinkable alcohol by bootleggers was often incomplete. From 1925 to 1929, forty people in every million died from poisoned liquor.[33]

The production of wine also increased during Prohibition. One estimate was that it increased by two thirds. Despite the increase in domestic production levels, the price of booze increased two to ten times over its pre-Prohibition level.[34] This was largely to pay for the unprecedented level of graft. New York speakeasy owners alone paid more than $50 million per year to policemen, prosecutors, federal agents and others.[35] In the first eleven years of Prohibition, about 18,000 prohibition agents were appointed and nearly 14,000 resigned or were fired for corruption.[36]

The Cook County State's Attorney, who was elected in 1921, increased his budget, added a thousand men to the police force and obtained an increase in judges from six to twenty. None of this produced more convictions. In his first two terms, 349 people were murdered; 215 of them gangsters. Only 128 people were convicted of murder and none of them were gangsters. No one was convicted for any of the 369 bombings.[37]

As James Ostrowski recently noted: "The murder rate rose with the start of Prohibition, remained high during Prohibition, then declined for eleven consecutive years when Prohibition ended. The rate of assaults with a firearm rose with Prohibition and declined for ten consecutive years after Prohibition."[38]

Despite these massive costs, prohibitionists demanded more and more resources for the law-enforcement effort—and got them. Convictions under the National Prohibition Act increased from about 18,000 in 1921 to about 61,000 in 1932.[39] The enforcement budget more than doubled from 1921 to 1930.[40] As Prohibition wore on, prison terms increased in length. Penalties for prohibition violations were increased in 1929. The number of stills seized rose from 32,000 in 1920 to nearly 282,000 in 1930.[41] Then, as now, the more money spent on law enforcement, the worse the problems seemed to become. Then, as now, the prohibitionists argued that each failure somehow demonstrated that we were turning the corner, and all we needed to do was spend more money and exert more determination in the effort.

In 1933, alcohol prohibition was repealed.

Effect of Alcohol Prohibition on Current Drug Policy

The United States outlawed Western Civilization's drug of choice—alcohol—after opium and cocaine use had fallen out of fashion. During the 1920s, the United States created a generation of young people that most other Western nations never developed, a generation that took its relief in illegal alcohol and other illicit foreign drugs. There were some behavioral norms for consumption of bootleg whiskey, but there were no cultural and scant legal controls for the foreign narcotics. In the first decade of the twentieth century, states that prohibited consumption, manufacture or sale of alcohol saw morphine sales increase 150 percent.[42] When access to alcohol was restricted, a few Americans turned to other drugs because the social limits on their use were less well defined.

At the same time as alcohol prohibition encouraged use of narcotics, it gave American criminal enterprises the seed capital and organizational foundation that they later would use to develop new profit centers in drugs when repeal put them out of the booze business. The Supreme Court's 1919 *Webb* decision had a long-term effect: the underworld took over where the Court had forbidden medical doctors to tread, in the maintenance of addicts.

During alcohol prohibition, the United States underwent a revolution in federal law enforcement. Oddly, however, the main victims of the newly aggressive law enforcement were Harrison Act violators, not alcohol bootleggers. In October of 1919 the Volstead Act gave the Internal Revenue Bureau a Prohibition Unit. A subunit was called the Narcotics Division.[43] At the outset, the Volstead Act was enforced by 2,500 prohibition agents. By contrast there were only 170 narcotics officers in 1920; 270 in 1929. The annual budget of the Narcotics Unit in this period was between a half and three quarters of a million dollars.[44] Despite their inadequate resources, the first narcotics officers gave the country value for its money. By mid-1928, almost a third of the 7,700 prisoners in the federal penitentiaries were Harrison Act violators, more than the combined total for the next two categories—liquor prohibition and car theft. There were so many narcotics prisoners that the Public Health Service was directed to create addict "farms," at Fort Worth, Texas, and Lexington, Kentucky. (The former opened in 1938, the latter in 1935.[45])

Thus, drug prohibition began to strain the capacity of the prison system soon after passage of the Harrison Act. This problem is still with us and grows worse every day. The drug problem as we know it today quickly began to take shape during alcohol prohibition.

Was Alcohol Prohibition a Failure?

For many years, the nearly universal opinion has been that alcohol prohibition was a grave mistake, bordering on folly, wisely if too belatedly corrected by repeal. Drug-legalization advocates trade on this belief when they point to the failure of alcohol prohibition as a reason to repeal the rest of prohibition. In response, a few scholars have emerged who claim that alcohol prohibition was not all that bad. At least, they claim, Prohibition succeeded in reducing alcohol consumption. Mark Moore, for example, points to evidence that cirrhosis death rates for men dropped from 29.5 per hundred thousand in 1911 to 10.7 in 1929. Additionally he claims, "Admissions to state mental hospitals for alcoholic psychosis declined from 10.1 per hundred thousand in 1919 to 4.7 in 1928."[46]

While the view that alcohol consumption diminished during Prohibition is the prevailing one, even that is debatable.

Moore's data about the drop in death rates from cirrhosis of the liver are suggestive, but little more. The time gap between the onset of drinking and death from cirrhosis is unclear. Moreover, the fact that admissions to state hospitals for alcohol psychoses were reduced by half can be explained by differences in diagnostic criteria, bed space, and other variables. As Ethan Nadelmann has pointed out, alcoholic admissions to New York State hospitals dropped even more sharply in the years *prior* to Prohibition than they did during Prohibition.[47] Nadelmann also notes that in Britain, the death rate from cirrhosis was cut in half in six years, from 1914 to 1920, a reduction at least as great as any experienced in America, and Britain didn't *have* prohibition![48] While the linkage between alcohol consumption and cirrhosis and psychosis is clear, the reduction in the diseases could be explained in part by different attitudes toward alcoholism and drunkenness. In the pre-Prohibition era, it was commonly asserted, and even believed, that alcoholics were helpless to control their drinking; they were entirely in the grip of the disease.[49] That view probably changed during Prohibition, with the result that many alcoholics cut down on their self-destructive drinking. In any event, persons inclined to cirrhosis or to alcohol psychoses are a fraction of any population of drinkers. Trends in their drinking hardly justify broad conclusions about the drinking patterns of the entire society of which they were a part.

There are also data that point in the opposite direction. Arrest rates for public drunkenness steadily increased from 1920 to 1927.[50] Domestic production of spirits, wine and beer skyrocketed and there were speakeasies on almost every corner in the large cities. Women also became public drinkers in large numbers during Prohibition.

While the consumption of alcohol clearly decreased during the first years of Prohibition—there was very little available in the cities and it took time to develop smuggling organizations and moonshine factories—the trends were such that even if the consumption rates at the end of Prohibition were lower than they were at the beginning, a few more years of Prohibition would have wiped out the difference. There were many other factors at work during the thirteen years of Prohibition. For example, we suffered the worst depression in our history. It began in 1929, four years before the end of Prohibition. Millions of Americans lacked food, much less the money to buy artificially overpriced booze.

Prohibitionists also argue that the consumption of alcohol increased sharply after the repeal of Prohibition, from which they deduce that Prohibition had some deterrent effect on drinking habits. But a lot of other things happened following the repeal that contributed to this increase. The popular media promoted the use and abuse of alcohol after repeal. For example, many magazines published drink recipes, and popular performers such as W. C. Fields made drinking appear glamorous—or at least charmingly amusing—by drinking to excess both on and off screen. Relatively few media voices spoke of the negative consequences of abusing alcohol until we were in the 1980s. Alcohol policies also encouraged consumption by undertaxing the product.

The basic facts about Prohibition are indisputable: if consumption of alcohol was reduced, it wasn't by much; the costs of enforcement, in money, corruption, crime, disrespect for law, alcohol and related poisonings far exceeded, by virtually anyone's measurements, the tiny gains in alcohol control.

Reefer Madness

When alcohol prohibition was repealed in 1933 and Congress acted in 1937 to outlaw marijuana, the main features of the current picture were largely in place.

There are two popular theories about why and how marijuana became contraband, when Congress passed the Marihuana Tax Act (MTA) of 1937. The leading text on the subject, Jerome L. Himmelstein's *The Strange Career of Marihuana,* calls these two theories the "Anslinger hypothesis" and the "Mexican hypothesis."[51] The Anslinger hypothesis, as expounded by Howard Becker in the early 1950s, maintains that Congress passed the MTA as a result of intense lobbying by Harry Anslinger.[52] (Anslinger directed the Federal Bureau of Narcotics from its founding in 1930 until he retired in 1962.) One version of the Anslinger hypothesis is that the MTA was the result of entrepreneurial lawmaking, calculated to feather an existing bureaucratic nest by increasing responsibilities and budget of the Federal Bureau of Narcotics. The "Mexican hypothesis," as expounded by David Musto, claims that the MTA was motivated by Southwestern Anglo fears that marijuana inspired Mexican-Americans to commit crimes and act violently.[53]

In the scenarios suggested by both theories, the advocates of the law whipped up public hysteria, either as a reason to expand the FBN or as an element in the racist propaganda against an ethnic minority. Each hypothesis provides a neat explanation of why marijuana was made illegal. Unfortunately, Himmelstein provides rather persuasive evidence that the Anslinger hypothesis—in its bureaucratic aggrandizement version—is wrong and that the Mexican hypothesis is simplistic.

Himmelstein attempted to find out what people actually were being told about the drug in the years before and since passage of the anti-marijuana law. He examined all the articles listed in the *Reader's Guide to Periodical Literature* under the topic of marijuana and under the topic of alcohol, from the 1890s to 1977. He found that there was very little interest in marijuana until the middle of the 1930s. In the forty-six-year period from 1890 to 1935, America's newsstands were graced by only seven articles about marijuana. In contrast, over the same period, American magazines published 968 articles—about twenty-one per year—on the topic of alcohol. In the years 1935 to 1937, two articles per year were written about marijuana; yet more than twenty-five times that many articles were written about alcohol during the same period. Between 1937 and 1939, the number of marijuana articles jumped only to eight per year, even though 1937 was the year that the MTA was passed. Still, there were almost six times as many alcohol articles as marijuana articles between 1937 and 1939.[54]

Himmelstein examined the twenty-two articles in the *Reader's*

Guide sample from 1935 to 1940 and found that most of them repeated propaganda put out by Anslinger and the FBN, stressing lurid accounts of violence allegedly caused by marijuana. One of the earlier articles was explicitly authored by Anslinger, and seven others credit the Bureau as their source of information. The same Bureau examples of "marijuana crimes" were repeated in article after article. There was the "Texas hitchhiker who murdered a motorist, the West Virginian man who raped a nine-year-old girl, the Florida youth who murdered his family with an ax, the Ohio juvenile gang that committed thirty-eight armed robberies."[55] "In sum," says Himmelstein, "sixteen of the twenty-two articles . . . bear the mark of the FBN or its favored sources."[56] Besides tales of marijuana-induced violence, the articles stressed the spreading of marijuana to America's children and implied that the violence would erupt throughout society as use of the weed itself spread.

The Anslinger hypothesis was right in attributing the passage of the federal marijuana statute to Anslinger-induced propaganda. But it was wrong, Himmelstein argues, in the version which includes the turf-expanding motivation. Himmelstein notes that while Anslinger created the reefer madness mentality and the belief that marijuana causes people to commit violent crimes, he did so not to enlarge his own bureaucratic fiefdom but, rather, to persuade the states to enact anti-marijuana laws and to relieve the FBN of enforcement responsibility for marijuana. Anslinger expressly opposed federal marijuana legislation in the early thirties while he and his agents aggressively sought to persuade the states to handle the matter. Unfortunately, Anslinger underestimated his own persuasiveness. He not only convinced the states to enact anti-marijuana legislation, he generated congressional interest as well. Confronted by the rising tide of congressional concern, Anslinger then changed course and actively sought the federal legislation he had so recently opposed. Himmelstein concludes that the FBN's "subsequent support for federal legislation appears to be an unintended consequence of this earlier activity."[57] Anslinger had oversold the marijuana menace.[58]

If Anslinger later forgot that the menace was mostly a creation of the FBN itself and thus failed to discount the reports he was receiving, it would not have been the first time a bureaucrat was convinced by his own propaganda, but that was apparently not the case. Shortly after the MTA was passed, Anslinger and the FBN did a second reversal of field. Says Himmelstein, "the FBN quickly dropped the tone of panic from its reports," and suggested that the marijuana problem "was being brought under control." The Bureau "also actively discouraged the kind of sensational publicity that it had purveyed just a few years before." [59] Little was heard about marijuana for the next quarter century.

And what of the "Mexican hypothesis"—that the MTA was the result of prejudice against Mexican-Americans which caused local officials to pressure federal officials for an anti-marijuana law? It is a plausible theory, Himmelstein says, but there is little evidence that any such local pressures were brought to bear at the federal level. Himmelstein acknowledges that "there was widespread anti-Mexican sentiment in the Southwest [in the late 1920s and early 1930s]." However, he concludes that "marijuana was an insignificant issue in anti-Mexican movements and on its own." [60]

What then ultimately accounts for the passage of the MTA? Himmelstein argues that legislators turned their attention to marijuana when they began to perceive the drug as a threat to non-Mexican youth. The fear, as expressed in the scare movie *Reefer Madness,* was that marijuana use was spreading to middle-class Anglo children. The false syllogism at work here is: Mexicans and fringe users in the Southwest and New Orleans are violent people. They smoke marijuana. Therefore if "our youth" smoke marijuana, they will become violent too. The fear was that Anglo youth would be infected by the alleged Mexican predilection to use the "killer weed." Himmelstein concludes, "The images of 'killer weed' and 'infection,' however, were shaped by the drug's association with Mexican laborers and other lower-class groups. Only when marijuana became unambiguously associated with middle-class youth in the 1960s did the image fundamentally change." [61]

The Mafia Connection

After repeal of alcohol prohibition, the Mafia partially compensated for the lost profit center by abandoning its ethical dictum against participating in prostitution. As alcohol prohibition was winding down, a Sicilian-American gangster—Salvatore C. "Lucky" Luciano—aggressively pursued a marketing strategy that artfully combined prostitution and narcotics peddling. Luciano is credited with introducing a business innovation that would allow the Mafia to maintain prostitute discipline with a greatly reduced overhead of pimps: get the prostitutes hooked on drugs, thereby creating a work force that is easily manipulated by a small disciplined cadre of pimps and dope pushers.

Lucky Luciano's new idea transformed prostitution from a cottage industry, which had been plagued by the deadweight of too many unproductive managers (the pimps), into a business suitable for management by organized crime. His idea also established a connection between drug abuse and prostitution that has survived to this day and contributes to the spread of AIDS.

The Mafia's participation in the drug business was temporarily interrupted when World War II interfered with access to raw materials, the opium poppies growing in Iran, Turkey and Southeast Asia.

THE PAX LUCIANO (1945 TO 1964)

After World War II, America's drug history entered its third phase. During this period, Luciano reinstated the heroin trade and organized illicit-drug syndicates patterned upon the efficient models that had worked for bootleggers during alcohol prohibition. The result was that, during many of the years following World War II, America's drug business was smoothly run by a disciplined international criminal enterprise that had begun to mature decades before in the alcohol business. Mafia families had their turf wars, but unlike modern crack gangs, most Mafiosi used violence only as a last resort and then tried to avoid creating "civilian" casualties.

The McCoy Thesis

In 1972, a book by Alfred W. McCoy, *The Politics of Heroin in Southeast Asia,* developed and documented the then controversial thesis that America's intelligence forces and those of other nations had for decades cooperated with international drug smugglers.[62] The McCoy thesis directly pointed an accusatory finger at Vietnamese Air Force general Nguyen Cao Ky, the Vice Premier of the Republic of Vietnam. McCoy also presented evidence that Nguyen Van Thieu, the Prime Minister of the Republic of Vietnam, indirectly collected graft from heroin merchants and smugglers. At a time when President Nixon was telling the world that the United States would continue to support South Vietnam in the most unpopular war this country had ever fought, here was a claim that the top leaders of our Vietnamese ally were personally profiting from selling drugs to our soldiers in the field and our citizens back home. The commotion caused by the McCoy thesis is understandable, in the context of reliable news reports that between 10 and 20 percent of our soldiers in Vietnam were hooked on high-grade heroin that they were buying both on and off base.[63]

Back in 1972, claims such as those made by McCoy greatly embarrassed the United States government and became an important issue in the debates about America's involvement in the Vietnam war.[64] Although South Vietnamese leaders denied the accusations, much of the McCoy thesis has been independently verified. Now few drug historians disagree with his major conclusions.[65]

McCoy claimed that the heroin problems in 1972 could be traced to the last days of World War II. His thesis begins with the assumption that American heroin use was almost eradicated by the war.[66] World War II disrupted all international commerce. Submarine warfare by the Axis powers and Japanese occupation of Southeast Asia and much of China caused American shortages of street heroin, along with rubber, silk and petroleum. Measures taken to prevent spies from entering the country and saboteurs from destroying naval installations effectively deterred smuggling.[67] Those addicts who could not draw on the limited supply of brown heroin from Mexico simply dropped their heroin habit. The number of heroin addicts in the United States is reputed to have been as low as an estimated 20,000 in 1945.[68] At that point, Lucky Luciano used his entrepreneurial acumen to rebuild the Mafia's heroin business.

In the 1930s, soon after Luciano had initiated his narcotics enterprise, aggressive prosecutors in the United States and political oppressors in Italy had sent the Mafia into a serious decline. In 1936, New York prosecutor Thomas Dewey used the testimony of three prostitutes to put Luciano in jail for a thirty-to-fifty-year sentence. Meanwhile, in Sicily itself, during the 1920s and 1930s, Mussolini waged a brutal campaign of arrests, torture and executions against the Mafia. Then, during the early years of World War II, sabotage on the New York docks set in train a series of events that would restore the fortunes of Lucky Luciano and the Mafia.

When the French liner *Normandie* burned shortly before completion of its conversion to an allied troop ship, the Office of Naval Intelligence (ONI) decided to take drastic measures to secure the New York docks from apparent sabotage. Unable to establish an effective intelligence network of its own on the docks, the ONI first cut a deal with mafia chieftain Joseph Lanza to protect the East Side piers. The ONI eventually made a similar deal regarding the West Side piers with Luciano, who was then doing time in Dannemora Prison.[69] The quid pro quo was that the gangster would immediately be moved to a more comfortable jail in New York's penal system, where he would have visits from naval intelligence officers and his criminal associate Meyer Lansky.

Luciano apparently kept his side of the bargain with the Navy. The New York docks operated smoothly and safely for the remainder of World War II. Luciano also helped in obtaining the services of the Sicilian Mafia as a resistance force against Mussolini.[70] General George Patton's hundred-mile advance to Palermo took only four days, in part because Luciano's friend Don Calogero Vizzini (Zu Calo) had used his "family" to clear the road of the Italian Army, its snipers and its land mines.

Luciano never completed his prison sentence. Instead, his ONI handlers helped him win deportation to Sicily, where he linked up with Mafiosi who had done very well in the last days of the war.[71] The American occupation forces in Sicily had installed Mafiosi in positions of civil authority; numerous Mafiosi were appointed mayors of their villages. Luciano's effort to rebuild the heroin business was greatly facilitated by the Sicilian Mafiosi who had prospered under the American occupation. Diverting heroin legally manufactured by the Schiaparelli Pharmaceutical Company, Luciano quickly organized a drug-smuggling operation that revived heroin use in America. By 1952 it was estimated that the number of American addicts had risen to 60,000, three times as many as there had been at the end of the war.[72]

The French Connection

When the Italian government later tightened its controls of the legal manufacture of heroin, the Mafia entered into an arrangement with Corsican syndicates in Marseilles that is now popularly termed the "French connection." Here, too, McCoy contends that machinations by intelligence agencies played a crucial role in facilitating drug commerce. The Corsican mobsters helped United States and French intelligence forces in the postwar years by breaking Communist-led strikes in Marseilles. In particular, the CIA's Corsican surrogates helped break strikes on the Marseilles docks that threatened both the success of the Marshall Plan and the war against Ho Chi Minh's effort to oust the French from their colony in Vietnam.

Aside from the money that the CIA directly paid the Corsican strikebreakers, their reward was political influence and a purge of Communists from the Marseilles police. This made the police available for strikebreaking duties and removed from the force those officers who had most stridently suppressed activities of the Corsican criminal syndicates. Two enterprising brothers, Antoine and Barthélemy Guerini, whose henchmen protected scab dock workers and assassinated picketers, emerged from the labor unrest as the underworld bosses of the Marseilles waterfront. This control of the docks would prove to be a crucial asset to the heroin smuggling business that the Guerini brothers controlled.

In approximately the same period, in the 1950s, international pressure convinced the French imperial government in Indochina to gradually abolish the state-run opium monopoly that supplied drugs to the colony's addicts. Opium profits historically had been the financial mainstay of the colonial administration. Hence, this measure caused budget deficits, which left the colonial government underfinanced. However, this gave French intelligence agencies a financial windfall, since the Deuxième Bureau (French military intelligence) and the Service de Documentation Extérieure et du Contre-Espionage (SDECE) (an approximate equivalent of America's CIA) solved the problem of financing their surveillance of the Viet Minh by taking over facets of the opium business as quickly as the colonial government abandoned them. The French intelligence services called their opium business "Operation X," and its existence was considered so secret and sensitive that knowledge of its existence was limited to top officials of the government. Saigon's Corsican gangsters and Binh Xuyen river pirates conspired with the French intelligence agencies to conduct Operation X.

The Vietnamese could use only so much opium, and the growing regions of Southeast Asia were producing bumper poppy crops. Saigon's Corsican mobsters eventually decided to use their deep connections with friends and family back home to smuggle the drug to Marseilles. There it was refined further into heroin by clandestine laboratories, whose influence with the police and the government provided protection. In turn, connections with French intelligence agents further provided cover for the refining of the Mafia's Persian and Turkish opium. By tacit agreement, none of the heroin was sold in France, but was transshipped mostly to America via Cuba, South America and Canada.

This arrangement worked very well until the late 1960s and early 1970s, when the Guerini brothers' control of the heroin business was overcome by a gang war and a prosecution that left Antoine dead and Barthélemy in jail. After the brothers lost control of the Marseilles heroin business, heroin began to show up on the streets of France. Since the smugglers may have broken the agreement by selling in France, one theory suggests that the French government no longer felt compelled to overlook drug smuggling. That is when Colonel Paul Fournier, an agent of SDECE, was indicted by the United States for heroin smuggling, and the French connection became common knowledge and the stuff of motion picture entertainment.

The exposure of the French connection was the beginning of the end of the Pax Luciano—the period of stability and growth the international narcotics business had enjoyed in the quarter century after World War II. During the Pax Luciano, governments and narcotics merchants had made mutually beneficial accommodations regarding the illicit-drug business. Under this informal arrangement, corrupt officials around the world collected bribes, and intelligence agencies used the drug black market as an instrument in their pursuit of anti-Communist foreign-policy objectives.

During the Vietnam war, when the United States replaced France in Southeast Asian politics and intrigue, a substantial piece of the SDECE's drug business went with the territory. According to McCoy, various CIA agents in the field could not possibly have been unaware of the opium poppies growing in the mountainous area of Thailand, Burma and Laos known as the Golden Triangle. Meanwhile, probably from 1949, when the People's Red Army pushed them out of China, the remnants of Chiang Kai-shek's Kuomintang (KMT) army, operating as warlords in the Golden Triangle, helped support themselves by guarding opium-carrying donkey caravans on their trek from the hills to places such as Vientiane, Laos.

McCoy admits that on the surface "the KMT's involvement in the Burmese opium trade seems to be just another case of a CIA client taking advantage of the agency's political protection to enrich itself from the narcotics trade." However, McCoy says that "upon closer examination, the CIA appears to be much more seriously compromised in this affair." He concludes, "There is no question of CIA ignorance or naïveté, for as early as 1952 *The New York Times* and other major American newspapers published detailed accounts of the KMT's role in the narcotics trade."[73]

Warlord armies that the CIA sporadically hired to oppose forces such as the Khmer Rouge, the Viet Cong and the North Vietnamese Army often did more opium trading than fighting. The peasant populations in the contested areas had a choice between raising subsistence rice or a cash crop of opium poppies. The opium-poppy crop was often the more economically astute choice, and several CIA-supported mercenary armies in Southeast Asia collected protection money that they called taxes from the opium growers. As recently as 1989, warlord General Khun Sa, who has earned the nickname "the Money Tree of Burma," all but admitted to *Newsweek* correspondent Melinda Liu that he still supported his Shan secessionist army and his lifestyle by collecting this tax from opium growers.[74]

A Question of Priorities

An argument can be made that United States intelligence agencies acted appropriately in cooperating with Luciano, the Corsican syndicate and the opium-trading mercenaries of Southeast Asia. In foreign relations, governments routinely act in ways that would be immoral—and even illegal—for individuals. They often operate on the assumption that even murder is justified as an instrument of foreign policy. By comparison to murder and destroying villages, supporting drug dealing is a peccadillo.

In the foregoing instances, government agents decided that their military and political objectives were more important than interfering with drug commerce. Can this be defended as a choice of lesser evils? In the unpopular Vietnam War, the alternative to aiding and abetting Southeast Asian mercenaries in their drug dealings would have been to commit several hundred thousand more GIs to theaters of the Vietnam war where American soldiers generally didn't go. CIA connivance in drug traffic was therefore a way to fight the Vietnam war on the cheap, saving lives as well as money. Regular infantry troopers—not small numbers of CIA agents and Special Forces—would have died in substantial numbers in Laos and the northern areas of Burma and Thailand. American taxpayers also would have been asked to underwrite a much more expensive war. Someone whose house was burglarized to pay for illicit drugs was in a sense paying a hidden tax to keep mercenaries in the field in Southeast Asia.

American drug users were in effect providing proxy soldiers by buying the drugs that the mercenaries sold.

The Pax Luciano demonstrates that America's antidrug policies are routinely subordinated to interests and objectives that seem more pressing or more important. No matter how often our presidents declare wars on drugs, such wars are still metaphors. Real wars, even when conducted by other countries with nothing more than sub rosa involvement by the United States, will usually take priority in any conflict of American policies.

THE AGE OF AQUARIUS (1964 TO 1978)

The Pax Luciano did little direct harm to most Americans. However, everything changed when the illicit-drug commerce appeared to spread beyond the Mafia's traditional market: poor minorities. Beginning in the 1960s, the crimes that had long plagued inner cities began to creep into the suburbs. Worse, the children of the suburbs began to express an interest in drugs. The final straw was the heroin epidemic among United States soldiers in Vietnam.

Vietnam veterans have been even more threatening and difficult to reabsorb into society than were veterans of earlier wars, because they were exposed to hideous atrocities, they are disproportionately minorities and they lost an intensely unpopular war. The fear inspired by a group of such veterans, 10 to 20 percent of whom were addicted to heroin, was immense. Having lost the real war, President Nixon declared a war against drugs.

Drug use continued to expand out to a major subgroup of the majority culture. During the late 1960s and 1970s, a sizable proportion of the generation born after World War II developed favorable attitudes toward the use of some illicit drugs. In 1979, 68.2 percent of eighteen-to-twenty-five-year-olds admitted to government surveyors that they had used marijuana or hashish at least once, and 27.5 percent of that age group admitted having used cocaine.[75] Among intellectuals and artists, a favorable attitude toward drugs was pronounced, and the consequence was an upsurge in pro-drug propaganda. Throughout the Western world, in fact, use of certain drugs became identified with otherwise legitimate political and cultural movements, weakening taboos about drug use. Heroin still had many negative connotations and cocaine—though very popular—seems never to have been used by a majority of any age group polled by the

National Institute of Drug Abuse. However, use of marijuana, synthetic hallucinogens—such as LSD—and natural hallucinogens—such as peyote—nearly attained the status of a folk sacrament.

This development disturbed the equilibrium of the previous Pax Luciano in two ways. First, the Age of Aquarius greatly expanded the number of people involved in drug commerce and brought many new players into the game who were not loyal to the smuggling organizations set up by Luciano and other Mafiosi. The business lost its discipline and has not regained it. Second, the rising of the Aquarian subgroup made drug use, previously confined largely to the ghetto, seem truly threatening to the rest of society. What then followed was a major reversal of the intellectual community's glorification of drugs, but not before snorting a South American product—cocaine—had become a chic way for some people to flaunt high status and wealth. This brought us to our present period, the Age of Narco Glitz.

THE AGE OF NARCO GLITZ (1978 TO THE PRESENT)

Since the beginning of the Age of Narco Glitz, in the late 1970s, the topic of drug smuggling and interdiction has been a staple of lowbrow motion-picture and television entertainment and a surefire ratings-getter for the nightly news and documentaries. At one point cocaine had its own television series, "Miami Vice." Drugs were and still are major box office boosters. In September 1986, CBS News received the highest rating for a network documentary in more than five and a half years for "48 Hours on Crack Street." According to Adam Weisman in *The New Republic,* that documentary captured 15 million viewers, or "three times the highest estimate for regular cocaine users in America." [76]

In Western society, virtually all fashions eventually work their way down the economic ladder. Just as Henry Ford used the assembly line to make the automobile accessible to the common person, narcotics entrepreneurs developed crack to make cocaine more affordable. Because the Mafia is no longer in control of the drug business, arrangements with corrupt government officials are no longer as stable as they once were, and upstart urban gangs compete for market share. As a consequence, America's borders and city streets are now war zones. Until some of the street gangs are shaken out of the business by more skillful or ruthless rivals, we will have children shooting each other with Uzis and AK-47s.

The unprecedented gang warfare on America's streets has intensi-fied a fear that often has accompanied the democratization of a drug. As mentioned earlier, England did not perceive a drug problem when opium was used exclusively by gentry on their estates. Similarly, at the beginning of the Age of Narco Glitz, cocaine commerce was not greatly threatening to the social order because the cost of the drug kept it out of the nostrils of the underclass.

Then along came crack, greatly decreasing the cost of a high and raising the specter of disenfranchised, unemployed ghetto youth run-ning amok under the influence of a drug. This was a matter fraught with as much peril as the dreaded return of combat-hardened, heroin-addicted Vietnam veterans. It was time to escalate the drug war. Cocaine—a foreign influence more insidious than the Communist infiltrators whom Senator Joseph McCarthy had railed against—was threatening to defeat us from within. Although much of the fear of drugs was initially unwarranted, our drug policies have acted as self-fulfilling prophecies to create the very real problems that we now face.

CHAPTER 6

The Crime Caused by Prohibition

Prohibition is an awful flop.
We like it.
It can't stop what it's meant to stop.
We like it.
It's left a trail of graft and slime
It don't prohibit worth a dime
It's filled our land with vice and crime,
Nevertheless, we're for it.[1]

"THE WICKERSHAM REPORT," A 1931 POEM WHICH
MOCKED THE FINDINGS OF THE WICKERSHAM
COMMISSION, A PANEL APPOINTED BY PRESIDENT
HERBERT HOOVER TO STUDY OUR BAN ON
ALCOHOL

BEFORE 1914, most states allowed the sale and possession of cocaine and opiates, and in those states nobody was behind bars for violating drug prohibition. Today, America's penal institutions house about one third of a million drug-prohibition prisoners (roughly 25 to 30 percent of the entire penal population),[2] whose offense—drug trafficking or possession—did not even exist eight decades ago. At least a hundred thousand additional inmates are incarcerated for crimes committed to obtain drug money.

103

Property-crime rates have tripled since the mid-1960s, and violent crime rates have more than doubled. This was despite the fact that the rates began to level off and even to recede around 1980, as the proportion of teenagers in the population diminished. About 1985, however, near the crest of the cocaine epidemic, the rates resumed their climb.

There is a disturbing relationship between crime rates and hard-drug usage. The more hard drugs we consume, the more crimes we seem to commit. This undergirds the fallacy that drug intoxication triggers violence in the user and directly leads to crime. However, as we saw in Chapters 3 and 4, while the legal drug alcohol may directly cause crime (as may barbiturates, available on prescription), it is doubtful that most of the other illegal drugs have such criminogenic effects. Neither marijuana nor heroin causes acute personality changes that incline the user toward violence or other aggression; quite the opposite. Some users of cocaine or amphetamines may be moved to violence by the pharmacological effects of the drug, but such effects are far less common than the violence triggered by alcohol. Most of the violence pharmacologically associated with cocaine, even crack, is related to the effects the drug has on the user's need to get money with which to buy more cocaine rather than to the chemical unleashing of violent propensities. Withdrawal dysphoria rather than intoxication accounts for this acute need to obtain money.

Indeed, there is little evidence that any of the illegal drugs create the reckless state of mind commonly linked to alcohol. None of the illegal drugs seem to interfere with cognitive functioning as dangerously as does alcohol. While one strongly under the influence of marijuana, heroin or LSD is in no shape to drive a car or pilot an airplane, consumers of such drugs are usually aware of their impaired condition and rarely take such risks. Drunks, on the other hand, are cognitively impaired and do not appreciate how their perceptual and motor skills have diminished under the influence of the drug. They will often even believe that their skills have improved. Cocaine creates no such cognitive impairments—at least in its normal or usual effects.

Most of the pleasure drugs provide their users with temporary pleasure and thus, at least in the short run, make their users' lives more bearable. The use of such drugs may even dampen the rage that so often erupts in violent crime. Offsetting such balming effects, however, is the fact that using pleasure drugs often produces dependence that cripples the life of the user and inflicts pain and deprivation on the user's family and associates. Those whose lives are wrecked by drug or alcohol abuse sometimes become outcasts, unable to function effectively in society. They then gravitate toward antisocial or parasitic groups and activities.

Whether, on balance, the pharmacological effects of pleasure drugs enlarge or diminish the overall antisocial behavior in a given society is unknowable. One thing, however, is clear: even if the net effect of individual drug use is antisocial or criminal activity, such effects are minuscule when compared to the social havoc wrought by attempts to .prohibit such drug use.

Many—perhaps most—of the millions of robberies, burglaries and thefts in American society would not have occurred but for the *prohibition* of drugs. Many of the murders and attempted murders, arsons and assaults, are also prohibition-caused. As a result of drug prohibition, billions of dollars are annually lost to embezzlers, swindlers and other cheats.

Our prohibition experiment roiled up what had been a relatively benign drug market. Today, prohibition-inspired crime ripples through our social order, just as waves emanate from a pebble tossed into a still pond. Successive waves of crime radiate from the original decision to prohibit drugs.

THE FIRST CRIME WAVE: DIRECT VIOLATIONS OF PROHIBITION

Eight decades of drug prohibition and several decades of escalating the intensity of the drug war have still left about 26 million Americans using illegal drugs, still violating federal and state criminal law. About three quarters of a million of those users—about 3 percent of the total—are criminally prosecuted every year for their drug use.

Drug prohibition has also resulted in the creation of several other hitherto unimagined crimes, such as money laundering, failure to make currency reports, possession and distribution of precursor chemicals. Violations of these criminal provisions number in the millions. There is nothing inherently wrong with these activities apart from the fact that they are prohibited or required by laws ancillary to drug prohibition, but once drugs are criminalized, a vast number of other crimes are generated. The fact that violations of laws prohibiting drug possession and use, money laundering and the like are almost as common as jaywalking has several serious criminogenic effects:

• *Undermining the Moral Message of the Criminal Law.* A major function of the criminal law is to help preserve a society's consensus about what is "wrong" and what is not; to clarify the boundaries between that which the society condemns and that which it tolerates; between what it regards as good and what it views as evil. If we include in our definitions of serious crime conduct that is engaged in by a large portion of our society without serious social condemnation or punitive consequences, we blur the boundaries we seek to maintain by the criminal law. Criminalizing behavior that is commonly engaged in by a substantial segment of a society inevitably debases the currency of criminal proscriptions. If a legal system declares that both drug use and robbery are reprehensible, it is not only making a moral statement about drug use, it is making a moral statement about robbery. If people who use illegal drugs in such a system are commonly not prosecuted, then robbery, which is similarly condemned, cannot be so bad either. In short, the currency of criminal prohibitions can be squandered if devoted to morally debatable or neutral behavior, which almost all drug and other "victimless" criminal activity is.

If both adult participants in a consensual exchange are pleased with the transaction, it is hard in the long run for a society to succeed in condemning it. If such an attempt fails, yet the legal proscriptions are left intact, a society's condemnatory message about other criminal behavior is weakened. Zealous prohibitionists seek to establish societal disapproval of consensual activities by ranking them with murder and other atrocious crimes. That is what former First Lady Nancy Reagan was trying to accomplish when she opined "if you're a casual drug user, you are an accomplice to murder."[3] Such a moral enterprise is doomed where illicit drugs are concerned, however, because it is deeply hypocritical. The use of marijuana, cocaine or heroin cannot be the moral equivalent of murder while the smoking of tobacco and the drinking of liquor are lawful. The hypocrisy is too transparent. Drug prohibition undermines rather than strengthens our morals and our fidelity to criminal law.

• *Encouragement of Arbitrary Enforcement.* When there is a large gap between patterns of violation and patterns of enforcement; where most violators, most of the time, are not criminally punished, illegitimate criteria for selection are ineluctably introduced. People will not be prosecuted for the crime they committed but for who or what they are. Racism and other bigotry will inevitably be instrumental in highly discretionary decisions to invoke the criminal process. The threat of a drug prosecution can be used by the police to obtain other benefits, including sexual favors, money and other property. The risks inherent in excessive discretion exist whenever victimless behavior is criminalized. But the risks are exacerbated in drug crimes because of the severity of the potential punishment.

Drug crime is also one of the few kinds of victimless crime that is engaged in by all segments of society, both genders, all races, all ethnic groups, all levels of income and social status. It is therefore a crime for which everyone is especially vulnerable to a frame or plant by the police (or others).

• *Distractive Effects.* Since drug transactions take place between willing buyers and sellers, both of whom are motivated to avoid detection, law enforcement lacks its staunchest ally, the victim, who is motivated not only to report the crime but to testify against the perpetrator. Drug crimes are therefore difficult to ferret out and to prove.

A successful investigation therefore gobbles law-enforcement resources. Police efforts to detect, prevent or prosecute drug and drug-related crimes between willing, consenting adults distract the police from their more conventional yet far more important tasks: preventing and prosecuting predatory crime. Even if his criminal activities are otherwise unrelated to drugs, the professional robber or burglar will find his work less risky and more profitable because the police are diverted from their traditional tasks by drug crime. Such a criminal is less likely to get caught; if caught, is less likely to be severely punished than he otherwise would be. The courts are too clogged with drug cases to make a serious effort to convict him, forcing a plea bargain or a dismissal. Moreover, to find room for him in a jail or prison, a drug offender may have to be released, and that is inconsistent with a "war on drugs." Robbers, burglars, rapists and murderers soon learn that if they avoid drugs or activities that look drug-related, they virtually have a hunting license in a society that is engaged in a drug war.[4]

The distractive effects of drug prohibition are not limited to crimes over which the police have primary enforcement responsibilities. For example, the Internal Revenue Service has often been conscripted into the war against drugs, at great cost to the taxpayer. Instead of collecting the billions of dollars in taxes unpaid by ordinary taxpayers, the IRS wastes time and money chasing suspected drug dealers. As part of President Nixon's drug war, the IRS targeted 1,011 suspected drug dealers for tax investigations. Investigations were completed only in 238 cases. Only 43 resulted in indictments and only 13 in convictions.

The special IRS antidrug effort spent about $12 million and yet convicted only 1.5 percent of its targets.[5] Had such resources been devoted to ordinary investigations, the results would have been far more productive.

SECOND CRIME WAVE: CRIMES TO GET DRUG MONEY

Drug prohibition fails to make drugs unavailable, but it does make them far more expensive than they otherwise would be. Drug-enforcement officials often measure their success by increases in drug prices. They believe that raising prices depresses demand and thereby reduces the incidence and therefore the negative consequences of drug abuse. Unfortunately, prohibition can increase the price of drugs without substantially decreasing demand, because the demand for drugs is less elastic—less responsive to price changes—than the demand for many other products. If a drug habit can be fed only at great expense, and if the demand for drugs is relatively inelastic, then crimes to obtain the money to buy drugs are inevitable. Achieving the prohibitionists' goal—higher drug prices—does not decrease the negative consequences of drug abuse; it increases the society's total ration of misery.

Although the use of heroin disinclines the user to engage in violence, the appetite for such use—in a state of prohibition—exerts a strong upward lift on crime rates. Heroin addicts rarely commit murder, and, apart from prostitution, virtually never commit sex crimes, but the theft of money and property is a way of life, simply because the addict has no other way to pay for the drugs needed to stave off withdrawal symptoms. The average heroin addict uses more than $10,000 worth of heroin per year.[6] The vast majority of them are unemployed. Several studies show that nearly one hundred percent of heroin addicts commit predatory crimes.[7] The typical addict earns about half his or her cash income from such crime, principally theft. A substantial part of the other half is made from prostitution and selling drugs.

The amount of predatory crime for which such addicts are responsible is huge. In a study of 356 male and female heroin users in Miami, James Inciardi found that they admitted committing nearly 120,000 crimes (an average of 332 per person) during a single year.[8] In a study of 237 Baltimore addicts, researchers found that the group had committed more than 500,000 property crimes during their average of eleven years on the street.[9] In another study of 573 Miami heroin users, Inciardi found them responsible for about 215,000 offenses during the previous year (an average of 375 per person). Included in the totals were 82,000 drug sales, 25,000 shopliftings, 45,000 other crimes of larceny and fraud, 6,000 robberies and assaults, and 6,700 burglaries.[10] In virtually all studies of addict crime, nonviolent, cash-generating crimes predominate; violent crime is comparatively rare. In the latter Miami study, for example, violent crimes comprised only 2.8 percent of the total. When addicts commit so many crimes, however, a small percentage of violent crime is still significant: 6,000 robberies and assaults in one year by 573 persons, an average of more than 10 each, is a lot of robberies and assaults.

There are fewer studies of cocaine users, since the epidemic is newer than the heroin problem. Cocaine-dependent Americans commonly spend several hundred dollars per week, and many spend thousands. Unlike heroin addicts, many are employed or in legitimate businesses. They commonly steal from employers, family, friends, clients or others who trust them. Many commit sophisticated predatory crimes such as bank or credit card fraud, or forgery. In a survey of 500 callers to a cocaine hotline, 45 percent reported they had stolen to buy cocaine.[11] In a nationwide sample of 1,500 adolescents, those who admitted cocaine use, only 1.3 percent of the sample, accounted for 40 percent of the serious crimes committed by the entire sample.[12] In a study of 3,500 drug-abuse patients in 27 states, J. Collins, R. Hubbard and J. Rachal found that frequency of cocaine use was strongly associated with the commission of income-generating crime.[13] Another study of non-narcotic-drug users that included cocaine users found types of crime and crime rates similar to those committed by heroin addicts. Inciardi found that 429 non-narcotic drug users admitted to more than 137,000 offenses during the previous year (an average of 320 crimes per person/year). Of the offenses, drug sales comprised 28 percent; prostitution, 18 percent; burglary, shoplifting and other theft, 27.4 percent; trading in stolen goods, 8.7 percent; and miscellaneous crimes, 17.9 percent (including violent crimes, 1.5 percent).[14]

In several studies of drug use by persons imprisoned, 65 to 80 percent of persons convicted of serious property crimes admitted to regular or lifetime illicit-drug use.[15] This is a far greater rate of drug use than among the population at large. Even among the group in which crime rates are highest—young males—regular illicit-drug users are a small minority.[16]

The fact that most predatory crimes are committed by illicit-drug users does not in itself prove that the crimes are the result of prohibition. Some of the drug users who commit predatory crimes would continue to do so even if they quit using drugs or their drugs were free. But as we noted in Chapter 4, evidence strongly links changes in drug consumption with changes in predatory crime rates, and even correlates increases or decreases in drug prices to similar changes in crime rates. There is no room for doubt that much crime is committed by regular drug users only because the price of drugs is inflated by prohibition. Perhaps the best evidence of that is the testimony of the criminals themselves. In a recent survey of prison inmates conducted by the Bureau of Justice Statistics, "nearly 1 in 3 robbers and burglars said they had committed their crimes to obtain money for drugs."[17]

The FBI estimates that there were nearly 13 million property crimes in the United States in 1991, an all-time high, 8 percent above 1987, 11 percent above 1982.[18] The total dollar losses from property crime are estimated at more than $16 billion.[19] This does not include robbery, involving direct losses of $562 million, and countless personal injuries and deaths.[20] Nor does it include embezzlement, fraud, con games, tax evasion or other white collar crime. At least $10 billion is probably lost in such crimes committed to obtain drug money.

THIRD CRIME WAVE: SYSTEMIC VIOLENCE

City after American city, in 1991 and 1992, experienced record homicide rates, despite continued aging of the population and consequent reduction in the proportions of violence-prone youngsters. In 1989, in our nation's capital, there were more than seven times as many homicides as there were that year in hostilities between Catholics and Protestants in the whole of Northern Ireland.[21] Rival drug gangs engaged in war over drug-selling turf are responsible for a substantial portion of the killings in many of our urban areas. In some cities, such as New Haven, the majority of recent homicides are attributed to hostilities between drug-dealing gangs. In Chicago, about 40 percent of homicides are of that type.[22]

Much homicide is attributable to other systemic aspects of drug trafficking, which engender a Wild West form of justice. Contractual obligations among drug dealers or between drug dealers and their customers are not enforceable in court. Nor can a dispute between street-level dealers be resolved in a sit-down with a Mafia don. There are rarely any higher authorities that can be invoked to mediate disputes among such drug traffickers. Hence the need for violence. Settling disputes or enforcing obligations through violence is also less risky among drug dealers than with legitimate citizens, for the drug dealers or drug customers who are subjected to violence are not situated to seek the protection of the police or the retribution of the criminal justice system.

Some people believe that if drug dealers kill other drug dealers or their customers, this is a desirable deterrent against participating in the drug business, far less expensive to society than lengthy imprisonments. It even can be viewed as an alternative system of capital punishment, involving no lengthy delays, few law-enforcement costs, no gnawing spectacles of condemned persons pleading for justice on network television the day before their execution.

But there is severe myopia in such a perspective. A large proportion—half in some areas—of the victims in drug-related shootings are innocent bystanders who just happened to be in the line of fire. The murders even take place on school grounds, in parks and fast-food restaurants; innocent children are struck down. Victims of such violence are also often potential witnesses for the prosecution who are being silenced by prospective defendants.

Moreover, if drug disputes are effectively resolved by violence, the result is the rewarding of violence, lending support to the most ruthless criminals. Violence and its threat makes criminal prosecution of drug trafficking extremely difficult. Since violence is an essential weapon of the successful drug dealer, it will tend over time to be structured into protective gangs and other organizations, embryonic successors to La Cosa Nostra. If we want to foster organized crime, we need only encourage internecine drug violence.

FOURTH CRIME WAVE: PROLIFERATION OF DEADLY WEAPONS

Criminals who deal in large quantities of contraband and illicit cash are especially vulnerable to predatory outlaws. They are often robbed, even kidnapped for ransom.[23] They are not only disabled from seeking help from the police, they can't even use the services of a bank or an armored car company. They need weapons, more deadly or more numerous than those possessed by their predators. Drug money provides the funds with which to purchase them.

As drug proceeds mushroomed during the seventies and early

eighties, midlevel drug distributors were able to buy not only rifles and handguns, but automatic weapons, bazookas, grenades, even rockets. Bulletproofing of cars, houses and clothing became an important industry. To counteract such offensive and defensive power, other more powerful weaponry is marketed, and so on up the spiral. Virtually everyone who deals in drugs or drug money has at least a handgun. Stash houses and laboratories are arsenals.

Many of those who wield such weaponry, often the same people who distribute the drugs or collect the proceeds, are children. Packing a weapon by a teenager has become, in the inner cities, a badge of manhood, much as carrying a condom was during more tranquil times.

At least 400,000 American youngsters take guns to school. One in five high school students carries a weapon. Says James Brady, "As the violence rises, more kids turn to guns in the false hope the weapons will protect them. Day after day, we hear of children murdered for their sneakers or leather jackets, or shot simply because they looked at somebody the wrong way. . . . Schools are spending millions of dollars to install metal detectors, hire additional security personnel and even build concrete walls around the schools to keep out the violence plaguing the streets. Our places of learning have become fortresses."[24] A decade ago, 10 to 15 percent of teenagers who got into serious trouble in New York were carrying guns. Now, it is 60 to 65 percent.[25]

As William Finnegan put it in a pair of *New Yorker* articles on drugs in New Haven, it is "primarily cocaine money that finances the proliferation of guns, but once the guns are in circulation they take on a life of their own. Among teen-age boys, especially, they become status items. . . . And they end up settling petty disputes that until recently were settled with fists."[26]

The drug business and the violence associated with it have also produced a growing trend toward the acquisition of weapons for defensive purposes. People not even remotely involved in the drug trade feel the need to carry a weapon in reaction to drug-prohibition-related violence. In city after city across the country, girls and their grandmothers are taking lessons in how to kill people with a handgun.[27] The gun lobby may be correct that carrying a gun for self-defense is a fundamental right, but it is a right that is exercised at a ghastly cost. The NRA's implicit claim that bearing arms will help to solve the crime problem[28] is preposterous. The more people carry guns, the more people get killed.

There are about 200 million guns in civilian hands in America, more guns than adults. Each year, 4 to 5 million more are added to that number. The annual sale of handguns has quadrupled from a half million a year in the 1950s to 2 million a year since the early 1970s. And, since guns don't wear out, the number of guns in circulation has increased drastically in the past few decades. The total number of guns in the hands of American civilians doubled between 1950 and 1970, and doubled again between 1970 and 1990.[29] Guns are almost as easy to buy as ice cream, in some cases easier. In one Chicago neighborhood where the Good Humor Man used to come, he has been replaced by the "Gun Man," who drives through the streets selling pistols from the back of a light blue van.[30]

Handguns are used in more than 600,000 crimes of violence every year in the United States, and in about 60 percent of the 24,000 homicides.[31] Guns would be a serious problem even if there were no drug prohibition, but the drug business, a creature of prohibition, provides an expanding, capacious market for guns, especially weapons capable of mass destruction, and in turn provides a powerful reason for citizens to arm themselves. This proliferation of armaments bears a causal connection to thousands of crimes which would otherwise appear unrelated to drugs.

While there are many regulations of gun trafficking and possession that could help, such as gun ownership registration, the possession and use of guns can no more be prevented by prohibition than can the possession and use of drugs. America's frenzied return to the murderous ways of the Wild West can be reversed only when it becomes irrational to keep or carry a gun for self-defense. That will occur when—and not before—predatory crime rates take a deep and permanent plunge. The *only* way that can happen in the near future is by decriminalizing drugs.

Fifth Crime Wave: Corruption of the Criminal Justice System

Our law-enforcement officers, our judges, our lawyers, have been pervasively corrupted by drug money. Nothing in our law-enforcement history rivals such a sorry state other than alcohol prohibition, when the vast majority of law-enforcement officers were apparently on the take.

Policemen in virtually every American city are on the payrolls of drug merchants, earning their pay by tipping off drug dealers about raids or searches, about "snitches" and the like. Some police even engage in the drug trade themselves. Hundreds of law-enforcement officials have been convicted of taking bribes, stealing from drug dealers, even selling their drugs.

In the late 1980s, over eighty Miami police officers were convicted of criminal offenses raging from murder to robbery to extortion in connection with drug investigations. In 1989, eighteen Los Angeles County deputy sheriffs were suspended for systematically siphoning off cash seized in drug raids.[32] In 1985, sheriffs in rural East Tennessee were charged with recycling drugs seized in raids.[33] In 1989, forty-four-year-old Edmund O'Brien, a respected senior officer who had worked on the legendary French-connection busts, was arrested with three other DEA agents on various charges of drug corruption.[34] In April 1991, Darnell Garcia, a former DEA agent, was convicted by a Los Angeles jury of various charges of drug dealing and money laundering. Two of his co-conspirators, also former DEA agents, testified against him. According to them, they all began a crime spree in 1982 when they skimmed $16,000 from money seized in a drug raid. In 1983, they substituted baking soda for two pounds of cocaine seized in a raid and sold the drug for $21,000. They graduated to the big time in 1986, when they found nearly four hundred pounds of cocaine in a Pasadena garage. They shipped it to a New York drug dealer who resold it for them. Eventually, they deposited $2 million in secret accounts in Switzerland.[35] In May 1992, a group of New York policemen were arrested and charged with conducting their own large-scale cocaine-distribution ring, one of the largest in the area. Their methods of doing business allegedly included murder.[36]

Corruption is not limited to the police. Defense lawyers often participate in bribery. Some even act as house counsel to drug distributors. Lawyers are commonly the architects of money-laundering schemes, setting up offshore corporations and secret bank accounts, papering over drug money. Jail and prison officials are commonly bribed with drug money. Even federal prosecutors and judges have fallen. An Assistant United States Attorney in the Southern District of New York was convicted of stealing drugs and money from government supplies.[37] Federal judge Robert F. Collins was recently convicted of bribery in a drug case and judge Walter Nixon was convicted of perjury in an investigation of a drug case.[38]

Corruption is inevitable where such large sums of cash are omnipresent and where only criminals can dispute the policeman's accounts. Drug prohibition encourages police corruption in other ways too. Drug policemen eventually realize that little good is accomplished by honest, resourceful police work. If a drug dealer is imprisoned, he is immediately replaced by another, often more violent and unscrupulous than his predecessor. If an honest cop does an effective job, what is perceived as "the drug problem" only gets worse. Neighborhoods still decline, crime rates continue to climb, and the officer's job even becomes more hazardous. Not only are the drug dealers more dangerous when law enforcement is "effective," the honest cops must worry that they or their informants may be murdered as a result of corrupt leaks.

The entire process is demoralizing and bribery and theft are easily rationalized. Honest cops can't meet their mortgage payments while fellow cops drive BMWs and send their children to private schools. Corrupt cops may even get more commendations and promotions because their co-conspirators help them arrest their competitors. Finally, when corruption is commonplace, even honest cops are routinely suspected, even accused, of corruption. In the presence of such pressures, drug-enforcement officers who remain honest almost qualify for sainthood.

It is impossible to quantify the corruption thus far produced by drug prohibition. Some scholars believe that the problem is not yet as pervasive as it was during alcohol prohibition.[39] Even that may be questioned. About half of the federal narcotic agents in New York were indicted or discharged on grounds of corruption during the early 1970s, and the Knapp Commission investigation into New York City police indicated that corruption was even worse in that department.[40] There is far more money available today. When drug dealers can post millions of dollars in bail and still afford to flee; when single drug transactions commonly involve hundreds of thousands of dollars; when the entire illicit-drug industry swallows perhaps $100 billion per year, corrupt drug enforcement agents can surely make a million dollars or more in bribes per year, which is about what they stand to earn in salary for their entire careers. The sums of money available to be stolen by cops are also growing at accelerated rates. Between 1984 and 1988, cash seizures actually turned in by the Los Angeles Sheriff's Department grew by more than 1100 percent, from $2.77 million in 1984 to $33 million in 1988.[41] The amount of cash reported seized by the DEA alone in 1990 was more than $363 million.[42] The problem can only get worse.

The corruption produced by alcohol prohibition made the entire criminal justice system a bad joke. It took little more than a decade for Americans to realize that a legal system so undermined was infected with a deadly cancer that could result in revolution or anarchy. We excised the cancer of alcohol prohibition. Americans should now realize that the cancer's root remained and has invaded the marrow of America in the form of drug prohibition. It too should be extirpated.

SIXTH CRIME WAVE: UNDERCOVER CRIME

Since drug crimes have no complaining victims and the stakes are so high, investigating them is difficult, time-consuming and often unproductive. Hence the need for "undercover" police who pretend to be crooks to infiltrate criminal organizations. This is the most exciting, glamorous, dangerous and potentially rewarding form of police work. It is also criminogenic.

Undercover infiltration is not possible without proving oneself as a criminal. Whether or not it is true that La Cosa Nostra and other criminal organizations require a recruit to commit murder to prove his worthiness for membership, one clearly cannot be a valuable "undercover" member of a criminal organization without committing many serious crimes. There is something especially disturbing about law-enforcement officers committing robberies, burglaries, murders and drug deals in the name of law enforcement. For that reason, such crimes are covered up. FBI agent Joseph Pistone wrote a bestselling book about his undercover life in the Mafia, but he left out of the story virtually all of the crime he committed during his six-year Mafia association.[43]

Even more criminogenic than undercover activity itself may be the training in mendacity and crime that such activities provide. An effective undercover operative not only has to live a lie about his identity, he has to adopt the values of the underworld, at least temporarily. Yet the combination of carefully crafted deceit and the adoption of criminal values is contagious. Undercover police not only talk like crooks and act like crooks, they often *become* crooks.[44] Such casualties of undercover operations are kept largely hidden from the public.

Even if one emerges from an undercover tour of duty still capable of seeing a difference between right and wrong, the skill acquired in using deceit to bag criminals is all but impossible to discard. Undercover cops who have lied to infiltrate a drug gang will almost instinctively lie in court to help break up such a gang or put its leaders in jail. And that brings us to the next wave of prohibition-induced crime.

SEVENTH CRIME WAVE: POLICE PERJURY, OBSTRUCTIONS OF JUSTICE AND OTHER PERVERSIONS OF JUSTICE

Because we are engaged in a war against drugs, almost anything goes. We not only dispense with civil liberties, we tolerate the deepest perversions of criminal justice in the name of law enforcement.

There are constitutional and even statutory restrictions on how police can gather evidence. When those rules are transgressed, the illegally obtained evidence is supposed to be "suppressed," that is, not used to help convict the person whose rights were violated. But whether the police acted lawfully, whether a person's rights were or were not violated, depends on the context, on the *facts*. For example, if a person "consents" to a search by the police, they need not have a warrant. The search is made lawful by the consent alone. If a suspect throws on the ground or into a hedge something he was carrying on his person, he has "abandoned" it and no warrant or other excuse is needed for the police to appropriate it, whereas they might have no lawful basis for examining the object if it remained in the suspect's pocket. If a suspect behaves suspiciously, as by running away when the police appear, this may justify a stop-and-frisk. Thus, if the police search the person or car or home of suspects and find drugs, the police can use what they found as evidence in court provided the suspects "consented" to the searches, or "abandoned" the drugs, or "fled." If, on the other hand, they searched the suspects' cars or homes arbitrarily without warrants, the "fruits" of the searches must be "suppressed."

Contrary to common belief, drug-seizure evidence is almost *never* suppressed.[45] In part, that is because the Supreme Court, recently self-enlisted in the war against drugs, has changed its interpretations of what the Constitution requires of the police. The dominant reason, however, is probably police perjury. Police routinely lie about the existence of consent, abandonment ("dropsy") or other excuses for a search.

In his book *The Best Defense,* Harvard law professor Alan Dershowitz set forth some unwritten rules that "govern the justice game in America today." Among them are:

Rule IV: Almost all police lie about whether they violated the Constitution in order to convict guilty defendants.

Rule V: All prosecutors, judges, and defense attorneys are aware of Rule IV.

Rule VI: Many prosecutors implicitly encourage police to lie about whether they violated the Constitution in order to convict guilty defendants.

Rule VII: All judges are aware of Rule VI.

Rule VIII: Most trial judges pretend to believe police officers who they know are lying.[46]

A few judges were outraged that Dershowitz was willing to contribute to the disrepute in which the criminal justice system is held by telling the truth about it, but few, if any, disputed the veracity of any of his "rules." Not only have we heard prosecutors admit that police routinely lie about Constitutional issues, the only police that ever seem to be prosecuted for perjury are those who testify in support of a *defendant's* motion to suppress evidence. A cop who does that is almost certain to be indicted.

Why do the police lie with such impunity to convict defendants, especially in drug cases? The fact that they are *expected* to do so explains a lot, and so does the fact that many of them became trained habitual liars in the course of undercover work. However, there is another reason, not quite so obvious. Police who testify in ways that support defendants' motions to suppress draw suspicion upon themselves that they have been bought; that their testimony is tailored to produce acquittals for which they expect to be richly rewarded. Lying, therefore, is a way of averting suspicion of corruption. Thus, ironically, police corruption by drug dealers causes police to commit perjury *against* alleged drug dealers who have not paid for the police testimony. This also accounts in part for the attitudes of prosecutors and judges in drug cases. The more hostility they display toward drug defendants and their rights, the more righteous and incorruptible they appear.

EIGHTH CRIME WAVE: THE VIGILANTE REFLEX

The deterioration of law enforcement leads to a further criminogenic consequence of prohibition. Frustrated by the failure of the police to control crime, Americans are increasingly turning to vigilantes, many of whom violate the law in the name of crime prevention. In Detroit, arsonists openly torched what they believed to be crack houses and were applauded by the local and national media for having done so. Instead of going to prison, the Detroit arsonists appeared on "60 Minutes" and signed a six-figure movie contract.[47] Only a few months before, however, another Detroit arsonist burned what he believed was a drug dealer's property and incinerated an eight-year-old girl who lived inside.[48] In city after city, houses that are believed to be drug havens are illegally boarded up, burned or bulldozed by irate citizens "fed up" with crime. Paramilitary groups such as the Guardian Angels and the Nation of Islam receive favorable publicity for menacing alleged drug dealers in ways that would not be tolerated if done by the police. Movie after movie extols the virtues of vigilante murderers who kill criminals in the name of law and order. The Chief Justice of the West Virginia Supreme Court promotes vigilantism to high school boys. Speaking at a Boys State function in 1989, Richard Neely told the boys that "there is nothing the police and courts can do about drugs" and that "it's time for citizens like you and me to go home and get our baseball bats!" They should not be worried about legal repercussions, he implied, because people in Miami and Detroit have not been punished for burning down crack houses.[49]

Although resort to vigilantism is understandable, it is dangerous. Episodic, disorganized adventures in vigilantism are likely to produce grave errors in the selection of targets for punishment. Vigilantism circumvents legal and constitutional protections and is fundamentally uncivilized. The vigilantes often get hurt or killed themselves.

Vigilante groups are inherently unstable. To achieve staying power, they must have a financial base. Frequently, this consists of "contributions" from the householders and businesses in the areas the vigilantes patrol. At best, this deteriorates into justice for sale. At worst, it becomes extortion. Organized vigilantes are hard to distinguish from criminal groups. Many crime organizations sell "peace" of one kind or another and represent the ultimate danger of corrupted vigilantism. Unrestrained by due process and not accountable to political institutions, vigilante groups can become engines of crime themselves. Like the death squads in El Salvador who murdered priests, vigilantes can attack any person whose politics displeases them. They often turn on the very people who earlier recruited them.

NINTH CRIME WAVE: SOCIAL DETERIORATION

For every violent crime committed, hundreds are feared. As crime rates increase in a neighborhood, fear takes over and decline and disorder begin.[50] Inhabitants who can afford to do so flee to safer neighborhoods. Those unable to leave barricade themselves in their houses and apartments, fearful of going out. In some neighborhoods, people sleep in their bathtubs to reduce the risk of being killed by a stray bullet. The streets, parks and playgrounds are surrendered to hoodlums. The streets are filthy; cars and other possessions are abandoned, and the inhabitants lose a sense of responsibility for the well-being of their neighbors. Small businesses are covered with iron bars and, ultimately, closed. Crimes are no longer reported, since there is a sense of futility about it, exacerbated by the appearance of decline and disorder in the neighborhood.[51] Crime begets more crime. Life becomes all but unlivable to those who have lost control of the neighborhood to criminal elements. Property values plummet and landlords abandon dwelling after dwelling. Drug dealers and prostitutes move in, and even the police virtually give up.

Drug prohibition is not the only cause of the decline of the inner cities. The failure of our government to educate inner-city children, to provide employment opportunities for them and their parents, to provide decent housing, to curtail the flight to suburbia and technological factors all have contributed, but drug prohibition has made these difficult problems all but insurmountable. It is the major cause of the crime in the inner cities and the major cause of their disorder and decline.

The result is that the children who remain in the blighted, crime-infested inner cities have virtually no employment opportunities— unemployment rates are 60 to 70 percent among male youths in many of these areas—and no real educational opportunities exist. The schools are underfinanced and controlled by armed hoodlums. The only opportunity for a decent life presented to most of these youngsters is connected with the drug business. It is virtually the only job available to most of the young men who are looking for employment. We should not be surprised that they accept it. What is surprising is that the majority do not.

It is often asserted that 50 percent of all crime is drug-related.[52] Some experts, such as New Haven police chief Nicholas Pastore, put that figure as high as 80 percent.[53] Such estimates can neither be substantiated nor refuted. It *is* clear, however, that virtually all of the drug-related crime would not exist without drug prohibition. It is also clear that the lives of everyone in America would be immensely safer if drug prohibition were repealed. Our cities—and their inhabitants—can be rescued by using great effort, resources and commitment, but only if the plague of crime can be radically reduced. No one has yet suggested a plausible way of accomplishing that goal under a system of drug prohibition. We can save our cities or we can maintain our war against drugs. We cannot do both.

CHAPTER 7

Freedom Costs

*"Experience should teach us to be most on our guard
to protect liberty when the Government's purposes
are beneficent. Men born to freedom are naturally
alert to repel invasion of their liberty by evil-minded
rulers. The greatest dangers to liberty lurk in
insidious encroachment by men of zeal,
well-meaning but without understanding."*

JUSTICE LOUIS D. BRANDEIS, DISSENTING FROM A
UNITED STATES SUPREME COURT DECISION THAT
PERMITTED WIRETAPPING TO AID ENFORCEMENT
OF ALCOHOL PROHIBITION.[1]

AT 2 A.M. on June 29, 1991, Tracy White of Los Angeles was awakened by the explosion of a diversionary grenade set off in a trash can outside her front door. She stumbled out into the upstairs hallway and was met by a shaft of light and a man's voice. "Freeze," he said. "Police." At that moment, her bedroom windows shattered and two men clad in black hoods swung into the room. Her three infants shrieked in fright. Several guns were pointed at her. More men dressed in black bounded through the bathroom window. One ran into an adjoining bedroom and pinned Tracy's sister Yolanda and her twelve-year-old daughter behind a door. The youngster tried to squirm free

122

and found the barrel of a pistol against her head. She closed her eyes and urinated on herself. "I thought," she said, "he was going to kill me."

The police had been searching for Ms. White's cousin, a reputed gang member, who did not live there and was not there when the raid occurred. The White apartment was left in shambles. Almost all the windows were gone, crystal glassware was reduced to shards, and a chunk was missing from a couch armrest.

Six months after the raid, Ms. White and her children still refused to move back into the old apartment, unable to find peace of mind in a place that reminded them of hooded men crashing through their windows.[2]

The injuries inflicted on the Whites were mostly psychological, but some searches are lethal. In Atlanta, in 1991, a pre-Christmas raid by nine cops with guns drawn awakened Bobby Bowman as they broke down his door with a battering ram. Bowman, who says he thought he was being robbed, opened fire with a shotgun. A gunfight ensued, and Bowman's eight-year-old stepson, Xavier, who had been sleeping in the front room, was killed by a detective's bullet. The police found $780 worth of crack in Bowman's apartment. Teresa Nelson, Georgia director of the American Civil Liberties Union, questioned whether it was worth the life of an innocent eight-year-old to get evidence in a drug case, but Atlanta police defended the tactics, as do police across the country.[3] They claim that surprise and overwhelming force is necessary to minimize destruction of evidence. Many also make the debatable claim that violent attacks reduce the danger to the police from counterattacks.

THE FOURTH AMENDMENT: A DRUG-WAR CASUALTY

Such raids and ransackings are standard procedure in most large cities and, except in the most outrageous cases, they receive the approval of courts. Police can get search warrants on the flimsiest of suspicion— even the word of an anonymous informant.[4] In many cases, though, the police don't even bother to get a warrant, since they are virtually unfettered by the risk of successful suits or other sanctions, especially if they confine their warrantless invasions to poor members of minority groups.

The Fourth Amendment of the United States Constitution, which guarantees against "unreasonable searches and seizures" and prohibits warrants on anything but "probable cause," is a casualty of the drug war.[5]

Since the early 1970s, almost all the searches and seizures reaching the United States Supreme Court have been upheld. The Court has held, for example, that a search made on an invalid warrant does not require any remedy so long as the police acted in "good faith."[6] People may be stopped in their cars, in airports, trains or buses, and submitted to questioning and dog sniffs of their persons and possessions.[7] Police may search an open field without warrant or cause, even if it has "no trespassing" signs and the police trespass is a criminal offense.[8] They may also, as in Orwell's *Nineteen Eighty-Four,*[9] conduct close helicopter surveillance of our homes and backyards.[10] If it is outside the house, they may also search our garbage without cause.[11] If they have "reasonable suspicion," the police may even search our persons and possessions. Mobile homes, closed containers within cars,[12] as well as cars themselves may be searched without a warrant.

The Court has also held that an international traveler, if a suspected "balloon swallower," may, without warrant or probable cause, be seized as she arrives at the airport, strip-searched and ordered to remain incommunicado until she defecates over a wastebasket under the watchful eye of two matrons. In sanctioning such an eighteen-hour ordeal, Chief Justice Rehnquist unabashedly listed other invasions that the Court had upheld: "[F]irst class mail may be opened without a warrant on less than probable cause. . . . Automotive travelers may be stopped . . . near the border without individualized suspicion even if the stop is based largely on ethnicity . . . and boats on inland waters with ready access to the sea may be hailed and boarded with no suspicion whatever."[13]

Those incursions as well as detention for defecation, Chief Justice Rehnquist said, are responsive to "the veritable national crises in law enforcement caused by smuggling of illegal narcotics."[14]

In the compulsory defecation case, as in countless others, searches or seizures have been upheld on nothing more than "reasonable" or even "articulable" suspicion that drugs are being transported. That level of suspicion can be achieved by matching up the victim of the search or seizure with a few of the characteristics contained in secret "drug courier profiles" that rely heavily upon ethnic stereotypes. As a result of such profiles, hundreds of innocent people are subjected to indignities every day. Twenty-seven-year-old Kurt Disser is an example. A diamond dealer, he frequently drives between San Diego and Los Angeles on business. Sixty-six miles from the Mexican border, on

Interstate Route 5, near San Clemente, the Immigration Service maintains a checkpoint, allegedly to detect illegal aliens, but increasingly serving in the drug war. Most of the 115,000 drivers who pass through the checkpoint each day are merely required to slow down while an officer glances at them. Disser, however, was stopped and searched fifteen of the thirty times he traversed the route during a seventeen-month period. On several occasions, he was frisked and his car trunk was searched. Drug-sniffing dogs were given repeated whiffs of Disser's car. Several times, agents told him the dogs detected drugs and this led to a full search. No evidence of drugs or criminality of any kind was ever found. Disser has no criminal record. He was stopped and searched solely because of his appearance (he has long hair and drives an elderly Cadillac, both characteristics apparently found in the profiles).[15]

Hispanics and "hippie types" bear the major brunt of the profiles near our southern border, but young African-Americans suffer from it wherever they go. An African-American who drives a car with an out-of-state license plate is likely to be stopped almost anywhere he goes in America. A survey of car stoppings on the New Jersey turnpike revealed that although only 4.7 percent of the cars were driven by blacks with out-of-state plates, 80 percent of the drug arrests were of such people.[16] The *Pittsburgh Press* examined 121 cases in which travelers were searched and no drugs were found. Seventy-seven percent of the people were black, Hispanic or Asian.[17] In Memphis, about 75 percent of the air travelers stopped by drug police in 1989 were black, yet only 4 percent of the flying public is black.[18]

Almost as offensive as relying on racial characteristics in a profile to justify searches or seizures is permitting the trivial and subjective profile characteristics to count as "reasonable" or "articulable" suspicion. Federal circuit judge Warren Ferguson observed that the DEA's profiles have a "chameleon-like way of adapting to any particular set of observations."[19] In one case, a suspicious circumstance (profile characteristic) was deplaning first.[20] In another, it was deplaning last.[21] In a third, it was deplaning in the middle.[22] A one-way ticket was said to be a suspicious circumstance in one case;[23] a round-trip ticket was suspicious in another.[24] Taking a nonstop flight was suspicious in one case,[25] while changing planes was suspicious in another.[26] Traveling alone fit a profile in one case;[27] having a companion did so in another.[28] Behaving nervously was a tipoff in one case;[29] acting calmly was the tipoff in another.[30]

Another favorite basis for suspicion is that the suspect is traveling to or from a major source city for drugs, yet every city in America with a major airport is such a city.[31] Even the same agents take contradictory positions. In Tennessee, an agent testified that he was leery of a man because he "walked quickly through the airport." Six weeks later, the same agent swore that his suspicions were aroused by a man because he "walked with intentional slowness after getting off the bus."[32]

As even their users admit, the profiles are self-fulfilling. If the profiles are based on who is searched and found guilty, the guilty will necessarily fit the profiles. The DEA claims to catch 3,000 or more drug violators through the profiles,[33] but no records are kept of how many people are hassled, detained or searched to produce the 3,000. Amazingly, the DEA keeps no records of the *failures* of the profile system.

Some numbers, however, are available. Rudy Sandoval, a commander of Denver's vice bureau, estimated that his police conducted 2,000 airport searches in 1990, yielding only 49 arrests. In Pittsburgh, where records were kept, 527 people were searched in 1990, and 49 were arrested.[34] In the Buffalo airport, in 1989, 600 people were stopped by police and only 10 were arrested. Said federal circuit judge George Pratt: "It appears that they have sacrificed the Fourth Amendment by detaining 590 innocent people in order to arrest 10 who are not—all in the name of the 'war on drugs.' When, pray tell, will it end? Where are we going?"[35]

And what of the cherished constitutional right to the privacy of bedroom and telephone conversations? An elaborate federal statute seeks to prohibit most interceptions of such conversations that are not approved by a court order, upon an application establishing probable cause, necessity and several other requirements.[36] The granting of wiretap and eavesdropping applications, however, appears to be even more routine than rubber-stamping of search warrants. In 1991, 856 requests were submitted to federal judges; *each and every one* of the applications was approved.[37] Even the procurers of search warrants cannot claim a batting average of 1000. The only reason there weren't ten times as many wiretaps and buggings is that they cost money to administer. Somebody, after all, has to listen. The average electronic surveillance cost $45,000 in 1991.[38] Sixty-one percent of the surveillances were of suspected drug dealers.[39] The total cost of electronic surveillance in drug cases, therefore, was about $23.5 million.

Not all of the court rulings against Fourth Amendment rights have occurred in drug cases, but most of them have, and the drug war fuels the attack on privacy even in cases not directly dealing with drugs. The pressure to uphold police activities in drug cases generates new "principles" that thereafter apply to everyone, whether or not drugs are involved. Moreover, if the police can search for drugs on suspicion, they can also search for evidence of tax evasion, gambling, mail fraud, pornography, bribery and any other criminality. The ostensible object of a police search does not limit what they can confiscate and use. If police conduct a lawful search, they can take and use any evidence they see, however unrelated it may be to what got them into the home—or the body—in the first place.

The Supreme Court has not stopped at amending the Fourth Amendment's "probable cause" to mean, in most cases, only "reasonable suspicion," and creating a half dozen outright exceptions to the search warrant requirement; it has also eliminated most legal remedies for those few searches that *are* still illegal. The exclusionary rule—which forbids use of illegally obtained evidence—has been restricted to the point of absurdity.[40] The Court has held that the rule does not apply to grand jury proceedings, to civil cases or even to sentencing procedures. It does not apply even in a criminal trial if the defendant has the temerity to testify in his own defense, for the illegally obtained evidence can then be used to "impeach" the defendant as a witness.[41] Thus, the police have strong incentives to violate the meager Fourth Amendment rights that remain intact, because there is in most cases no practical remedy for their violations.

Students and Other Quasi-People

Although students in our public schools are "people" protected in theory by the Bill of Rights, they are treated otherwise in practice. The Supreme Court approved the search of a high school student's purse on reasonable "suspicion" that the search will turn up evidence that the student has violated either the law or the rules of the school.[42] Courts uphold searches of lockers and even college dorm rooms on the same flimsy justification.[43] Students have been subjected to strip-searches,[44] to having their activities in a bathroom recorded on film[45] and, in a parochial school, to routine urine tests.[46] A court even upheld the strip-search of a male student because his crotch, a teacher thought, was "too well-endowed." (The search revealed no contraband.)[47] Douglas Wilder, Governor of Virginia, proposed that all Virginia college students be subjected to mandatory drug testing.[48]

If students get only a diluted version of an already watered Fourth

Amendment, at least they have standing to complain. But nonresident aliens who are searched abroad by our drug agents seem to have no rights at all. Upholding the warrantless search of a defendant's home in Mexico by American DEA agents, Chief Justice Rehnquist declared that nonresident aliens are not "people" protected by the Constitution even if, as in the case before the Court, the victim of the search had been taken to the United States and was being held here for trial while the search was conducted in Mexico to help convict him here.[49] Thus, unless they are acting against American citizens or resident aliens, our police can do anything abroad to anyone and the Constitution is seemingly inoperative.

It is not even clear that our own citizens have any constitutional rights outside our borders. In June 1992, the Supreme Court upheld the DEA-supervised kidnapping of a doctor suspected of assisting in the torture of a DEA agent in Mexico. Nothing in either the Constitution or the extradition treaty with Mexico, the Court held, required any remedy for the doctor's forceful abduction to the United States for trial.[50] While the defendant in that case was a nonresident alien, the principle of the case, extending a precedent more than a century old,[51] is unlimited: it doesn't matter whom the police kidnap, or where they kidnap them, or how they do it; the kidnapping will not prevent the victim's own criminal trial. (Mexican authorities were outraged at the kidnapping-doesn't-matter case and expressed their resentments in diplomatic channels. Other Mexican officials retaliated in kind, crossing our border on the same day as the Supreme Court's decision and kidnapping two fugitives at gunpoint, returning them to Mexico.[52])

THE BEST OFFENSE: GET THE DEFENSE COUNSEL

What the drug war has done to the Fourth Amendment, it has also done to the Sixth. The Sixth Amendment guarantees, among other things, that in "all criminal prosecutions" the accused shall enjoy "the Assistance of Counsel for his Defense." No other right is as precious to one accused of crime as the right of counsel. A loyal, competent lawyer is essential for the protection of every other right the defendant has, including the right to a fair trial.

In recognition of that fact, the definition of the enemy in the war against drugs has been expanded. Not only are drug sellers and drug users targets, so are their lawyers."[53] Criminal-defense lawyers, especially if they practice in federal courts, have increasingly come to expect their law offices to be searched, their phones to be tapped or their offices bugged. They are rarely surprised when they get IRS summonses seeking information about their criminal clients, about themselves or about both. Prosecutors frequently serve subpoenas on defense lawyers prior to trial, requiring them to produce documents and testify about their client before a grand jury, in secret.[54] Having thus driven a wedge between client and attorney, creating a disqualifying conflict of interest at worst and mistrust of the lawyer at least, the prosecutor is then in a strong position to coerce a guilty plea or, in intractable cases, to seek disqualification of the lawyer on the eve of trial, when no other lawyer has time to prepare a defense. The courts have upheld all these practices, the effect of which is to deprive the accused of his only real defensive armament.[55]

The Supreme Court added a powerful missile to the government's arsenal when it held in 1989 that federal authorities could freeze and later obtain the forfeiture of the assets of a person *accused* of a drug crime, so that he would have no money with which to pay a lawyer.[56]

The centuries-old tradition that confidential conversations between a lawyer and client cannot be divulged without the consent of the client also seems headed for the basement of American legal history. Courts have held that because "monitoring" of conversations in jails and prisons is well-known, any attorney-client conversations that are eavesdropped upon—or tapped—are fair game—they have been implicitly "consented" to. This absurd fiction was even applied to Colonel Manuel Noriega, who barely speaks English. After he was kidnapped in Panama and thrown in a Miami jail, his phone conversations with his lawyers were "monitored." A federal court found he waived his rights by talking on the phone.[57]

Courts have expanded other exceptions to the attorney-client privilege to the point that little is left of the privilege in criminal prosecutions. Two exceptions together almost swallow the privilege: (1) if the attorney's services were sought, in whole or in part, to aid in the commission of a crime or a fraud, the crime-fraud exception applies; (2) if necessary to clear himself of suspicion, the attorney can disclose privileged confidential communications, even if they bury the client. In short, if the interests of attorney and client are in conflict, the interests of the attorney prevail. Anyone accused of being involved with illegal drugs who is (or ever has been) guilty of the crime charged or any other acquisitive crime and hires a lawyer is necessarily seeking, at least in part, to cover up past crimes and to avoid future claims against his assets, such as tax claims, forfeiture claims and the like. These are usually regarded as impermissible objectives. It is not possible to separate consultations concerning past money-making crimes, as to which the attorney-client privilege supposedly still applies, and consultations about future crimes or frauds as to which the privilege does not apply. Faced with such overlaps, courts commonly find there is no privilege.[58] But if the defendant hasn't been convicted of the crime, how can anyone decide in advance of trial that the client was seeking, in his communication with counsel, help in hiding assets or otherwise perpetrating a "crime or fraud"? Courts have ruled that it is enough if there is "probable cause" to believe that such is his objective. The court that considers the claim of privilege may even rely on the supposedly confidential conversations themselves to find that probable cause exists.[59] Alternatively, if the attorney, rather than asserting the privilege on behalf of the client, secretly discloses the confidential matters to the prosecutors or a grand jury, a court can later hold, if the disclosure is discovered and challenged by the client, that the disclosure itself proves that the privilege never applied in the first place. In such a case, the client has no remedy for his lawyer's betrayal of trust.

Even if the crime-fraud exception does not destroy the privilege, the second, save-the-lawyer-at-any-cost exception often will. A prosecutor can apparently trump the privilege simply by making insinuations about the complicity of counsel in the client's alleged criminal activities. The lawyer can then betray the client to clear himself. That this rule permits the prosecutor to destroy the accused's privilege by a mere insinuation seems not to bother either courts or experts on legal ethics.[60]

Unpunished Prosecutorial Crimes Against Defendants

Some prosecutors don't stop at making grand jury witnesses out of criminal-defense counsel. They even arm traitorous defense lawyers with bugging devices and direct them to get incriminating admissions directly from their client's lips. Novelist Scott Turow, when a federal prosecutor in Chicago, did exactly that. An attorney named Marvin Glass came under suspicion in the federal corruption investigation dubbed operation Greylord. To help himself, he cut a deal with Turow to provide information incriminating his clients. Among others, Glass was representing Ronald Ofshe, who had been arrested on cocaine charges in Florida. Turow equipped Glass with a body bug and directed him to talk with his client, Ofshe, while agents listened in. Glass continued to represent Ofshe for ten months, all the while secretly helping the government convict him and others. The federal appeals court held that while the prosecutors' behavior was "reprehensible," it did not require any remedy; Ofshe had not been "prejudiced" by the fact that the person passed off to him as his lawyer was really a government informant.[61]

Even more reprehensible was a conspiracy between prosecutors, drug agents, and a Los Angeles defense lawyer named Ron Minkin. After representing drug defendants for twenty years, Minkin became an imposter lawyer, working for the government while pretending to defendants that he was their lawyer. He would suggest to the prosecutors whom they should investigate, and even provide evidence against them. When it arrested them, the Government would then encourage the defendants to hire Minkin as their counsel, for which he would collect large fees. Minkin also profited in other ways from "unsuccessful defenses" of his clients. He provided information about a former client, Seth Booky, that led to Booky's arrest. Minkin then "represented" Booky and turned him into a paid government informant; worse, Minkin was to get one third of all the money Booky received from the government for his services, including any shares of forfeited property.

Minkin and Booky, assisted by federal agents, then set out to trap new drug defendants and to confiscate their property. One of their targets was an associate of Booky's named Steven Marshank. They pretended that Minkin was conducting a vigorous defense of Booky and that Booky needed help with Minkin's attorney fees. Marshank "helped" and Minkin pocketed the proceeds. Minkin then proceeded to put together a case against Marshank, even arranging to have him arrested, and putatively became his attorney. Minkin continued to provide detailed information about conversations he had with Marshank for months, and even testified against him before a grand jury. This conspiracy to deprive Marshank—and Minkin's other clients— of their constitutional rights was too much for the court to take. San Francisco federal judge Marilyn Patel dismissed the indictment for "outrageous" governmental misconduct.[62]

The conduct of the government and the defense lawyers in the Ofshe and Marshank cases is not only outrageous, it is clearly a felonious criminal conspiracy, yet we have never heard of a case like those where *any* proceedings of any kind were brought against the prosecutors. In most cases, nothing whatever is done. If such a conspiracy comes to light and the defendant complains, the court may agree that the accused was denied his Sixth Amendment right to counsel, but then, as in Ofshe's case, it usually holds that such a violation was "harmless" to the defendant. This is because the Supreme Court held, in a drug case, that even "egregious behavior of . . . Government agents" warrants no remedy for the victim unless he can show that he might not have been convicted had the violation not occurred.[63] The reason, the Court said in another case, is that to impose a sanction against the prosecution for such behavior would fail to give sufficient weight to the "unfortunate necessity of undercover work and the value it often has to effective law enforcement."[64]

Defending a Client Becomes a Crime

Courts have also upheld recent requirements that criminal-defense lawyers report to the IRS anyone who pays them $10,000 or more in cash, whether a client or a third party. Attorneys who have refused to make such reports about their clients have been jailed.[65] As of 1986, it is also a felony for anyone, including a lawyer, to accept money or property in excess of $10,000 which was derived from specified unlawful activity.[66] It is no defense to a lawyer or any other recipient that the money or property was received for legitimate goods or services, even essential legal services. Nor is it a defense that the attorney had nothing to do with the illegal activity that generated the money or property. Nor is it a defense that the attorney was unaware of the specific kind of criminal activity that produced the money.[67] It is not even a defense to the attorney that he had no actual knowledge that the money or property was illegally derived. "Willful blindness" is a substitute for knowledge, and the lifestyle of the client—fitting stereotypes of how drug dealers comport themselves—may go far toward establishing the attorney's guilty "knowledge," or "willful blindness." Thus, an attorney who represents a person who is charged with a drug offense who "looks like" a drug dealer is at risk of being indicted also.[68]

Defense lawyers therefore risk losing not only their fee but their freedom and their license to practice law for trying to protect the constitutional rights of their clients. The possible charges against lawyers are not limited to accepting "tainted" money as payment of a fee.

Lawyers who help their clients avoid indictment or who represent them in business dealings, such as real estate transactions, can be indicted, with the client, for money laundering, tax evasion or even drug trafficking.[69] Attorneys who confine their professional activities solely to defending clients who have already been arrested on charges still risk their own indictment, for "obstruction of justice," if nothing else. Nobody knows what the limits of that crime are. Many prosecutors think that anything a defense attorney does that might be helpful in defending the client is such an obstruction. Courts have not yet embraced that interpretation, but neither have they repudiated it. According to Columbia law professor H. Richard Uviller, a former prosecutor, "it is almost possible to say that the statute threatens a five-year penalty for virtually any conduct during the pendency of a judicial proceeding that the government deems evasive, abusive, or inconvenient."[70]

It has always been difficult for persons accused of drug crimes to find competent attorneys willing to bear the stigma of being "a drug dealer's lawyer," but now that such attorneys also risk losing both their fees and their freedom, privately retained drug-defense lawyers are on their way to extinction—which is what the Congress and the Supreme Court appear to want.

THE ROT BENEATH THE VENEER

Court opinions that chisel away at specific constitutional guarantees ought to be alarming to all who value liberty, but such decisions are at least visible and are subject to intense scrutiny and criticism. Legal scholar Steven Wisotsky, for example, calls the result of this chiseling process "the Emerging 'Drug Exception' to the Bill of Rights."[71] A less visible and therefore more ominous "drug exception" corrodes the amorphous rights to a fair trial protected by the Fifth and Fourteenth Amendments' due process clauses. In most drug prosecutions, the trial proceedings are ignored by the press and no opinions are written by the trial judges justifying or explaining their rulings. Those accused of crime must rely on the integrity of appellate judges to scrutinize the record and assure that the trial proceedings were fair and consistent with due process. Yet in many courts criminal convictions and long prison sentences are routinely upheld without even hearing argument of the appeal, and without even the writing of an appellate opinion. In such cases, there is no basis for believing that the appellate judges bothered to read the briefs or understood the issues, much less that they dealt with them fairly.[72] The prevailing—although rarely acknowledged— attitude in American courts is that almost any trial is too good for a person accused of a drug crime. That attitude was succinctly displayed in a remark made in 1987 by one of the most liberal Supreme Court Justices. In an interview with *Life* magazine, Thurgood Marshall, a lifelong defender of the Bill of Rights, said, "If it's a dope case, I won't even read the petition. I ain't giving no break to no dope dealer. . . ."[73] That statement caught the attention of some in the legal profession, but it produced neither a bark of criticism nor a paragraph of protest. What would have happened if Justice Marshall had said the same thing about petitions from politicians convicted of bribery? Or those of securities dealers convicted of stock fraud? Or even petitions from the government, disappointed that a lower court had the nerve to *reverse* a drug conviction? There would have been raucous demands for his impeachment.

A System Without Respect

The pressures that the drug war have brought to bear on already overburdened courts have produced a breakdown in both their integrity and the respect in which they are held. Many defense lawyers and scholars are convinced that appellate judges will say anything to uphold a drug conviction. If such judges don't affirm without writing any opinion at all, they often issue unsigned opinions and, because such opinions are so shoddy, forbid their publication. The courts will not even allow lawyers to cite such "opinions" as precedent in other cases. Finally, when they do publish their opinions, judges often invent nonexistent "facts" to support their affirmances. Respect for the American judiciary by lawyers who appear before them has probably never been lower.

Occasionally, a judge rails against the trampling of rights under the tanks of the drug war. Usually, this is done as part of a multi-judge panel, where a judge can "dissent" from the decision of the majority while having no discernible effect on the outcome. Such dissenting opinions are free—they can ring the bells of freedom while the majority orders the defendant packed off to prison. The dissenter has little responsibility for what he says, since he is not deciding the case. Protests by judges at the trial level—where a single judge is responsible for the outcome—are rare. One such judge was U.S. magistrate Peter

Nimkoff of Miami, Florida. Nimkoff frequently offended prosecutors and other judges by granting bail to defendants accused of major drug crimes. Most judges either order the defendant detained without any bail at all—a power given to them by the 1984 "Bail Reform Act"[74]— or find out how much bail the defendant can post and then set bail at five or ten times that amount.[75] Nimkoff asserted that the Constitution presumes the innocence of all persons accused of crime, even a drug crime. He also blasted as "outrageous" the tactics of a DEA agent who, posing as a friend of a lawyer's client, tried to get the Miami attorney to divulge confidential communications from his client. DEA agents then tried to implicate the lawyer himself in an escape plot. Failing that, they obtained a search warrant on a fraudulent affidavit and thus were able to read privileged letters between attorney and client.[76]

In another case, Nimkoff denounced the DEA's use of a female informant who "set up" at least forty men, enticing them into drug deals after developing a sexual relationship with them. The "boyfriend" would be busted and the "girlfriend" would get paid by the DEA.[77]

Finally, in 1986, Nimkoff had enough. He resigned to protest the relentless erosion of rights and the governmental abuses of power with which he was daily confronted. In a press conference, he decried the view "that there are two constitutions—one for criminal cases generally and another for drug cases." Such a view is not only "wrong," he said, it "invites police officers to behave like criminals. And they do."[78] Nimkoff's lamentations had the impact of a flower falling in the forest. Miami's major newspaper, the *Herald,* found nothing about his resignation or his press conference that warranted reporting.

THE FORFEITURE FROLIC: WHAT BECAME OF THE RIGHT OF PROPERTY?

The signers of the Declaration of Independence believed, with John Locke, that the right of property was fundamental, inalienable, an aspect of humanity. They regarded liberty as impossible without property, which was the guardian of every other right.[79] These beliefs are reflected in constitutional text. The Fifth Amendment declares that "No person shall be deprived of life, liberty or property without due process of law; nor shall private property be taken for public use, without just compensation." Under forfeiture statutes enacted since

1970, however, both deprivations occur routinely, with the approval—sometimes reluctant—of courts.

Under federal statutes, any property is subject to forfeiture if it is "used, or intended to be used, in any manner or part, to commit or to facilitate the commission" of a drug crime.[80] No one need be convicted or even accused of a crime for forfeiture to occur. Indeed, in 80 percent or more of drug forfeitures, no one is ever charged with a crime.[81]

Forfeiture is a "civil" matter. Title vests in the government instantly upon the existence of the "use" or the "intention" to use the property in connection with a drug offense.[82] All the government needs to establish its right to seize the property is "probable cause," the same flimsy standard needed to get a search warrant. The government can take a home on no stronger a showing than it needs to take a look inside. Hearsay or even an anonymous informant can suffice. No legal proceedings are required before personal property may be seized. If the police have "probable cause" concerning a car, a boat or an airplane, they just grab it.[83] Although property may not be repossessed at the behest of a conditional seller,[84] a driver's license may not be revoked,[85] welfare benefits may not be terminated[86] and a state employee cannot be fired without a hearing *before* the action is taken,[87] persons can have their motor homes confiscated without any proceedings of any kind, if the confiscation is a drug forfeiture.[88] There may be a right to contest the forfeiture after the seizure, but even this right is lost if not promptly asserted. Moreover, the costs of hiring a lawyer and suing to recover the seized property may be prohibitive unless the property seized is of great value.

As construed by the courts, the forfeiture statutes also encourage police to make blatantly unconstitutional seizures. Property may be seized without probable cause—on a naked hunch—and still be retained, and still be forfeited. The reason: courts hold that illegally seized property need not be returned but may be forfeited if the police can establish probable cause at the forfeiture proceeding itself.[89] It doesn't matter that there was no cause whatever for the seizure; it doesn't matter that the seizure was illegal, even unconstitutional. If the government can later establish probable cause (through the seized property itself or investigation occurring after the seizure), that is sufficient to uphold a forfeiture.

If the government wants to seize real property without notice, it has to get a court's approval, but that is as easy as getting a search warrant. A seizure warrant is obtained in the same way as a search warrant, and on the same hearsay grounds. A six-story apartment building in New York, containing forty-one apartments, was seized on such a warrant, which the appellate court upheld.[90]

No civilized country imposes criminal punishment for mere evil intentions; but the forfeiture statutes—since they are "civil," not "criminal"—are apparently subject to no such limitation. A court recently held that a home was forfeitable because the owner, when he applied for a home equity loan, "intended" to use the proceeds to buy drugs. By the time the loan actually came through, he had used other funds for that purpose, but that didn't matter, the court said, because he had *intended* to use the home to secure a loan, the proceeds of which he *intended* to use for drugs. The home was therefore no longer his.[91] It would apparently have made no difference if he never even applied for the loan, as long as he thought about it.

Any activities within a home that relate to drugs are sufficient for forfeiture of the home: a phone call to or from a source; the possession of chemicals, wrappers, paraphernalia of any kind; the storing or reading of any how-to books on the cultivation or production of drugs. The operative question is whether any of these activities was "intended" to facilitate a drug offense.[92]

If a car is driven to or from a place where drugs are bought or sold and is then parked in a garage attached to a home, the home has then been used to store the car, which facilitated the transaction, and is probably forfeitable along with the car. If the home is located on a 120-acre farm, the entire farm goes as well.[93] If only a few square feet of land in a remote section of a farm are devoted to marijuana plants, the grower loses not only the entire farm, but—if it is on the same land as the farm—his home as well.[94]

It is hard to see any ending point. Once any property qualifies for forfeiture, almost any other property owned or possessed by the same person can fall into the forfeiture pot. Notions about how otherwise "innocent" property can "facilitate" illegal activities are almost limitless. When drug proceeds were deposited in a bank account that contained several hundred thousand dollars in "clean" funds, the entire account was declared forfeit on the theory that the "clean" funds facilitated the laundering of the tainted funds.[95] Where a drug dealer owned and operated a ranch, his quarter horses—all twenty-seven of them—were forfeited on the theory that as part of a legitimate business, the livestock were part of a "front" for the owner's illegal activities.[96] On this theory, the more "innocent" one's use of property is, the more effective it is as a "front" or "cover" and therefore the more clearly forfeitable.

Entire hotels have been forfeited because one or more rooms of the hotel have been used by guests for drug transactions.[97] Entire apartment houses have been lost because drug activities occurred in *some* apartments.[98] Proceedings were brought to forfeit fraternity houses at the University of Virginia because some of the "brothers" sold drugs therein.[99] Those seizures created a stir, but they pale when compared to the potential. Imagine the government taking over New York's Plaza Hotel or one of the giant casino hotels in Atlantic City or Las Vegas on the same theory. Or taking over a company town because of a single drug sale or backyard marijuana plant. Harvard University is also available for the taking. There are certainly drug sales, drug use, even drug manufacturing taking place on campus.

No one has yet gone after Harvard, but they have hit the University of California. A Scripps Oceanographic Institute vessel was seized because a marijuana "roach," less than a gram, was found in the locker of a sailor who had long since been fired.

Dozens of people have lost their homes for growing a few marijuana plants for personal use, including James Burton, a glaucoma sufferer who needed the marijuana to keep from going blind. Burton lost not only his home but his ninety-acre Kentucky farm as well.[100] Thousands of car owners have forfeited their cars because they, or someone else to whom they lent the car, used the car to buy or attempt to buy a small quantity of drugs for personal consumption.[101] Boats and airplanes worth millions of dollars have been forfeited because minute quantities of marijuana were found on board.*

In the New Haven area, Assistant United States Attorney Leslie Ohta gained national recognition for her aggressive pursuit of forfeiture, taking homes of parents and even octogenarian grandparents whose children or grandchildren sold marijuana and stored it in their homes. Ohta insisted, with great success, that the owners of a home had a duty to know what was going on inside, even in the rooms of children or grandchildren. In December 1989, however, Ohta's own

---

*The Supreme Court recently held that forfeiture, although "civil" and not "criminal," is nonetheless "payment to a sovereign as punishment for [an] offense," and is therefore subject to the Eighth Amendment's prohibition against "excessive fines." *Austin v. United States*, 113 S. Ct. 2801 (June 28, 1993). Whether that ruling will eventually curb excessive forfeitures is problematic.

son was arrested for possessing marijuana and for selling LSD out of her car. Court papers also disclosed that an undercover agent had bought marijuana from Ohta's son in his parents' Glastonbury, Connecticut home. Ms. Ohta was allowed to keep her car and her home, but she is no longer working on forfeitures.[102]

Sheriff Robert Vogel, Jr., of Volusia County, Florida, routinely stops cars and searches them. If substantial sums of money are found, the money is confiscated, whether or not any drugs are found. The theory is that the money is probably drug related. Sheriff Vogel says that in most cases the drivers are so happy that they aren't arrested, they don't even ask for a receipt. Such forfeitures are almost never contested.[103]

Police commonly use trained dogs to sniff in and around cars. The dogs usually react positively to cash and therefore suggest the presence of cocaine. This produces a full search and, often, discovery of cash, which is confiscated.

There are serious problems with forfeiting cash on the theory it is drug money. The fact that there is cocaine on the cash is meaningless. Eighty to 90 percent of *all* cash in America has cocaine on it.[104] Moreover, there are lots of reasons, other than drug dealing, why people carry large sums of cash.

The difference between such routine seizures of cash and armed robbery is either nonexistent or paper thin. It is unconstitutional, but who cares? It is almost certainly criminal, but who prosecutes the confiscators, especially if the prosecutor gets part of the proceeds?

Innocent Owners

What about innocent owners whose property is used (or "intended to be used") illegally, without their knowledge or consent? Such owners of conveyances, such as boats and cars, were defenseless before 1988, since the theory of forfeiture is the preposterous fiction that the property, not the owner, is the wrongdoer. Accordingly, the Supreme Court said in 1974, the "innocence" of the owner is irrelevant.[105] Such a fiction may have been tolerable as long as forfeitures against innocent owners were rare, but in March 1988, the Customs Service and the Coast Guard went berserk under a "zero tolerance" program and began enforcing the forfeiture law as it was written. They began seizing boats, cars and airplanes whenever any detectable amount of any controlled drug was found aboard. Yachts and fishing vessels worth millions were seized merely because a crew member may have possessed a small amount of marijuana. The Administration obstinately defended its approach despite expressions of outrage from congressmen who had enacted the law. Representative Gerry Studs, whose district includes the home of the oceanographic research vessel *Atlantis,* which was seized upon the finding of a single marijuana cigarette in the crew quarters, branded the seizures "lunacy."[106] The result was an "innocent owner" defense for conveyances (there already was one for real property) included in the otherwise hysterical Anti-Drug Abuse Act of 1988. Now owners of any property seized under civil forfeiture proceedings can defeat forfeiture if they can prove either that the claimed offending use did not occur and was not even intended (a defense that was always available) or that the offending use occurred or was intended "without the knowledge or consent of that owner." Unfortunately, even this seemingly clear provision provides little protection for innocent owners. Courts have treated "knowledge" and "willful blindness" as equivalents and have then merged "willful blindness" into "negligence." Despite the plain language of the statute, most courts are unwilling to lift a forfeiture unless the owners can prove that the offending activity not only occurred without their knowledge or consent, but also that they did all they "reasonably could be expected to prevent the proscribed use of the property."[107] The owner has been conscripted as a policeman to assure that no improper use is made of the property. In a Milwaukee case, the owner of a thirty-six-unit apartment building plagued by dope dealing evicted ten tenants suspected of drug use, gave a master key to the police, forwarded tips to the police and even hired two security firms. The city seized the building anyway.[108]

Property owners who decide that what their lessees do in rented premises, cars or planes is none of their business as long as they don't damage the property, who conclude that renters as well as owners are entitled to privacy in their day-to-day activities, risk losing their property. Such people might lack "knowledge" of drug activities in the traditional sense, but not be able to prove that they did all they should have to prevent the proscribed use. To protect their property rights, owners may conduct background investigations of their tenants, permitting only those who are above suspicion to use the property. In a nation of 26 million illegal-drug users and even more former illegal-drug users, hardly anyone is above suspicion of drug use. If property owners' suspicions are aroused, however, and they seek reassurances that no illegal use is to be made of the property, they may only be digging holes for themselves, for seeking reassurances can be taken as manifestation of owners' otherwise secret, unprovable suspicions.[109] In short, nothing property owners do or do not do is likely to establish that they lacked "knowledge" of offending uses. Whatever they do or do not do can undermine their claims of ignorance.

If, then, owners discover that their property is being used to "facilitate" drug use or sale, what can they do to assure that they will not lose their property to forfeiture? Nothing, probably. If they call the police and inform on their tenants, they have established their "knowledge," as of the date they informed, which will usually be sufficient for forfeiture. Informing the police may go far toward establishing that owners did not "consent" to the illicit use, but many courts have held that the owner must *both* lack knowledge *and* not consent to the illicit use.[110] Courts that do allow a nonconsent defense by those who had knowledge require active efforts on the part of owners to get rid of the offending tenants and to prevent their replacement. Fear of repercussions does not excuse the failure to exert such efforts. A battered wife, whose husband had murdered his previous wife and who had threatened to kill her, failed to establish the defense even though the trial court found she was her husband's "slave." The appellate court held that she had still "consented" to her husband's illegal use of her property because she could have fled and reported her husband to the police.[111]

Innocent Acquirers of Tainted Property

Once an offending use is made or intended to be made of property (or it is acquired with tainted proceeds), title automatically passes to the government. Unless the innocent-owner provisions apply, no ownership can thereafter be conveyed to anyone else, however ignorant that person may be of the improper use to which the property was put. Thus a bona fide purchaser who pays full value for the property can lose it to forfeiture. So can a bank that lends money on the property and takes back a mortgage on it. Whether such persons are protected at all by the innocent owner defense is unclear. Many courts have declared that the only person who can be an innocent owner is a person who had an interest in the property *at the time* the offending use occurred. Anyone who acquired the property thereafter would not be an innocent "owner" since no title whatever would have been conveyed. Although there is slight textual support for this view, it renders the innocent owner provision almost empty.

If innocent owners cannot convey good title to another, even a bona fide purchaser, their "ownership" doesn't count for much, and their "innocence" is not respected. Hence, the innocent owner defense, such as it is, ought to apply not only to one who owned the property when the offending use occurred, but also to one whom such an owner conveyed the property. If after-acquirers can prove that their predecessors in title, during the period of illicit use, were innocent owners, the after-acquirers should defeat forfeiture.

A generous interpretation would also permit those who lack knowledge of the offending use at the time they acquire the property to get good title even from guilty grantors. Guilty grantors who had no title could create one by transferring defective title to one who was ignorant of the defect. Thus, after-acquirers would have alternative defenses: (1) my grantor was an innocent owner or, (2) even if the grantor wasn't, I was innocent when I acquired the property and should therefore be treated as an innocent owner. The Supreme Court recently seemed to accept the latter claim, holding that one who had received a gift of money from a drug dealer and thereafter bought a house with it could retain the house if she could prove she had no knowledge of the source of the funds at the time she received the gift. Unfortunately, no majority of the Court could agree on the rationale for its decision.[112]

The forfeiture provisions are not only horribly unjust, they inflict great damage to the inner cities. They encourage drug dealers and even drug users to invade the property of strangers rather than conducting their activities on their own premises and thus they increase the uncertainties of property ownership in declining neighborhoods. Property owners are always at risk of losing everything to forfeiture. Bankers have incentives, in addition to the risk of declines in property values, to refuse to lend money on property in such areas, for there is a significant chance that the bank itself will lose its security interest in the property. If the offending use took place before the mortgage interest was acquired, there may have been no such interest to convey. If the illicit use occurred after the mortgage was in place, a bank may be faulted for not taking all available measures to assure that such use did not occur, as by background investigations of its mortgagors, random inspections and so forth. There is no way that a bank can effectively regulate the uses to which mortgaged property is put. The only way to protect itself is to avoid lending the money in the first place. The conversion of our cities into ghost towns continues. Even more dangerous than the destruction of property values involved in the civil drug forfeiture schemes is the capacity of the forfeiture concept to expand to all other criminal activities. When it is so extended, the punishment becomes drastically disproportionate to the offense and the constitutional safeguards of criminal procedure are circumvented. Already, federal forfeiture statutes apply to pornography, gambling and several other offenses, as well as drugs.[113] Many state statutes apply to property used in *any* felony. The forfeiture of cars used in sex offenses is commonplace.[114] Hartford, Connecticut, recently began confiscating the cars of johns who cruise neighborhoods looking for prostitutes.[115] Some states take one's car for drunk driving.[116] Where will it end? Why not extend it to income tax evasion and take the homes of the millions—some say as many as 30 million—who cheat on their taxes? The statutory basis for forfeiting homes and businesses of tax evaders is already in place. The Internal Revenue Code reads: "It shall be unlawful to have or possess any property intended for use in violating the provisions of the Internal Revenue Service Laws . . . or which has been so used, and no property rights shall exist in any such property."[117] Although use of this provision has mainly been limited to seizures of moonshine and gambling equipment, and sometimes businesses, there is no reason—given the breadth of the drug forfeiture decisions—why it can't be employed to take the homes and offices of tax evaders and even those of their accountants and lawyers. A congressman who failed to pay social security tax on wages of his housekeeper could lose his home. Moreover, unlike drug forfeiture, the tax forfeiture statutes have no innocent owner defense.[118]

How to Get Rich: Become an Informant

The Supreme Court held in 1927 that it was a violation of Due Process to try a person, even for a traffic offense, before a judge who had a financial interest in the outcome.[119] In 1962, the United States Court of Appeals for the Fifth Circuit extended that principle to a case made by a criminal informant.[120] There, a bootlegger made a deal with treasury agents to help them "catch" specified bootlegger suspects by buying moonshine from them. The informant was to be paid $200 for each of the suspects he could "catch" plus $10 per day and travel expenses. He made the purchases and the suspects were convicted. Saying that such a contingent fee agreement "might tend to a 'frame-up' or to cause an informant to induce otherwise innocent persons to commit" a crime, the Court said the "opportunities for abuse are too obvious" and held that no conviction could be based upon the services of an informant who stood to receive a contingent fee.

Times—and the law—have changed. Instead of receiving $10 per day and a bonus of a few hundred dollars, informants now commonly receive a salary, bonuses for information and/or convictions and up to 25 percent of all property forfeitures attributable to their "assistance." [121] Some informants have made more than $1,000,000 under such arrangements.[122] Informants in a single case, that of Manuel Noriega, were paid almost $4 million and forgiven hundreds of years of prison time.[123] Altogether, federal and state agencies pay over $100 million to informants every year.[124] Despite the vastly increased motivation informants have to frame others, the 1962 decision invalidating convictions based on contingent-fee informers was expressly overruled in 1987.[125] It now doesn't matter that the evidence for a forfeiture was the tip of an informant who stood to make hundreds of thousands for a successful seizure. Nor does it matter that a defendant is convicted on the testimony of such an informant, who stands to receive a bonus if the defendant is convicted.[126] The contingent-fee crook can plant marijuana in the far corners of a farm, or place some leaf under the seat of a car, in the hold of a ship, or on the floor of a million-dollar Learjet, "drop a dime" and become rich overnight. He probably won't even have to testify, because even if the forfeiture is contested, the forfeiture stands unless the owners can prove that they had no knowledge of the drugs. Their mere protestations of ignorance, even if uncontradicted, need not be—and usually are not—believed.

Informants are not the only ones who directly profit from forfeitures. Police and prosecutors do too. Most of the assets and money obtained from forfeitures stays with the police and prosecutors who are responsible for the forfeitures. The funds are supposed to be spent for extra-budget needs, but personal benefit inevitably accrues. Police and prosecutors are often seen driving fancy sports cars, flying airplanes and piloting boats obtained by forfeiture. James M. Catterson, Suffolk County New York district attorney, for example, drives a BMW, obtained by forfeiture, which he spruced up on forfeiture funds, even adding a new stripe.[127] Catterson claims that he is not accountable to anyone for forfeited assets or funds. Acknowledging that what Catterson does is legal, *The New York Times* says, "doesn't make it right." The *Times* also questions "the wisdom of asset forfeiture that gives prosecutors and police a financial interest in the criminals they chase." Giving police and prosecutors discretion over forfeiture money also "insults good government."[128]

Perhaps the most ominous example of the corruptive power of drug forfeiture law is the killing of Donald Scott, a rich, reclusive resident of a 200-acre ranch in Malibu. Thirty state and federal authorities conducted a commando-style raid of his home early in the morning of October 2, 1992. Awakened from sleep, the sixty-one-year-old Mr. Scott emerged from his bedroom gun in hand, apparently believing he was under armed attack. He was shot and killed by a deputy sheriff. No drugs were found on the property and the only basis for the raid had been the preposterous claim of a federal agent that, with naked eyes, he had seen marijuana growing while flying 1,000 feet over the ranch. The major motivation for the raid was the hope of adding the $5 million ranch to the assets of the invaders. They had even had it appraised before the raid.[129]

One of the many ironies of the drug war is that while we are engaged in an unprecedented campaign to confiscate the property of Americans, Russia is beginning to return property to its citizens.[130]

If there is a shard of moral justification for forfeiture, it is that an owner, duly forewarned, chooses to use or permit his property to be used illegally and therefore voluntarily "waives" his constitutional rights of property. But such a "waiver" theory can be extended to destroy all rights and all liberty. It is a cancer on the Constitution, certain to metastasize if not eliminated soon.

CHAPTER 8

Autonomy Costs

> *"[A]dmission into the closed circle of officially recognized drug-law experts is contingent on shunning [basic questions]. Instead, the would-be debater of the drug problem is expected to accept, as a premise, that it is the duty of the federal government to limit the free trade in drugs. All that can be debated is which drugs should be controlled and how they should be controlled."*
>
> THOMAS SZASZ[1]

THE CORE difference between America and totalitarian regimes is that Americans have rights to make wrong choices; rights to do things that are not good for them. They also have rights to do things that are not good for other people.

The English philosopher John Stuart Mill stated a principle a century and a half ago that still has considerable force in America:

The only purpose for which power can be rightfully exercised over any member of a civilized community, against his will, is to prevent harm to others. His own good, either physical or moral, is not a sufficient warrant. He cannot rightfully be compelled to do or forbear because it will be better for him to do so, because it will make him happier, because, in the opinions of others, to do so would be wise, or even right.[2]

146

Mill had drug prohibition in mind when he wrote those words. In fact, he objected to laws in some American states that prohibited the sale of alcohol in the middle of the nineteenth century. This development, he declared, was a "gross usurpation upon the liberty of private life"[3] and an "important example of illegitimate interference with the rightful liberty of the individual."[4]

OTHER CANDIDATES FOR PROHIBITION

Myriad activities of Americans are dangerous or unhealthy yet not prohibited. Swimming drowns 5,000 people per year[5] but is permitted, even in remote lakes and rivers. Motorcycles killed 3,328 riders in 1990 and injured 84,000. Per mile traveled, a motorcyclist is twenty times more likely to die in a crash than is the driver of an automobile.[6] Motorcycles probably don't even conserve fuel, since much motorcycle riding is probably recreational and does not replace automobile travel. Yet no state seriously considers banning motorcycles.

There are at least 30 million obese people in the United States. Obesity is almost as deadly as alcohol abuse. Obese adults are twice as likely as those who aren't to have heart attacks.[7] Obesity severely damages self-esteem, job security and earning power,[8] yet obesity is not only entirely lawful, government makes almost no effort to discourage it. A legal prohibition against obesity would, in some respects, be easier to enforce than drug prohibition. People could be required, as highway trucks now are, to weigh-in periodically. At the outset, upon a brief physical examination, an "appropriate" weight could be determined and, on subsequent anniversaries, the scales would establish the guilt or innocence of the subject. The weigh-in would be easier and much less expensive to administer than drug testing, far more accurate, and much less invasive. One who exceeded the target weight could then be confined in a literal "weight control center" and "treated" with low-calorie food until "recovery" was achieved. Repeat offenders could be punished. Such a law, if enforced, might save more lives in a few years than have been spared by drug prohibition during its entire history.

A better case can arguably be made for the government to coerce citizens to trim down than to prohibit them from choosing which drugs to use. Weight reduction would be for their own good, both physically and psychologically—almost no one wants to be fat. (In a survey of forty-seven formerly fat people, 91 percent said they would rather lose a leg than be fat again; 89 percent said they would rather be blind.[9]) Most of us who are overweight find it painfully difficult even to maintain our weight at the same level of obesity. Diet programs, which annually waste billions of dollars, are colossal failures.[10] Hardly anyone who loses weight on a diet program succeeds in keeping the weight off. The diet usually makes the problem worse.[11]

The biological and psychological sources of obesity are immensely powerful, qualifying as an "addiction" by any but the narrowest definition.[12] If governmental coercion is needed to deter people from using drugs, it also is needed to help them lose weight and keep it off. Unlike obese people, who usually find themselves unable to control their ingestion of food, most illicit-drug users are not so burdened; nor do they feel drug dependent. Only about 5 percent of such users— certainly not more than 10 percent—are drug dependent[13] and in that respect are analogous to almost all obese overeaters. The victims of obesity are easily identified and government coercion could be restricted entirely to them. Persons who have no problem with obesity would be left free to eat whatever and whenever they liked. Drug prohibition, in contrast, denies the freedom of all to choose whether to use a drug because a very small minority of users are unable to resist overindulgence.

An ordinary cost-benefit analysis might suggest that before we use governmental coercion to control the consumer's choice of drugs, we should employ such resources to control the weight of those afflicted by obesity. Yet if anyone has ever seriously suggested that government devote its coercive apparatus to reducing obesity, or to a "war on fat," we have not heard it. Nor do we expect to.*

The Television "Drug"

Some critics assert that the most serious American "narcotic" is not a chemical at all; it is television.[16] The average American family watches television seven hours a day.[17] Average Americans spend 40 percent of their free time watching television. The trends are also

---

*Should our argument be taken out of context and misunderstood, any "reformer" interested in legislating a coercive weight control program should be prepared to show not merely that there are many probable benefits from it but that there are no unacceptable costs. No one knows what kinds of physical and psychological damage would be inflicted on the subjects of such a program by its coercive aspects. Our preoccupation with thinness already accounts for some of the use—mainly by women—of tobacco, cocaine, and other drugs[14] and is implicated in anorexia and bulimia.[15]

disquieting. Women spend 70 percent more time viewing television than they did in 1965, and men spend 35 percent more.[18] They watch mindless, repetitive soaps or sports events: racing, football, basketball, baseball, fake wrestling. America's "addiction" to television is bad for physical health, destructive of "family values" and arguably pathological. Almost everyone would be better off watching less. If parents turned off the set and spent half their television time studying and self-improving and the other half nurturing and educating their children, America might quickly regain its hegemony in the world economy. Nobody, however, suggests that government has any business trying to regulate the amount of television each of us watches. We have fundamental rights to waste our lives on twaddle.

A century and a half after Mill's *On Liberty,* governmental efforts to prohibit or even strongly to discourage swimming, motorcycling, obesity or excessive television viewing would rightly be regarded as unthinkable totalitarianism, a "gross usurpation" of Mill's concept of liberty. Why, then, do most of us accept the legitimacy of drug prohibition? The answer is unclear.

Mill's principle has lost much of its edge since it was laid down. Under the modern welfare state, society accepts responsibility for the basic needs of those unable to care for themselves. Accordingly, it is commonly argued, society has a right to interfere with or to prohibit self-harming conduct that is likely to make self-harmers or others who are dependent upon them wards of the state.[19] This may justify requiring automobile travelers to use their safety belts, for example. But in safety belt legislation, the imposition on the driver and passengers is *de minimus,* and the resultant protection is great. Wearing seat belts reduces the risk of fatal or serious injury to front seat passengers by 50 percent.[20] In 1990, safety belt use prevented about 125,000 moderate to critical injuries and 4,800 deaths. Yet fewer than 50 percent of Americans wore their belts. If Americans, like Canadians, could be induced to use their safety belts at a rate of 85 percent, perhaps 10,000 more American lives could be saved every year.[21] Mandatory safety belt legislation imposes insignificant burdens on automobile passengers while cutting in half their risk of getting killed or seriously injured. That is an incursion on Mill's principles the rightness of which is hard to deny (yet there are many who still contend that there is a fundamental right to ignore a car safety belt).

Government's right to prohibit use of psychoactive drugs cannot be sustained by analogy to mandatory seat belt use. It is doubtful that a drug prohibition that exempts alcohol could even be beneficial to health. In any event, the lives saved by drug prohibition, if any, are fewer than those lost to motorcycles, swimming or obesity.* The analogy to compulsory seat belt use would have appeal only on the assumption that denying the right to use drugs, like denying the right to ignore a seat belt, is a trivial deprivation. The nontriviality of that interest, however, is clear. Even nonaddicts are willing to spend hundreds, even thousands, of dollars a year on illicit drugs, to risk criminal prosecution, to risk forfeiture of their property, even to risk losing their jobs, for the privilege of occasionally consuming illicit drugs. The consumer obviously finds the benefits of psychoactive drug use to be considerable.

Some of our prominent prohibitionists frankly admit that the reason for banning drugs is less for the protection of health than for preservation of the "soul" or "morality." UCLA professor James Q. Wilson, for example, asserts that the justification for prohibiting the drugs we do prohibit "rests in part on their immorality." He says, "Tobacco shortens one's life, cocaine debases it. Nicotine alters one's habits, cocaine alters one's soul. The heavy use of crack, unlike the heavy use of tobacco, corrodes those natural sentiments of sympathy and duty that constitute our human nature and make possible our social life."[22] Note, however, that the corrosive effect of drugs on the "soul" observed by Professor Wilson is limited to "heavy users." No serious claim can be made that occasional use of *any* drug corrodes the soul or corrupts morals per se. Yet since 90 to 95 percent of all illicit-drug users are not addicts or abusers, Professor Wilson would deny access of all to nonprescription psychoactive drugs (other than alcohol and tobacco) because of the fear that 5 to 10 percent of their users will have their souls corrupted by drug addiction. He apparently believes that slowly killing the body with tobacco smoke has no appreciable adverse effect on the soul or on "morality." He also seemingly believes that alcohol addiction, unlike cocaine addiction, leaves the soul alone, for it is clear that if we were able to eliminate all illegal drugs, their would-be abusers would be abusing whatever remained available, i.e., alcohol.

---

*As it actually works in America, drug prohibition kills thousands more people than it saves, as the chapter on crime shows. Based on current consumption rates, a hypothetical drug prohibition which actually eliminated use of presently illegal drugs and had negligible external costs would save fewer than 6,000 lives (see Chapter 4), assuming, contrary to reality, that those deprived of illegal drugs would not transfer their appetites to alcohol. When the likely transferees to alcohol are taken into account, a fully effective prohibition would save few, if any, lives.

Almost any common activity produces abusers, persons who become obsessively preoccupied with the activity to the detriment of their physical and mental health, their jobs, their financial security, their families. Examples are eating, drinking alcohol, running,[23] television, sex,[24] golf, pornography, gambling;[25] even reading has its share of "addicts," as does, of course, work. Mill's principles (if not our societal interest in survival) would clearly reject efforts to prohibit everyone from engaging in these activities merely to protect a few who lack the self-discipline to resist excessive indulgence.

THEN WHY PROHIBIT DRUGS?

The impulses for prohibiting psychoactive drug use—other than alcohol and tobacco—are both deep and mysterious.

As an act of paternalism—protecting us from harming ourselves—drug prohibition is hard to distinguish from coercive governmental prohibition of obesity, excess television viewing, loafing, wasting money on unneeded luxuries and infinite other ways in which people seem to act contrary to their own long-term best interests. Even the nature of the self-harm is similar. The main cost of using drugs excessively is not poor health but an unrewarding life. Drug abusers, like other obsessive or addictive persons, neglect their social and work obligations and their duties to friends and family and as a result receive fewer benefits in such relationships. Whatever the drug or other obsession, if family, friends or employers disapprove, a pattern of lying and deceit almost always develops. The same things can be said of one who falls in love.[26] People who are in love often focus obsessively on their loved one and ignore the claims of friends and family for attention and affection. If access to a love object is restricted, deceit is commonly employed to increase access. There is truth to Professor Wilson's observation that excessive drug use "corrodes those natural sentiments of sympathy and duty that . . . make possible our social life," but precisely the same thing applies to any other activity obsessively pursued. Abusers themselves realize this, and most of them spontaneously recover from their obsessions, without either punishment or treatment. The obsession is itself punishment enough. As long as a nation generally refrains from coercing its people in their choice of lifestyles, it has little basis for drawing the line at drug use.

Apart from such notions of symmetry, there are many other moral objections to drug prohibition (even assuming hypothetically that it would be free of external costs and would also be effective). Among them are:

The Right to Choose How to Live One's Life Includes the Right to Choose Which Drugs Are to Be Ingested.

The signers of the Declaration of Independence declared that the right to "life, liberty and the pursuit of happiness" is "inalienable" and "self-evident." No exception was made for drugs. The right to choose which drugs to use, and whether to use them at all, is arguably as fundamental as the right to decide where to live, where to work, whether to marry, whether to have children, how much education to seek and how to raise one's children. Many of these rights are said by the Supreme Court to be constitutionally protected, usually but not always under the rubric of "right of privacy."[27] The Supreme Court has repeatedly held that a person has a constitutional right to refuse treatment by psychotropic or mind-altering drugs, even though the purpose of the compulsory drug administration is benign or therapeutic.[28] Inflicting psychotropic drugs on an unwilling recipient is an effort at "mind control" appropriate for a totalitarian regime, but alien to the American Constitution.[29] The right to control how one feels by taking psychotropic drugs is the flipside of the same coin. There is essentially only one right at issue—autonomy over the basic operations of one's mind.[30]

The Judgment of Individuals About the Value of Their Drug Taking Is Far More Reliable Than the Judgment of the State.

One must concede, as even Mill did in the case of children, that some people are handicapped in making fundamental choices in their lives. They are not adequately informed. They do not rationally consider even the costs and benefits known to them; they engage in "denial" or wishful thinking concerning some of the perceived costs or benefits. Many—mainly but not exclusively children—have poorly developed senses of time and are incapable of rationally weighing future costs or lost benefits against present satisfactions.[31] Government might justifiably make the decision for such persons, or provide coercive "assistance," if it knew better than they what they would choose if they had their mature wits about them. Government lacks that omniscience.

Except in a case like seat belts, where both costs and benefits are virtually the same for all automobilists and the benefits *greatly* outweigh the costs, government is poorly equipped to act as surrogate for the individual. People are unique. They vary enormously in their needs, the satisfactions they get from particular activities, their capacities to resist their impulses to excess. It bears repeating that, in the case of illegal drugs, the vast majority of users are casual, not problem, users. There may be some drugs which are so addictive or so dangerous that virtually no rational person, informed of their dangers, would use them at all. In such a case, if the state is correct about the facts, prohibition may be warranted, but that certainly cannot be said of marijuana, or even heroin and cocaine. If there are such drugs, there is good reason to believe that honest education about the hazards of casual use or experimentation with the drug would soon send it into exile as a recreational drug. Most drug users are not suicidal. Those who use drugs as a way to die can find countless ways to commit suicide without resorting to a particular drug.

Deciding Whether to Use Psychoactive Drugs Is Important to the Full Development of Individual Potential; It Is Part of the Process of Life.

The use of mind-altering drugs may contribute importantly to the awareness of one's essence. Even if we do not want to use such drugs, or to use some drugs but not others (the choice of the vast majority of Americans), considering the temptation and responding to it are important aspects of our human development. As Professor Charles Reich argues, it is essential that government be compelled to respect the "personal space" of the individual where the individual reigns supreme, in order to develop our full potential as human beings.[32] If we treat people like children, "protecting" them from the necessity of choice, they will remain children, and the vitality of the nation will be at risk.

Many users of psychedelics such as mescaline or LSD and even, occasionally, marijuana, claim that they have experienced powerful creative insights while under the influence.[33] Artists, musicians, writers and other creators often report that using such drugs contributes positively to their creative endeavors.[34] Others believe that the experience of some form of euphoria amidst a sea of misery is invaluable in the psychic survival of persons suffering such pain. It is at least plausible that the experience of chemically induced euphoria can provide motivation for achievement, for gaining access to nonchemical intoxication. Government simply has no idea what the benefits of illegal-drug use are. Since the Drug War escalations in recent decades, the subject has been largely ignored by serious scholars and participants in drug-policy debates out of fear that even mentioning the subject may brand the broacher an advocate of indiscriminate drug use.[35] A prohibitionist writer recently claimed that most of those who favor legalizing drugs have a "hidden agenda" to "justify their own use of drugs, a throwback of course to the 1960s. What they want are chemical pleasures brought to them without risk and, more important, without moral stigma."[36] Hence, anyone who suggests that there may be positive benefits to the use of illegal drugs must expect to be accused of being a closet drug user.

Still, the truth is that drugs provide great pleasures to many, including many who are not in any sense addicted. Those who feel that they are more creative or insightful or self-aware while under the influence of psychedelics or other drugs may be delusional or they may be right. Prohibitionists commonly *assume* that such claimants are delusional, but proof of that assumption is entirely absent.[37] It is riskier to a society in the long run to prohibit access to drugs which have that potential than it is to permit such access.

DRUG PROHIBITION IN THE UNITED STATES

The foregoing objections to drug prohibition are fairly conventional libertarian objections that transcend time, place and society. Their persuasiveness does not depend upon the particular characteristics of a culture. Similar arguments are ably explored in two recent books: Douglas Husak's *Drugs and Rights*[38] and Thomas Szasz's *Our Right to Drugs: The Case for a Free Market*.[39] A number of other objections are more tailored to time and place: they are objections to drug prohibition in America, in the late twentieth century. Paradoxically, they may also explain why we have such prohibition. One person's objection to prohibition is another person's motivation. These objections include:

Punitive Drug Prohibition Is Motivated in Part by Racism.

America's experience with prohibition suggests that the "drug problem" is widely viewed as a social or medical problem when, as in the sixties and seventies, drug use pervaded the middle and upper classes. But prohibition becomes more punitive, deadly serious in fact, when illicit-drug use is disproportionately concentrated among ethnic and racial minorities. Trafficking in even small quantities of heroin has been considered a major felony in the United States since the end of World War II because it has always been popular only among ethnic minorities, chiefly blacks. Cocaine became more "serious" a problem than heroin only after the mass marketing of crack in 1985, when cocaine rapidly invaded the lower classes. Middle and upper class interest in cocaine began to wane about 1980 and has now shifted to new fads like "smart drugs" (mainly minerals, vitamins, amino acids and herbs)[40] and bottled water. As cocaine use has become more concentrated in the lower classes, our enthusiasm for imprisoning drug traffickers and drug users has grown exponentially. The correlations are not coincidental.

Drug Prohibition Is Elitist.

There is a direct connection between the misery and bleakness of one's ordinary existence and the pull of psychotropic drugs. Such drugs ease pain, both physical and psychological. They also act as tranquilizers and sedatives and can be a sure source of euphoria, a state of mind hard to achieve in the ghettos and barrios of America without the assistance of chemicals. A person who has the money to visit a psychiatrist or other medical doctor can legally obtain virtually any state of mind achievable by ingesting illicit drugs. There is a long list of prescription psychoactives that can provide euphoria similar to that induced by cocaine or the tranquillity triggered by heroin or morphine. Much of what passes for drug abuse in the underclass is "medication" in the middle class. The major difference, apart from the legalities, is that the prescription drugs have different names and somewhat different pharmacological properties than those available in the inner city. But to deny that much drug-taking is self-medication is to deny reality.[41] The differences are primarily those of status, not of pharmacology.

We cast our indigent mentally ill into the streets to fend for themselves, without access to the psychotropics that they received when institutionalized. They need drugs to feel—and sometimes to be—normal. The only drugs available to them, very often, are illegal ones. For a society to deny poor people—because they are poor—access to doctors, hospitals and prescription drugs and then to insist that they surrender all right to self-medication is callous cruelty.

Prohibition Is Akin to Religious Persecution.

Karl Marx said, "Religion is the opium of the people." The reverse is probably more true: opium (or other psychoactive drugs) may be a substitute for religion. Intense religious experience is often joyful, intoxicating, beautiful, enriching and rewarding. Hearing a well-sung *Ave Maria* in an ornate cathedral is, to many, the near-equivalent of a shot of speed. The use of psychoactive drugs presents a challenge to mainstream religions. The challenge has several strands. The duality or separateness of mind/soul and body, a tenet of many fundamentalist Christians, is belied by psychoactive-drug taking, which demonstrates that profound changes in mind can be produced by a physical process—ingesting chemicals. The notion that mind or mentality is independent of the body is difficult to maintain in the face of such evidence. Moreover, with respect to hallucinogenic drugs like LSD, peyote and psychedelic mushrooms, responsible religious scholars have plausibly opined that the mystical consciousness produced by these drugs not only facilitates religious experience, it *is* a religious experience.[42] Precisely because the two psychic experiences, religion and drugs, are competitive, the use of drugs is often declared morally evil or blasphemous.

Because of its deep historical and biblical roots, and perhaps its limited capacity to produce a mystical consciousness, alcohol has been incorporated into the dogma of mainstream Christianity and Judaism.* Wine, especially, enjoys lofty roles in religious sacraments. The use of other drugs is a challenge both to the special religious status of alcohol and to the religions that confer such status upon it. The condemnation of drug use other than alcohol, therefore, supports majoritarian American religions. Thomas Szasz makes this point in *Ceremonial Chemistry*,[43] his study of the symbolic uses of drugs.

The nexus between drug use and religious experience is often legally recognized. During alcohol prohibition, the sale of wine for use in religious observances was exempt from the prohibition laws.[44] By long

---

*Orthodox Jews are even obligated to become drunk on *Purim,* so that they "should not be able to differentiate between 'Cursed be Haman' and 'Blessed be Mordecai.'" Rabbi Solomon Gangfried, *Code of Jewish Law* (New York: Hebrew Publishing Company, revd. ed. 1927), pp. 120–121.

tradition, moreover, the use of peyote in religious ceremonies of the Native American Church has been permitted, either through specific statutory exemption or as a matter of constitutional law: the First Amendment's guaranty of free exercise of religion or its prohibition of the establishment of religion were held to require deference to the use of peyote in the traditional ceremonies of the church.

In 1990, however, the Supreme Court declared an end to that long tradition. It held, in *Employment Division v. Smith*,[45] that an Oregon law criminalizing the use of controlled drugs could be applied to members of the Native American Church for using peyote during sacramental ceremonies. Since the law banning the drug was one of general applicability, Justice Scalia said, it does not violate the free exercise or the establishment of religion clauses of the First Amendment to criminalize the use of peyote in Native American religious ceremonies. "[W]e cannot afford the luxury," he said, even to demand that such a law have a compelling governmental interest behind it before allowing it to snuff out a traditional religious practice.[46] Leaving the matter to "the political process will place at a relative disadvantage those religious practices that are not widely engaged in; but that [is] an unavoidable consequence of democratic government. . . ."[47]

The free exercise of religion thus became another casualty of the drug war. After the *Smith* case, said USC law professor Erwin Chemerinsky, "it is hard to imagine a claim of infringement of free exercise that would succeed."[48] For whatever reassurance it is worth, fundamentalist Christians in West Virginia and elsewhere remain unmolested by the law as they kill themselves while demonstrating their faith by handling rattlesnakes and drinking strychnine.[49] Moreover, there can be little doubt that if a state or county were to criminalize possession of wine without a religious exemption, the Court, if asked to on behalf of a Christian or Jewish religious organization, would find constitutional protection. The Constitution may be color-blind, but its interpreters are fully aware of the numbers of voters who hold particular religious beliefs.

Prohibition May Protect the Status Quo from New Ideas.

The 1960s, with its love-ins, flower children, sexual liberation and social protest, was a time of intellectual and moral ferment. Virtually every idea and every institution was questioned. One institution subjected to intense scrutiny was drug prohibition. The questioning was so effective that numerous states decriminalized marijuana, and virtually everyone between the ages of fifteen and thirty tried the drug. This social protest contributed greatly to progress in civil rights and put an end to the Vietnam war.

Most of those who are now in control of the drug war were frightened by the sixties, and still are.[50] Illicit-drug use has become, in the minds of many, a symbol of the sixties and the ferment that accompanied it. Drug prohibition is motivated in part by a fear of the resurgence of the essence of the sixties, which was social revolution.[51] Some fear that drug use was a cause of the social revolution rather than a result. They thus worry that drug use may generate new ideas and new values that undermine the status quo. Even though few, if any, who were actively involved in or even fondly recall the sixties believe that drugs had a substantial causal role, many of those who feared and loathed the sixties believe otherwise. That provides fuel for today's war on drugs.*

Drug Prohibition Causes the Government to Deceive Its Citizens.

The history of America's drug prohibition crusade demonstrates that drug prohibition brings out the worst of government evils. The federal government seems incapable of telling the truth about the drugs that it prohibits or about any related issues. The web of deceit reaches into the highest levels, as illustrated by the elaborate charade we described in the preface, a charade pulled off by the DEA, the White House staff and President Bush in his first televised speech.

The government does a good job of making Americans aware of deaths from drug overdoses, "drug-related" robberies and murders and the corruptive power of "drug money" on America's youth. But the government goes to great efforts to keep Americans from understanding that most deaths from drug overdoses are the products of prohibition, not the intrinsic qualities of the drugs themselves; that virtually all of the drug-related crime is the result of prohibition, not the pharmacological properties of the drugs; that the drug business as we know it is solely and entirely the consequence of prohibition. As

---

*Iran's fear of revolutionary ideas has another target: Western popular music. Such music is outlawed because it is believed to cause disorderly conduct and sexual excess and, ultimately, undesirable moral and social changes. James B. Bakalar and Lester Grinspoon, *Drug Control in a Free Society* (New York: Cambridge University Press, 1984), 19.

a result, most Americans attribute the evils of prohibition to illicit drugs themselves. The government calculatedly promotes such false beliefs. For example, when he was "drug czar," William Bennett gave speech after speech *denying* the claims of the critics of prohibition that crime and the black market were caused by drug prohibition.[52] As long as the public continues to believe what the government's propaganda machine wants it to believe, we will continue to escalate the "War on Drugs." And if the government repeatedly lies to us about drugs, what else will it lie to us about? How can we believe anything the government says?

The objections to prohibition that we have sketched above differ from the other costs of prohibition, which we discuss in other chapters, in that they are virtually unrelated to whether prohibition works and whether it has unacceptable external costs. They presuppose a society in which the command of the law is immediately and universally obeyed. Even in that wholly hypothetical society, we think, the case for prohibition is uneasy indeed. It may be an exaggeration to assert, as does Professor Steven Wisotsky, that prohibition is "profoundly totalitarian,"[53] but prohibition is clearly at odds with much lofty American ideology. Its continuation has a corrosive effect on that ideology. That in itself is a substantial cost.

CHAPTER 9

Social Costs

IN ADDITION to the crime, freedom and health costs we have described, the drug war burdens our social order in countless other ways. Other major burdens include exacerbation of racial division, promotion of a form of intolerance that we call "drug McCarthyism," and the strangulation of our courts and prisons.

RACIAL MISTRUST AND HOSTILITY

The greatest social problem plaguing the United States near the end of the twentieth century is the same one that has plagued the continent for five centuries: racism. The drug war didn't cause that problem and nothing done about drugs will solve it. The drug war, however, makes progress impossible. As shown in Chapter 6, prohibition makes a massive contribution to the destruction of our cities. Anything that harms our inner cities worsens racial inequality. There are many other ways in which the drug war widens the divisions and deepens the mistrust between the races.

160

As Ron Harris of the *Los Angeles Times* observed in an article for which more than one hundred drug warriors, defense attorneys and members of black communities across America were interviewed, "Maybe no one planned it, maybe no one wanted it and certainly few saw it coming, but around the country, politicians, public officials and even many police officers and judges say, the nation's war on drugs has in effect become a war on black people."[1] The vast majority of illegal drug users are white, yet in the media, in the prisons, in the courts, and even in some hospitals, the drug problem sometimes appears to be almost entirely a black problem.

Racial Differences in Illicit-Drug Consumption

The National Institute on Drug Abuse estimates that 9 million whites were current illegal-drug users in 1991, while only a little over 2 million blacks and one million Hispanics currently used illicit drugs. (NIDA's survey classifies as "current users" those who used a drug during the past month.) Thus, current white drug users are nearly three times more numerous than blacks and Hispanics combined.

Nonetheless, a higher percentage of minority than majority Americans use illicit drugs. According to the 1991 NIDA survey, 9.4 percent of African-Americans and 6.4 percent of Hispanics were current users of at least one illicit drug,[2] while 5.8 percent of whites used an illicit drug during the previous month.*

During much of the 1980s, both illicit- and legal-drug use declined for the total United States population. But the overall decline did not affect all segments of the American population equally. The graph below explains. It depicts the change, from 1988 to 1991, in the estimated percent of current illicit-drug users for the three ethnic groups—Hispanics, blacks and whites. Whites and Hispanics decreased their overall current drug use significantly during the

---

*Although preliminary reports of the government's 1992 surveys were becoming available as this book went to press, we make our inter-racial comparisons on the basis of data from 1991 and earlier. The accuracy of the estimates of African-American drug use obtained by the 1992 Household Survey has been seriously questioned. Expressing concern about "an unusual pattern of decline among blacks in the use of both licit and illicit drugs between 1991 and 1992," the government's Office of Applied Studies formed a peer review committee to assess the validity of the 1992 measures of African-American drug use. The committee recommended "that comparisons of the [1992] rates for blacks to previous surveys' results should be made with caution due to the observed inconsistencies." Substance Abuse and Mental Health Services Administration, Office of Applied Studies, *Preliminary Estimates from the 1992 National Household Survey on Drug Abuse: Selected Excerpts,* 1993, 14–15.

offensive. Meanwhile, African-Americans significantly *increased* their use of illicit drugs.

With respect to cocaine, a disturbing ethnic hierarchy appears to be developing. Between 1988 and 1991, whites cut their current use of cocaine nearly in half, while Hispanics reduced their use by somewhat more than a third. During the same period, African-Americans chipped off only one percent of their monthly cocaine use, a decline that was too small to be statistically significant. As matters stood by 1991, the prevalence of monthly use of cocaine for both Hispanics and African-Americans was more than twice as great as it was for whites.

The fact that blacks and Hispanics are disproportionate users of cocaine and (probably heroin) relative to whites only begins to tell the story of disproportionality. The disparities are even greater when we compare frequent users (once a week or more), which is a rough gauge

ILLICIT DRUG USE TRENDS 1988–1991

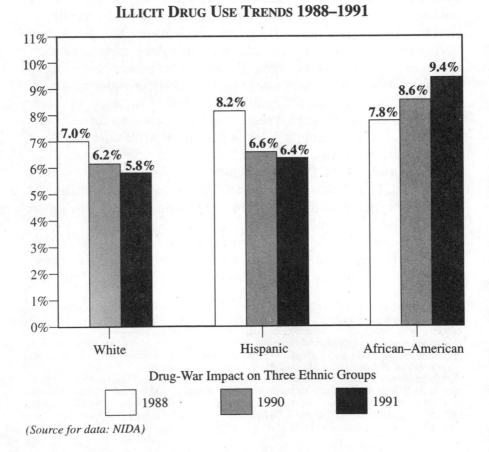

Drug-War Impact on Three Ethnic Groups

☐ 1988   ▨ 1990   ■ 1991

(Source for data: NIDA)

of cocaine dependency. According to NIDA, Hispanics were more than twice as likely to be frequent users as whites in 1991,[3] and blacks were almost four times as likely as whites to be frequent users.[4] Since racial minorities are also more commonly poor and not covered by health insurance, the deleterious effects of cocaine use on the health of minority users is magnified. Due in part to the interaction of poverty and abuse of drugs, blacks rank well below whites in virtually all health measures, such as life expectancy,[5] AIDS death rates,[6] infant mortality,[7] accidental and violent death rates[8] and occurrence of serious chronic diseases (e.g., heart disease, arthritis, hypertension).[9]

Black inner-city residents are also victims of drug-related crime at a far greater rate than is proportionate to their share of the population. Retail distribution of illicit drugs is heavily concentrated in inner-city neighborhoods. That is where the systemic murdering occurs and is also the situs of most thefts, robberies, burglaries and related assaults and killings.

Conspiracy Theories

By almost any measure, blacks suffer disproportionately from drug prohibition. They are more drug-dependent than whites, more likely to get AIDS, syphilis, hepatitis B and other diseases in the course of feeding their dependencies (or interacting with infected drug abusers). They are far more often than whites the victims of drug-systemic violence. It is the residents of inner-city black and Hispanic communities who see their children seduced by drug money into a life on the street instead of a classroom; who see their children murdered or maimed; who see their parents, children, spouses and neighbors packed off to prison for increasingly lengthy terms, leaving shattered families behind. The prevalence of cocaine and heroin in inner-city communities would be a grave problem without drug prohibition, but the drug war converts a serious health problem into a pervasive series of burdens that collectively resemble a pogrom. Because whites are the major consumers of illicit drugs (and most of the consumers that come into the inner city to buy their drugs), while the costs of prohibition fall disproportionately on members of minority groups, sinister racial inferences are all but inevitable. Louis Farrakhan, head of the Nation of Islam, opines that "The epidemic of drugs and violence in the black community stems from a calculated attempt by whites to foster black self-destruction."[10] His conspiracy theory is shared by many.

The fantasy of pop culture melds with reality to support such conspiracy theories. A scene from *The Godfather,* in which Mafia dons decide to market drugs exclusively in the black ghetto, is cited by black filmmaker Spike Lee and others as though it were historical fact rather than fiction.[11] But adherents to the theory cite real events, too. Government investigations of black elected officials, such as former Washington, D.C., mayor Marion Barry, are controversial fragments of nonfictional evidence. Proponents of the conspiracy theory say that the travail of Mayor Barry, who was given cocaine by his seductive ex-girlfriend acting as a secret government agent, and was then prosecuted, convicted and sentenced to jail for drug possession, was part of an orchestrated scheme to discredit all black leaders.

Racial inequality is fertile ground for conspiracy theories. It even provides support for paranoid fantasy. Black professor Leonard Jeffries, of City University of New York, and others even claim that genocidal white conspirators—already implicated in the drug cabal—simultaneously concocted the AIDS virus in a laboratory and purposely spread it among minorities.[12] The Central Intelligence Agency is usually blamed for this element of the conspiracy. Mark Riley, who hosts a New York talk-radio show with a largely black audience, told a *New York Times* writer that many of his callers "believe the twin epidemics of AIDS and crack are the product of an active white conspiracy."[13]

A *New York Times*/WCBS-TV poll in late 1990 revealed that substantial numbers of African-American New Yorkers believe various parts of the AIDS conspiracy theory.[14] Only 10 percent of the 408 blacks surveyed said that the AIDS virus definitely was a plot against them, but another 19 percent thought that it might be. *The New York Times* further reported, however, that "[a] quarter of the blacks polled said that the government deliberately makes sure that drugs are easily available in poor black neighborhoods in order to harm black people."[15] Another third of those surveyed believed that the availability of drugs might be the result of deliberate government activity.

Most intellectuals—black and white—reject the theories but note the level of despair that their existence manifests. Harvard psychiatry professor Alvin Poussaint,[16] Yale Law School professor Stephen Carter,[17] *Washington Post* columnist William Raspberry[18] and columnist Clarence Page[19] are African-Americans who acknowledge the depth of black suspicion but repudiate the theories.

A Factual Basis for the Drug-Conspiracy Theories

Major support for conspiracy theories, as they apply to drugs, seems to lie in the fact that racial minorities suffer from drugs and drug prohibition vastly out of proportion to their representation in the population, while drug dealing openly occurs on the streets of their neighborhoods, seemingly tolerated by the police. People who would not think of relieving their bladders in public buy or sell drugs in full view of children and whoever else is in the neighborhood, sometimes including police. Further support for the theory inheres in the fact that very few of those who import the drugs or participate in large-scale wholesale distribution are black. They are white, Hispanic or Asian. Non-blacks are profiting from the drug-related misery of inner-city blacks.

It should not be hard to understand why some conclude that there is a conspiracy afoot. If the United States Government were omnipotent, then any problem as immense, as notorious and as lasting as "the drug problem" would be the result of a deliberate decision somewhere in Washington, D.C. A government that can vanquish the Iraqi Army in a few weeks, that can send men to the moon and cameras to Mars, that can contemplate construction of a gigantic shield to keep invading missiles out ("Star Wars"), has at least a colorable claim to omnipotence, especially when the problem requires only the manipulation or coercion of human behavior.

It is not only believers in a white conspiracy who claim that the government could keep drugs from being smuggled into the country if it really wanted to. Drug warriors have been telling us that for decades (a false claim, as we show in Chapter 11). They say that the tens of billions of dollars we have spent trying to do just that simply have not been enough. Even if the government cannot keep the drugs out of the country, it should at least be able to put a stop to open-air drug markets in blighted inner-city neighborhoods. The government does, after all, prevent street-level sales of drugs in white neighborhoods. Since the major consumers of illicit drugs are whites, it would make sense to take the product to them, like the sandwich wagon or the Good Humor Man, but this doesn't happen. Why? Because white people and the police wouldn't stand for it. A dealer who peddled drugs on New York's Central Park South wouldn't last five minutes.

Such is the mix of reasoning and fact that undergirds the conspiracy theory. The truth is more complex. Drug dealing and the evil that accompanies it are tolerated more in lower-class than in upper-class neighborhoods, but police bigotry is not the primary cause of that disparity. Residents of the drug-dealing neighborhoods are themselves ambivalent about arresting drug dealers. Speaking of "addicts" but including retail drug dealers, black Yale Law professor Harlon Dalton says, "We despise them. We despise them because they hurt us and because they *are* us. They are a constant reminder of how close we all are to the edge. And 'they' are 'us' literally as well as figuratively; they are our sons and daughters, our sisters and our brothers. Can we possibly cast out the demons without casting out our own kin?"[20]

Some nondealer residents of drug-marketing areas—family and friends of the dealers themselves—have a financial stake in the drug dealing. If none of the dealers are providing direct support to nondealing residents, some of the drug money still trickles down to others in the community. Wise dealers see to that.

Fear is also a factor. One who lives in a neighborhood infested with drug dealers risks her life—or those of her children—if she calls the police or informs. If she testifies for the prosecution, her life in that neighborhood, and perhaps in any, is over. The police cannot rely on eyewitnesses to street-level drug crimes. They usually must either observe the crime themselves or establish it by undercover purchases. It is difficult to prove a drug crime by observation. An apparent hand-to-hand exchange *may* be a drug deal but more proof than appearance is required. Even if a search of a suspected buyer or seller yields drugs, that does not establish that he just completed a sale or a purchase in an observed exchange. Undercover purchases are therefore almost essential, but they are expensive. Why should undercover resources be devoted to street-level purchases of a few grams of a drug when that same undercover operation could be aimed at the wholesale drug trade, which might produce multikilo drug seizures, favorable publicity, even forfeiture of large sums of cash? Drug-enforcement police can hardly be faulted for wanting to employ their limited resources in efforts to catch and punish wholesalers or at least "higher-ups" in the drug-distribution scheme. With dozens of street sellers in a single neighborhood, the arrest and conviction of a few will have no impact on the trade.

Still, the residents of the most affected communities are right in concluding that if the authorities cared *enough,* they could drive the drug dealers out of any neighborhood. But that possibility is much easier to conceptualize than to carry out. Experimental programs where a neighborhood is saturated with undercover buyers and full enforcement takes place have had very limited success.[21] The dealers adapt to the programs, sometimes moving their drug deals, or at least their deliveries, indoors, where they cannot be observed and danger to undercover buyers is magnified.[22] Even if such a program drives out some of the drug dealers, it is usually only to an adjoining neighborhood, where the process must be repeated, again and again. There simply are not enough police—and never will be—to saturate every conceivable venue where drugs might be sold.

Intensive enforcement against street-level drug sales, moreover, generates virulent hostility from many of the residents of the affected neighborhoods, especially from those who are related to or financially dependent upon the drug-dealer targets. Police are likely to find themselves attacked as "racist" for investigating and prosecuting drug dealing in the neighborhood. Many of the conspiracy theorists adopt the line that the drug problem can be solved by attacking drug commerce "at the source." If drugs were not imported, the argument runs, there would be no drug problem in minority communities. It is, therefore, the nonblack growers and smugglers who should be punished rather than their black "victims," whether the latter are consumers or distributors, or both. Thus, street-level enforcement is viewed by some conspiracy theorists as manifestations of the conspiracy the more so when it is intense and committed. Given such reactions, street-level enforcement is not only inefficient but frustrating and demoralizing to the police. Those factors, rather than a genocidal conspiracy, may account for much of the disparity in enforcement.

Some blacks and Hispanics agree with Catholic priest Father John Clements, who campaigns against drug use by black Chicagoans. Clements says, "I'm all for whatever tactics have to be used; if that means trampling on civil liberties, so be it. I deal in funerals. I feel that they're not being strict enough."[23] Two prominent black political leaders, Representative Charles Rangel and Reverend Jesse Jackson, also staunchly support the drug war, complaining that it has not been waged aggressively enough.

Other minority leaders, such as black defense attorney Randolph N. Stone, of Chicago, make the opposite charge, saying, "The ongoing 'war on drugs' is a serious threat to the survival of the African American community."[24] Baltimore mayor Kurt Schmoke, who is black and who was an effective drug-law prosecutor, has become a prominent proponent of drug decriminalization. Representative

George W. Crockett,[25] of Michigan, and New York State legislator Joseph L. Galiber, of the Bronx,[26] are both African-Americans who advocate drug legalization.

These sharp differences reflect the confusion, ambivalence and suspicion that are generated by the racial differences in patterns of drug dealing, drug consumption and drug enforcement. They are part and parcel of drug prohibition.

Disappearance of Civil Liberties in the War Zone

As we noted in Chapter 7, the drug war is rapidly corroding what remains of the Bill of Rights. The drug war rationalizes trampling upon or circumvention of virtually every liberty protected by the Constitution. Nowhere is this felt more strongly than in minority communities and the trampling is itself supportive of racial hostility and mistrust. If young black men have any rights left against arbitrary intrusion by the police, such rights are hard to identify. Young blacks are routinely stopped, interrogated and searched wherever they go in middle or upper class neighborhoods, as if just being there were itself an offense.[27]

Other residents of minority communities suffer routinely from police invasions of their basic liberties. A few examples:

- "street sweeps" by New York's Tactical Narcotics Teams (TNT), which arrest and arraign all in sight, regardless of evidence;[28]
- routine, unwarranted searches of homes in public housing projects;[29]
- "lockups," in which Chicago housing-project residents are forbidden to have overnight guests and, apartheid-style, are required to show security guards their "papers" to get into their own homes;[30]
- in 1991, in Los Angeles, use of the excuse that he appeared high on PCP as justification for the brutal police beating of defenseless black arrestee Rodney King;[31]
- the trashing by narcotics officers of apartments and houses in the course of drug searches—almost always occurring in homes of poor members of racial minorities.

Quasi-entrapment of Inner-City Youths

American drug prohibition also roughly resembles "entrapment" of youthful residents of minority neighborhoods. Criminal law recognizes a defense to a charge of crime which is called the entrapment defense. That doctrine holds that if the police cause a person to commit a crime by blandishing inducements that "create a substantial risk that such an offense will be committed by persons other than those ready to commit it,"[32] then the person who responds to such inducements cannot be convicted. America of the 1990s provides almost no hope for inner-city youngsters of ever making a decent living and otherwise enjoying what the media suggest is their birthright as Americans—unless they succumb to the omnipresent temptations, created by drug prohibition, to sell drugs. Sixty to 70 percent of the youngsters in many inner-city communities are unemployed and they lack the skills needed to get decent jobs. Even if they had the skills, there are few such jobs in the inner city where they live. Even if there were decent jobs, the prejudice against young black men is so palpable and pervasive that merely looking for a job is degrading.

On almost every street corner in the neighborhood, however, a job is waiting, a job that not only pays a decent income—sometimes far more than that—but one that carries some prestige and entrepreneurial promise—dealing drugs.[33] Such systemic pressure toward criminality is not a sufficient enticement to be recognized legally as entrapment, but it resonates with the ethical underpinnings of the concept. Failed prohibition both provides the enticement of drug dealing and has helped to eliminate other meaningful opportunities for inner-city youngsters. If this appears to some as evidence of systematic racism, they may be mistaken but they are hardly delusional.

Racially Unequal Enforcement of Drug Prohibition

There are twice as many black males in New York's prisons as there are in its colleges.[34] Nationwide, one out of four black males in his twenties is in prison or under some form of court supervision, such as probation or parole.[35] Of black males aged eighteen to thirty-five, the court-enmeshed figure is 42 percent in Washington, D.C.,[36] and a mind-boggling 56 percent in Baltimore.[37] Fewer than one in sixteen white males of the same age are caught up in the criminal justice system.

As many as 70 percent of black men in Washington, D.C., are arrested before they turn thirty-five.[38] Although about 77 percent of current illegal-drug users are white and less than 17 percent are black, of 13,000 drug arrests in Baltimore in 1991, 11,000, about 85 percent, were of blacks.[39] Nationwide, about 45 percent of drug arrests are of African-Americans."[40]

Such gross disparities in criminal-law enforcement are not necessarily racist. They are often responsive in part to demands from residents of the inner-city communities for an escalated attack on drug dealing in their neighborhoods. But some view this concentration of law enforcement—largely against young black men—as itself a manifestation of a genocidal conspiracy. Young black men are routinely sent to prison for succumbing to the temptations presented by the neighborhood drug dealer. The sentences imposed on such youths are nothing short of savage. In federal court, anyone who assists in the distribution of even a small quantity of hard drugs like heroin or cocaine, even by acting as a lookout or a "mule," can expect a no-parole prison sentence of five years or more.[41] For large quantities, the mandatory minimum is ten years.[42] An enterprising youngster who hires a few of his friends to help him distribute drugs (even marijuana) can be convicted as a "drug kingpin" and receive a life sentence without possibility of parole.[43] Many have. Some states, such as Michigan, routinely hand out life, no-parole sentences.[44]

The friends and families of many of the young people who are imprisoned for a decade or more are at least perplexed by a criminal process that imposes such draconian penalties yet produces no apparent benefits to their communities. The young people who are punished more severely than many murderers, rapists or bank robbers lose any residual opportunities for a productive life and are taken from their mates and their children. Many forces help to produce the deplorable absence of fathers in the rearing of America's black children, but a major force is drug prohibition. The fathers are prisoners of war—our civil war against drugs.

Young black men make up only about 2 percent of our population, but they make up about *half* of our prison population. American Civil Liberties Union lawyers John Powell and Eileen Hershenov observe, "If the goal of our nation's drug policy is to warehouse young minorities while militarizing the inner-city, it is indeed successful. Black men are now four times more likely to be incarcerated in the United States than they are in South Africa: of every 100,000 black males in the United States, 3,109 are incarcerated, while the comparable figure for South Africa is 729."[45]

Whenever a disadvantage is imposed upon a racial group, some will see racism. This was even taken to a ridiculous extreme in 1986 when the New York branch of the National Association for the Advancement of Colored People opposed ordinances limiting or forbidding smoking in public places on the grounds that they discriminate against black people. Why? A slightly higher proportion of blacks than whites smoke cigarettes. Thus, it was alleged, blacks are disproportionately disadvantaged. As Yale law professor Stephen Carter observed, this ignores the fact that blacks are also disproportionately killing themselves with cigarettes and thus disproportionately *benefit* from such ordinances.[46]

The taproot support for black suspicions is racial history.[47] Blacks have suffered from bigotry, poverty, poor health, inadequate education and disadvantage on virtually every measure of well-being in America since the first blacks were brought here in chains. Moreover, as we note elsewhere, racism has been linked to drug prohibition throughout its history in America.[48] The many blacks who suspect racist motivations in everything the white majority does have history on their side. Such attitudes are unlikely to disappear so long as there is plausible support for them. When a society creates or permits the *appearance* of racism in its criminal process, it feeds racial hatred and mistrust. That is a major evil of drug prohibition. However it is administered, drug prohibition cannot avoid creating appearances of racism and thus fostering racial division and mistrust.

The unequal enforcement of the criminal law against blacks also self-validates white prejudice. As noted, only 2 percent of the population are young black males, yet 45 percent of the persons accused of drug crimes are from that small group; and more than half of all prison inmates are black. Such figures support venomous stereotypes about the criminal propensities of African-Americans.

DRUG MCCARTHYISM

American history has many examples of violations of civil liberties for the purpose of defeating a feared enemy. In a wartime emergency, a country can rationalize many outrages that would otherwise be intolerable. During the Civil War, Abraham Lincoln suspended habeas corpus rights. During World War II, Franklin Roosevelt interned innocent Japanese-American citizens in concentration camps. In the name of the drug war, echoes of the worst American traditions of Salem witch-hunts and the McCarthy era's hysterical suspicions are reverberating.

Enforcement of Drug Orthodoxy

Like the fear of communism during the McCarthy era, the antidrug hysteria of today enforces orthodoxy of belief and association by rooting out of public life and sensitive occupations those who are either "soft on drugs" or "sympathizers."

Former Los Angeles police chief Daryl Gates declared casual drug users guilty of "treason."[49] Shortly after federal district judge Robert Sweet gave a speech expressing his support for drug legalization, the Washington Legal Foundation filed an ethics complaint, alleging that he had violated canons of judicial conduct by stating his view.[50] Although the Judicial Council of the Court of Appeals dismissed the complaint, Judge Sweet subjected himself to political attack by exercising his right to free expression on the topic of drugs.

In the late 1980s, drug toughness and drug purity became standard tests for domestic political office. Ronald Reagan and his entire cabinet voluntarily submitted to urine tests,[51] apparently to convince the rest of us that we also should surrender our Fourth Amendment freedoms against unwarranted drug searches. When Mayor Coleman Young of Detroit was campaigning for his fifth term as Detroit's mayor, he gathered local reporters so they could personally witness him urinating for a drug test.[52]

The youthful drug peccadillos of politicians and public servants can be disqualifications from office. When Ronald Reagan nominated Federal Judge Douglas H. Ginsburg to be Associate Justice of the United States Supreme Court, disclosure of Ginsburg's marijuana smoking as a young law professor in the 1970s quashed the appointment.[53]

The charge of drug use or even of softness toward drug users is a common smear tactic in a political campaign. In the 1990 Democratic gubernatorial primary in Texas, candidate Ann Richards refused to answer questions about prior illegal drug use. Her rival, Jim Mattox, then ran campaign ads with her photograph, asking, "Did she use marijuana, or something worse like cocaine?"[54] A federal prosecutor such as Rudolph W. Giuliani, who was a relentless drug buster, ought to be immune to accusations of drug softness. However, when he campaigned for the 1989 New York mayoralty race, his Republican primary opponent, Ronald Lauder, charged that Giuliani had once advocated a pardon for a drug dealer and received a $700,000-per-year salary at a law firm that represented (among hundreds of clients) a Panamanian bank under investigation for laundering drug money.[55]

Even former drug czar William Bennett and former Vice President Dan Quayle fell victim to the drug McCarthyism that they promoted while in office. In 1989, cartoonist Garry Trudeau produced a series of Doonesbury cartoons ridiculing the drug czar's addiction to nicotine. Then, in November and December 1991, Trudeau produced another series that claimed the DEA had covered up charges (by federal prisoners) that Dan Quayle had used marijuana and cocaine.[56]

Two of the most sympathetic victims to suffer from drug McCarthyism, however, were fourteen-year-old Dana Merry and Michelle Wines, of Hamilton, Ohio. Both were suspended from junior high school because Dana gave two Tylenol capsules to Michelle, who had a headache.[57]

The International Struggle Against Drug Disloyalty

Drug McCarthyism has emulated the earlier political McCarthyism by assuming a dominant role in much of our nation's foreign affairs. During the past several decades, United States relations with Turkey, Iran, Lebanon, Southeast Asia, China, Central America, Colombia, Peru, Ecuador, Jamaica, Cuba, Haiti and Mexico have been tinged by American insinuations that those countries or regions have been responsible for our drug problems. The implication is that the governments and the people of those nations are morally deficient because they have profited from supplying the United States' demand for drugs. Senators and others have even proposed military invasions against drug-producing nations.[58] Drug McCarthyism feeds jingoistic international scapegoating by our policymakers.

Snitching on Family and Friends

Even more than the anti-Communist witch-hunts of the 1950s, drug McCarthyism turns citizens and family members against each other. Government and media campaigns encourage irresponsible accusations of drug use and drug dealing. In Anderson County, South Carolina, Sheriff Taylor's Operation Rollover solicited donations for billboards reading, "Need cash? Drop a dime on a drug dealer."[59] Drug warriors have asked all of us to turn in our friends and neighbors, and one campaign included public-service advertisements in newspapers, which include a form to clip out and use for anonymous tips to the police about suspected drug activities.

A 1987 *Glamour* magazine poll revealed that 56 percent of young women believe that it is desirable for children to inform on drug-using parents.[60] When he was drug czar, William Bennett told a group of Miami middle-school students that exposing drug-using parents "isn't snitching . . . It's an act of true loyalty—of friendship."[61]

Such acts of "true loyalty" are all but structured into many school programs. Eleven-year-old Crystal Grendell of Searsport, Maine, was part of a drug-education class taught by the Chief of Police in 1991. He asked the class of fifth graders if they knew anyone who used drugs. Crystal said nothing at the time but later met with the chief and told him she knew two people who smoked marijuana: her parents. Crystal was whisked away and hidden by the police. Her parents were arrested for growing forty-nine marijuana plants in their bedroom. Mrs. Grendell was fired from her job as a school bus driver and teacher's assistant and Mr. Grendell pleaded guilty to cultivating marijuana. The family bonds are still in tatters. "I would never tell again," says Crystal, a once outgoing student who is now withdrawn and gets lower marks in school. "Never. Never."[62]

Crystal's snitching was wormed from her in a course in drug education. The antidrug program, called Project DARE (Drug Abuse Resistance Education), is the most popular drug-education program in the United States. The program is taught by police officers in the school systems of nearly 5,000 communities nationwide. DARE proponents deny that the police make any systematic effort to cause their students to snitch. DARE is not "a program to spy on families," says Captain Patrick Froehle, commander of the Los Angeles Police Department's DARE division. "The main purpose is to curb drug abuse." The police argue, however, that they would be remiss to ignore information about drug-using parents that they learn in the course of the project. Sergeant Robert Gates, DARE's national coordinator, defends snitching on parents. Where parents use drugs, he says, "there are usually no morals, values or training for the child . . . an arrest is the best thing that could ever happen to that parent. Marijuana could lead to harder drugs, which, in turn, could ultimately lead to death. What may turn out to be negative for the parent is positive for society."[63]

For the government to encourage denouncing one's family members is not only poisonous to the "family values" that were the theme of the Republican campaign for the presidency in 1992, it may even be dangerous. In the 1690s, a group of impressionable children in Salem, Massachusetts, was encouraged to make accusations of wrongdoing against their elders, and as a result a witchcraft tribunal hanged several of the colony's citizens. Antidrug "snitch" programs and the popular support for informing are reminiscent of Chairman Mao's Red Guard and Nazi Germany's Hitler Youth, which made public denunciations of loved ones a mandatory civic duty and a public virtue.

Drug McCarthyism May Have Peaked

Joseph McCarthy had his comeuppance. In the years since McCarthy was censured by his Senate colleagues, red-baiting waned, and America still won the cold war. A similar decline of drug McCarthyism may already be underway. Although our nation carries the historical blemish of witch-hanging, most Americans are resistant to mass hysteria. There is ground for optimism that our nation will shed drug McCarthyism. When Judge Douglas Ginsburg's Supreme Court nomination went up in smoke, only 26 percent of the respondents to a *Newsweek* poll thought that his past use of marijuana should disqualify him from a seat on the Court.[64] Sixty-nine percent felt it should not. And while only 17 percent of the respondents to the *Newsweek* poll thought that marijuana should be made legal, only 4 percent of the respondents said that they would report a marijuana user to the authorities. A full 40 percent said they would accept a person's use of marijuana as his or her personal decision. Shortly after the Ginsburg fiasco, presidential candidates Bruce Babbitt and Albert Gore went public with their own youthful marijuana indiscretions. Those confessions did not seem to hurt their political careers.[65] By 1991, American public sentiment already had regained some balance; Clarence Thomas' drug indiscretions did not impede his confirmation as a Supreme Court justice.

Today, both the President of the United States and the Vice President are confessed marijuana smokers. Today's orthodoxy for politicians, according to columnist Anna Quindlen, is to "say they only did it once or twice and that they didn't enjoy it." Even that, she says, seems "foolish and shortsighted." Instead of "insisting that they didn't like it, why not admit that part of the allure of drugs is that they've been known to make you feel temporarily terrific?"[66]

We haven't come that far. It is still dangerous to say anything positive about illicit drugs. Jefferson Morley smoked crack and wrote an article about it for *The New Republic*. Although he experienced euphoria and craving, he did not find the experience, on the whole, pleasant. However, he said, "If all you have in life is bad choices, crack may not be the most unpleasant of them." Drug czar William Bennett immediately denounced the article as "garbage" and labeled its author "a defector in the drug war." R. Emmett Tyrrell, Jr., editor of *The American Spectator,* called Morley's article "contemptible" because he did not express support for the drug war.[67]

As Dr. Lester Grinspoon has noted, drugs don't always make their users behave irrationally, but they "cause many nonusers to behave that way."[68] It is impossible in many quarters even to discuss drugs rationally. When two psychologists from the University of California at Berkeley published the results of a study of adolescents that showed that those who had engaged in drug experimentation (primarily with marijuana) were better adjusted psychologically than both frequent drug users and *nonusers,*[69] a storm erupted. The researchers were attacked as "irresponsible" for suggesting that dabbling with drugs was anything short of catastrophic.[70] The same study concluded that problem drug use is a symptom rather than a cause of personal and social maladjustment and that drug-prevention efforts are misguided which focus on symptoms rather than the psychological syndrome underlying drug abuse. An article in *Pride Quarterly* in the summer of 1990 called such a conclusion "outrageous."[71] Dr. Grinspoon himself felt the disapproval of academic colleagues for arguing that marijuana is less dangerous than alcohol and cigarettes.[72]

It remains to be discovered whether the nation will accept in its public servants a past that includes abuse of hard drugs. This seems to be the case in New York, however. In his autobiography, circulated in December 1992, Joseph Fernandez, former head of the New York City school system, revealed that he had been a mainlining heroin addict in his youth.[73] No one demanded that he be fired for that revelation.[74] A few weeks after that disclosure, Raymond Diaz, another admitted former heroin addict, was named by the Mayor to become New York City's drug czar.[75]

In the meantime, applicants for federal jobs, including judgeships, and even temporary law student jobs with United States Attorney's offices, are still required to answer questionnaires reminiscent of the McCarthy era's, "Are you now or have you ever . . ." The common understanding among applicants for such jobs is that an affirmative answer to past marijuana use will not necessarily disqualify but that admitting the use of heroin or cocaine will produce automatic disqualification. Since many of today's young attorneys did in fact sample cocaine during the early 1980s, they either don't apply for such jobs or, probably more commonly, lie about past drug use. As a result, the Department of Justice and, to some extent, the judiciary, is being staffed with people who committed a serious federal crime—lying to the government[76]—before even starting their government jobs.

THE COURTS ARE CHOKING ON DRUG CASES

The burden of drug-law enforcement is swamping the judicial system, according to legal scholars[77] and members of both the state[78] and federal[79] judiciary. In many court systems, the right to trial by jury has all but disappeared, especially in civil cases. Indeed, since criminal cases have priority, many courts are unable to reach their civil dockets at all. Persons who can't wait ten or more years to have a civil dispute decided are forced to "rent" a retired judge or a lawyer, or even to resort to arbitration. Such remedies are not only expensive and inconsistent with constitutional guarantees, they are heavily dependent upon the cooperation of both sides of the dispute. A defendant who wants to postpone the inevitable plaintiff's judgment is usually able to do so, almost forever in some drug-congested systems. The effects, especially on elderly plaintiffs, are devastating. The difference between the status quo and a state of anarchy becomes murkier every day.[80]

The vast majority of drug cases are handled in state courts. These drug cases made up 14 percent of criminal trials in 1980. By 1990, that percentage had more than tripled, to 44 percent.[81] The federal courts also have felt the strain of the drug war. Between 1980 and 1992, the number of federal drug cases quadrupled, rising from 3,127 to 12,433.[82] The problem looks worse as you go up the ladder in the federal system to the appeal courts; by 1989, more than half of the appeals filed in federal court were drug cases. In his annual report for 1989, Chief Justice of the United States Supreme Court William Rehnquist wrote, "Some [federal] courts, especially in border states, are approaching the outer limits of caseload and fatigue from handling drug-related criminal cases."[83] Chief Justice Rehnquist complained that the glut of drug cases is delaying important litigation about business disputes, the environment, civil rights and bankruptcy.

On the state level, the problem of court overburdening is even more severe. In Houston's Harris County courthouse, twenty-two Texas judges heard more than 40,000 drug cases in 1991.[84] Crack defendants, wearing prison jump suits and chained together in long lines, troop through the corridors whenever the Harris County courts are in session. "Less than one gram should be treated as a class-A misdemeanor," says Texas District Court judge Norman Lanford, in frustration.[85] Reducing cocaine possession from a felony to a class-A misdemeanor would give that crime a maximum sentence of one year and make its penalty identical with that for marijuana possession. Thus, the drug war's burden on the Texas courts is so severe that it ironically may cause a partial decriminalization of cocaine. Allocating court resources to the drug war also creates a de facto decriminalization of other serious crimes, such as rape, murder and robbery or, at the very least, results in inappropriately lenient sentences for them. Judge Lanford explains, "We are shoving . . . the minuscule cocaine cases into the prison system; [meanwhile] we're shoving people out the back door of the prison that perhaps ought to be there, because they have demonstrated that they are dangerous to the rest of us."[86]

With the California courts in a similar quandary, Malcolm M. Lucas, the Chief Justice of that state's Supreme Court, has asked for additional resources to deal with the overflow caused by the ever-growing docket of drug cases.[87] The president of California's judges association, Judge Candace D. Cooper, complained that a "substantial majority" of the 1980's growth in the Los Angeles criminal case load is attributable to drug prosecutions.[88] The annual number of felony criminal cases handled by downtown Los Angeles courts quadrupled between 1981 and 1992: up from 7,648 prosecutions in 1981 to 28,951 in 1992.[89] Judge Cooper warned that she and her colleagues on the California bench soon will need to talk so fast to keep up with the accelerating pace of drug-related cases they will "sound like a chorus of Alvin and the Chipmunks."[90]

What is true in federal courts and in Texas and California is true virtually everywhere in America. At the midwinter meeting of the American Bar Association in February 1993, its criminal justice section reported that our justice system "is on a fast track to collapse" because of the avalanche of drug prosecutions and the severe prison sentences meted out to drug violators.[91]

THE DRUG GULAGS

Conditions in the correctional institutions maintained by our criminal justice system may be even worse than those of the courts. The American penal system is one of the world's largest and least commodious hotel chains. In 1990 the penal system housed more than one million occupants, 710,054 residents in the state and federal prisons and an average of 395,553 in the local jails.[92] According to a study by the Sentencing Project, the "United States now has the world's highest known rate of incarceration, with 426 prisoners per 100,000 population."[93] There were 254,176 employees[94] at the 670 American prisons in 1989.[95] As of the summer of 1988, an additional 99,631 employees worked at the 3,316 local jails,[96] bringing the grand total to around 350,000 correctional employees.

During the 1970s, total prison and jail population grew by 30 percent from 325,630 in 1970 to 468,686 by 1980.[97] Between 1980 and 1990, however, the population behind bars more than doubled, to 1,105,607.[98] Experts predict that by 1994, the number of prison inmates will have increased by 200 percent over 1980.[99]

Anyone who is not profoundly disturbed by the exponential rate of growth in the United States prison population should be. If the present rate of increase merely continues, rather than accelerating as it has during the past two decades, the United States will have more than 2 million inmates by the year 2000.

Drug sentences represent the largest segment of growth for the penal population. In Florida, the proportion of drug sentences increased from 15 percent to 35 percent of the total between 1985 and 1988.[100] As of 1989, drug possessors and traffickers represented roughly 21 percent to 24 percent of the 395,553 inmates of the nation's county and municipal jails[101] and an estimated 25 percent to 35 percent of the 710,054 convicts serving sentences in the state and federal prisons.[102] Thus, in 1989, drug prohibition forced our penal institutions to warehouse somewhere between 260,000 and 343,000 people, who otherwise would not have burdened that system. If we add those who were imprisoned not for drug crimes but for drug-related crimes (such as crimes to get drug money, or murders and assaults arising out of the drug business) we could include at least another 150,000 to the total. Thus, about half of our penal population is there because of drug prohibition.

When subjected to analysis, the data are even more disquieting. Economist Peter Reuter points out that the intensity of our punitive avalanche is indicated not merely by the increasing numbers of drug arrests, but also by aggravation in the nature or seriousness of the charges.[103] The number of state and local arrests for drug offenses has not only doubled from 1980 to 1990, their seriousness also changed substantially. In 1980, only 30 percent of the arrests were for drugs other than marijuana whereas more than 60 percent were for drugs other than marijuana in 1990. Distribution charges accounted for only 18 percent of the arrests in 1990; they now comprise 27 percent.[104] As one would expect, the numbers of prison sentences also soared. In a two-year period in 1986–88, the number of persons receiving state prison sentences nearly doubled.[105]

Federal sentencing trends are even more alarming. Reuter explains that when you combine (1) the increase in numbers of drug cases with (2) the increase in the average length of prison sentences actually imposed with (3) the abolition of parole in the federal system, you find that the "expected prison time" imposed in 1990 is *ten times* what it was in 1980.[106] This is insane. Many judges recognize this. One federal judge resigned rather than impose the mandatory sentences he was required to impose in drug cases.[107] Another suggested that in the future, judges who impose such sentences may be asserting the Nuremberg defense ("I was just following orders") to charges of human-rights violations.[108] Others simply refuse to accept drug cases.[109]

Maintaining America's drug gulag is expensive. The estimated annual cost to incarcerate each prisoner in California is $28,000.[110] In New York City, the cost is $50,000 per year.[111] By comparison, for the 1992 to 1993 academic year, undergraduate tuition at Harvard cost $16,454.[112] The total operating budget for federal, state and local prisons in the 1990 fiscal year was a staggering $11 billion.[113]

Forty states and the District of Columbia are under court orders to alleviate prison overcrowding.[114] The United States Constitution's ban against cruel and unusual punishment motivates courts to order relief of overcrowding. If courts continue to adhere to the human-rights principle that punishment must be humane, states will have to reduce the prison population by measures such as drug decriminalization or decriminalization of rape or murder, or build more prisons. In recent years many states have floated multibillion-dollar bond issues to finance the construction of new prisons; the total national building budget for the 1990 fiscal year alone was around $3 billion.[115] At a cost of $50,000 per cell, state taxpayers will have spent an estimated $35 billion on prison construction between 1990 and 1995.[116] Once built, the upkeep of those buildings will become another gigantic public expense. The United States cannot afford—morally, pragmatically or economically—the horrific increases in incarceration mandated by the drug war.

CHAPTER 10

Health and Safety Costs

"[Our approach to drugs should be] led by the Surgeon General, not the Attorney General."

KURT L. SCHMOKE[1]

CONSIDERING THE physical harm that drug abuse can cause, an ironic consequence of drug prohibition is that it causes far more. Most of the sickness, accidents and deaths attributed to the taking of illegal drugs are products of prohibition itself, and this does not include the fatal diseases acquired by nonusers from users, nor the suffering of persons whose illnesses are unrelated to drug taking but whose treatment would be improved if controlled drugs were more available.

Prohibition causes two distinct types of health problems:

- It limits or forbids access to therapeutic substances. America's drug policy subordinates the health of the afflicted to the unachievable purpose of preventing recreational use.
- It makes the recreational use of drugs far more dangerous than would have been the case if drugs were not contraband.

THE CRUELTY OF THERAPY DENIED

If the dose is sufficiently large, most medicinal drugs are toxic. Aspirin is an example. In 1990, American medical examiners mentioned aspirin as at least one of the possible causes of 111 drug deaths.[2] They also labeled it the *sole* cause of eighteen drug deaths.[3] There is no doubt that aspirin is an abused drug, and that aspirin kills. Yet aspirin is a true wonder drug that not only relieves pain, it reduces fever and inflammation and even reduces risks of heart attacks, strokes and colon cancer. The risks of abuse, fatal accidents and fetal injury are significant but cannot compare to the beneficial effects of making aspirin available in virtually every store at low cost. Had aspirin been a tightly controlled drug, many of its health benefits would never have been discovered.

Most drugs have some unwanted side effects. For instance, many antihistamines, which relieve allergy symptoms, also cause drowsiness, making it dangerous for some users to drive or operate equipment. Despite these risks, antihistamines are freely available.

If a drug's therapeutic benefits sufficiently outweigh the harm or risk of its side effects, then the Food and Drug Administration permits its sale over-the-counter despite the unwanted consequences of use—as is the case with antihistamines and aspirin. Other drugs can be sold on prescription. Users are warned of possible adverse reactions, and discontinuance is counseled if side effects become severe or dangerous. Toxicity and side effects are inevitable in drug therapy. The medicolegal community constantly weighs costs against benefits and often attempts to cope with unwanted effects rather than forgoing the therapeutic benefits of a drug.

Some of the presently illegal drugs have one or more firmly established medical uses—heroin as a painkiller, marijuana as an antidote to the nausea associated with cancer chemotherapy and cocaine as a local anesthetic. However, our law forbids medical use of marijuana or heroin. The fear allegedly is that recreational users would divert the heroin or marijuana from their legitimate medical applications, or medical users would become recreational users. Such fears cannot justify making these drugs unavailable for therapy. The real reasons for the medical bans are symbolic and political.

Marijuana in the Medicine Cabinet

Many disease victims have had their well-being sacrificed for the sake of our unsuccessful marijuana prohibition. Two examples are Barbra and Kenneth Jenks, a young Florida couple, now deceased.[4] Mrs. Jenks suffered from nausea, due to AIDS, which she acquired from her hemophiliac husband, who had been infected with AIDS by transfusion of tainted blood. Following the advice of a member of her AIDS support group to smoke marijuana to improve her appetite, she regained forty pounds. She otherwise would have starved to death. However, anonymous informants tipped off the police. Vice-squad cops broke down the door to the Jenks' house trailer, held a gun to Barbra's head and confiscated their two marijuana plants. Their medical-necessity defense was rejected and they were sentenced to one year of probation.[5] A Florida appeals court later reversed their conviction and upheld their medical-necessity defense.[6]

Although thirty-five states have statutes that in one way or another permit the medical use of marijuana,[7] sufferers like the Jenks are trapped by federal supremacy. Federal laws take precedence over state laws when drugs are concerned. Thus, the federal Controlled Substances Act of 1970[8] means that sick people can get legal access to their medicine only if federal agencies want them to have it. Several government agencies, including the U.S. Public Health Service (USPHS), the Food and Drug Administration (FDA), the National Institute on Drug Abuse (NIDA) and the Drug Enforcement Administration (DEA), have control of the medicinal marijuana supply for people with illnesses that could be helped by marijuana.

The Public Health Service did have a "compassionate-use" program, which provided marijuana grown on a government farm in Mississippi. However, as of early 1992 just fourteen disease victims had persevered in their battles against the bureaucracy to obtain supplies of this federally grown medicine.[9]

Disease sufferers could legally obtain marijuana for medicine only if physicians are willing to seek permission to conduct experimental research on what the FDA calls an "Investigational New Drug" (IND). But doctors are not enthusiastically volunteering to sponsor IND patients. Because of drug-war fervor, many research physicians are reluctant to have themselves stigmatized as advocates of marijuana therapeutics. DEA harassment of the researcher is a possibility, and their government research grants stand in jeopardy. They also lack support by foundations, universities or drug companies to conduct research.

Irvin Rosenfeld, who needs marijuana to help treat a rare disease that causes bone tumors, labored four and one half years from the time he resolved to obtain legal marijuana until he won an FDA permit.[10] It took political lobbying and the credible threat of a lawsuit to achieve his enrollment in the compassionate-use program.

The final irony in Rosenfeld's case was that his effort was rewarded by the legal obligation to do business with an unreliable drug supplier. NIDA frequently provides him marijuana of insufficient potency or fails to make scheduled deliveries at all.[11] Other clients of the "compassionate-use" program report that not only is NIDA an inept and slipshod apothecary,[12] its marijuana is third-rate.[13] Often the medicinally active ingredients of NIDA-supplied dope are degraded and useless because the product is several years old when delivered.[14] No private-sector pharmaceutical company could stay in business if it provided the quality of service and product attributed to NIDA.

The Drug Enforcement Administration justifies the obstacles it has placed upon the drug's therapeutic use by claiming that marijuana is unsafe. Research discussed in Chapter 4 strongly suggests that the adverse health risks of marijuana use are minor relative to most other drugs. Whether those risks warrant prohibition of marijuana for recreational use, however, is not the issue; the relevant question is whether marijuana's health risks are outweighed by its medicinal benefits.

The DEA's own administrative-law court considered this very question. On September 6, 1988, Francis L. Young, chief administrative law judge of the Drug Enforcement Administration, completed a full review of the evidence about marijuana as medicine. The evidence included documents and witnesses on all sides of the issue, vigorous cross-examination and submission of extensive briefs, over a period of many months. Citing compelling medical evidence that marijuana could be prescribed safely, Judge Young recommended that marijuana be rescheduled, which would allow doctors to use the drug in medicine and to prescribe its use. He wrote: "The evidence in this record clearly shows that marijuana has been accepted as capable of relieving the distress of great numbers of very ill people, and doing so with safety under medical supervision. It would be unreasonable, arbitrary and capricious for the DEA to continue to stand between those sufferers and the benefits of this substance in light of the evidence."[15]

John C. Lawn, the administrator of the Drug Enforcement Administration, rejected Young's recommendations. Lawn ordered that marijuana's Schedule I classification be retained.[16] As a Schedule I drug, marijuana is stigmatized as a dangerous drug for which there is no recognized medicinal use. By contrast, cocaine and morphine are less restricted Schedule II drugs, which physicians can prescribe for medical use.

Among Judge Young's findings, which the DEA disregarded:

• Marijuana has been used for more than 5,000 years by very large numbers of people, yet, Young writes, "There is no record in the extensive medical literature describing a proven, documented cannabis-induced fatality."[17] Although NIDA's Drug Abuse Warning Network (DAWN) states that in 1990 medical examiners mentioned marijuana in 209 death reports,[18] this simply means that the drug was found in the system, not that it had lethal effects. As noted, even aspirin appeared on 111 death reports (and caffeine appeared in fifty-four).

• It is more hazardous to consume many common foods than it is to use marijuana. Young explains: "[E]ating ten raw potatoes can result in a toxic response. By comparison, it is physically impossible to eat enough marijuana to induce death."[19] Standard medical tests to determine lethal doses of drugs suggest that "[a] smoker would theoretically have to consume nearly 1,500 pounds of marijuana within about fifteen minutes to induce a lethal response."[20]

Marijuana's Therapeutic Efficacy

Clinical and research evidence has established that marijuana has clear therapeutic value for some illnesses. For others, marijuana has potential value that may be established by further experimentation. The principal medical applications of marijuana that have been confirmed or are being seriously debated are:

• *Alleviating the Nausea of Chemotherapy.* The most widely accepted and best-documented medical use of marijuana is the alleviation of nausea that accompanies use of some chemotherapy drugs.[21] Experiments reported in *The New England Journal of Medicine,*[22] and the *Annals of Internal Medicine,*[23] along with at least fourteen court affidavits by oncologists, cancer patients and others,[24] unambiguously establish such value of marijuana in cancer treatment.

Some cancer-chemotherapy drugs are extremely toxic substances, which often cause patients to retch violently.[25] The vomiting is so overpowering and uncomfortable that many cancer patients develop anticipatory nausea, which eventually makes it impossible for them to participate in chemotherapy. Marijuana—provided illegally by compassionate nurses, doctors, family members or friends—has prolonged or saved the lives of many cancer victims.

Marijuana is "probably the most effective anti-nausea drug we have," asserts chemotherapy specialist Dr. Ivan Silverberg.[26] Almost two thirds of Dr. Silverberg's colleagues agree with him that marijuana is an effective antidote to nausea, according to a 1991 survey that randomly sampled roughly 10 percent of America's oncologists.[27] Rick Doblin and Mark Kleiman, the researchers from the Kennedy School of Government who conducted the survey of 1,035 Members of the American Society of Clinical Oncology, also discovered that 44 percent of those cancer specialists had at least once been willing to risk criminal sanctions by advising chemotherapy patients to obtain marijuana by whatever means necessary. Nearly half (48 percent) of the sample of oncologists said they would prescribe the drug as an antiemetic if it were legal to do so.

Yet pharmacists now cannot legally stock a gram of this drug in its raw form, carrying instead synthetic THC capsules which *are* legally available. Roxane Laboratories, a marketing partner of Unimed, Inc., sells THC capsules under the trade name Marinol,[28] which is used by nearly 100,000 chemotherapy patients.[29]

However, smokable marijuana is superior to the THC capsules as an antiemetic, according to more than three quarters of the oncologists who responded to the question on that issue in the Doblin and Kleiman survey.[30] The opinion of the oncologists is supported by a study published in 1988 by Dr. Vincent Vinciguerra and two other researchers, in *The New York State Journal of Medicine,* which found that 29 percent of patients whose nausea was not relieved by THC were able to obtain relief by smoking marijuana.[31] Marijuana contains many compounds other than THC, and those substances may account for much of the antiemetic effect. More importantly, patients who need the drug explain that their persistent vomiting prevents them from retaining the capsules long enough for the medication to do any good. Marijuana smoke, on the other hand, does not itself cause nausea like the capsules do, and its active ingredients enter the bloodstream through the pulmonary system far more rapidly than the oral THC can enter through the stomach wall. Thus, the patient gets relief sooner and is able to self-titrate the dose very accurately, by smoking only until the nausea symptoms subside.

• *Glaucoma Treatment.* Millions of Americans suffer from glaucoma, a disease in which the force exerted by the fluid inside the eyes (intraocular pressure) damages the optic nerve. The disease is progressive, and for approximately 7,000 Americans per year the outcome is blindness. Eighty to 90 percent of glaucoma victims are able to control the disease by taking conventional drugs that reduce the intraocular pressure. For the remaining 10 to 20 percent, the drugs fail to control the pressure, and surgery once was the only recourse. Surgery, however, can itself cause blindness. The use of marijuana might reduce intraocular pressure to acceptable levels for patients whose glaucoma would otherwise require the vision-threatening surgical intervention.[32]

The celebrated case of Robert Randall, who since 1975 has legally smoked up to ten marijuana cigarettes per day to avoid blindness, demonstrates that marijuana can reduce the intraocular pressure of glaucoma.[33] Randall has successfully fought the law several times: first to win acquittal on a marijuana-possession charge by using the medical necessity defense[34] and then to obtain a settlement with the U.S. government, allowing him legal access to the medicine which has preserved his eyesight.[35] His marijuana therapy apparently has not caused any adverse side effects.[36] He also has avoided glaucoma surgery.[37] Numerous other glaucoma sufferers have obtained similar benefits from use of legally or illegally obtained marijuana, according to courtroom testimony by physicians.[38]

Despite the promise of marijuana in glaucoma treatment, leaders of the American ophthalmology profession still seem reluctant to advocate medicinal availability. The official position of the American Academy of Ophthalmology is that more research is needed on marijuana's "possible" value for glaucoma treatment.[39]

• *Relieving Chronic Pain.* During the last half of the nineteenth century, doctors prescribed marijuana as a painkiller.[40] Its use for that purpose was sufficiently common that medical textbooks and journals of the day identified the types of pain for which it should be used[41] and debated the appropriate dosages[42].

At the onset of the twentieth century, physicians largely abandoned marijuana as an analgesic, opting instead to inject opiates[43] or to prescribe the recently developed drug aspirin. (Injection of water-soluble opiates via the hypodermic syringe was a treatment method developed in the 1850s.[44]) Physicians of the period came to prefer opiate injection over marijuana use because its effects were both more predictable and more profound.[45]

Principally as a result of its recreational use since the 1960s, marijuana's ability to relieve surgical, migraine and menstrual pain has been rediscovered.[46]

• *Controlling Multiple Sclerosis Spasms.* There is no known cure for multiple sclerosis, a nerve disorder which can result in severe loss of muscle control. Presently, spasm control is the most that can be done to help the MS sufferer, and even that attempt at symptomatic relief is usually unsuccessful. Two drugs are approved by the FDA for spasm control, but neither of them is very effective and they both are highly toxic.[47]

At least one study has found that smoking marijuana impaired motor performance of both multiple sclerosis patients and healthy subjects.[48] However, other studies have shown that THC can decrease spasticity[49] and tremors[50] of multiple sclerosis patients. Further, case histories, described in court testimony[51] and a pharmacology-journal article[52] by neurological researcher Denis Petro, M.D., indicate that marijuana can lessen the pain and muscle spasticity of multiple sclerosis, cerebral palsy and spinal injury. Marijuana is not a cure for those neurological disorders, but it appears to control muscle spasms sufficiently to allow some patients to resume nearly normal lives. For some of these patients, marijuana also appears to control the socially and psychologically debilitating symptom of incontinence.[53]

• *Controlling Some Epileptic Seizures.* Medical researchers have found that cannabidiol (CBD) and other closely related marijuana constituents can effectively control several types of epileptic seizures[54] with important advantages over the more conventional antiepilepsy drugs. The marijuana extracts have "fewer unwanted side effects and related risks to health at effective dosage levels, less potential for causing seizures in some individuals, and less likelihood of gradually losing anticonvulsant effectiveness over time."[55]

• *Other Ailments.* Some research intimates that marijuana could retard tumor growth, reduce anxiety, induce sleep for insomniacs, combat depression, calm surgery patients before receiving anesthesia, control high blood pressure, diminish inflammation of joints and tissue and even fight infection as an antibiotic.[56] Marijuana has even been proposed as an asthma drug[57] and as a medication in alcohol and drug-dependency treatment.[58]

In spite of the impressive list of its established and potential therapeutic uses, University of California, Los Angeles, psychiatrist Sidney Cohen observes, "Marijuana is not a panacea."[59] It may not prove to be as beneficial for some proposed applications as it is for combating nausea. It may even be counterproductive for some of its proposed uses. Much remains to be learned.

However, the present prohibitory system impedes even the experimentation that the Food and Drug Administration claims to permit. Under current restrictions, researchers may never be able to learn whether marijuana truly could be used to treat symptoms or illnesses other than nausea. Here, as often occurs when freedom is denied, prohibition blocks the advance of science.

The Intoxication Objection

Even the government's argument that marijuana has the side effect of causing intoxication has little merit.

First, the government's stance regarding intoxication is inconsistent. It allows more than 100,000 patients to use THC, while it virtually forbids medicinal use of raw marijuana. Yet THC is the marijuana ingredient that causes most of the high. Many patients who use THC find the intoxication caused by this concentrated psychotropic drug to be extremely unpleasant. Marijuana, which often contains as little as 2 percent THC, is a much milder and less intoxicating substance than chemical THC.

Second, although marijuana usually has a consciousness-altering effect for its *recreational* users, according to physician John P. Morgan and City University of New York pharmacology professor Lynn Zimmer, "Smokers of marijuana for medical relief do not spend their days 'stoned.' "[60] Morgan and Zimmer elaborate in a *Newsday* opinion piece: "Research has repeatedly shown that much of the marijuana high is socially constructed, dependent upon users' expectations and the social circumstances in which it is consumed. Just as the chronic pain patient may consume opiates without impairment, patients who take medical marijuana feel little intoxication and remain capable of conducting normal daily activities."[61]

Why Is Medicinal Marijuana So Vehemently Opposed?

Why does the U.S. government ignore scientific evidence and perpetuate needless suffering? Have bureaucrats been bamboozled by pharmaceutical-company lobbying? There is little evidence of that. But it is clear that none of the pharmaceutical companies have any economic interest in promoting the medical use of marijuana (or heroin, for that matter), since they can acquire no patent for the product.

The political cost of permitting marijuana's rescheduling would be an admission that the government has been consistently wrong since 1937, when it first outlawed a drug with already known medicinal usefulness.

Since 1937, admitting the mistake has become progressively more costly for politicians. This cost is an artifact of earlier political cleavages that resonate into the 1990s. During the 1960s and 1970s, marijuana became symbolic of youthful rebellion and resistance to authority. Social and political moralists of the religious right railed against marijuana as vehemently as their predecessors had excoriated Demon Rum. Liberals and radicals flaunted marijuana use to demonstrate their disdain for conventional morality. The claims of medical necessity have been smothered by the intense politicization of the plant.

Protectors of the marijuana status quo have also been influenced by the presence in the marijuana-as-medicine debates of people who seem to care more about the recreational benefits of marijuana than they do about the medical issues. They support rescheduling pleas in the hope that a victory on that front will topple the entire regulatory edifice. As irrational as that belief seems to be, the rigid prohibitionists in the government seem to believe it also. Their extreme antimedical stance can best be understood in that light.

The soundest approach would be to treat the issues of recreational and medical uses as distinct. There is no reason why permitting medical prescription should make it substantially more difficult to control recreational use. Indeed, the prohibitionist position might even gather strength from a more limited reach, since it would not then be as utterly indefensible as it now is.

But neither compassion nor rationality reigns. Despite marijuana's therapeutic efficacy and its safety, long recognized in the "compassionate-use" program, not only has the DEA refused to reclassify marijuana so as to permit a doctor to prescribe it, it has persuaded the Public Health Service to terminate the compassionate-use program. In May 1992, James O. Mason, head of the Public Health Service, announced that the program was being phased out. No new applications would be approved. The thirteen on the program would be continued, but no one would be added, despite the flood of applications from AIDS victims like the Jenks. Dr. Mason was fairly candid about the reasons. Giving out marijuana as medicine might create the "perception that this stuff can't be so bad."[62]

Robert Randall, who has been able to retain his eyesight by using marijuana, condemned the decision as reflecting "ideological signals" rather than an interest "in the welfare of desperately ill people." Mark Kleiman, Harvard professor and drug analyst, commented on the written explanations for the decision: "I'm mostly a hawk in the war on drugs, but this is gibberish."[63]

NATURE'S BEST CHEMICAL PAINKILLER: THE OPIATES

Drug prohibition also interferes with severe-pain management. Victims of trauma and terminally ill patients in the advanced stages of cancer or AIDS are often denied access to the opiates—principally morphine or heroin—that might make their pain bearable. In a 1990 *Scientific American* article, Ronald Melzack, a McGill University psychologist who was a codeveloper of the famous "gate control" theory of pain, complained that physicians excessively fear "turning patients into addicts."[64] Melzack reasons that the doctors respond to their fear by delivering "amounts [of morphine] that are too small or spaced too widely to control pain."[65]

The historical record suggests that physicians' wariness of opiate prescription may be rooted more in a fear of legal sanctions than the need to avoid harming patients. The Harrison Narcotics Act,[66] as passed in 1914, permitted medical practitioners to prescribe opiates in "good faith" and to possess those drugs for the "legitimate practice" of their professions. Many physicians construed these exceptions to condone maintaining addict comfort by providing them opiates. This view is implicit in the theory behind present-day American methadone-maintenance programs and British heroin-weaning programs.

The Internal Revenue Bureau, which enforced the Harrison Act during its early years, disagreed that addict maintenance was "good-faith" prescription. Medical practitioners were among the defendants in some of the earliest and most aggressive prosecutions under the Harrison Act. Physicians and pharmacists fought for their privileges to prescribe or sell opiates in accordance with their own professional judgment. (No doubt, some of these members of the medical community also were fighting to retain the profit center in prescribing and selling opiates to addicts, a market which is now controlled by the underworld.) In 1916, a Supreme Court case[67] made it appear that the physicians would win their dispute with the Internal Revenue Bureau, but in two other Court decisions,[68] handed down three years later, the doctors lost their right to prescribe opiates in accord with their own medical judgment. Since March 1919, the prospect that a doctor or pharmacist could go to jail for a false step in opiate prescription has been a fact of their professional lives.

Melzack asserts that physicians' caution about creating addicts is excessive because "when patients take morphine to combat pain, it is rare to see addiction—which is characterized by physical craving for a substance and, when the substance is suddenly removed, by the development of withdrawal symptoms (for example, sweating, aches and nausea)."[69] Physicians who deal with pain estimate that fewer than one tenth of one percent of patients who receive any painkillers become addicted to them.[70] Melzack says, "Addiction seems to arise only in some fraction of morphine users who take the drug for its psychological effects."[71]

Heroin, which is superior to morphine for some pain sufferers, can be prescribed in Great Britain,[72] but is unavailable from legal sources in the United States. Thus, the Committee to Treat Intractable Pain in Washington, D.C., now lobbies for the legalization of heroin for medicinal use.

The 1991 "Hospice Six" case is symptomatic of the pain-management problems caused by drug-war perspectives.[73] Six nurses at the Hospice of Saint Peter's, in Helena, Montana, had routinely stockpiled morphine, which had been left unused by deceased cancer patients. State regulations require that leftover drugs be destroyed when a patient dies, but the nurses instead retained the morphine to give to subsequent terminally ill cancer patients at pain-crisis times when pharmacies were closed or doctors could not personally sign for the drugs. The nurses broke the letter of Montana's drug-control laws, even though they claimed that they always obtained at least telephone authorization from a physician before providing drugs from their illegal supply.

State Prosecutor Steven Shapiro saw the matter quite differently. He brought license-suspension proceedings against them before the Montana State Board of Nursing, and scrutinized medical records to see if he could build homicide cases against them for shortening the lives of any patients.

In a rare display of resistance to drug-war paranoia, residents of Helena rallied to the side of the nurses, writing hundreds of supportive letters, buying newspaper advertisements on behalf of the nurses and wearing buttons that demanded, "Free the Hospice Six!" The state board eventually punished the nurses with only probationary suspensions of their licenses, but the net result of the entire incident was that government once again subordinated compassion and common sense to a mindless application of drug-prohibition policies.

How Prohibition Causes Death by Disease and Accident

Aside from denying access to therapeutic drugs and depriving pain victims of relief, current drug policy adds new and more horrible dimensions to the baseline drug-abuse problem in at least three other important ways:

- Prohibition is implicated in the spread of a lethal epidemic, AIDS, and many other infectious and often deadly diseases.
- Prohibition eliminates any possibility of regulating the safety, potency or purity of drugs. Overdoses and toxic reactions to drugs are far more common under drug prohibition than they would otherwise be.
- Illegal-drug abusers avoid the health-care system, making them a danger to themselves and to the rest of us.

Spreading Disease and Death

"Twenty dollars can keep one hundred addicts AIDS free for a week; twenty dollars won't buy you an hour in the hospital," says John Parker, of Boston.[74] A graduate student and recovering heroin addict, Parker put his own freedom in jeopardy when he organized a program to distribute sterile needles to New England heroin addicts. The program led to Parker's arrest and trial, in which he was acquitted.[75]

Given public attitudes toward drugs, it is not surprising that programs to distribute clean needles have their critics. Greg Mykland, of the Tacoma, Washington, City Council, expresses a common view: "I think it sends a message [that] you've got a drug habit; we'll help you along with that; we'll give you clean needles so that you can keep going."[76]

But advocates of needle-exchange programs claim that the contact required to obtain a needle increases the probability that an intravenous-drug user will get into drug rehabilitation. Further, such advocates as Dr. Stephen Joseph, former New York City Health Commissioner, who headed an experimental needle-exchange program in New York, says, "This is not a program that causes harm;

we've learned that in a year in New York City, and our data show it." [77]

Still, the prohibition of drugs makes it difficult to take common-sense hygienic measures to cope with an emergency, such as the AIDS epidemic. About 3,500 AIDS patients in America die annually who acquired their disease from contaminated needles, and people who use no recreational drugs needlessly die. Intravenous-drug users have been identified as the group that introduced AIDS to females, infants and heterosexual males, three populations whose risk otherwise might have remained relatively low.

Virtually all these deaths are attributable to prohibition. Drug users use the needles because the drugs are too costly to consume in a less efficient but safer manner. Clean needles themselves are illegal contraband and are therefore expensive. Users go to "shooting galleries" to take their drugs with borrowed needles. In Hong Kong, where needles are legal and cheap, there is no drug-related AIDS. [78]

Spreading of infectious diseases is not limited to the use of contaminated needles. Illegal heroin and cocaine, and even marijuana sometimes contain disease viruses and bacteria. In addition to AIDS, illegal-drug users get pulmonary infections, endocarditis, bacteremia, hepatitis, tetanus, malaria and numerous other diseases. Some of these are acquired through snorting or eating the drugs. Legal drugs would be sterilized.

Unregulated Drugs

Under prohibition, all contraband-drug sales are illegal; hence, the quality—and more importantly the safety—of marijuana, heroin and cocaine are completely unregulated. There is no underground equivalent of the Food and Drug Administration to protect consumers of illegal drugs and no Federal Trade Commission to police false advertising. Nor are there any tort remedies against dishonest sellers. Anarchy reigns in the marketplace. Sellers of illegal drugs are often prosecuted, but hardly ever for selling drugs that turn out to be something more potent, dangerous or poisonous than they claimed. *Caveat emptor.*

Illegality makes the most rudimentary forms of customer warnings and education impossible to require. If there is a potential for allergic reactions to a drug, the contraband merchant cannot be expected to alert customers to that possibility. Unlike cigarette and alcohol packaging, which must carry warnings to pregnant women and others, no consumer warnings accompany cocaine to discourage the birth of crack babies.

In fact, although it is well known that alcohol combined with heroin or cocaine can kill, there are no warnings of that on any *alcohol* labels. Indeed, while the combination of barbiturates and many other drugs with either cocaine or heroin can be lethal, the government does not require that such a warning be placed on legal-drug packaging. This seems due to one or both of the following assumptions: (1) to require such warnings would implicitly condone the use of cocaine or heroin, (2) the government shouldn't help people reduce their risks of dying from cocaine or heroin but rather should try to keep those risks as high as possible. The first assumption is false; the second is vicious.

In addition to negating the government's ability (or willingness in the case of absent warnings on legal drugs) to regulate drug safety, prohibition actually encourages intervention by the government to make drugs more dangerous. Since the late 1970s, the United States has prevailed on Mexico to aerially spray remote marijuana plantations with the herbicide paraquat,[79] which has been shown to damage lungs.[80] Such spraying programs are unlikely to eradicate entire crops, and much paraquat-tainted marijuana entered the marketplace. A 1989 DEA study found that 7 percent of the nation's marijuana is contaminated by paraquat.[81] Thus our government has been willing to expose millions of America's pot smokers to poisoning by a toxic chemical.

In a less direct government contribution to the danger of drugs, the unregulated market for the contraband substances makes overdoses far more probable than they would be in a legal market. When you buy alcoholic beverages, the strength of the drug you receive is standardized by market forces, excise-tax rates that are proportional to alcohol concentration, and laws governing the definition of products (as in the case of wine and beer). Extra-potent wines and ales are identifiable as such and are now marketed as "fortified" wine and "malt liquors." In the case of "hard" liquor, concentration or "proof" is plainly labeled on the bottle. Who knows what the "proof" of an illegal drug is? The user can only guess, and guessing wrong can be fatal.

Ironically, the illegality of recreational drugs creates economic motives for increasing the potency of the product. Some of the marijuana in today's market is substantially more potent than the product of the

1960s and 1970s. Growers have hybridized and cultivated their plants to increase their concentration of THC. Garden-variety marijuana has lost much of its market share to sinsemilla—a seedless variant of the plant which is substantially more potent. This is because the price for the product is directly linked to its potency while the costs of producing and distributing it (including the costs of criminal prosecution) are closely related to its *volume*.

Similarly, prohibition accounts for the fact that virtually all illegal trade in opiates in this country is confined to the most potent and most dangerous of the family: heroin. Since it is far more powerful than any other natural opiate, it is easier and less conspicuous to smuggle and to transfer down the drug-distribution chain than any of its weaker siblings.

The existence of cheaper though more dangerous forms of various drugs may also be attributable to the illegality of the substances from which they are derived. Cocaine is expensive because it is illegal, and crack was developed to make the drug affordable by America's underclass.[82] Using ingredients and equipment available in virtually every kitchen, a single gram of street cocaine, which may cost several hundred dollars, can be transformed into many rocks of smokable crack. Beyond a certain point, snorting more cocaine powder is wasteful, because the powder causes the blood vessels of the nasal mucosa to constrict, inherently limiting their ability to get the powder's active ingredients into play. The lungs, however, are richly endowed with alveoli, which can get the active ingredients of smokable crack cocaine into the bloodstream with greater haste and less waste than snorting the powder can. Thus, each rock of crack gives the smoker a high that is comparable in intensity to the intoxication caused by snorting the entire gram of powder. The synthesis of crack stretches the original investment in cocaine; the total market value of the affordable rocks made from a gram of cocaine is much greater than the cost of the cocaine. The invention of crack is to the drug business what the development of the Ford assembly line was to the automobile business. Crack's discovery was breakthrough technology; it made mass marketing of cocaine economically feasible. However, the rapidity of the crack high and the lungs' greater capacity to get active ingredients into the blood also make crack more dangerous than powder cocaine. Thus, by creating market forces that favor crack over powder, prohibition again promoted a more dangerous use.

Repeal of drug prohibition would make the use of drugs far safer in many ways. During the alcohol prohibition of the 1920s, liquor poisonings were commonplace. Each year of Prohibition, about 40 out of every million Americans discovered to their extreme detriment that the liquor they had imbibed was lethally poisonous.[83] Since Prohibition was repealed in 1933, alcohol poisonings of Americans have become rare—about 4 per million between 1980 and 1983.[84] In contrast, in the former Soviet Union, where economic conditions and deliberate government policies created shortages of legal alcohol that amounted to de facto prohibition, moonshiners in 1979 caused fifty times as many poisonings as contemporaneously occurred in America.[85]

The vast majority of drug users will seek safe sources, modes of ingestion and doses of drugs if they are given legal means to do so. During alcohol prohibition, there was a trend away from beer and wine toward hard liquor, for the same reason we now have sinsemilla, heroin and crack—higher potency at lower cost. But when alcohol prohibition was repealed, the consumption of hard liquor dropped by two thirds. Even drinkers who stayed with hard liquor reduced the proofs of the liquor they bought, and many reverted to beer. The consumption of wine, which had increased during Prohibition, also dropped sharply.[86]

Similar movements would occur if drug prohibition were repealed. Most people who use recreational drugs do not want to die or become addicted; they simply assume the risk of doing so because they have little choice other than forgoing the drug. Were prohibition repealed, many people who now smoke crack, snort cocaine powder or mainline heroin would revert to the forms of these drugs that existed prior to the Harrison Act: liquid potions like the original Coca Cola, laudanum, or Mariani's wine; or low-potency tablets. These diluted forms of cocaine and opiates are far safer and less addictive than the forms that prohibition has produced.

Aliens to the Health-Care System

Before drug prohibition in this country, addicts usually functioned productively and could afford the necessities of life. They were not regarded as evil or as outcasts. Today, the addict is a marginal person in American society. Drug abusers are often members of the large segment of the American populace who do not have access to adequate health care. Drug prohibition contributes to the alienation of drug users from the health-care system in two ways. First, the users spend all or most of their disposable income on drugs, the prices of which are inflated by prohibition, rather than on medical care or medical insurance. Second, the users become part of the criminal underclass, for whom contact with health-care agencies might get them in trouble with the law. They are often in possession of drugs or their bodies carry such signs of drug use as the needle tracks caused by intravenous drug use. If they surface to seek medical attention, they risk contact with police agencies. Unhealthy lifestyles and the lack of money for food and shelter make the health care missed by drug abusers that much more necessary. In the fervor of the drug war, we have become increasingly hostile to drug users. Our drug policies drive users underground and separate them from the very health care that might offer a solution to addiction problems.

As part of the strategy for the drug war, several prominent politicians—such as California attorney general Daniel Lungren[87] and Maryland governor William D. Schaefer[88]—have advocated draconian measures, such as putting drug users in prison, confiscating their property and barring them from licenses, loans and employment. Former Los Angeles police chief Daryl Gates tops them all, recommending to the Senate Judiciary Committee that "casual drug users" should "be taken out and shot."[89] Such attitudes seem to underlie much of our drug policy. One who believes the death penalty is appropriate for a drug user has no sympathy for the user who is poisoned by adulterants and loses the life-or-death drug lottery. The more drug users who die, the greater the "deterrent" to drug use. Murderous drug dealers who spike their drugs with poison have become soldiers in the drug-war army.

The savagery of our attitudes toward drug users and their health and safety also myopically ignores the consequences such attitudes inflict upon innocent nonusers. The infectious diseases that drug users acquire from contaminated drugs, needles, and filthy crack houses and shooting galleries are not only transmitted to their children and their sexual partners but to the population at large. Moreover, most drug users who overdose, are poisoned or acquire disease do not die—at least not immediately. They get AIDS and damaged brains, lungs, hearts, livers, kidneys. They slowly lose their grip on life and become huge drains on our public health-care system, reducing the health services available to many others in need of them.

Not all societies take this punitive approach to a health problem.

Various analysts[90] have suggested that English, Dutch, Italian and German public-health approaches to confronting drug problems have been more successful than the moralistic American approach of criminalizing the problem.

The Netherlands enforces its laws against heroin traffickers, while it has instituted progressive programs to draw heroin addicts into its health-care system.[91] In Amsterdam, in neighborhoods where heroin users congregate, state-sponsored methadone buses make regular visits to dispense that heroin substitute and enroll addicts in withdrawal programs.[92] Dutch health-care officials estimate that most—possibly as many as 90 percent—of the heroin addicts in the Netherlands have thereby been registered with the government, which makes sure that they receive conventional health care in addition to drug counseling and treatment. Amsterdam police do not arrest people for possession of personal drug supplies. Sterile needles are readily available. Marijuana use also is tolerated at Dutch coffee shops and taverns, where varieties of that drug are actually on the menu.

According to a report by senior officials of the United States Embassy in the Hague, the results of the Dutch drug policy are salutary.[93] Dutch youngsters are increasingly indifferent toward marijuana. The number of Dutch users of cocaine and heroin is also declining. The average age of heroin users is increasing, suggesting that the tolerant policy does not lead Dutch youth to become heroin addicts. Meanwhile, the needle exchange programs in the Netherlands have virtually eliminated intravenous drug use as a source of HIV and hepatitis infections.

Baltimore mayor Kurt Schmoke has challenged America to adopt a drug strategy which is "led by the Surgeon General, not the Attorney General."[94] European policies appear to adhere to the mayor's advice; our own disastrous policies do not.

CHAPTER 11

The Drug War Cannot Succeed

"We continue to pursue a policy that does not and cannot work."

MATHEA FALCO, ASSISTANT SECRETARY OF STATE FOR
INTERNATIONAL NARCOTICS MATTERS 1977 TO 1981[1]

THE IMPOSSIBLE goal of the drug war is "a drug free society."[2] Drug-war strategies in pursuit of that goal are grouped into two major categories: supply reduction and demand reduction. Supply reduction has been and must continue to be a colossal failure. Demand reduction has prospects of limited success, but it can never produce a victory.

SUPPLY-REDUCTION STRATEGIES AND THEIR LIMITATIONS

The government's current battle plans for the drug war simultaneously pursue four major supply-eradication strategies:

· attacking production capabilities;[3]
· interdiction of smuggling;[4]
· preventing distribution;[5]
· disruption of suppliers' finance and control systems.[6]

200

STRATEGY 1: ATTACKING PRODUCTION

This effort includes eradicating crops of opium poppies, coca and marijuana in producer countries; supporting crop-substitution programs; destroying laboratories and processing facilities; arresting producers; and denying producers the use of transportation networks. It also includes attempts to control the distribution of precursor chemicals, such as methyl-ethyl ketone (MEK), which is used in cocaine processing. Assisting and prodding law-enforcement authorities in producer countries to arrest leaders and employees of the illicit-drug enterprises is another strategy by which our government attempts to fight production.

Domestic suppliers in the United States produce commercially important quantities of some drugs—most notably marijuana and methamphetamine. Hence, the United States itself has been the venue for some major law-enforcement operations, such as the Campaign Against Marijuana Production (CAMP), in Humboldt County, California. However, most antiproduction campaigns take place in foreign countries, where about 80 percent of marijuana supplies and nearly 100 percent of the cocaine and heroin supplies are produced.[7]

In 1989, Congress appropriated $2.2 billion for the Bush administration's five-year program to attack drug production (mostly cocaine manufacture and coca growing) in Bolivia, Colombia and Peru.[8] Under this "Andean strategy," the United States provides financial assistance and "advice" to law-enforcement officers and the military establishment in the three countries. The United States aid also theoretically promotes economic development that will reduce the countries' dependence on the drug business.

However, international relations, objections to U.S. violations of sovereignty, world politics, cultural differences and commercial trade questions complicate the already daunting task of attacking production, which can be conducted virtually anywhere on earth. Much of the production takes place openly in regions like the Golden Triangle of Southeast Asia or the Maoist, Shining Path–dominated areas of Peru, where unstable governments make it difficult or impossible to project either the producing nation's or the United States' law-enforcement power. Many government officials and citizens in source countries such as Peru and Bolivia are also unsympathetic to our objectives. They understand, as our drug warriors do not, that the only thing that eradication programs can possibly affect is not whether coca and opium will be grown, but where and by whom. They believe that our use of a drug produced in their country is our problem, not theirs. This view coincides with their economic self-interest. Both Bolivia and Peru are in the worst economic condition in their histories. The Peruvian coca industry brings in about $1 billion a year and employs some 15 percent of the national work force.[9] Bolivian dependence on coca is even more extreme. Coca revenues account for about half of Bolivia's exports and the industry employs 20 percent of the work force.[10] If the governments, bribed by American money and helped by American "advisers," destroy crops in their countries, they also destroy the livelihoods of peasant farmers, at least until the farmers can plant new crops, either in the same place or nearby.

The damage inflicted by our efforts at crop eradication is often unrelated to drugs. For example, when the United States induces the governments of the producing nations to spray herbicides on drug crops, both legitimate and illicit crops are damaged. In Guatemala, an American-sponsored program to spray chemicals in the Cuilco valley was designed to eradicate opium poppies. Instead, peasants in the valley claim, the spraying destroyed much of their tomato crop and annihilated the bees which produce commercial honey and pollinate all other crops in the valley.[11]

Some features of the Andean strategy amount to ecological warfare which the producer nations have wisely resisted. Spraying drug crops harms the environment of the producer nations. Ultimately, it could harm the entire planet by promoting deforestation, which is believed to cause global warming. Even conventional eradication methods, which do not involve spraying, may contribute to these problems. When drug eradication pushes coca production deeper into the jungle, deforestation is promoted. South American researcher Roberto Lerner claims that ". . . at least 10% of the [rain-forest] deforestation has been caused by coca growing and coca expansion."[12]

Successful eradication in one area may have the paradoxical effect of damaging the economic prospects of the farming we would like the producer countries to substitute. Growing coffee instead of coca only increases the glut of coffee, further depressing its price and hurting traditional, established coffee growers. Meanwhile, the coca supply is slightly diminished by the substitution, raising coca's price and making it worthwhile to plant it in places where government control is weak. Police actions sponsored by the United States merely play into the hands of insurgent groups, such as the Sendero Luminoso (Shining Path) guerrillas in Peru, who protect coca growers and purposely disrupt alternative economic development by terrorist actions such as blowing up electrical-transmission lines. Such disruption of economic development provides another reason why the coca crop is essential to the economic well-being of the campesinos: there are no alternative jobs.

What is the net result of the eradication strategy? Although we have been promoting crop eradication in the Andean region for decades, the State Department reported in March 1992 that there were sharp increases in worldwide production of coca.[13] Calling the programs against production "[T]he least promising approach," Rensselaer W. Lee, of the Foreign Policy Research Institute, says, "We've spent billions on international assistance programs, and have nothing to show for it."[14] The capabilities and output of drug producers have not been diminished either by the recent drug-war escalation or the decades of prohibition that preceded it. All the money and effort expended on the Andean Strategy has been squandered.

A few facts should reveal the futility of efforts to prevent production. Marijuana plants can be and are grown virtually everywhere, including every one of the United States.[15] Coca and opium poppies can be grown in almost any warm climate. The State Department estimates that record production of both coca and opium has been produced on only about 510,000 acres devoted to the growing of coca in South America and another 560,000 acres devoted to the opium poppy worldwide.[16] This acreage could easily be increased 1,000 times over. Yet a mere 200 square miles (128,000 acres) of coca and another twenty-five square miles (16,000 acres) of opium poppy are all that is needed to supply America's entire markets for cocaine and heroin.[17] It is doubtful that crop eradication programs can succeed even in notably increasing the costs of production.

STRATEGY 2: INTERDICTION

The interdiction strategy consists of all the familiar efforts to combat smuggling of illicit drugs into the United States. These include undercover operations to infiltrate smuggling organizations, border searches by the Customs Service, Coast Guard and Navy inspections of vessels on the high seas, radar tracking and interception of aircraft, and investigations designed to locate landing facilities and warehouses in the United States. Both ideological concerns and logistical difficulties impede these interdiction efforts, giving them a poor prognosis for success.

Effective drug interdiction is at odds with the high value that many

Americans still place on freedom and human rights. Because of the searches involved, drug interdiction interferes with both the privacy and the convenience of international travelers and the efficient progress of international commerce. During the late 1980s, interdiction efforts were militarized, reversing a more-than-100-year-old American tradition that denied a law-enforcement role to the armed forces.

With or without the military, the logistical impediments to interdiction are insurmountable. In addition to 354 official border-crossing points,[18] which handle close to 500 million legal entries to the United States each year,[19] there are millions of places where an unlawful entry is feasible. It is a relatively simple matter to walk, drive, wade, swim, sail or fly illegally across our 1,933-mile Mexican border or our two separate borders with Canada, which total 5,525 miles. In fiscal year 1991, the Border Patrol captured 1,132,933 people who had entered the country illegally, and that agency officially admits it apprehends only about half of the undocumented entrants.[20] Nearly 60,000 commercial vessels, over 85,000 private boats and approximately 4,500 military ships *legally* entered United States harbors in 1991.[21] In all this nautical confusion, countless other craft doubtless sneaked ashore illegally at various places on our 12,383-mile coastline. Low-flying drug-smuggling planes can easily conceal themselves among the half million or so general-aviation, commercial and military flights entering United States airspace every year.[22] Any pedestrian, vehicle, vessel or aircraft that enters the country, legally or illegally, can be carrying drugs.

Any letter, package, bulk-cargo container or traveler's baggage can include drugs. The federal government's National Narcotics Intelligence Consumers Committee (NNICC) has reported heroin seizures ranging from 4.4 pounds (2 kilograms) to 32 pounds (14.5 kilograms), which were secreted in "[n]ew and unusual . . ." places, such as "the walls (insulation areas) of two office-type refrigerators, . . . boxes of electrical cords, and . . . a shipment of lace."[23] In each of those cases, the smugglers sent their shipment as checked baggage on commercial airline flights.

The ratio of dollar value to bulk of drug cargoes is extremely high: as much as $240,000 to each kilogram (2.2 pounds) of wholesale heroin.[24] This makes it possible to conceal commercially meaningful quantities of illicit substances in virtually any hiding place.

Some 8 million cargo containers legitimately enter this country every year. Only a small fraction are even checked by customs. Within these large containers are an almost infinite variety of products, such as fruit, furniture, and chemicals. Cocaine or heroin secreted inside these objects is virtually certain to get through in the absence of an informant.

In a study he conducted for the Department of Defense, Peter Reuter of the RAND Corporation concluded that it would be "extremely difficult to reduce cocaine consumption in this country by even as little as 5 percent through a more stringent interdiction program."[25] Reuter gives three major reasons for his conclusion:

1. *Smugglers adapt successfully to changed conditions.* There is a cadre of experienced smugglers who *actually benefit* from more intense interdiction efforts. These veterans have survived as smugglers because they long ago learned how to stay a jump ahead of the interdictors; more stringent control of the border merely knocks novices out of the trade, reducing competition and increasing profits for the survivors.

2. *Smugglers have developed widely variable and flexible trade routes and concealment methods.* This resourcefulness is bounded only by the impressive imagination of the drug smugglers. One group of smugglers transported many tons of cocaine through a tunnel they dug between Mexican entrepreneur Rafael Francisco Camarena's luxury house in Agua Prieta, Mexico, and his warehouse in Douglas, Arizona.[26] Seismologists from the United States Army eventually detected the tunnel with high-tech equipment, and a binational police team raided the passageway in May 1990. The reinforced concrete tunnel was 273 feet long by five feet high, was burrowed thirty feet below the surface, was kept dry by electric sump pumps, and had a trolley and sophisticated winches to move merchandise. The completely lined passageway, which is only one of many thought to cross our borders, had an entry on the Mexican end that was concealed by a mechanically raised concrete floor underneath a pool table. It cost an estimated $1.5 million to construct, and it was engineered to professional standards. American drug-enforcement officials characterized the structure as "something out of a James Bond movie."[27]

Cocaine smugglers have poured their product into small holes drilled into lumber planks, even secreted half a ton of it inside 252 drums of powdered lye. Two tons of cocaine bricks were wrapped in lead to foil X-rays, but the lead triggered metal detectors. Next time, the smugglers switched to heavy plastic wrappers.[28] Some South

American drug importers mastered the technology necessary to form cocaine into a plasticlike material that they made into the portable kennels used for canine air travel.[29] Nobody knows how many other plastic products imported to the United States are made of cocaine.

For decades, smugglers have evaded border interdiction above ground—aboard airplanes, on foot and in motor vehicles. The sophistication of this effort defies detection by measures as silly and discriminatory as drug-courier profiles. Fifty-three-year-old Marvin D. Harris and his sixty-year-old wife, Raquel—by every indication a bourgeois and respectable elderly couple on vacation—were apprehended on July 9, 1991, as they attempted to drive across the United States border at Nogales, Arizona, with $68 million worth of cocaine concealed in their motor home.[30] When grandpa and grandma in a motor home can be smugglers, there is no serious prospect of interdicting drugs by border searches. The Customs Service lacks the resources to tear apart every vehicle.

A novel method of smuggling heroin from Southeast Asia during the Vietnam war was to secrete it in the coffins of dead American soldiers. Live bodies have been a favorite smuggling device for decades. For example, Colombian smugglers induced Juan Manuel Contento-Pachon, a Bogotá taxi driver, to enter the United States on a commercial flight after swallowing 129 balloons filled with cocaine.[31] Yet Contento-Pachon would not qualify for the *Guinness Book of Records*. That honor belongs to a smuggler of heroin.[32] According to the NNICC report, "The record [heroin] seizure obtained from a 'swallower' was 227 balloons with an estimated gross weight of 2.9 pounds (1.3 kilograms)."[33] Projecting from 1990 wholesale values of heroin,[34] the swallower cited by NNICC was transporting between $84,500 and $312,000 worth of heroin in his intestines.

Smugglers conscientiously protect their merchandise, too. NNICC describes standard operating procedure of a Nigerian heroin ring that operated, in 1990, out of an international airport in Senegal: "Three to five couriers would board an aircraft along with an 'expediter' who might denounce a courier to customs if it appeared that inspection was tight to distract attention away from other couriers. A 'convoying officer' unknown to the couriers was often aboard to ensure that the couriers did not disappear."[35]

A great fount of smuggler resourcefulness still remains to be tapped. Peter Reuter suggests that drug smugglers may someday (if they don't already) use radio-controlled model airplanes to cross the border with economically meaningful drug payloads, if the financial risks of human-piloted flights ever become unacceptable.[36] Model airplanes, which are smaller than many birds, would be virtually impossible to track by either radar or visual observation because of their size and ability to fly very low. Reuter's idea of airplanes is well within the technological and financial capabilities of drug dealers who dig million-dollar tunnels: the airplanes can be simply purchased at toy or hobby stores.

3. *The economics of the drug business favors the smuggler over the interdictor.* No one seriously contends that any law-enforcement effort can keep drugs out of the country. The only realistic goal of interdiction is to raise drug prices, but even that effort is rendered unrewarding by the economics of the illicit market. Both merchandise and labor are relatively inexpensive for smugglers. Production accounts for only about $1,000 of the price of a kilogram of cocaine, which in the first half of 1991 had a street-retail value of $40,000 to $150,000.[37] Transportation is more costly than production, but still adds only marginally to the final price when interdiction efforts cause extraordinary shipping disruptions. Reuter believes that aircraft pilots—the aristocrats among the cocaine mules who may earn more than fifteen times as much as crew members on drug ships—charge only about $250,000 for an illegal flight carrying a cargo worth many millions of dollars. According to Reuter, if enhanced interdiction efforts made drug flights so risky that smugglers were forced to triple the amount they pay pilots, the retail price of cocaine still would increase by only one percent.

Experts agree that the DEA and Customs are able to interdict no more than 10 percent of the drugs smuggled into this country every year.[38] The value of the drug at the point of interdiction is low, a very small fraction of its street value. A seized shipment of drugs, and the courier that brought it, are easily replaced.

STRATEGY 3: PREVENT DISTRIBUTION

Drug supplies are theoretically vulnerable to interruption at any point during the chain of transactions which conveys the merchandise from the initial importer to the wholesaler, the middlemen, the retailers and finally the end consumers.

At the street level, drug transactions can be prevented by massive police presence in high-volume sales territories. As with similar programs aimed at preventing streetwalking prostitutes, however, such efforts largely succeed only in forcing the activity to move into adjoining territory. Intensive police presence, if continued indefinitely, can improve the quality of a neighborhood (as it destroys the quality of another), but it cannot substantially interfere with drug trafficking.

At higher levels involving wholesale distribution, prevention is even more difficult. Transactions are conducted in secret and both buyer and seller are motivated to avoid detection. A significant police presence can be achieved only by laborious undercover operations, in which a person acts as a customer who is really a police operative, either an undercover officer or a former drug buyer who has been "turned" by the police. An undercover transaction must be closely monitored by officers so that a provable case is created and no one is injured during the controlled purchase. The quantity of wholesale transactions, involving subkilo quantities of cocaine or heroin, is so enormous and undercover work so tedious and costly that such efforts cannot hope to interfere more than marginally with the distribution of the drugs. At best, they merely create apprehension and thus reduce the efficiency of the process.

STRATEGY 4: DISRUPT FINANCIAL AND CONTROL SYSTEMS

The final supply-reduction strategy is to attack the managerial and financial systems of the underground business. Presently, this attack takes three forms: money-laundering controls, forfeitures of drug-related assets and criminal prosecution of the drug-marketing conspirators under the Racketeer Influenced and Corrupt Organization (RICO)[39] law and federal and state drug statutes.

Money laundering. Street-level drug transactions are conducted in small denominations of cash. As the cash makes its way up the drug-distribution ladder, it becomes more and more unwieldy, conspicuous to law enforcement and attractive to robbers and thieves. There is a strong need to convert it into bank instruments such as cashier's checks or interbank transfers. Alternatively, the cash can be exchanged for hard assets such as cars, planes and boats, which can then be transported out of the country and reconverted into cash equivalents or bartered for more drugs. Converting drug proceeds into apparently legitimate spendable cash or usable assets is referred to as money laundering. If money laundering could be prevented, the drug business would be wrecked. Unfortunately, money laundering is as inevitable and unstoppable as drug smuggling itself.

The techniques for laundering drug money are virtually limitless. Typically, a drug retailer turns over his cash to a professional money launderer, who employs a group of runners or couriers who carry cash to banks in amounts sufficiently small to avoid reporting requirements and exchange the cash for a bank money order, cashier's check or similar bank instrument. These are then deposited to the account of a shell company operated by the money launderer and in turn wire transferred to a secret foreign account. The money is then available to the drug smuggler who lives and works abroad or it can be "repatriated" for the benefit of a domestic drug merchant (or a foreigner who wishes to bank or invest here) by a reverse bank transfer. The funds flowing back into this country can even be disguised as a "loan," thus evading income tax and permitting tax deductions of phony "interest" payments on the "loans."

Rather than using a professional money launderer, the drug merchant can acquire control of his own bank; deal with a corrupt bank; set up a front such as a casino, a grocery store or some other cash-generating business. The drug money can then be comingled with the legitimately obtained cash and converted into laundered bank credits. Alternatively, the drug dealer or money launderer can run a check-cashing business, exchanging drug cash for the customer's checks, which can then be deposited in a bank, free of currency reporting requirements.

To make these transactions risky, the government employs agents and informers worldwide to get inside information about transactions and to inform on the suspicious ones. It negotiates treaties and agreements that hopefully limit foreign bank secrecy. Unfortunately, there are millions of banking transactions every *day* and it is impossible to monitor even a fraction of them. Since 1970, regulations have required domestic financial institutions and businesses to file reports on currency transactions "of more than $10,000." The reporting requirements, however, have often been ignored by the institutions required to make the reports. It has taken criminal prosecutions of several bankers to sensitize bankers to the requirements. Reporting is more common today. It is still possible, although irksome and costly, to avoid the requirements simply by keeping each transaction below the $10,000 limit. Hence the utility of the professional money launderer described above.

A 1986 federal statute sought to tighten control of money laundering by making the practice not only reportable but a criminal offense.[40] Anyone who engages in a business transaction of any kind involving property he knows to have been the proceeds of unlawful activity may himself have committed a serious felony. These provisions do not add any significant deterrent to money laundering. They may even discourage compliance with reporting requirements, since the reporters may be incriminating not only their customers but now themselves as well.

The duty to sift through millions of financial transactions and to read, analyze and conduct follow-up investigations on the ocean of currency reports (about 70,000 per *day*) is primarily the task of about 350 Internal Revenue Agents.[41] As a result, *no one* reads the reports. A currency report is examined only when a tip or some other information singles out a suspect or a series of suspicious transactions. Only then is the information retrieved from the computer.[42] At most, then, the currency reporting system is an irritant and an incremental cost to the drug trafficker.

If currency reporting requirements and other risks of depositing large sums of cash in banks is sufficiently burdensome, the cash-choked drug merchant can always put the cash in a suitcase and take a sojourn to the Caribbean, either on a regular airline or in a chartered craft. If extra cautious, he can use his own airplane to move the money to the Caribbean, Panama or some other laundry center. If averse to flying, he can place the cash in a van and drive it into Mexico or Canada, where he can then bank it, "layer" it with a few crisscrossing international wire transfers and then send it back to the United States. Smuggling contraband into the United States is easy, but getting cash out of the United States is a joke. United States officials care relatively little about what goes out of the country, and Mexican border officials are indifferent to what comes into their country from the United States. Canadians are not consistently curious about what is imported into their country either. Neither Mexico nor Canada has an economic interest in discouraging a flow of American currency out of America and into the bordering country.

Since it is impossible to control money laundering in the United States, we spend huge sums of money and effort trying to prevent money laundering assistance by foreign banks and the governments in which those banks are located. Those efforts have been notorious failures. One of the major reasons for the Bush administration's invasion of Panama and its kidnapping of Manuel Noriega was to stop what it claimed was Noriega's aid of drug smugglers by providing a transshipment or refueling site for them and permitting Panama's banks to launder drug money.[43] The Bush administration sent 27,000 invading American troops to Panama. Twenty-three Americans and hundreds, if not thousands, of Panamanians were killed.[44] The United States invasion was condemned by numerous international organizations, and America's respect for international law was cast into grave doubt.[45] We then spent millions prosecuting Noriega in Miami, and, because we had such a shabby case against him, we had to buy (with money, protection and freedom) the testimony of more than a dozen drug smugglers and dealers, many of whom were guilty of worse drug offenses than Noriega himself.[46] The net result, according to a GAO report issued in the summer of 1991, was that "drug trafficking may be increasing" in Panama,[47] which "continues to be a haven for money laundering."[48]

Forfeiture. About a billion dollars' worth of assets including cash are seized by law-enforcement officials annually. Most of these seizures are loosely drug-related, but it is unclear how much of the assets seized actually constitute the proceeds from drugs, are drug-trafficking equipment or are otherwise involved in the drug business. Since the federal statutes authorize seizure of any property used in any way in connection with the sale *or possession* of illegal drugs, luxury yachts, million-dollar homes, ranches, airplanes, hotels and office buildings can be seized if a small quantity of illicit drugs is found on the premises. The seizure will stick unless the owner can prove that the drug got there without his knowledge or consent. As we noted in Chapter 7, these provisions are Orwellian and need have no connection with drug trafficking. Owners of forfeited property need never have bought, sold or used drugs in order to lose their property.

Even if we assume counterfactually that the entire billion dollars in annual forfeitures are actually extracted from persons in the drug business, such costs are easily absorbed and reflected in price increases. Forfeitures represent less than 2 percent of America's illegal-drug market.

Criminal prosecutions. As happened during alcohol prohibition, our drug-war failures have resulted in spiraling increases in prosecutions for drug offenses and much longer prison terms for those convicted. Although there is talk of imposing the death penalty on drug dealers, that is likely to remain just talk. We will not follow the lead of Iran, which hanged 1,762 possessors of opiates in a seventeen-month period in 1989–1991,[49] nor of China, which has executed hundreds of drug traffickers, including thirty-one that were tried, sentenced, and executed in a mass rally on the same day in June 1992.[50] Here, however, life terms without parole are commonplace. That kind of a sentence, together with the ruinous fines, forfeitures and defense costs often connected to a criminal drug prosecution, are draconian indeed. But regardless of the penalties, there will always be a new drug dealer waiting to replace one removed by the drug warriors. Street-level dealers in America have little to lose by selling drugs. They have no legitimate job, no stable home, no marketable skills, bleak future prospects. Many are in daily jeopardy from another's knife or gun whether or not they are involved in drugs or other crimes. Their lives are disposable to society and cheap to themselves. Prison is not a prospect that engenders great fear. At higher levels of the drug business, where vast fortunes can be made in a brief time, the temptations are overwhelming. At any but the highest levels, the drug business does not require much sophistication, education or skill. What it requires is cunning, resourcefulness, and, as the drug war increases the risks of participation, recklessness and savagery.

At virtually any level of the drug business, the risks of a dealer's getting killed by a competitor, customer or employer, combined with the risks of criminal conviction and lengthy imprisonment, are high. As the drug war intensifies, they become higher. These risks are costs of doing business and are reflected in higher prices for the drugs.

There are numerous ways, however, that imaginative drug merchants can reduce their costs and enhance their profits. One way is to employ "cheaper" human capital, including children who cannot get jobs paying the minimum wage, undereducated members of minority groups, illegal immigrants and persons with extensive criminal records. Workers can also be recruited who do not fit drug courier profiles and are thus less likely to be apprehended, such as pregnant women or older people. Such workers are also less likely to receive severe sentences if convicted, thus reducing punishment costs as well. Drug smugglers and distributors can also increase the quantities of the drugs they smuggle and distribute, introducing economies of scale. They can respond to law-enforcement efforts by changing their own distributional methods in other respects. They can escalate their own violence and terrorism to eliminate witnesses or compensate for the coercion employed against potential witnesses by law enforcement.

They can step up their levels of bribery if this is more cost-effective than submitting their dealers to long prison sentences. They can also become better organized. As economist David Henderson notes, one of the many ironies of an intense drug war is that "civilized" drug dealers are driven out and are replaced by ruthless criminal organizations.[51] We learned this during alcohol prohibition, when the Mafia strengthened its influence over American society, an influence that persists to the present day. The role the Mafia played in alcohol prohibition is beginning to be assumed by a group of national and international criminal gangs in the drug business.[52]

An example of how multinational criminal organizations can successfully adapt to law enforcement can be found in Colombia, where drug-cartel leaders Pablo Escobar and Jorge Ochoa made the *Forbes* 1987 list of the world's billionaires.

Drug cartels killed more than fifty Colombian judges and 170 other employees of that country's criminal-justice system during the 1980s.[53] In 1984, Colombian *narcotraficantes* assassinated Justice Minister Rodrigo Lara Bonilla on a Bogotá street. In 1985, M-19 guerrillas, believed to be under contract to the Medellín cartels, invaded Colombia's Palace of Justice and assassinated eleven of the twenty-four Supreme Court justices. At least eighty-four others (including many of the attackers) also died. In 1989 the *narcotraficantes* even blew up an Avianca airliner on takeoff, killing all 107 passengers.

In August of 1989, members of the Medellín cartel, calling themselves "the Extraditables" to underscore their dread of standing trial in the United States, assassinated the favored candidate for the Colombian presidency—Senator Luis Carlos Galan. During the same month, the gang also murdered a colonel of the national police in Medellín and a well-known Bogotá magistrate. In effect, the Medellín cartel had declared all out-war against the government of Colombia; 550 lower-court judges promptly abandoned their calling.

The assassinations in August 1989 went a step too far; Colombian president Virgilio Barco Vargas reinstated Colombia's previously repudiated treaty of extradition with the United States. That was quickly followed by arrests of over 11,000 suspected members of the cartel, seizures of drugs and luxury properties of the Medellín drug lords, a spate of extraditions, $65 million in military aid from the United States and violent retaliations by Colombia's *narcotraficantes*. On one day in August 1989, the Extraditables bombed nine banks, including seven owned by the government.

On September 2, 1989, a truck bomb exploded outside the Bogotá offices of *El Espectador,* Colombia's second-largest daily newspaper and an outspoken advocate of putting the drug barons behind bars. The bomb blast killed a part-time reporter, wounded eighty-three others and left the editorial and production facilities of the newspaper in shambles.

The all-out Colombia drug war continued. Hundreds more died in violence related to conflicts among the U.S.-goaded Colombia government and the rival Medellín and Cali drug cartels. Top-rank *narcotraficantes,* such as Pablo Escobar and Jorge Ochoa, remained at large for the next two years.

Then, in 1991, negotiations between the Colombian government and the drug lords resulted in Pablo Escobar's "plea-bargained" guilty plea to relatively minor charges. Under the plea-bargain, Colombia amended its constitution to abrogate the extradition treaty with the United States, while Escobar and several of his higher-ranking associates peacefully submitted to custody in a specially built, inmate-approved, luxury "prison," where they were safe from further government harassment, safe from kidnapping by or extradition to the United States and safe from lethal attacks by rival *narcotraficantes.* In 1992 they escaped.

Escobar's cartel, which once controlled 90 percent of Colombia's drug trade, is crippled, but the Colombian drug industry has been left unimpaired by the unprecedented international law-enforcement effort. Indeed, it seems to have been strengthened by the resulting dominance of the Cali cartel. The Cali cartel, which now controls about 75 percent of the trade, has replaced Escobar's thuggish and crude Medellín organization. The Cali cartel is much more sophisticated. It eschews the indiscriminate terrorism of the Medellín's and recruits for its upper echelon Colombians trained in business management and engineering. It also spends vast sums of money pleasing powerful politicos. According to Robert Bonner, DEA administrator, "The Cali cartel is the most powerful criminal organization in the world. No drug organization rivals them today or perhaps any time in history."[54]

The Cali cartel is not reluctant to engage in assassinations; it merely uses that tool as a last resort, recognizing the enormous political costs that such activities bear. To reduce its need to rely on murder, the cartel is vertically integrated, handling major distributions in this country and abroad with its own Colombian employees. These distributors are not only well trained, they are well motivated to succeed, for most of them have families who remain in Colombia. If they are arrested and cooperate, their families will be killed. The Cali mob makes its killing count.[55]

The Evidence of Supply-Side Failure

Total seizures of cocaine by customs have increased every year but two since 1977. There were 952 pounds seized in 1977 and almost 165,000 pounds seized in 1990, for an increase of more than 1700%.[56] During the early part of this period, from about 1977 to 1985, the increases roughly correspond to the growth in the numbers of frequent cocaine users, suggesting that the seizures simply reflect increased consumption and, hence, increased imports.[57] During the later part of the period, the increases in seizures were sharper than increases in use, but prices generally were down. Again, the best explanation of the increased seizures poundage is increased importation. If increases in seizures actually reflected a substantial reduction in the cocaine available for consumption in the United States, one would expect the price to go up as the numbers of frequent users remained fairly constant, as has been the case since 1985. Instead, the prices remained even or decreased, implying that successful importations have more than kept pace with the seizures.[58]

During the same period, there has been an escalation in the *size* of record seizures. In May 1991, for example, Customs seized 1,080 pounds of heroin arriving in San Francisco.[59] Two months later, 73 *tons* of hashish were seized on the high Pacific. In November 1991, the second-highest cocaine seizure on record, 23,641 pounds, was seized.[60] This suggests that the product is becoming increasingly inexpensive to smugglers, so that they can afford to risk large quantities in a single shipment. It does not support a claim that the interdiction strategies are working. Typically the reports of record seizures include self-serving statements by drug warriors that their successful drug bust had just dealt a devastating blow to the business. Yet Michael Massing pointed out in *The Christian Science Monitor* that record-setting drug seizures are evidence of prohibition's failure, not its success.[61] Ever larger confiscations just demonstrate the logistic capabilities and the magnitude of the production resources of the worldwide drug business.

Despite periodic claims in the media that seizures have dented the market, the government's statistics suggest that drug productivity and supply continue to meet or exceed demand. Thus, it is clear that the foregoing strategies to reduce supply have been singularly unsuccessful. These efforts do not fail as a result of corruption or incompetence or lack of will. They fail for a few fundamental reasons far beyond the capacity of any drug warrior to change.

OVERALL EFFECTS OF SUPPLY-SIDE STRATEGIES ON DRUG CONSUMPTION

All of the supply-side reduction strategies have one overall impact on the supply of illicit drugs: drugs remain available, but at a much higher price than would be the case were their marketing lawful. The price increase attributable to the drug war varies, among other things, with the bulk and potency of the drug. Marijuana probably feels the impact as sharply as other illegal drugs even though it can easily be home-grown, is not addictive and is relatively benign. Since marijuana is a weed that will luxuriate in almost any climate or soil conditions, the costs of production in a free market would, on a weight basis, be comparable to the costs of producing cabbage. Since marijuana today costs between $100 and $400 per ounce,[62] the markup is 10,000 percent or more.

The illegality tariff on cocaine can best be gauged by comparing it with another Colombian product, coffee. In Colombia itself, cocaine can be bought for approximately $3,000 per kilogram. The price to the distributor/consumer per gram in the United States is about $75, or $113,400 per kilogram, a markup of about 3780 percent. The price of a pound of coffee, by comparison, is increased during its trip from Colombia to our supermarket shelves by about 300 percent. Illegality, therefore, accounts for at least 80 percent of the markup in cocaine prices.[63] The drug war markup on heroin is probably even greater than on cocaine. It sells for about 20,000 percent of what it would cost in a free market.[64]

Price increases almost certainly have a negative effect on the consumption of the drug whose price has risen. Such effects are minor in the short run with respect to a highly addictive or dependency-producing drug like heroin or cocaine. Addicts will pay almost any price to get their drug of choice, if it is within their power to raise the money. It is true that their ability to meet the demands of their drug dependency by thefts, burglaries or prostitution has upper limits—higher for some than for others, but addicts can almost always raise the needed cash by selling drugs: as the cost of the drug they consume goes up, so also, proportionately, does the price of the drugs they sell, and hence their profits. Ironically, reasonably effective supply-side deterrents not only raise the price of the drugs, they add leverage to the incentives of drug users to become drug distributors themselves. As distributors devote more energy to drug distribution, supplies are increased and prices tend to return to where they started.

Price does have some effect, however, with marginal or casual drug users. Many of them simply do not find enough pleasure in the illegal drugs to warrant their price, especially when alcohol (which provides roughly similar euphoria) is both legal and inexpensive. Therefore, imposing higher costs on drug distributors, *all other things being equal,* probably reduces both the numbers of casual users and the amounts they use. Even that achievement has a limited effect on total consumption because casual users do not account for more than a small fraction of total drug consumption. A good rule of thumb—with most pleasure drugs, legal and illegal—is that 80 percent of the supply is consumed by the top 20 percent of users—the addicts and other compulsive abusers.[65]

But even the tendency of drug prohibition to reduce drug consumption by driving up prices can easily be exaggerated. In any drug war, some drugs are targeted as more dangerous or otherwise evil than others and receive priority emphasis from law enforcement. Less problematic drugs are neglected. Supply-side strategies aimed at priority drugs, such as cocaine today, can, if they don't elevate the prices, at least keep them from sinking precipitously, and cocaine consumption can be negatively affected. But the high cocaine prices will nudge drug users in the direction of different, neglected drugs, and the consumption of these drugs will tend to increase. As cocaine use diminished in recent years, for example, the use of LSD, methamphetamines, heroin and inhalants has reportedly edged upward. The net effect of a program that increases the prices of one drug, therefore, may not be nearly as dramatic as an isolated examination of the data dealing with that particular drug might suggest. *Overall* drug consumption can be reduced by punitive strategies (as long as they remain in effect), but much less so than is commonly assumed. Alcohol prohibition, it may be recalled, introduced some people to marijuana. Marijuana eradication turned some users on to cocaine. And, although the interdependence of alcohol and other drug consumption is complex, our present drug prohibition is probably responsible for much liquor consumption.

THE UNWINNABLE WAR

Despite alarmist claims that our culture's survival is at stake, there are myriad reasons why the supply-side drug war cannot be carried on indefinitely. The costs of such a war are astronomical, not only in money, crime, deaths and misery, but in the corruption and erosion of our constitutional system. Moreover, we are not in control of the supply; the rest of the world is. The economic viability of several Latin American countries rests on their receiving billions of dollars of drug profits. Even if that were not true, economic interests in the drug-export business are so strong that, at the very least, efforts to eradicate the crops or otherwise terminate the South American role in drugs wreaks havoc on governmental structures in the producer countries. There are limits to how far we as a nation are prepared to go to cut off supply, and there are limits to how far our neighbor nations will permit us to go. This means that no drug war will ever be anything but a limited war. Even if this were not so, however, and all-out, total war were waged, it could not help but end in failure. The reasons are few and fundamental:

1. *The Permanence of Demand.* As psychopharmacologist Ronald K. Siegel argues cogently in his book *Intoxication,* the urge for intoxication is innate in human beings (and most other animals). It is as basic as the other primal urges. It has existed in all societies. There are many ways to achieve intoxication without ingesting chemicals, but some, like skydiving and car and boat racing, are dangerous and expensive. Others, like running the marathon, are time consuming, require discipline and are sometimes painful. Some sedentary types get sufficient intoxication from sex, gambling, music, religious experience or even old-fashioned achievement. But socially approved ways of intoxication are unavailable to or don't work for many, and some are riskier or more damaging than almost any drug. Gamblers often lose their homes, jobs and families. Other adventurers, following Winston Churchill's dictum that nothing is quite so exhilarating as getting shot at and missed, get shot at and hit. Some seekers of nonchemical thrills have even discovered that self-strangulation can be exhilarating, but the point of no return is unclear to them, as many medical examiners can attest.

The lure of a chemically assisted high is powerful in American society, where a majority of us consistently, and with society's approval, get intoxicated on alcohol, and 50 million get hourly fixes on cigarettes. Whether the drug is alcohol, heroin, cocaine or another, the euphoric effects are predictable, quick and available almost any time, anywhere, with relatively little cost or risk in comparison to the alternative, nonchemical ways to achieve euphoria. The possibility that most of us will be persuaded by a drug war to surrender our appetites for chemical intoxication is nonexistent.

Even if drug-dependent users are denied access not only to their drug of choice but to their preferred substitutes, they can get by tolerably well on alcohol, and most of them do. Even if the addict is locked up in an unusual prison where drugs are not available, moreover, he will, unless successfully treated, carry a powerful addiction indefinitely. Many heroin addicts report that when imprisoned, they lost all apparent desire for heroin, but as soon as they were released, they felt a powerful craving for it. A dormant craving becomes intense when the possibility of satisfying it arises.

When people are accustomed to seeking euphoria through chemicals, that conditioning cannot be eradicated merely by denying them access to their drug of choice.

2. *The Cornucopia of Competing Drugs.* Although we commonly think of the demand for drugs like heroin as inelastic, that is, largely unresponsive to increases in price, this is true only to the extent that competing or substitute drugs are also subject to proportionate increases in price. There are, in fact, many drugs which are acceptable substitutes for heroin addicts, morphine being the most obvious. Since morphine is valuable in the practice of medicine, it and other opiates are likely to remain available as controlled drugs for the foreseeable future. Since the war is not against morphine or other opiates but against heroin (and to some extent against blackmarket pharmaceutical opiates), other opiates will become increasingly available if and as the price of heroin increases. Pharmaceutical suppliers of these controlled drugs will find their inventories diverted to the black market.

The same is true of cocaine. There are many common pharmaceutical drugs that compete on the blackmarket with cocaine for the user's affections. As the price of cocaine rises, the availability of quasi-legitimate substitutes increases to meet the newly created demand for them.

If the government's efforts at restricting supplies of cocaine and heroin ever succeeded in driving their prices much above their present levels, that achievement would be a rueful one. There would be a flock of chemical competitors to meet the demand and, in the process, exacerbate the illicit-drug problem.

The demand for cocaine can be largely met with methamphetamines, which can be, and are, domestically manufactured in basement laboratories, much as bathtub gin was produced during alcohol prohibition. The intoxication produced by crystal meth is all but indistinguishable from the high of cocaine, except that instead of lasting twenty minutes, it may last eight hours. A smokable form of methamphetamine, "ice," is on the market and competes with crack. In Hawaii, ice is reputed to be far more popular than crack.[66] Amphetamines are also the most serious drug problem today in places as diverse as Japan[67] and England.[68] The paranoia, depression, dependence, and other *sequelae* are almost certainly more common with ice than with crack.

There are also synthetic opiates that will do virtually everything for the user that heroin does, and more.[69] One of them, fentanyl, is about 50 to 500 times more powerful than heroin. It too can be manufactured in basement laboratories. (Some synthetics are up to 3,000 times the potency of heroin!)[70]

Synthetic substitutes for cocaine and heroin can also be diverted from legitimate pharmaceutical manufacturers. In 1989 an industrial chemist was arrested with 10 million doses of fentanyl is his possession, enough to supply 10,000 heroin addicts for an entire year.[71] Many of the synthetics, unlike heroin, can be prescribed and bought in a drugstore, producing opportunities for blackmarketeering through corruption of health professionals. Fentanyl, for example, a schedule II drug, is currently being marketed in a transdermal patch, like a nicotine patch. These will no doubt be immensely popular among opiate addicts. Fentanyl is a short-acting drug and, like heroin, must be replenished in the system of the addict every few hours to stave off withdrawal symptoms. The fentanyl patch will solve this problem. An addict can wear a patch inconspicuously, get a steady dose of the drug, and avoid AIDS, hepatitis and other diseases from intravenous drug consumption in the process. There is only one reason that fentanyl and other synthetic opiates are not common in the street life of addicts: these drugs cost more than heroin on the black market. If heroin prices greatly increase from present levels, fentanyl and other synthetics will quickly replace it. It may be a matter of time before the synthetics replace the plant drugs, in any event.[72]

Recreational diversion of such powerful synthetics can be deadly.

According to H. Wayne Carver II, Chief Medical Examiner of Connecticut, a batch of "heroin" hit the streets in Brooklyn on Friday evening, February 1, 1991. It was labeled with the brand name "Tango and Cash" in honor of the recently released police movie of the same name. Within hours, a user died in New York. The next morning, in Hartford, more than 100 miles away, another user died. Before the week was out, two Tango and Cash users had died in Connecticut, twelve in New Jersey and eight in New York City. By Sunday, police were patrolling affected neighborhoods warning residents through loudspeakers. Despite this, some addicts continued to ask for Tango and Cash by name, seeking the ultimate high. Subsequent analysis of the drug by the DEA disclosed that it was not heroin at all, but fentanyl, and had been diverted from a pharmaceutical source.[73]

Beyond the nearly unlimited numbers of plant and synthetic drugs that can be employed to satisfy a desire for intoxication are hundreds of common household products that aren't even "drugs." More popular among today's youngsters than cocaine—three times as many twelve-to-seventeen-year-olds have used inhalants than have used cocaine[74]—the inhalation of gases and fumes from household products is increasingly popular—and deadly—among our teenagers.[75] The practice, known as "huffing," extends to any gas under pressure, whether in a spray paint can or a can of whipped cream. Also huffed are gasoline fumes, propane, nitrous oxide (used to inflate balloons), refrigerant, Wite Out, canned "air" (Freon) used to blow dust from cameras and computers and Scotchgard, a fabric protector. Authorities estimate that there are about 1,200 common household products that can be huffed for intoxication.[76] Many of these gases and fumes are deadly. Inhalations of Freon or Scotchgard can kill the inhaler and often do.[77] Since the intoxicating effects from the use of many of these products often results from the fact that they block oxygen rather than any inherent intoxicating effects, brain damage is common. Spasms of the larynx, cardiac arrhythmia, destruction of lung tissue and kidney failure are also common. Some analysts estimate that as many as 1,200 deaths per year are attributable to inhalants.[78] The use of these products is far riskier to human health than the use of any popular recreational drug, yet since the products have legitimate and important uses, they cannot, as a practical matter, be controlled as drugs. To the extent our drug war efforts have turned youngsters away from marijuana or cocaine and on to Freon, butane and Scotchgard, we have hardly made progress.

Those who regard cocaine and heroin as a plague should realize that the worst conceivable outcome from that perspective would be for the government's interdiction/eradication efforts to succeed.

3. *Push-down/Pop-up Phenomenon.* The market for illegal drugs is like a balloon. Squeeze it here, and it bulges out over there. Ethan Nadelmann calls this the "push-down/pop-up phenomenon."[79] It has several facets:

- In the 1970s, when the French connection busts and the Nixon administration's successful diplomatic efforts to reduce Turkish heroin production disrupted traditional Middle Eastern supplies of that drug, Mexican and Southeast Asian producers quickly took over the business.[80] In the late 1970s, Colombians and domestic producers became major players in the marijuana business, when, at the behest of the United States, the Mexican government sprayed its crop with the toxic herbicide paraquat, reducing both the availability and the desirability of Mexican marijuana.[81]

  The same thing has happened with every illicit drug. The primary source of the drug is constantly shifting geographically, both in the places where the raw material is produced and the locations where the drugs are refined. Production is a moving target. At least one fourth of the planet is hospitable to the cultivation of coca or heroin. Yet most of the coca now used to make cocaine is grown in parts of only two countries, Peru and Bolivia. If eradication efforts in either of these two countries were ever moderately successful, or threatened to become such, there would be new plantings around the globe. Indeed, recent plantings have been observed in Brazil, Ecuador and Venezuela.[82] For a most recent example, the Cali cartel, the kings of cocaine distribution, have decided to diversify and have planted some 7,400 acres of opium poppies in Colombia.[83] High production—and distribution—costs and lower prices of cocaine in America and elsewhere have made branching out into another lucrative drug attractive to the Colombians.

  If the government were to achieve the impossible and temporarily stop the importation of all marijuana, cocaine and heroin, that would be an empty victory, even if it didn't produce explosive growth in the blackmarketing of synthetics. All the marijuana needed by domestic consumers can be grown here. Coca and opium poppies can be grown here, too.[84] Both could be cultivated anywhere in greenhouses, as high-grade marijuana is today. Whether domestic production of coca and opium would ever become an economically feasible source of the drug is uncertain, since it has never been necessary for drug merchants to try it. The genius of American agriculturalists, however, should not be underestimated. They learned to grow a variety of marijuana, sinsemilla, that is far more potent than the imported variety. Through further genetic manipulation and hydroponics, they have learned to grow marijuana indoors, year-round, in forms that are more than ten times as potent as the old-fashioned out-door variety. Responding to outdoor eradication and surveillance techniques, modern marijuana growers can make $250,000 per year from a single room or basement of a house.[85]

It seems likely that similar techniques could be employed in growing coca or opium poppies but they will probably never be necessary until a Star Wars device is invented that will automatically destroy all illegal coca and opium products as they cross our borders.

The point is not merely that supplies of these drugs are almost unlimited, but that sophisticated cartels can stay several jumps ahead of the eradicators and have new crops coming into production before the eradication efforts elsewhere are successful. By the time the eradicators discover that their enemy has moved and start deploying their forces to the new battleground, the enemy will move elsewhere, start new plantings and so forth. Eventually, Peru and Bolivia will be forgotten by the drug warriors, and the cocaine cartels will return there and the cycle will start over.

• When drug-war efforts against marijuana began to heat up, smugglers began to change their product mix from bulky, relatively inexpensive marijuana to concentrated, expensive cocaine. The risk/reward ratios favor the most concentrated, potent, expensive, dangerous drug. A by-product of our war against marijuana, some believe, was the beginning of the cocaine epidemic.

Interdiction is not only counterproductive in that it results in the marketing of more potent and, often, more addictive drugs, but every aspect of the drug-distribution enterprise is fluid. The enemy never digs into the trenches.

While efforts to interdict or eradicate a specific drug can, for a short time, show some signs of success, it will often result in the resurgence or discovery of another drug that had enjoyed less popularity and, partly as a result of its lack of popularity (because of diseconomies of scale), is relatively expensive and therefore more profitable to smuggle. To the extent that the drug war was responsible for a consumer movement from marijuana to cocaine, we need no more such victories.

• As we noted, the manner and means of smuggling drugs into this country are limitless. Technological advances in interdiction are slow and are usually offset by similar advances available to the smugglers. In the mid-1980s, the Reagan administration committed enormous resources to the DEA's South Florida Task Force. This made the South Florida route risky, so the smugglers moved elsewhere, mainly to our border with Mexico.[86] Changes in methods are also inherent in changes in products. Methods appropriate for smuggling marijuana are less appropriate for smuggling cocaine or heroin. But whether the changes are deliberately tactical or more related to the nature of the cargo, the effect is to make interdiction efforts more difficult. Moreover, as in the case of the ability to alter places of production or refining for the drugs, the variability in smuggling methods greatly increases the costs and decreases the effectiveness of law-enforcement intelligence. Most of the information that is acquired from informants is obsolete soon after, if not before, it is bought.

Two Demand-Reduction Strategies

In addition to the supply-reduction strategies, the *National Drug Control Strategy* also includes two major demand-reduction strategies. We attempt to decrease drug demand by:

• penalizing drug use;[87]
• reducing drug demand through public education and treatment of drug abusers.[88]

STRATEGY 5: PENALIZING USERS

Although compassion seems to be a rare commodity in a country that tolerates the homelessness of millions of its people, some Americans probably still think that drug addicts are worthy of pity. Such Americans would probably like to believe that police and prosecutors spend

most of their time chasing drug dealers, while referring their victims—
the users—to social workers and treatment centers. In fact, the opposite is true. The vast majority of drug defendants are apparently users,
not dealers. During each year of the 1980s about 75 percent of drug
arrests were for mere possession, while only about 25 percent were for
drug trafficking.[89] The user, not the dealer, bears the brunt of domestic
drug-war strategy.*

To suggest, as many do, that drug users are as responsible for the
deterioration of our drug-choked, crime-ridden cities as are the smugglers and dealers, makes pragmatic sense if you are a drug warrior
trying to persuade others that you are winning the war by arresting
users. It makes theoretical sense if there is no moral difference between
buying a drug for your own use and selling that drug—even a large
quantity—to another. Yet the more the user's and the seller's moral
responsibilities are equated, the less evil the seller appears, for there
are millions of casual illicit-drug users who are otherwise law-abiding
citizens, good parents, even public servants. Most of them do not have
criminal records and are not otherwise involved in criminal activities.
Prosecution of drug users, therefore, may undermine or confuse the
moral message sought to be imparted by criminal prosecutions.

The standard argument supporting the criminal culpability of drug
users is that they provide the market for the drug distributors: if there
were no buyers, there would be no sellers; no drugs would be available. Whether such an argument is profound or specious, however, it
probably has little to do with the disproportionate presence of drug
possessors in the arrest statistics. Rather than reflecting a considered
comparison and equation of the culpability of drug users and drug
dealers, the data reflect the relative ease of making arrests for mere
possession. In a nation of 26 million illicit-drug users (used within past
year),[90] drivers whose cars are searched, for any reason, are often
found to possess illicit drugs. Pedestrians, strollers or loiterers who
are frisked, for any reason, are often carrying drugs. In many high-
intensity drug areas in the inner cities, both drug commerce and drug
use are conducted in the open. If there is a sweep, it is likely to catch
many more users than dealers, not only because there are far greater
numbers of them but because possession is much easier to prove than
trafficking. A simple physical fact makes the case: the presence of illicit

---

*Some of those arrested for possession were probably dealers, but there is no basis for believing
that the majority of them were.

drugs on or near the accused. Drug-trafficking prosecutions, in contrast, require costly investigation, undercover infiltration of drug dealerships, careful monitoring of drug purchases and serious risks to human life.

No one can seriously contend that arresting 3 percent of our drug users every year saps the vitality of the drug business or otherwise makes a substantial contribution to the war effort.

There is little evidence that punishing casual use of drugs has any significant effect on either demand or supply of the drug. As John Kaplan observed, the marijuana laws provide a dramatic illustration of the ineffectiveness of user punishment. In recent years, eleven states repealed their criminalization of small-scale possession and use of marijuana. Several studies show that such repeals "had no discernible effect on the number of users or on their frequency of use. In those states which repealed their laws creating use crimes, marijuana use increased no more than it did in comparable states which continued to apprehend and prosecute users."[91]

Punishing drug addicts cannot have any important effects on their demand for drugs since, as addicts, they are not responsive to threats. Casual drug users, on the other hand, could in theory be influenced to give up or reduce their consumption of illegal drugs if they ran a serious risk of criminal punishment for casual drug use. Since most casual drug users are middle class, in school or employed, and have social and economic stakes in society, the risk of a drug arrest and a jail term could be a weighty factor, along with the price of the drugs, entering into their cost/benefit calculations. Such risks, however, are minuscule. Middle- or upper-class drug users can avoid open purchase, use or possession of their drug of choice. They can send an emissary to the inner-city market to buy enough drugs for their social group, or even arrange to conduct the transaction in an unlikely area for a drug deal. As a consequence, the drug user who would be deterred by criminal prosecution is almost never arrested for drug use. There are, for example, at least 20 million white users of illicit drugs.[92] If we assume that the average white drug-user possesses illicit drugs sixty days during the year, then out of 1.2 billion drug possessions by this group, there are fewer than 500,000 arrests,[93] an arrest rate of about 1/2400. Such a risk appears to many to approximate the chance of being hit by lightning. It is not a significant deterrent to casual drug use, even among the potentially most deterrable group of users.

Punishment of drug users who are not dealers is a serious misallocation of law-enforcement resources. Even though much less costly than the prosecution of drug traffickers, prosecuting drug users is still very costly. Unless the arrested users are frequently convicted and imprisoned, the user prosecutions trivialize the crime and undermine any deterrent effect that might be expected. If users are often jailed, however, the space they occupy must be found by freeing a drug trafficker, a robber or a rapist. Little is gained; much is lost by such a process.

The only way that prosecutions of users could have any important impact on drug demand or supply would be to step them up dramatically, so that criminal prosecution was a significant risk of using drugs. Instead of 750,000 arrests, we might need 5 million. There would be no room in our overstuffed jails and prisons for such defendants and the results would be politically intolerable.

While the usual rationale for blaming drug users for the drug problem is that they provide a market for the despised products of the drug trafficker, President Bush's 1992 *National Drug Control Strategy* suggested a different basis. According to that document, the casual user "bears a major responsibility for the spread of drug use, because that person imparts the message that you can use drugs and still do well in school or maintain a career and family."[94] Accordingly, the *Strategy* tautologically concludes, we must make sure that the message imparted is untrue: we must damage the users' lives by "providing clear consequences for possessing or using illegal drugs."[95]

In the service of that enterprise, the *Strategy* recommends not only that we criminally punish users, but that we punish them civilly and socially as well. Among the required or recommended techniques are not only civil forfeitures, but eviction from public housing,[96] firm antidrug policies in public schools and higher education,[97] employer drug testing and loss of employment for those failing the tests,[98] denial of federal benefits such as student financial aid, pilot's licenses, and so forth.[99] States are also encouraged to deny benefits to convicted drug users and to impose other sanctions.[100]

Even if it ever became feasible—because the drug war had reached the hysterical state—to deny federal and state benefits to those convicted or suspected of drug use—this outlawry approach to social problems, reminiscent of the ways of the Puritans, would be dubious indeed. Our most serious drug abusers are those with little education, few job skills, little or no income from legitimate employment, few connections to mainstream society. In short, they are most in need of governmental assistance. The civil and societal sanctions proposed by the 1992 *Drug Control Strategy*, explicitly designed to wreck the user's life, could not have been better designed to turn casual users into addicts or to keep addicts from controlling their addiction. If we ever take seriously this part of the strategy, we will be in the kamikaze stage of the drug war.

STRATEGY 6: TREATMENT AND EDUCATION

Treatment and education, both essentially nonpunitive, constitute the second basic demand-reduction strategy. It is the only strategy that poses any possibility of fundamentally altering America's appetite for chemical euphoria and therefore the only strategy that contains the slightest basis for optimism. It is, however, the last in line when funds are allocated. During the 1980s and 1990s, federal expenditures for enforcement and interdiction consistently have absorbed 70 percent of the federal drug budget.

We deal separately in the final chapter with what is promising, what works, what doesn't work, and what remains to be learned about drug education and treatment. It is sufficient to note here that many aspects of the drug war are inconsistent with enduring drug education. A state of war traditionally produces and justifies propaganda or "disinformation." The war metaphor therefore explains and to some extent justifies the government's lengthy history of lies about drugs. Marijuana was said to create crazed killers, then to produce inert masses of laziness, devoid of energy, useless. Heroin too went through a phase of being the crazed-killer drug. That crown has now been transferred to crack cocaine. Said to be instantly addictive and to create homicidal maniacs, crack is now the drug to be feared above all others. Not only does the government propagate such falsehoods, it pays millions of dollars a year to have them, or similar fictions, supported by "scientific research." It then urges schools to inculcate powerful fears of illicit drugs. To some extent, at least in the short run, such warlike propaganda may be effective in persuading its audience to accept such audacious claims. (Many of us were even convinced by the government in World War II that Americans of Japanese ancestry were traitors and thus should be interned without accusation, proof or trial.) Eventually, however, if it consistently lies, the government loses its credibility on drug issues. Few of our youngsters believe what they are "taught" about drugs because they or others whom they trust know otherwise. The government has cried wolf too often.

Much money is expended on drug "education," but not enough is spent on objective efforts to determine the truth about illicit drugs and to inform our youth and our public about the truth. If we end the war, and treat the drug problem as a public health problem, integrating it into other health and safety education programs, we can hope to have some lasting successes. We will never eliminate recreational-drug use, but we may achieve a society that is more willing and able to seek intoxication in healthier, less antisocial ways than many of us now do.

Treatment programs are shockingly underfunded in the otherwise bloated drug-war budget. By the government's own estimate, there are at least 2.77 million drug users in America "who need and can benefit from drug treatment."[101] There are, however, fewer than 600,000 "slots" in the nation's treatment system.[102] The delays between the expression of a desire for treatment and the opening of an available slot are unconscionable, running as much as a year in some areas. In keeping with its generally negative attitude toward governmental support of health care, the 1991 *President's Drug Strategy* asserted that "paying for drug treatment has been and must largely remain the responsibility of individuals, third-party insurers, private organizations, and State and local governments."[103] As a result, the federal government pays for only about one fourth of drug treatment, the states pay for another fourth, and private sources pay for the other half.[104] This is hardly a sensible approach to a problem that ostensibly warrants the waging of war. The Clinton administration has a much more favorable attitude toward governmental support of health care and is publicly committed to "treatment on demand." However, that attitude has been slow to translate into greater financial support for drug treatment.

Apart from its stingy allocations of funds to support drug treatment, the drug war is, in some respects, inconsistent with the goals of treatment. The intensive criminalization of both drug trafficking and drug use provides a deterrent against voluntary efforts to obtain treatment. It also overlays the stigma of criminality upon the stigma of disease: the drug addict is simultaneously both a serious criminal and seriously sick. Since, as some have asserted, the best treatment for many drug addicts may be a good job, doubly stigmatizing drug-dependent users hardly helps them get that job and rehabilitate their lives.

Like most aspects of the drug problem, however, there is another perspective. When discussing the criminalization of drug users, we noted that part of the strategy is to wreck the lives of users to demonstrate that even casual use of drugs is devastating to the user's life. Since there is nothing inherent in the use of drugs that warrants such a claim, the drug warriors must make it true by inflicting the horrible consequences that drug use does not itself impose on the user.

That perspective also has a perverse treatment rationale. As John Kaplan noted, criminal punishment of addicts helps to reduce them to "a sorry state" where they recognize their need for treatment.[105] This notion is reminiscent of the Vietnam war, where an officer justified the decision to bomb a town by telling reporter Peter Arnett, "In order to save the town, it became necessary to destroy it."[106] If destroying addicts in order to save them doesn't persuade them that they need help, criminal punishment can provide strong leverage to coerce participation in a treatment program. The addict can be given the choice of submitting to treatment or going to jail. The strategy has been responsible for many treatment successes. It is, however, a misallocation of scarce treatment resources, since it artificially inflates and thus prioritizes the treatment needs of the 3 percent or so of users who get caught, to the disadvantage of the remaining 97 percent, many of whose lives are already in shabby shape and who remain outside the treatment system.

Chapter 12

The Legalization Option

"How can you conserve the basic values, how can you conserve the fabric of your life if you do not have the courage to change when what you're doing is tearing the heart out of your country?"

Presidential candidate Bill Clinton, in a speech to the National Urban League, San Diego, July 27, 1992[1]

Drug prohibition has not worked in the past, does not work now and will not work in the future. Recognition of that truth eventually will force drug-policy makers to legalize or at least de facto decriminalize the drugs now prohibited. What are the benefits and costs of the legalization option?

Benefits

Legalization will lead to at least eight beneficial outcomes:

Benefit Number One: A Saving of $200 Billion or More per Year

The federal, state and local governments spend about $100 billion a year on law-enforcement and criminal-justice programs. About $35

231

billion of that is directly related to drug-law enforcement. Probably another $15 billion is related to crimes committed to obtain drug money or is otherwise systemically related to drug commerce. Hence, about $50 billion per year spent on law enforcement could be saved if drugs were legalized.

As Gore Vidal put it, "fighting drugs is nearly as big a business as pushing them."[2] Drug legalization threatens the jobs and career trajectories of police officers and politician-drug warriors. Defense attorneys and prosecutors, who make their living on drug cases, will also lose from drug legalization. Drug Enforcement Administration (DEA) officer Michael Levine exaggerated when he told CBS News: "The whole drug war is a political grab bag, in that everybody has got their arm in looking for that political jackpot that will either win them an election, win them a lucrative position as a consultant or you name it,"[3] but serious de-escalation of the drug war—to say nothing of legalization—does threaten tens of thousands of careers that the taxpayers would no longer need to support. That is a major impediment to legalization. Nonetheless, many law-enforcement officers are well ahead of politicians in recognizing the futility and economic wastefulness of the drug war. As Robert Stutman, previously a high official of the DEA, says, "Those of us who carry a badge learned a long time ago we're not going to solve the problem, and yet an awful lot of policy makers continue to depend on us, and we keep telling them we can't do it."[4]

Ralph Salerno, a famous organized-crime expert and long-time drug warrior himself, goes further. He says that the drug war not only "will never work" but that police on the front line, risking their lives and their physical, psychological and moral health, "are being lied to, just as I was lied to 20 years ago."[5] Among the lies:

[P]olice officers and all other Americans are being told by our political leaders that if the coca crop in Peru and Bolivia can be curtailed it will be all over, ignoring the botanical fact that coca can be grown in many parts of the world. We are told that if the chemicals can be cut off from the purification plants in Colombia it will all be over. The chemicals are derivatives of the oil industry and there are wells in many parts of the world. We are told that if we can incarcerate the Medellin and Cali cartels it will all be over, and that is another lie. The Latin American *narcotraficantes* will be replaced by others as easily as were the American mafiosi.[6]

The waste of the public fisc on law enforcement pales in comparison to the costs of the drug war borne by individual citizens. Estimates of the yearly earnings of the illicit-drug business range as high as $100 billion. Sixty billion dollars may be a conservative estimate. Thus, if the principal recreational drugs were legal, drug consumers might save $60 to $100 billion each year.

Although nonusers may have difficulty sympathizing with a program that would make drug use more economical, in fact nonusers have a personal financial stake in drastic reductions in drug prices. Nonusers provide much of the money spent on drugs when they are innocent victims of crime. If $10 billion of the money spent to buy drugs comes from stolen tangible property—a rough estimate—property owners may lose $50 billion worth of property to provide the thieves with $10 billion in cash or equivalents with which to buy drugs (stolen property is sold at steep discounts). Nonusers also indirectly bear much of the cost of high drug prices when they pay high premiums for theft insurance, when they purchase security systems, when they pay high taxes for police protection and when they pay a premium to live in gated communities or suburbs. Inner-city landlords pay when their tenants move out to escape the hellishness of their surroundings.

Those users who do not perpetrate property crimes must spend their legitimate earnings on drugs. This often deprives their families of the money needed to survive. The non-drug-using public ends up paying for much of that distress, too. Welfare and public-health budgets also bear heavy burdens. Much of the $60 billion or more collected by drug traffickers from customers comes indirectly from the pockets of nonusers.

Adding the money squandered on the ineffective drug-suppression activities of state and federal governments to the money we all lose as a result of the unnaturally high price of drugs, the total probably would come to well over $150 billion per year, perhaps twice that. Drug legalization could save us most of that cost.

Moreover, as we observed in Chapter 6, drug prohibition is a major contributor to the destruction of our inner cities. Drug legalization could produce an increase in property values in the cities that would make all other savings minuscule in comparison. In city after city over the past several decades, hundreds of millions of dollars have been spent to "revitalize" or "renew" the inner city. Much of that money and most of the renewal projects only decelerated the decline that continued, apparently inexorably. Eliminating drug prohibition and the crime and insecurity it causes would do more to make the cities livable than everything spent on urban renewal in the past half century. The resulting increases in property values could number in the trillions of dollars.

Legalization will not alone solve the problem of inner-city decay and disintegration. It could even temporarily exacerbate the problem in some areas, where many of the residents survive on the drug trade: they sell drugs not only to other inner-city residents but, directly and indirectly, to white upper-class suburbanites.[7] While it saps resources from virtually every user sector, the drug trade also produces an important flow of money from the suburbs to sections of the inner city. Government and private agencies will have to replace some of that urban income in the form of jobs, training programs, public assistance and other investments in human capital. Even if the menace of drug-related crime is eliminated, the residents of the inner city must still have jobs, housing and quality schools in order for the cities to prosper. What legalization promises is a climate in which such basic elements for survival—and prosperity—are possible.

Benefit Number Two: Reduced Crime and Safer Neighborhoods

The full costs of drug-prohibition crimes are measured in lives lost, neighborhoods destroyed, families shattered and the psychological penalties of living in a police state required to "protect" a society under siege. In neighborhoods both rich and poor, the specter of crime is omnipresent. In America's most disadvantaged neighborhoods, open-air drug markets and gang violence related to drug-turf battles make life miserable. Possibly as much as half of our violent and property crimes—certainly a very large portion—would be eliminated by legalization.

The present prohibitionist policy has created a distorted and perverse economy in our inner cities. For the youngster growing up there, the models of upward mobility are not people who go to school to learn professions and trades, but drug peddlers who flash expensive jewelry and clothing. An enormous amount of human capital is being wasted. In the most obscene cases, children not yet in their teens are recruited as gofers and even assassins for drug gangs because they work cheaply and their juvenile status makes them immune to the full force of the law. An end to prohibition would remove both the model of the criminal entrepreneur and many of the incentives for infantile criminality. A reallocation of resources from drug interdiction to education and economic development of the inner city could create role models consistent with the high value our country places on the work ethic.

When the illicit drug business leaves the cities, our homes, streets and schools will become far safer. It may even become possible to educate children in urban public schools.

Benefit Number Three: Elimination of Drug-Related Corruption and Waste

Our drug laws are a major source of the corruption of public officials and law-enforcement officers. Respect for law is impossible when corruption is ubiquitous. Legalization would make a great source of official temptation disappear overnight.

Even if all public officials and law-enforcement officers were scrupulously honest, the war on drugs still would be extremely wasteful. Seizure of the assets of drug suspects is an example of the sort of drug-war inefficiency that is draining the national economy. One would think that the authority to take property without any due process would make drug-enforcement largely self-sustaining, if not actually profitable. However, this is not the case. The government's cash and noncash seizures in 1991 amounted to just over one billion dollars, or only 8.5 percent of the $12.5 billion the federal government spent on drug programs that year.[8]

Cash comprises only a fraction of the total appraised value of the assets seized. In 1991, approximately 64 percent of the dollar value of forfeitures was attributable to *non*cash assets—real estate, airplanes, motor vehicles, boats, negotiable instruments, jewelry.[9] When disposed of, these assets return a tiny fraction of their appraised value. General Accounting Office (GAO) investigators told Congress that the United States Customs actually lost money on over two thirds of the noncash items it seized between June 1987 and June 1989.[10]

How are such losses possible?

Customs had to remit $302 million worth of noncash, drug-war booty to the people from whom it was unjustly, illegally or improperly seized, and incurred storage and handling costs of $7.7 million in the process. Because so much of that property was seized illegally or taken from completely innocent bystanders, Customs was only able to charge remittees for $4.5 million of the handling costs, thereby realizing a net loss of $3.2 million on the returned property. Another $37.6 million worth of illegitimate seizures was "canceled" before Customs actually took possession, resulting in a loss of another $100,000 in handling costs.

Much of the property seized by Customs was worthless junk that was destroyed rather than sold, although its official appraised value came to $29 million. For instance, many of the automobiles seized by the customs service are in fact old clunkers that seizure-wary drug couriers tend to drive rather than the flashy cars we see in movies and on television.[11]

Customs keeps some of the property it seizes, and it gives some of that property to state and local law-enforcement agencies. Customs and the agencies also directly use the boats, vehicles and other equipment they retain. Accordingly, during the period covered by the GAO report, customs retained (or gave to other police agencies) property that had an appraised value of $27.8 million. From the administrative costs and from an estimated rate of return on other assets that have been sold, the GAO calculates that the federal and state governments' net gain on those $27.8 million worth of property was only $7.2 million.

During the two years covered by the GAO report, Customs managed to auction off less than 10 percent of the property it seized. But even then the financial waste was catastrophic. Contractors for the Customs Service sold $42.8 million worth of real estate, automobiles, boats, airplanes, jewelry, and appliances, but the taxpayer netted only $7.4 million or 17.2 percent of the property's appraised value. (One of the worst horror stories told to Congress involved a $170,000 boat that was sold for $13,500.[12]) Marketing and advertising costs—largely paid to government contractors—also contributed greatly to the government's losses on the Customs sales. And the government's warehousing costs are outrageous; the Customs Service has paid as much as $360 per month, for as long as a year, to store $1,000 drug boats.[13] The GAO reported that the U.S. Customs Service *lost* an average of $204 on each automobile seized, in the first three quarters of 1989.[14]

The final box score, according to GAO: "Property appraised at $438.9 million provided a return of 2 cents per dollar."[15] Only the government could perform so disastrously on a retail business for which all the merchandise is stolen from suppliers.

Legalization would put a stop to all this nonsense because it would terminate the property forfeitures.

Benefit Number Four: Room in Jails and Prisons for Real Criminals

About one third of the prisoners now stuffed into our penal institutions would not be there if it were no longer a crime to possess or traffic in the presently illicit drugs. An additional proportion of the other convicts—possibly another quarter—are in prison for property crimes committed to support drug habits. Still others are there for crimes of violence related to the drug business. If the drug-prohibition burden that has been superimposed on our penal system were removed, then the institutions would be available to punish the perpetrators of the sorts of crimes that truly threaten our security and freedom such as rape, murder, robbery and burglary.[16]

Benefit Number Five: Enhanced Public Health

Chapter 10 discusses various ways that drug prohibition deprives us of the medicinal use of marijuana, heroin and other drugs. That chapter also described how drug prohibition makes the inevitable use of psychotropic drugs more dangerous. Most overdoses and drug poisonings are attributable to the operation of the illicit market, not to the inherent qualities of drugs. Further, needle sharing by intravenous drug users now does as much or more to spread HIV and hepatitis infections as do unsafe sexual practices. And America's drug puritanism has widely blocked the implementation of clean-needle programs that clearly reduce the spread of AIDS and other deadly diseases.[17] Drug prohibition has also kept drug users from seeking treatment for many other medical conditions, many of which are communicable. The illegal status of drugs even makes it more difficult for drug abusers to seek treatment for drug addiction, the very condition that often inspires them to commit the crimes of drug possession and trafficking.

If drugs are legalized, the dangers to physical health from using heroin, cocaine, marijuana or other previously illegal drugs would be *greatly* reduced. Even if such drug use were to increase by a factor of two or three, the deaths and diseases caused by such drug use would still be lower than they are now. Also, since the economic factors pushing producers, traffickers and users toward more concentrated, more deadly and more addictive drugs would be eliminated by legalization, one can expect many users to confine their drug consumption to highly diluted forms, just as consumers of alcohol more often drank beer before and after alcohol prohibition than they did during Prohibition. This alone will greatly reduce the health risks and the addictive potential of drug use under a legalized system. If drug purities were standardized and clearly and accurately labeled, the likelihood of a person accidentally overdosing would be much less than it is under the present regime.

Legalizing heroin, cocaine and marijuana would probably produce a net reduction in the use of tobacco and alcohol, saving thousands of lives every year, perhaps tens of thousands. This reduction would come from two sources. First, as prohibitionists commonly argue, legalizing the illegal drugs would convey a message that the legal and illegal drugs are in the same socio-cultural-medical family. Some of the billions that the government has spent trying to convince us that illegal drugs are immoral, suicidal, treasonous, dumb and so forth will be symbolically transferred to legal drugs, causing some potential drinkers or smokers to think long and hard before using or abusing those drugs as well. Second, many of the illegal drugs are substitutes for alcohol, and vice versa. Studies demonstrate that when access to alcohol is restricted—as when the drinking age was raised from eighteen to twenty-one—there is a substantial corresponding increase in the consumption of marijuana, not otherwise explainable.[18] This strongly suggests that increased availability of marijuana would reduce alcohol consumption.

Similarly, when heroin addicts are deprived of heroin, they become alcohol abusers.[19] Making heroin more available would probably decrease the number of alcohol abusers. If legalization produces an increase in the consumption of illegal drugs, some of the increase may represent a transfer from alcohol or even tobacco. To the extent the switch is into marijuana, that would be a major plus, as far as health is concerned, and that could even be true of a switch from alcohol or tobacco to cocaine or heroin, hard as that may be for some to accept.[20] But even if no such transfers from legal to previously illegal drugs occurred, the first factor mentioned above might produce a reduction in smoking and drinking.

Benefit Number Six: Restored Civil Liberties and Respect for Law

Americans are less free than they were before drug prohibition began in 1914. Each year, as some supposed "loophole" used by drug dealers is closed, we all lose important civil liberties. Many Americans are persuaded by the claims of drug police and prosecutors that we must sacrifice constitutional safeguards in order to keep drug felons from escaping on "technicalities." However, the "technicalities" are the substance of our liberty, which took a revolution to establish. If drugs were legalized, there would be much less reason for police and prosecutors to seek, and for courts and legislatures to provide, easier standards for imposing criminal punishment, forfeitures and other deprivations of fundamental freedom.

Ridding our courts of the glut of drug and drug-related criminal cases will permit them to attend to civil matters, largely neglected in our escalated drug war. People who are injured in automobile or other accidents or are the victims of malpractice, fraud, rape or battery won't have to wait five to ten years for a court decision. Defendants who are accused of crime may once again entertain an expectation of getting a fair trial. Those who are convicted can even hope to obtain a fair and honest review of their convictions by courts of appeal.

Benefit Number Seven: Drug Prosecutions Will No Longer Destroy the Lives of Otherwise Productive Citizens

Most users of presently illegal drugs, like most users of tobacco and alcohol, are productive, generally law-abiding people. But making their drug consumption a serious crime makes it harder for them to be so, and makes it impossible for some to be so—those who are socially and economically marginal to begin with. Legalizing drugs would greatly increase the capacity of the 26 million users of presently illicit drugs to be productive citizens.

About 500,000 of our jail and prison inmates are there for illegal-drug or drug-related offenses. Possibly as many as 300,000 would not be there if drug prohibition were repealed because they would not be criminals under legalization. They would be available to their spouses and children, helping to raise families left parentless by imprisonment. Many of these people would be useful members of society rather than embittered criminals wracked with rage over their unjust punishment. No one who gets a prison term of any duration for using drugs and no one who gets a twenty-year prison term, or even a five-year term, for selling drugs to a willing buyer is likely to be persuaded that his punishment was deserved. Hundreds of thousands of Americans who might otherwise be integrated into the mainstream of society have that possibility virtually eliminated by a combination of embitterment and societal stigma, rendering their acceptance of and by the mainstream unlikely. This appalling waste of human lives, which far exceeds any plausible cost of illegal-drug use, would be eliminated by legalization.

Benefit Number Eight: Users Will Bear Most of the Costs

When reformers were lobbying for drug prohibition early in the twentieth century, they justified their proposal on the ground that it would protect drug users from the damage caused by their own folly or depravity. The prohibition laws obviously do not prevent moderately determined drug buyers from harming themselves with drugs, and in the waning years of the twentieth century, compassion for the less fortunate has become an increasingly difficult commodity to sell to the American public anyway. Hence, the major justification that prohibitionists now offer for continuing prohibition is that it protects *non*-users from harm. The harm that the prohibitionists wish to spare us takes two forms: victimization by crime and financial loss. Yet, we already have described how prohibition *causes* both categories of harm, rather than protecting us from them.

One of the most ironic consequences of prohibition is that it virtually guarantees that innocent victims will pay the financial cost of the harm that prohibition unsuccessfully seeks to prevent. This is because no taxes are collected on drug commerce, and law enforcement does everything it can to pauperize drug users, so they are not financially responsible for any of the damage they cause.

Scholars who study the relationship of law and economics have coined the term "cost externalization" to describe phenomena akin to this consequence of prohibition.[21] When the costs of a commodity are internalized, those who profit from producing the commodity are required to pay the costs for the damage that the commodity causes. Thus, when manufacturers are forced to pay for injuries caused by defective products, that particular cost of the enterprise has been internalized. To the extent that motorists, automobile manufacturers and oil companies pay less than the full costs of road construction, use of land for parking, automobile accidents and the damage caused by air pollution, they have externalized the costs of the activity from which they benefit.

As matters stand under drug prohibition, drug users and sellers can externalize almost all the harm costs of their activity. Prohibitionist propaganda over the past few years has suggested that asset forfeitures compensate the government for drug-enforcement costs. However, we saw earlier that the government actually loses money on many seizures, and makes little on most, so sellers and users even externalize the costs of enforcing prohibition. The general taxpayer picks up most of the tab. No tax money comes in from drug commerce to pay for the costs of drug education and treatment of drug abusers. Drug sellers and buyers pay no direct tax to offset the medicaid and welfare costs of supporting impoverished addicts. Drug dealers don't even pay income taxes on their profits.

Harvard Medical School professor Lester Grinspoon has proposed that America institute "harm taxes" to internalize some of the costs for the damage done by drugs.[22] His proposal is consistent with recent efforts to increase taxes on legal drugs, in order to internalize some of the harm caused by alcohol and tobacco. For instance, in 1988, California voters approved Proposition 99,[23] a referendum that imposed a quarter-per-pack tax increase on cigarettes and dedicated the revenue to antismoking public education and other measures to alleviate tobacco harm. Dr. Grinspoon's measure would work with regard to the now-contraband drugs only if they were legalized. Indeed, one of the principal benefits to be realized from drug legalization would be the ability to tax drugs so their harm costs might be partly internalized.

RISKS (COSTS) OF LEGALIZATION

Increased Consumption of Presently Illegal Drugs

Drug consumption could soar under legalization. Yet that prospect is extremely unlikely. Legalizing drugs would not be a reckless experiment.

During most of its history, this country had no drug prohibition, and drug abuse was never worse than it is now. There are few countries in the history of the world that ever had a majority of their populations hooked on any drug other than tobacco, and when they did, it was alcohol. Drugs are still at least de facto legal on much of the globe, as they have been throughout most of human history; yet if there is or ever has been a country that has 10 percent of its population abusing cocaine or heroin, we have not heard of it. Although there are legal prohibitions against drug trafficking in our neighbor to the south, Mexico, there is no serious enforcement against local distribution or consumption. Mexico is a major source of marijuana and heroin, and a major transshipment point for cocaine. The country is awash in inexpensive drugs. Yet our own State Department says that Mexico "does not have a serious drug problem."[24] Regular, heavy use of strong psychoactive do-it-yourself drugs is either an effort to treat mental illness or an effort to escape pain and despair, or both. The notion that any drug, if freely available, will enslave an entire population has no basis in fact or theory. It is prohibitionist fantasy.

Recent Netherlands experience suggests that abandoning suppression efforts need not even produce new users. That country de facto decriminalized marijuana. While possession and use of marijuana technically is still a crime in Holland, one can purchase hashish and marijuana there with impunity. Some Amsterdam cafés blatantly feature various forms of cannabis on their menus, and municipal recreational facilities for teenagers can sell as much as thirty grams to their young patrons without being prosecuted.[25] According to a 1989 report by the United States Embassy in the Hague[26] and a 1985 report by the Dutch government,[27] marijuana consumption in the Netherlands has *decreased* substantially since the decriminalization.

At various times, eleven American states more or less decriminalized possession and use of marijuana.[28] Yet marijuana consumption has declined at approximately the same rate in the states that decriminalized it as consumption has declined elsewhere in the United States.[29]

Marijuana has decreased in the Netherlands and in states that decriminalized for the same reasons its use has declined in places that have retained prohibition. People stopped using marijuana, or use it to a lesser extent, because "pot smoking" is simply less fashionable than it once was, and because of heightened health consciousness. What these experiences demonstrate is that extralegal, psychosocial forces account for changes in patterns of drug consumption far more than do prohibition efforts; that official suppression—or lack thereof—is a relatively uninfluential factor in drug-use trends and patterns. This is corroborated by a random telephone survey of 1,401 American adults conducted in 1990. Of those Americans polled, fewer than 1 in 100 who had not tried cocaine would do so if it were legal.[30]

Since eliminating (or greatly shrinking) the black market in drugs is the main object of legalization, drug prices under a system of legalization, even though taxed, must be kept much lower than they are now.

When most commodities become cheaper, more people use them and those who used them before use more of them. That is true to some extent when the commodity is a pleasure drug. We observed that with the invention of crack in the mid-1980s, when the cost of a cocaine high was drastically reduced, bringing in hordes of new users. In July 1992, *The New York Times* reported that due in part to the recent abundance of heroin and cocaine (despite decades of drug war aimed at preventing it), drug dealers had cut the price of a $10 or "dime" bag of heroin to $5 and, in some parts of the city, reduced the price of a dose of crack to an all-time low of 75 cents.[31] New York authorities believe that the reduced prices also accompanied increases in the numbers of both new users and abusers of cocaine. Heroin use also increased as prices declined, because users could afford to snort heroin rather than inject it and thus avoided the risk of AIDS and several other diseases related to intravenous drug use. Several studies show that the price of cigarettes—our most addictive drug—has a measurable impact upon consumption, especially long term: the higher the price, other things being equal, the less tobacco is smoked.[32] Reducing the amount of money it takes to buy a dose of a drug is not the only cost reduction to the user contemplated by legalization. The user under legalization will no longer be a felon for using drugs and will no longer feel pressured to commit crimes in order to pay for the drugs used. Thus, in a broad sense, the "price" of drug use under legalization will be vastly reduced. There is undoubtedly a causal relationship between drug usage and drug prices, especially over the short term.

Legalizing the use of a drug that was previously criminal is also likely to have some influence in the direction of increasing consumption beyond its effects on the availability of drugs. Laws still have some impact upon the behavior of some citizens, even if such laws are widely disregarded by large segments of society. While legalizing drugs is not a statement that using drugs is desirable—the government regularly propagandizes against many activities that are legal, including smoking, dropping out of school, unsafe sex and so forth—legalization can be interpreted by some potential drug users as withdrawing condemnation, even as morally equating the use of newly legalized drugs with those already legal, such as tobacco and alcohol. This too can have a contributing influence on the consumption of previously illegal drugs (and, as noted earlier, a negative influence on consumption of previously legal drugs).

There is, therefore, a substantial likelihood that, *all other things remaining equal,* legalization will be accompanied by an increase in the consumption of newly legalized drugs. But there is also little reason, and no support in what followed the repeal of alcohol prohibition, to suggest that legalizing the illegal drugs would produce a huge increase in the numbers of users of pleasure drugs or, more important, the numbers of *abusers* of such drugs. One who neither smokes tobacco nor drinks alcohol is extremely unlikely to become a user of any of the other pleasure drugs (caffeine aside). While there are surely some teetotalers or occasional light drinkers who would become addicted to heroin or cocaine under a system of legalization, their numbers are almost certainly small. The major reasons why people desist from smoking and drinking—health, social stigma, morality, aesthetics—are also applicable to other pleasure drugs.

The potential new users of legalized drugs are therefore people who are now deterred by the price of these drugs or by the criminality of their use, but who nonetheless drink or smoke cigarettes.* To the extent that such persons were to substitute newly legalized pleasure drugs for tobacco or alcohol, they would be better off from a bodily health standpoint, and so would those who come into contact with them. Cocaine or heroin users do not pollute the air and rarely beat up their spouses or children while intoxicated on those drugs.

Most of the people who would abuse cocaine or heroin if it were legalized, but who do not now abuse these drugs, are already abusing alcohol, killing themselves and others by the tens of thousands every year. They would be less likely to kill themselves with drugs if they used less alcohol, even if they used more cocaine or heroin, and would be much less likely to kill the rest of us.[33]

It seems clear that increased consumption of marijuana or heroin, all other conditions remaining the same, will result in a reduction in the consumption of alcohol. The psychoactive effects of such drugs are sufficiently similar to alcohol, among a large number of users, that they are to a substantial extent substitutes. What is less clear is whether such a relationship exists between cocaine and alcohol. A great many cocaine users also consume alcohol while taking cocaine; the two drugs are apparently complementary, one being a depressant

---

*Many nonusers—even though they smoke or drink—may also be deterred by the health risk of drug use, which would be greatly reduced under any rational system of legalization. Offsetting that factor, however, is that drugs would contain labels warning of the dangers of using the particular drug. Thus, drugs would be safer under legalization but their residual dangers would be better known and effectively advertised.

and the other a stimulant. Alcohol, which is cheap, may augment the effects of cocaine, which is expensive. Alcohol thus seems to play a role similar to that of Hamburger Helper. It is not as good as the real thing, but it helps to stretch out the real thing with tolerable diluting effects. We think it is likely, however, that increased use of cocaine will not be accompanied by an increased use of alcohol but rather a reduction. If cocaine is inexpensive, as it would be under legalization, there would be little incentive to use alcohol as a stretcher or helper of cocaine. More important, perhaps, combining either heroin and cocaine with alcohol is dangerous. Most deaths from "overdoses" of cocaine and heroin may in reality be overdoses of alcohol (or barbiturates) *and* cocaine or heroin (or both).[34] Users would be better informed about the risks of drug synergy under legalization. The kick or sensation that alcohol adds to cocaine would not be worth the risks in a legalized system, since cocaine itself would be approximately the same price per intoxicating dose as alcohol.

The very substantial reductions in numbers of alcohol and tobacco users over the past few decades demonstrates that people are capable of avoiding drugs that they know are bad for them, even if the government says they are legal and they are widely advertised as the key to success and happiness. As federal judge Robert W. Sweet observed in a 1989 speech urging drug legalization, "If our society can learn to stop using butter, it should be able to cut down on cocaine."[35]

Whether Americans choose to avoid recreational drugs in the first place or to quit using or abusing them is linked to the quality of their lives and their perceived prospects for a rewarding life without drug use or abuse. This is clearly demonstrated by recent data about illegal-drug use. Illegal-drug use has been reduced drastically in the past few years among white middle and upper classes—but hardly or not at all among ethnic minorities, who largely inhabit our inner cities. Many of those users see nothing but a bleak future before them. They have little to lose by drug abuse, and they proceed to lose it.

In sum, the drug market is already saturated with a combination of legal and illegal drugs. Virtually everyone who now wants to get high already does so. Legalization may significantly alter market shares among the now legal and illegal drugs, but it is unlikely to create a strong surge in *new* demand for psychoactive drugs. As Michael S. Gazzaniga, Professor of Neuroscience at Dartmouth Medical School, puts it, "There is a base rate of drug abuse, and it is [presently] achieved one way or another."[36]

Even if heroin, cocaine and marijuana legalization increased substantially the number of users of such drugs and even their total drug consumption, the number of abusers of such drugs could still be diminished by legalization. The drugs used would probably be less potent than those now available and therefore less addictive and less damaging. Users of legal drugs also have many advantages over users of illegal drugs that help them to resist frequent, heavy use. They need not be criminals or outcasts to use the drugs. They are less likely to acquire serious or incapacitating illnesses from drug use. They need not steal to buy their drugs; they can work at a regular, legitimate job. Legal-drug use, therefore, is far more compatible with the personal ties, extrinsic resources and general well-being that support efforts to resist drug abuse.

Other Risks

There are no other major risks of legalization apart from increased consumption of drugs. All other risks are subsidiaries. Some of the derivative risks deserve mention, however. If legalization were to produce major long-run increases in the numbers of psychoactive-drug abusers—an assumption we have difficulty making for reasons already set forth—a number of concrete adverse consequences might follow. Many heroin and cocaine abusers, like alcoholics, have difficulty holding jobs or handling other significant responsibilities. Some of them—like many alcoholics—seem all but immune to treatment or other therapeutic interventions. Such persons have more than their share of health problems, and could put an additional strain on our health care systems. If legalization were to produce hundreds of thousands of new addicts who were incapable of functioning in the society, along with the mentally ill, alcohol and other drug-abusing derelicts who already inhabit our cities, this would indeed be a major cost of legalization. But for reasons already discussed, neither common sense nor experience supports the likelihood of such a scenario.

Some say that legalization would be the equivalent of genocide on inner-city black communities. But to believe that members of a particular race of Americans are incapable of making their own decisions about what they want to put into their bodies is reminiscent of the attitudes that underlay a system of slavery. Urban blacks are disproportionately users and abusers of both crack and heroin. But it does not follow that there is something in their genes or even in black culture that preordains such drug usage. People—regardless of their race—abuse drugs for two reasons: (1) they got hooked accidentally and haven't yet mustered the motivation and external assistance to quit, and/or (2) such abuse provides temporary escape from a painful existence. Prohibition can't change either of those circumstances, but a caring society, using funds freed by legalization, can change them both. Drug abuse can produce dreadful disabilities, with resultant neglect of children, jobs, health and other responsibilities, but drugs are not viruses or even bacteria: they are substances that people choose to take into their bodies. The first step in reducing drug abuse is to make sure that those who make the decisions to take drugs are aware of the risks of doing so. (This was not the case with crack; the epidemic was well underway before the addictive qualities of crack were widely known.) The second step is to provide a society in which the risks of using the drugs are unacceptable because life has more to offer than a chemical high. The notion that inner-city blacks lack the capacity to resist their own self-destruction is preposterous, yet it is just beneath the surface in prohibitionist polemics linking legalization and genocide. In addition to their painful lives, a major reason why inner-city blacks are heavy users of cocaine and heroin is that they are inundated by these drugs and their users. Most retail drug markets in the nation are located on the streets of the inner cities, the same streets in which children are growing up and trying to play. The children are often recruited as dealers before they become users. These markets would disappear under legalization.

Another subsidiary risk is that, if use of newly legalized drugs became far more widespread than at present, there would be greatly enlarged safety risks to nonusers. Automobiles, trucks, airplanes, factory machinery would be operated by people whose capacities were significantly impaired by drugs. But as we have noted, the major impairments are produced by alcohol, not the other drugs. If legalization diverts users from alcohol, we may even have safer highways and airways as a result. But it is, in any event, possible to prohibit driving and piloting by drug-impaired persons in a state of legalization. In fact, it would be less difficult under legalization because impaired operators would have less reason than they now do—when mere use of the drugs is a serious crime—to hide their condition. Drug testing is now commonplace—far more so than we would like—but in a state of legalization, drug testing by employers and traffic police would be much less objectionable, since it would not expose the person tested to a charge of a serious felony. Moreover, modern technology is capable of producing portable devices to test cognitive, perceptual and motor capacities. Such tests are far more relevant to one's ability to operate machinery than a test to determine the presence, or even the quantity, of drugs in one's blood, breath or urine.

Legalizing drugs does not require that impaired driving also be made legal. Drivers who are seriously impaired, for whatever reasons, should not drive and should be punished if they do so.

It is sometimes said that legalization will produce more "crack babies" or other infants whose health is seriously damaged by their mothers' drug use during pregnancy.[37] But much—perhaps most—of the damage done to such babies comes from their mothers' neglect of nutrition and hygiene, combined with the fact that many of them have no prenatal medical care. Fear of criminal prosecution keeps many such mothers away from prenatal care when it is available. Moreover, most drug-treatment programs, believe it or not, refuse access to pregnant mothers![38] Such idiocy would stop under any rational system of legalization.

Finally, what about our children? Is it possible that the high cost of illegal drugs is a significant deterrent to drug experimentation by America's teenagers? If this cost were drastically reduced, a substantial segment of such deterrables might experiment with newly legalized drugs and become hooked. What we have already said about adults applies here as well. Children who do not drink or smoke will not use cocaine or heroin, however cheap it is. Many of those who do drink or smoke, and are interested in expanding their use of drugs, already have tried marijuana and many have tried cocaine. The price of experimental quantities of illegal drugs is already well within the reach of most teenagers.

Moreover, as difficult as it may be for some to contemplate, even if legalization produced a substantial increase in juvenile experimentation with marijuana, heroin or cocaine, the juveniles themselves, and the rest of society, might still be better off. Tobacco and alcohol are especially harmful to children's bodies; a reduction in the use of those drugs by juveniles would be a great advance, even if achieved by some increase in the use of other drugs.

We would continue to criminalize the distribution of drugs, including tobacco and alcohol, to children. But since drug use among adults would be lawful, we could concentrate our law-enforcement resources on purveyors of drugs to children, and we could be far more successful in that endeavor, having narrowed our focus, than we are today. It is not true that anything a society permits adults to do cannot effectively be denied children, and that, as a result, adults who encourage children to engage in such "adult" activities cannot be condemned. Sex between adults and children is severely condemned in America, while sex between unmarried adults is not even a misdemeanor in most states. We would treat the distribution of drugs to children like statutory rape, and put people in prison for it. Under today's prohibition that rarely happens.

THE BALANCE OF BENEFITS AND COSTS

We think almost any one of the eight benefits we have sketched above outweighs the risks of legalization—which are not great. When all benefits are combined, the case for legalization becomes overwhelming. If legalization is too large a leap, courageous governors and a courageous president could give us many of the benefits of legalization simply by de-escalating the war. Cut the drug-law-enforcement budgets by two thirds (as President Clinton cut the personnel of the "drug" czar's office), stop civil forfeitures, grant executive clemency to most of the nonviolent drug violators stuffing our prisons, and much of the evil of prohibition will disappear. When the benefits of de-escalation are experienced, the nation will then be ready for de jure reform.

The meekest among us must admit that the case for legalizing marijuana is overwhelming. Jimmy Carter was right when he proposed decriminalization during his presidency.[39] We would all be better off if he had succeeded. Marijuana poses some health risks, but far less than tobacco or alcohol, and it substitutes for and therefore competes with both alcohol and tobacco. Pending the legalization of marijuana, our nation's chief executives and law-enforcement officers should put a stop to all prosecution for marijuana possession or trafficking, and open the prison doors for all who are there solely for such offenses. Even an ardent prohibitionist ought to agree with this proposal. Everyone agrees that cocaine and heroin are worse drugs, by any standards, than marijuana. If marijuana is legalized, the drug warriors could then focus their resources on the war against "hard" drugs.

The case for legalization is strong; the case for de-escalating the drug war is overwhelming.

CHAPTER 13

Forms of Legalization

*"[We need to] free ourselves from the superstition
that that which is legal is, for that reason,
something we approve of."*

A COMMENT ABOUT DRUG LEGALIZATION BY
WILLIAM F. BUCKLEY, JR.[1]

UNITED STATES Representative Charles Rangel, the chairman of the
now-defunct House Select Committee on Narcotics and Drug Abuse,
opposes drug legalization. On a special "Koppel Report" on ABC,
Rangel rhetorically asked, "Which drugs are going to be legalized?
[In] which communities are they going to be dispensed? Is it going to
be a private sector initiative? Is it only going to be for the wealthy that
can afford to go to a doctor? Will we expand Medicaid for the poor,
Medicare for the aged? . . . How much do we give? . . . [W]ho
determines when you're high? And do you go into the question of
overdose? . . ."[2] This rhetoric, which diverts attention from the issue
of *whether* drugs should be legalized, marginalizes legalization proponents and implies that they have failed to think the matter through. It
is an effective debate tactic when the critics of prohibition are denied
an opportunity to reply. Representative Rangel is adept at asking such
questions in a rapid-fire manner and then loudly interrupting or
speaking over the answers.

The congressman has put a similar list of challenging questions into print.[3] At least one Drug Enforcement Administration document unleashed a similar barrage of questions,[4] and in a 1990 article for *Public Interest,* New York University professor James B. Jacobs asserted "that the debate over drug legalization ebbs and flows without a fleshed-out proposal for what drug legalization means and how it would work."[5]

In fact, the charge by Rangel, the DEA and Jacobs is incorrect. For years, its advocates have discussed how legalization might be implemented, in ways that would ameliorate most of the problems caused by prohibition. The Drug Policy Foundation, the Cato Institute, Baltimore mayor Kurt Schmoke,[6] *Reason* magazine,[7] *Hofstra Law Review,*[8] and the *University of California at Davis Law Review*[9] have all sponsored public discussions or published articles on this very topic. Legislator Joseph Galiber has even proposed a detailed drug-legalization bill to the New York State Senate.[10] Congressman Rangel and the DEA ignore these analyses and proposals. Professor Jacobs cites several of the legalization proposals but dismisses them as not "carefully drafted."[11]

One of the most useful synopses of the diverse recommendations offered by legalization advocates appeared in the October 1988 issue of *Reason.*[12] The magazine asked several prominent legalizers to describe their regimes for postprohibition drug distribution. Some of the results were as follows:

• Milton Friedman, a Nobel prize–winning economist, has publicly advocated drug legalization at least since 1972 when he wrote in a *Newsweek* opinion piece: "Prohibition is an attempted cure that makes matters worse—for both the addict and the rest of us."[13] In the *Reason* symposium, Friedman suggested that we legalize all drugs and permit their private-sector sale, while minimizing government interference with the operation of a free market. Friedman not only opposes a role for the Food and Drug Administration in regulating recreational drugs, he suggests that its other regulatory responsibilities be discontinued as well, in order to permit a free market in pharmaceuticals. However, Milton Friedman did agree that sale of drugs to children should be forbidden.

• David Boaz, Vice President of the Cato Institute, a Washington, D.C., think tank that has urged reform of our drug policies, gave the editors of *Reason* a more moderate proposal than Friedman's. Boaz suggested that our present methods of regulating distribution of alcohol be largely applied to the distribution of drugs that are now illicit. Thus, there would be warning labels, it would be illegal to sell to minors and advertising would be controlled.

• Norman E. Zinberg, Professor of Psychiatry at Harvard Medical School, also proposed a less permissive system of legalization than that suggested by Friedman. Zinberg suggested that we gradually decriminalize drugs rather than legalizing them outright. He proposed that educational and treatment programs be enhanced as the criminal penalties for the use of drugs or their distribution are removed.

• Georgette Bennett, the author of *Crime Warps: The Future of Crime in America,* presented the most comprehensive program in the *Reason* issue. She proposed:
   • regulations to remove the profits from the drug business
   • regulations to promote public health
   • civil as opposed to criminal controls of drug abuse
   • criminal sanctions for violation of the regulations

In general, the drug market she envisions would operate on a non-profit basis. She would prohibit brand-name advertising, would restrict sales to licensed government vendors and would have the government make commodity purchases of all drugs directly from foreign governments. Price controls and taxes would further stabilize the market, as would free distribution by government clinics to indigent drug users.

Essential features of the public-health component of her proposal were:

   • public education
   • quality control
   • bans on commercial advertising
   • drug education in the schools
   • minimum ages for drug purchases

Her system of civil controls envisions employers being responsible to establish job-related criteria for drug-abuse policies, which would be enforced by terminations of drug users. She would retain a few criminal sanctions for:

   • those who price-gouge on drugs
   • sale of drugs outside the authorized government channels
   • drug-impaired driving

• Ron Paul, a former Republican congressman from Texas who ran in the 1988 presidential campaign as the candidate of the Libertarian party, suggested the most radical form of legalization: unfettered distribution. "There should be no controls on production, supply or purchase (for adults)."

• Ethan Nadelmann, Assistant Professor of Politics and Public Affairs at Princeton, warns against repeating mistakes we already have made in our alcohol and tobacco policies. He suggested to *Reason* readers that drugs should not be sold in vending machines and that we not subsidize them as we do tobacco. He emphasized that the system should be designed to remove drug use from the underground to "enable the drug abuser or addict to improve the overall quality of his life and health."

• Ernest van Den Haag, formerly Professor of Jurisprudence and Public Policy at Fordham University, proposed that drugs "should be sold only to adults, in liquor and drug stores, without prescriptions." He also said, "They should be taxed as much as alcohol and the revenue should finance more and better educational efforts about drugs and alcohol."

• Charles Freund, a columnist for *The New Republic,* suggested that our new drug policies should rely on the kinds of social controls that are readily available for controlling alcohol use. He pointed out that social norms and cultural taboos have recently been very successful in bringing pressures against those who drink and drive. Similar informal cultural forces can be used to control the use of the presently illicit drugs. Freund opined that drugs are consumed now with little social control because they are available only through "outlaw subcultures."

• Arnold Trebach, president of the Drug Policy Foundation, suggested a legalization program relying primarily on education. He pointed to the successful reduction of tobacco use as a fruitful model for a drug-education policy in the postprohibition era.

Thus, a wide variety of politicians, concerned citizens, social scientists, psychiatrists, journalists, law professors and other scholars have constructively proposed how to control drugs after legalization. Many of their ideas have been worked out in considerable detail. Admittedly, as Professor Jacobs observed, the proposals disagree—some would have no regulation, some would have government regulation, some would have social controls, some would have a mixture of the above. But proponents of legalization have made and are making concrete implementation proposals and it should not be surprising that they disagree on the details.

OUR PROPOSAL

A comprehensive drug legalization proposal should answer at least these important questions:

1. Which drugs will be legalized?
2. Will the drug market be regulated?
3. Where will drug use be permitted?
4. What will we do about juvenile access?
5. What form will licensing and distribution take?
6. What will become of our pure-food-and-drug regulations?
7. Will drug advertising be permitted or restricted?
8. How will we cope with drug abuse in the workplace?
9. What residual law-enforcement demands will remain?

Which Drugs to Legalize

One option would be to legalize selectively. We might sate the public appetite for intoxicants by legalizing some illicit drugs while attempting to hold the line on more dangerous drugs. We might distinguish between marijuana, which is relatively benign, and cocaine, which is more hazardous. It seems likely that, when legalization arrives, it will do so incrementally and that marijuana is almost certainly the first important recreational drug that will be converted from contraband to legal status. But legalizing marijuana will not remove the evils of prohibition, or even greatly ameliorate them. Because marijuana is so easily home grown, its price per dose can never get very high for very long and the profits in it cannot support major black-market organizations.

The chief evils of prohibition are related to cocaine and heroin. We should legalize those drugs as well, in either the first or the second stage of legalization. Should we stop there? Some argue that we should not legalize drugs the prohibition of which does not create serious social problems. Thus, since there appears to be no huge problem associated with the consumption of and trafficking in PCP, LSD, amphetamines, or methadone, we should perhaps not legalize them, even though we can expect a significant black market to continue with those drugs, as with tranquilizers, barbiturates, codeine, other opiates and numerous designer drugs.

Such a halfway move toward legalization would not be advisable, other than as a cautionary step in the legalization process. The line remaining between legal and illegal drugs under such a scheme would make no more sense than the present dichotomy. There is little basis for distinguishing legally between amphetamines and cocaine, for example, other than the current consumer preference for cocaine, a preference which is almost certainly transitory. And it would be ludicrous to legalize the most potent, addictive and dangerous natural opiate, heroin, while continuing to criminalize trafficking in all the lesser opiates. Since one of the advantages of legalization is removal of the black-market incentives toward more powerful forms of drugs and thus encouraging drug consumers to use less potent, safer, less addictive forms, we should legalize all opiates and virtually all stimulants. We should certainly legalize coca when, if not before, we legalize cocaine.

It might be tempting to draw the legal line at crack and ice (smokable methamphetamine) because these drugs seem to be so addictive. This temptation should be resisted. Crack is easily manufactured by anyone who possesses cocaine, and ice can be manufactured in the basement or garage of anyone with elementary chemistry knowledge who can read a recipe book.[14] If there is a strong market for these drugs, prohibiting them is certain to fail. Market forces, however, are likely to take care of the problem. If the price of cocaine is greatly reduced, as it would be under legalization, the incentives for manufacturing and using crack or ice would also be greatly reduced. If crack is more addictive than cocaine in powder form, then consumers will eventually become aware of that (if they are not already) and will opt for the less addictive form of the drug. According to Dartmouth Medical School neuroscientist Michael S. Gazzaniga: "This is so because if cocaine were reduced to the same price as crack, the abuser, acknowledging the higher rate of addiction, might forgo the more intensive high of crack, opting for the slower high of cocaine. . . . [O]n another front—we know that 120-proof alcohol doesn't sell as readily as the 86 proof, not by a long shot, even though the higher the proof, the faster the psychological effect that alcohol users are seeking."[15]

Thus, market forces under legalization should largely eliminate crack and ice.

It is arguable that some psychoactive drugs should remain in the controlled category. Some synthetic opiates, for example, are so powerful and dangerous that they are analogous to grenades or other highly dangerous weapons that are effectively prohibited. If the most popular plant drugs are legalized, it is doubtful that any serious, lucrative market is likely to develop for a synthetic drug such as fentanyl that can be so deadly to its users. Hence, we would recommend that such drugs remain controlled at least until it is demonstrated that their prohibition creates worse problems than it prevents.

Many other drugs would remain available only on prescription and only through pharmacies. Any proprietary drug manufactured by a pharmaceutical company that maintains patent or other legal protection of its proprietary rights in the drug would not lose its privilege and responsibility for controlling the distribution of the drug. Such protection is a quid pro quo for holding the manufacturers of such drugs liable for the damage they inflict on users. We cannot hold the manufacturer of a drug liable for birth defects, sterility or other serious damage unless we permit the manufacturer to retain substantial control over the distribution of the drug. We also have to protect the proprietary rights of the drug manufacturer in order to provide an incentive for research and development of new drugs.

Some black-market activity will remain regarding any psychoactive drug that is available only on prescription. But such activities, which are rampant now, will be greatly diminished when many other psychoactive drugs are available on the open market. Minor black markets are manageable costs of necessary protection of the consumer and the manufacturer.

Where Drug Use Should Be Permitted

Between 1987 and 1992, Zurich, Switzerland, explicitly tolerated the unrestrained use of heroin and other drugs in Platzspitz Park.[16] Meanwhile, the possession and sale of drugs were ferociously suppressed elsewhere in Switzerland, and throughout much of Europe. When the Zurich experiment began, the park served as an open-air shooting gallery for just a few hundred regular habitués. However, the park's drug clientele eventually swelled to 20,000 drug users, one fourth of whom came from countries other than Switzerland. Once a beautiful family park, Platzspitz became dangerous, unhealthful and unsightly. By 1992, the disorder, the nonstop toxic-drug reactions, the crime, the discarded syringes and other litter strewn about, the use of the grounds as a public toilet and the general degeneracy that characterized Platzspitz Park led the Zurich City Council to rescind its permissive policy. The experiment's physical impact on the park was so severe that more than a year's labor was necessary to restore the property to normal park uses.

Drug regulations after legalization should avoid restricting use to a few outdoor venues. The regulations should permit use in the privacy of one's own home. However, public use either should be forbidden altogether or allowed in a sufficient number of locations to prevent problems of concentrated impact. Otherwise, the problems of drug immigration that destroyed Platzspitz Park will recur.

We recommend that drug consumption be prohibited not only in those places where alcohol cannot now be lawfully consumed (generally, in motor vehicles and in public places) but in semipublic places as well. There should be no "drug saloons" or the modern equivalents of opium dens. We see little reason why the consumption of newly legalized drugs should be permitted in restaurants, in public transportation facilities or in other public facilities. We would deny such uses to discourage consumption of pleasure drugs without paying the exorbitant costs of general prohibition.

Drug use in the workplace presents special problems. There is much to be said for prohibiting drug use in the workplace, especially if the work is hazardous. But much work is not hazardous to anyone and drug use would not actually injure co-workers, as cigarette smoke does. Heroin addicts, moreover, cannot be expected to go all day without a drug dose. To prohibit heroin addicts from taking heroin anywhere but in their own homes is to require them to work at home or not at all. Perhaps the matter would best be decided by agreement between employer and employees with employers allowed to designate semiprivate places where drugs in addition to tobacco can be consumed during breaktimes.

An alternative is to prohibit conventional drug use in the workplace but to permit heroin addicts or other drug addicts to take their drugs through transdermal patches (that could hardly be effectively prevented, in any event, without strip searches). The delivery of heroin through such a patch is probably practicable. The reason why such patches are not now available is that the technology for patch delivery of drugs is complex and is controlled by a few high-tech companies; the street doesn't yet know how to package heroin that way, and it is illegal for pharmaceutical companies to do so, since heroin is a Schedule I drug and cannot be prescribed for any legitimate purpose. Delivery of heroin through a patch would eliminate or reduce the rush produced by intravenous injection and would probably provide even less kick than would the snorting of heroin powder. Transdermal delivery, therefore, may be an inferior means of delivery for many addicts. If necessary to keep a good job, however, most addicts would probably be willing to accept the inferior form of delivery, especially since it is far safer than the others.

Restrictions on the places where drugs can be consumed are enforceable, as we have seen with alcohol and tobacco use regulations. Violations of place restrictions, unlike the acquisition and private consumption of drugs, have witnesses and victims who are willing to complain and to pressure officials to prosecute. Many Americans are repulsed by the public consumption of marijuana, cocaine or heroin, just as many of us are repulsed by public sexual activities. A society can legitimately protect us against such aesthetic assaults, and we think that it should do so. More important, those who are trying to quit using drugs, or trying to resist using them, are shielded from temptation if such consumption does not occur in public or semipublic places. The government should provide such a shield.

Such regulations of newly legalized drug use—essentially confining it to the home or semiprivate places—would involve substantial enforcement costs and would also be inconsistent with our more permissive stances on the consumption of tobacco and alcohol. While America is becoming much more restrictive on the places where tobacco can be smoked, and somewhat more restrictive about alcohol consumption, we are not close to confining the use of those drugs to the home. Such a policy with respect to those drugs would neither be feasible nor just. With 50 million of our residents addicted to cigarettes, it would be impossible to prohibit them from smoking on the street. It imposes suffering on cigarette addicts to prohibit their smoking in the workplace and that can only be justified on the ground that smoking physically harms co-workers or others.

The consumption of alcohol has been so socialized and accepted by our culture for so long that to prohibit drinking in restaurants or in bars, where customers gather to watch sports events and otherwise to socialize, would be both politically impossible and inadvisable. Our culture even proselytizes against "solitary drinking" and thus encourages "social drinking" as more healthy and less problematic. As long as such attitudes prevail, we must go slow in restricting the places where alcohol can be consumed.

But more restrictive regulations of newly legalized drugs is another matter. Users of such drugs are already accustomed to consuming their drugs in private, to avoid arrest. There would be nothing revolutionary in a system that required them to continue to so confine their consumption. The semipublic use of tobacco and alcohol is the norm in American society, whereas such use of marijuana, cocaine and heroin is the exception. We should try to keep it so, at least until our inability to do so is clearly established.

Preventing Juvenile Access

Most proponents of drug legalization propose to severely limit juvenile access to drugs. As things are now, children have varying degrees of access to each of the legal and illegal drugs. Under the present system, juvenile access to the legal drugs—alcohol and tobacco—is more limited than adult access. Meanwhile, in the absence of any regulation of the illegal-drug market, children can obtain heroin, cocaine, and marijuana as readily as adults can. Unfortunately, some of our youngsters probably always will be initiated to drug use before they are mature enough to handle the attendant risks.

Children can obtain alcohol by raiding mom and dad's liquor cabinet, by coaxing an older friend or sibling to purchase it for them or occasionally by purchasing alcohol directly from foolhardy retailers. However, a retailer risks loss of a lucrative license by selling alcohol to a minor. Alcohol licensing regulations, if enforced, could represent a powerful method of restricting access to such drugs by children. Experiments demonstrating the ease with which underage minors can purchase alcohol from retailers are among recent steps taken to pressure officials to enforce the laws against the sale of alcohol to minors.[17] Lax enforcement reflects, among other things, our preoccupation with illicit drugs. Acquiescence in underage drinking also reflects an implicit preference for one kind of illegal activity—underage drinking—over another one—illicit-drug use. Law-enforcement officers, parents and other interested citizens feel ambivalent about enforcing the alcohol control laws because of their fear of even worse temptations. The licensing laws, however, are a potent tool which could be effective if all recreational drugs were treated equally.

Access to cigarettes by children is virtually unlimited, in spite of laws that prohibit sales to minors. Law-enforcement agencies—in part because they are overwhelmed by drug-prohibition duties and ideology—ignore the statutes against selling tobacco to children.

A serious trend toward prevention of early smoking is underway, and if this effort accelerates it could attain a level of effectiveness at least as great as the partially enforced ban on drinking by children. Cigarette vending machines have been outlawed by approximately twenty Minnesota communities,[18] by a few California jurisdictions[19] and, surprisingly, by Raleigh, North Carolina.[20] Because children also buy or shoplift tobacco products from live retailers, Chanhassen, Minnesota, has even banned all self-service tobacco sales and requires stores to limit their stocks to closely guarded cigarettes at the cashier's counter.[21]

The tobacco industry fights back, mounting sometimes effective lawsuits and legislative lobbying campaigns against such restrictions. Often the tobacco industry creates "citizens" groups as front organizations or funds the efforts of merchants' associations in this struggle against regulation.

The tobacco industry also aggressively recruits juvenile smokers. The future of the nicotine business in America is absolutely dependent on finding children to replace adult Americans who defect from the ranks of smokers or die from the habit.[22] Ninety percent of all new American smokers are in their teens or younger.[23] Aware of the public-relations implications of pandering lethal drugs to children, R. J. Reynolds cynically publishes materials that purport to fight against teen smoking. Meanwhile, Reynolds' "Joe Camel" advertising campaign has radically improved the juvenile-market share of Camel cigarettes—previously a largely adult brand. In the first three years of the Joe Camel campaign, the proportion of smokers under eighteen who chose Camel cigarettes zoomed from 0.5 percent to 32.7 percent. The illegal sale of Camels to minors increased the earnings of R. J. Reynolds from that source nearly 80 times, from $6 million to $476 million,[24] as a consequence of omnipresent posters, billboards and adolescent promotions, which depict the urbane "smooth character" Joe Camel, an anthropomorphic caricature of a dromedary.[25] The *Journal of the American Medical Association* (*JAMA*) has published three separate studies on the Joe Camel campaign,[26] which cumulatively suggest that R. J. Reynolds intentionally is recruiting toddlers as customers. In addition to many other disturbing findings in the *JAMA* articles, one of the three studies indicated that 91.3 percent of six-year-olds could identify the cigarette's cartoon logo.[27] The study presented symbols of twelve miscellaneous products, including both "adult" and "children's" brands, and only Mickey Mouse—the logo for the Disney Channel—achieved recognition comparable to that of Joe Camel.

Under a comprehensive program of drug legalization, government could effectively reduce the access by children to all drugs. The program could maintain the present bans on alcohol sales to minors and stiffen penalties for others who provide alcohol to children. Drug legalization could incorporate major improvements over the present situation by:

1. Banning the sale of cigarettes and all other drugs through vending machines.
2. Enforcing existing bans on the sale or transfer of cigarettes to children.
3. Genuinely banning sale of the presently illegal drugs to children.

The sale of cigarettes, alcohol and newly legalized drugs to children could be made a serious felony. As with sex crimes against children, the seriousness of the felony could vary with the ages of the perpetrator and the victim. Noncommercial distribution to children could be made a lesser offense or, to avoid undue complexity, treated the same as a sale.

We would not stop at punishing the willful distribution of tobacco, alcohol and other drugs to children. We would encourage courts to hold parents and others civilly and even criminally responsible for negligently providing access to such drugs by children. The liquor cabinet, and the drug cabinet, if there is one, should be locked if there are children in the house. Since such drugs are dangerous to children's lives and health, it would not be a great stretch of legal principle to hold the possessors of such drugs to a duty to prevent children from obtaining them. One who leaves poison in the presence of children would hardly be surprised to learn that he was liable for the damage done to a child who took the poison. The same principles should be applied to pleasure drugs, with underage consumption itself regarded as actionable or punishable harm.

Modes of Regulation

Because the repeal of the Prohibition amendment to the Constitution restored most of the control over alcohol regulation to the states, we have many different models for drug regulation. We should examine these models in our search for the best way to repeal drug prohibition.

Let us first consider the proposal of Daniel Benjamin and Roger Miller. In *Undoing Drugs: Beyond Legalization*[28] they recommend that federal drug-prohibition statutes be repealed, leaving each state free to decide how it wants to deal with drugs: free availability, stringent prohibition or somewhere between those extremes. A similar proposal was recently made by Whitman Knapp, Senior United States Judge for the Southern District of New York.[29] There are two major advantages to this approach. First, since it does not itself result in either legalization or prohibition but just gives each voter in each state a greater voice in the drug policy that immediately concerns that voter, it may be politically feasible. The Benjamin and Miller proposal permits each state to have the kind of drug laws that it wants. Second, the proposal permits us to try many different approaches to the illicit-drug problem, to experiment, to discover and evaluate new ways of dealing with drugs. We already know much about how to deal with drugs, since we have experimented endlessly with alcohol regulation, but there are differences among drugs and always more to be learned. A single federal approach to the problem cuts off experimentation and creative competition in fashioning reactions to problems.

There is, however, a problem with this approach. As we learned with alcohol drinking age disparities, major differences between states concerning the legal availability of drugs create ugly stateline industries that cater to persons coming to buy and consume the drugs from states in which they are not legally available. Such differences encourage interstate travel under the influence of the sought-after drug. This dangerous condition, as it applies to drinking ages, was changed by federal legislation that effectively raised the minimum drinking age in all states to twenty-one.

Highway-safety considerations which warranted the change of drinking-ages would almost certainly be less powerful considerations where other drugs were concerned. As explained in Chapter 4, none of the three major illicit drugs is likely to impair driving capacity as greatly as does alcohol. Alcohol is also a far more popular recreational drug among teenagers than all the illicit drugs combined—by far. It is virtually inconceivable that this basic order of consumer preference would be reversed under legalization. Thus, the problem of state-line drug industries and impaired driving home from source states would almost certainly be less substantial than it is with respect to alcohol.

The likely outcome of the Benjamin and Miller scheme, if enacted, would be the gradual adoption of legalization, state by state. A few states would try it, if only for the revenue. Adjoining states would find their prohibition laws even less enforceable than they are now and, lustful for the loot, would align themselves with their more prescient neighbors. As the states that legalized experienced not only revenue enhancement but less crime, safer streets, increased property values and general improvements in the quality of life, the remaining states would fall in line like dominoes. We think the federal government should skip that step and not only legalize most of the drugs it now treats as "controlled," but at the same time deny the states the power to prohibit them. Some room can still be left for state regulations, as is now the case with most products, where the federal government and the states share regulatory responsibilities.

Licensing Production?

Should we try to license the production of plant-based drugs? It is possible to produce not only marijuana but coca and its derivatives and opium and its derivatives in the territorial confines of the United States. If we were to ban the importation of such drugs, we could give a boost to domestic farmers and exclude the Colombian *narcotraficantes* at the same time. That does not seem feasible, at least in the short run. Subtropical climates have natural advantages in the growing of coca and opium, and our farmers lack experience producing either crop. The harvesting of coca and especially opium is also very labor intensive. It is unlikely that American farmers could compete effectively with South American coca producers or with Indian, Pakistani or Southeast Asian opium producers, at least in the short to intermediate term. We would still have smuggling and still have major black markets if we tried to close our drug markets to importation.*

A more feasible possibility is the licensing of later stages of drug production, say from the coca or opium stages to refined production of cocaine or opium derivatives. While we could not effectively prevent the importation of coca, opium and all their derivatives from abroad, we might try to confine some refining activities to licensed American manufacturers. We could thus hope better to control the purity of the drugs and to reduce the risk of contaminated products.

---

*We probably *could* effectively prohibit importation of marijuana, since we can grow it cheaper and better than any country in the world, but there would be no need to do so. The market itself would produce that result.

Health and safety could thus be promoted. We do not do this with other drugs or food products, however, and it is hard to see why we should treat pleasure drugs differently. If foreign pharmaceutical companies can produce cheaper drugs than our manufacturers, and can satisfy Customs and the FDA that they have produced uncontaminated drugs, we see no reason—other than economic protectionism—why they should be prohibited from doing so.

Regulation of Domestic Distribution

The domestic distribution of pleasure drugs, like the distribution of pharmaceuticals, foods, alcohol, tobacco and every other product, should be subject to regulation by American law. The question is what kind of regulation. Several options are available:

Unfettered Distribution. Few but the most doctrinaire libertarians would favor this system for drug distribution, which threatens to replicate one of the worst problems that we now have with the largely unregulated distribution of cigarettes. Children would have easy access to drugs.

Under the present regime of drug prohibition, we have a de facto unregulated drug market. When buying from drug pushers, it is caveat emptor. Thus, the unfettered option also would possess many of the disadvantages of the present regime, in which the consumer has no protection against mislabeled drugs or products tainted by toxic adulterants. There is nothing wrong with—and much to be gained by—drug regulation short of prohibition.

Unrestrained drug trade also would lead to aggressive marketing to attract young customers, new-product development and creation of market niches for extra-potent forms (just as there now is a market niche for extra-potent beers—so-called malt liquors). Those aggressive marketing ploys would occur no matter how much tax the government put on the product. Paradoxically, many of the evils of prohibition would remain.

Government as Sole Distributor. One possible distribution system might be an exclusive federal-government dispensary system. By having the dispensaries run by the federal government, as opposed to the state governments, the problems of competition between neighboring states would be avoided. There would be one price-and-distribution system across the United States, and no interstate travel induced by the drug business. The effort to keep drugs out of the hands of juveniles would be greatly facilitated. Advertising could also be eliminated without any First Amendment problems. While private organizations may have constitutional rights to advertise their products, nothing *requires* the government to advertise.

There are, however, major disadvantages to government drug dispensaries. As we have learned from the Eastern Bloc countries, when government is the sole legal distributor of a commodity, competition and self-interest are not available to promote the efficient workings of the market. Thus, the Soviet Union and Eastern Europe experienced shortages, hoarding and black market distribution, which greatly contributed to the collapse of their economies and ultimately their governments. The temptation of government to increase profits by raising prices on a controversial product would also exacerbate the problems. Black markets that legalization was designed to prevent would develop parallel to the government drug-distribution system, just as illegal gambling organizations compete with state-run lotteries.

Finally, when the government has a financial interest in promoting vice, as it does in those states that have lotteries, states frequently engage in shameless promotions, even fraud, to induce their citizens to part with their money.[30] There is little of that in state-controlled alcohol dispensary systems, but the lottery example is another reason to worry about turning the drug business over to government-run monopolies.

A Prescription System. Another option for distribution would be a "medical system," in which prescriptions would be filled at pharmacies. This could provide a modicum of state regulation and some protection against consumption by minors and drug abusers, but in black-market consequences far more regulation and cost than is desirable. People who can afford to pay doctor's fees can already get a potpourri of drugs from unethical physicians who are at present a gray-market distribution system that competes with black marketeers. Legalizing the gray market and broadening its range of products would not solve prohibition's problems. It would merely make drug dealers out of our health professionals. Drug distribution as an adjunct to medical treatment or to maintain addicts as a health measure can be legitimate medical practice, but retailing recreational drugs manifestly is not. To impose that function on the medical profession would demoralize if not destroy the profession.

Licensed Suppliers. A third possible distribution system would be to license and regulate distributors and retailers who would sell psychoactive drugs as commercial products. New York State senator Joseph L. Galiber's proposed bill would implement essentially this system, while funding treatment and education programs from taxes on retail sales.[31]

Alcohol distribution, which is already licensed, and tobacco trade, which is largely unfettered, could be brought under this regulatory umbrella, too.

The main advantage of this system of distribution would be that it would be far more likely than government dispensaries or a prescription system to destroy the black market. A troubling disadvantage is that it would undermine the system by which psychotropic prescription drugs are distributed only by licensed pharmacists on written authorization of a medical doctor. But people who are reluctant to experiment or self-medicate with over-the-counter drugs will—if they can afford it—still seek the advice and guidance of a physician, so that the prescription system, although weakened, would not be destroyed. Doctors today prescribe medication that can be bought without prescription. They would continue to do so under a legalized drug regime. Also, as noted earlier, there would in any event be a large number of psychoactive proprietary drugs that could legally be bought only on prescription. Nor would the legalization of psychoactives be inconsistent with the prescription-only system for medicinal drugs such as antibiotics. Many of these are proprietary drugs and there is no significant black-market problem.

Distribution licenses could be conditioned on good character and proof of insurance or financial responsibility. Since a substantial benefit of legalization is that it would permit us to require drug distributors to sell uncontaminated and properly labeled products, distributors would have to establish their financial responsibility for defaulting on their obligations. This would be a major function of a licensing system. No monopolies or oligopolies should be created. Any person or organization meeting minimum requirements should get a license.

A commercial licensing system should also include mandatory warning labels, generic packaging (no brand names, slogans or touting) and detailed description of contents and purities. It might also be advisable to limit the quantities of drugs that any individual could purchase, to require records of sales, and to forbid quantity-price discounts. If those regulations—and others dealing with purity, potency and so forth—are complied with, the manufacturers and distributors of the drugs should receive immunity for the damage done by their drug. Alcohol and tobacco distributors now have the same immunity for the damage done by their products.[32] Otherwise, the price of drugs would have to reflect highly uncertain liability risks and would therefore be very high relative to production costs. A powerful black market would result.

A Practical Choice. Given drug prohibition's counterproductivity and the drawbacks of the other options we have described, the most practical alternative would be commercial licensing. While government regulation is not risk free, there is ample, successful precedent for regulating dangerous products and services. The government would regulate the drug marketplace in the public interest just as it regulates power companies, telecommunication companies, liquor sales and gambling.

The Role of the Food and Drug Administration

For the most part, the food and drug regulatory system accomplishes the goals that were set for it when it was first enacted in 1906. Prior to that, quackery was far more common than it is today, and the purveyors of patent medicines foisted on an unwary public myriad potions and medicines for ailments real and imagined. Often these remedies did more harm than the diseases they purported to treat. At best, many were harmless but ineffective.

Presently, a new drug must go through years of testing—often ten years or more—before it is approved for sale to the public. The FDA supervises testing to determine that the proposed drug product is both efficacious and safe; that it will do what it claims to do and that it will do no unacceptable harm to the patient if used as directed.

In recent years, the medical and pharmaceutical communities' authorized monopoly over medicinal drugs has been controversial. The FDA also has come under attack. During the 1960s and 1970s, the alleged cancer cure laetrile acquired a cult of advocates who warred against the FDA's refusal to approve that drug. In the late 1980s, there was controversy over scandals regarding the testing and regulation of generic drugs as substitutes for brand-name drugs. More recently, the drug L-tryptophan has been restricted, and advocates of its use claim the restrictions were unwarranted. Advocates for AIDS victims also frequently complain about FDA delays in approving AIDS drugs. Nonetheless, the Food and Drug Administration does much good by protecting the public from tainted food and unsafe drugs. The FDA also provides powerful protection of desperate sufferers from medical fraud. It ensures that those who have a disease for which there is effective treatment will not be sidetracked by worthless remedies.

No rational legalization proposal would subject well-established recreational drugs to the new-drug approval process of the FDA, for such drugs probably never could receive approval. Rather, the common recreational drugs that we would legalize should be "grandfathered" as were alcohol, tobacco and aspirin, none of which was ever subjected to that process. Newly discovered plant drugs or synthetics, however, would be subject to FDA scrutiny, as they now are, before they could be sold. They, too, would receive a patent monopoly and could be sold only on terms fixed by the proprietor of the drug. This would reward the drug companies for the research and the lengthy process of testing necessary to get FDA approval. As recreational drugs for the most part, they then would be sold over the counter as patented and trademarked products. The manufacturers could defend their patent rights against incursions by counterfeiters of their products.

The major difference between our scheme and the present scheme, insofar as newly discovered drugs are concerned, is that the FDA would have to approve drugs developed to provide intoxication, as well as those having "medical" value. This would provide substantial incentives to the pharmaceutical companies to develop safer and less addictive pleasure drugs than most of those now on the market. What should happen when the manufacturer's exclusive rights in such a drug expire? If the drug is a popular recreational drug, and no more dangerous than the drugs already available, such drugs should enter the generic market.

Banning Advertising: A Pesky Constitutional Question

An important dilemma for drug-legalization advocates has been expressed by Milton Friedman: "With respect to restrictions on advertising, I feel uneasy about either position. I shudder at the thought of a TV ad with a pretty woman saying, 'My brand will give you a high such as you've never experienced.' On the other hand, I have always been very hesitant about restrictions of freedom of advertising for general free speech reasons. But whatever my own hesitations, I have very little doubt that legalization would be impossible without substantial restrictions on advertising."[33]

A ban on all drug advertising, including cigarette and alcohol advertising, might be a worthwhile trade-off for the benefits of drug legalization. We already have a ban on broadcast advertising of cigarettes, the American Medical Association has endorsed extending that ban to print advertising,[34] and American distillers voluntarily keep their hard-liquor advertising off the air.[35] Certainly, the powerful alcohol and tobacco lobbies would fight legislation that would produce more radical restrictions on their advertising. Those lobbies would be joined by some civil liberties organizations as well. Whether the bans if enacted would then be upheld by courts is unclear. Despite earlier Supreme Court decisions suggesting that "purely commercial advertising" is not protected by the First Amendment,[36] the Court has several times rejected that theory. Plain and simple advertising is entitled to some protection by the First Amendment.

Drug advertising should perhaps be an exception, and there is precedent for that position. As recently as 1986, the Supreme Court held that Puerto Rico, although permitting gambling, could forbid advertising of gambling aimed at Puerto Ricans. Said Justice Rehnquist for a five-Justice majority, "the greater power to completely ban casino gambling necessarily includes the lesser power to ban advertising of casino gambling."[37] He added that it would be "a strange constitutional doctrine which would concede to the legislature the authority to totally ban a product or activity, but deny to the legislature the authority to forbid the stimulation of demand for the product or activity through advertising on behalf of those who would profit from such increased demand."[38] The Court also suggested that all advertising of cigarettes and alcoholic beverages could be banned in all media, on the same theory.[39]

The Puerto Rico case was an aberration, and the Court has usually rejected the greater-includes-the-lesser theory of the First Amendment. In *Virginia Board of Pharmacy v. Virginia Consumer Council,*[40] for example, the Court held that a licensed pharmacist had a First Amendment right to advertise truthfully the prices of prescription drugs. The Court has also invalidated restrictions on lawyer advertising[41] and on the posting of "for sale" signs on property.[42]

We are troubled by the free speech implications of a ban on drug advertising. Even if the Court would uphold such a ban, we would oppose it, especially if it did not include tobacco and alcohol, and probably even if it did so.

It is important under any drug regime—a legalized one like we propose or a dichotomous one like we have now—that there be free and open debate not only on the merits of legalization or prohibition, but on the merits, risks and evils of drugs themselves, either on their own footing or in comparison to other drugs. No one should worry about legal repercussions for advocating the use or nonuse of any drug. People should be encouraged to discuss, debate and explain the safe use of drugs, the dangers of combining particular drugs, as well as the joys or evils of such use. An all-media prohibition on drug advertising would have a chilling effect on such debate because the line between advertising and advocacy is murky.

The reasons why we have had little difficulty to date in distinguishing between advertising and advocacy is that in television and radio, where we have discouraged or banned alcohol and tobacco advertising, the costs of advertising are so high that it seldom makes sense for anyone to advertise who is not hawking a particular brand name in a thirty-second spot. In such an expensive medium, there is little doubt about what is and is not advertising. Very little private benefit accrues for advocating generic drugs.

Nonetheless, enterprising tobacco and liquor companies find ways of encouraging the audience to use tobacco and alcohol that escape bans on advertising. For example, the Partnership for a Drug-Free America campaign, which urges television, radio and print audiences to avoid "drugs," makes clear that the "drugs" they are crusading against do *not* include tobacco or alcohol. One reason: tobacco and alcohol companies are major financial contributors to the campaign.[43] Many of the advertising agencies that provide "pro bono" services to the campaign make much of their income servicing tobacco and alcohol companies. The tobacco and alcohol companies realize that presently illegal drugs are in competition with their own products and that the clearer a line is drawn between those products and theirs, the more beneficial it is to them. Hence, ironically, our largest drug manufacturers support campaigns against "drugs." We also see messages on public television, which eschews "advertising," that are difficult to distinguish from advertising. Programs are "sponsored" or "underwritten" by oil companies or other giant manufacturers or distributors of products and the viewers are so informed. This is apparently "public relations," not "advertising."

If a lot of money is to be made from advertising, a ban on it will encourage the creation of forms and modes of communication that come as close in function to advertising as is legally possible. The way to eliminate or greatly to curb advertising is not to ban it, but to make it unprofitable. If we prohibit the use of brand names on packaging or any other claims about the desirable effects of using a drug, confining descriptions to generic, chemical contents and explicit warnings about adverse consequences, we would eliminate most of the commercial incentive for advertising or its functional equivalent. We could also deny trademark protection with similar effects.

Manufacturers or distributors of marijuana might pool their resources and try to persuade potential customers to switch to marijuana from alcohol, and they might use sexual or other imagery in which to conduct that persuasion, but that would make economic sense only if most of the producers of marijuana could be induced to make a pro rata contribution to the "public relations fund." Otherwise, free riders could enjoy the benefits of the campaign without sharing any of the costs. We have some such campaigns by the tobacco industry or the beer industry because a small group of producers account for a large share of the total market, a state of affairs produced largely by brand-name advertising. If we make sure that there are no oligopolies in the marijuana business, there will be little pooling of resources for advertising. In a market where competition is mainly based upon price, there is little incentive for advertising anything *but* price. We should so structure the drug market that there are no excess funds to be spent on advertising. An alternative way to assure that there is little commercially motivated advocacy of particular generic drugs would be to require that any such advocacy by or on behalf of a manufacturer, distributor or retailer of a drug, or any organization of such persons, be accompanied by specified warnings. If the mode of advertising were print, the warnings could be required to be in no smaller type than the largest type in the ad (or one half of that size, if we want to be generous to the merchants). If the spoken word is the medium, the warnings would have to be repeated every thirty seconds, and so on. No one has a constitutional right to commit fraud or to purvey falsehood, and claims about the desirability of any product are arguably fraudulent if not offset by disclosure of effects, side effects and risks.

It is reasonably clear that we *can* legally prohibit advertising of drugs on radio and television, which are by far the most powerful advertising media for influencing children. There may be no First Amendment right to advertise on the airways because they are owned by the public. Just as none have the right to advertise their wares in the Supreme Court Building, neither do they have such rights on the public airways. That is not an entirely persuasive theory, but it appears to be well established in the courts.[44]

Residual Law Enforcement

When drugs are legal, there still will be many important law-enforcement functions. First and foremost, police can revive their neglected tasks of trying to solve and deter murder, rape, robbery, burglary, theft and other serious crimes. Police still will need to enforce the laws against intoxicated driving. However, drug legalization will offer a substantial advantage over prohibition. The police resources that are now wasted on unsuccessful interdiction and suppression will be available for policing impaired driving and impaired operation of other dangerous machinery.

Police still will be required to enforce regulated conditions of drug use, just as we now must enforce rules on where and when drugs like alcohol and tobacco may be used, and, most important, to enforce laws against access by juveniles.

As with alcohol now, under drug legalization, the state still will need to enforce the laws against nuisances. Just as it is not desirable to live next door to a rowdy bar, it may not be desirable to live next door to a drug dispensary. A person offended by a drug retailer's mode of operation can make complaints to authorities and can seek nuisance abatement in the courts, just as now can be done with obnoxious alcohol establishments. Zoning of neighborhoods and licensing of drug retailers can restrict placement of retail-drug establishments. State laws now specify how far liquor stores and bars must be from schools, houses of worship and residential neighborhoods. Officers of the state also will be called upon to enforce similar regulations regarding the location and operation of drug businesses.

Coping with Drug Abuse in the Workplace

Patricia Saiki, administrator of the Small Business Administration, reports that substance abuse costs the economy "more than $100 billion annually in lost productivity and wages."[45] Estimates of the cost to American business of drug-and-alcohol abuse vary, but some measures support Saiki's claim, putting the amount in the ballpark of one hundred billion dollars per year.[46] Consequently, during the late 1970s and early 1980s, federal government experts on workplace substance abuse developed a comprehensive system, called "employee assistance program" (EAP), that employers could use to deal with employee drug-and-alcohol problems if they affect an individual's job performance.

Many EAPs concentrate only on substance-abuse problems, while other so-called broad-brush EAPs also tackle other off-duty difficulties, such as compulsive gambling, family or marital strife, the stress of life and mismanagement of personal finances.

At its optimum, an EAP is a resource which an employee can tap for confidential help when substance abuse or other problems have gotten out of hand. Ideally, the employee makes a self-referral to the program, although supervisors generally also can refer a "problem" employee to the program. In return for self-referral or cooperation after supervisorial referral, the EAP is supposed to give the employee a measure of job protection. That is, so long as the employee carries out the program's reasonable recommendations for obtaining professional help and therapy, the employee usually will be able to retain his or her job. Such programs do not operate as a means for identifying and firing a problem person, but as a positive means to use the employee's drive for job survival to encourage that person to come to grips with important problems, including drug-abuse problems.

When EAPs operate properly, they are humane, legally defensible and fair. Employers like the programs because they protect legitimate interests of the employer, such as workplace safety and worker efficiency. Employees and unions like properly operating EAPs because they respect the workers' right to be left alone regarding off-the-job behavior as long as it does not affect on-the-job performance or safety. Under EAPs, law enforcement is left to the state rather than usurped by corporations.

EAPs encourage troubled workers to get outside help in a relatively nonpaternalistic manner that involves no more coercion than is justified by the employer's legitimate interests. Under an EAP, loss of a job is not punishment; it is an inevitable consequence of an employee's uncorrected performance deficits.

Professor Dale A. Masi of the University of Maryland was a pioneer in the development of such programs. From 1979 to 1984, he directed the model federal employee assistance program for the Department of Health and Human Resources. As Dr. Masi testified to the 1988 congressional committee hearings on drug legalization, "a majority of drug abusers (of both legal and illicit drugs) are in the workplace."[47] EAPs therefore could help reduce drug abuse by focusing attention where drug abusers are most likely to be found: on the job. EAPs succeed because holding on to productive and meaningful employment is a powerful incentive for a person troubled by substance abuse to become and remain sober.

According to general principles of behavioral psychology, the *inevitable* prospect of losing a good job as a result of a return to drug abuse is likely to "shape" sober behavior, while threat of punishment probably only would promote guile in continuing the drug-abusing behavior. If they are nothing else, successful EAPs are evidence that positive incentives can promote sobriety even though the entire coercive apparatus of the state has failed to keep contraband drugs off the market.

PUTTING DRUG-CONTROL MONEY WHERE IT WOULD DO SOME GOOD

During the past decade and a half, America has undergone a shocking amount of economic and social decay. An American merchant seaman who visited Calcutta in the 1930s recently reminisced that he was astonished to observe people sleeping on the streets in that city. In that respect, Calcutta of the 1930s is America of the 1990s. We have people sleeping on the streets, and it no longer shocks most of us. The gap between the wealthiest and the poorest in this country is growing, partly because middle-class blue-collar workers have lost jobs to foreign competition, partly because minority participation in the middle class declined as a result of cutbacks in government employment and white resistance to affirmative action, and partly because our educational systems have failed in their mission.

The surest way to deal with the problem of drug abuse in this country is to do something about the hopelessness felt by large portions of the American population. Instead of wasting its resources on futile drug prohibition, America needs to invest in economic development of its urban communities and in rebuilding our educational infrastructure. Every dime spent on Head Start is worth five dollars spent on drug prohibition. Any young person who sees hope for advancement and for a rewarding and useful life will have something better to do than obsessive pursuit of intoxication. One of the most important steps in a comprehensive drug-control program under legalization is to reestablish opportunities for America's underclass.

Six Steps for Change

The advocates of drug legalization should find some important lessons in the methods employed by other reformers who have successfully precipitated major change in American society. Six steps employed by the civil rights movement in the 1960s and the opponents of the Vietnam war in the 1970s are applicable to the drug-legalization campaign.

Generally, the steps include:

1. debate and discussion;
2. formation of advocacy groups, organizations which will lobby for drug legalization;
3. general education of the public;
4. study of concrete alternatives and planning;
5. petitioning, lobbying and campaigning for repeal legislation;
6. incremental implementation.

These steps overlap each other to a great extent, and much of the process is well launched already.

Debate and Discussion

Since 1988 there has been more debate and discussion of the drug-legalization option than there has been in the previous three quarters of a century of our war against drugs. Even advice columnist Ann Landers joined the debate in April 1990, with two days of "Dear Ann" letters both pro and con.[48] Her correspondents included William Bennett, who wrote to oppose the idea. Although she finally revealed her opposition to legalization, Landers provided a forum for both sides of the debate.[49]

Formation of Advocacy Groups

Organized groups favoring legalization already exist. The National Organization for the Reform of Marijuana Laws (NORML) advocates legalizing marijuana, although not necessarily other drugs. Eric E. Sterling left his position as counsel to the United States House of Representatives to form the pro-legalization National Drug Strategy Network because his own work on the largely punitive 1988 drug

legislation passed by the one hundredth Congress left him disillu-
sioned about the damage the drug war was doing to the American
institutions of law and justice.[50] Arnold Trebach's Drug Policy Foundation and libertarian groups such as the Cato Institute also include
drug legalization as part of their general reform proposals.

Education

Education is well underway. There has been an outpouring of articles
on the topic of drug legalization, including several opinion pieces and
editorials in the *Economist*,[51] a highly influential article by Ethan
Nadelmann in *Science*[52] and important writings by legal scholars such
as Steven Wisotsky[53] and Randy E. Barnett.[54]

Television, radio and newspapers also have shown interest in this
topic since 1988. Ted Koppel's "Nightline" has featured several programs on the topic. "David Brinkley's Journal" had a program on the
topic, and "The MacNeil/Lehrer NewsHour" had a segment on the
subject. William F. Buckley's "Firing Line" conducted a two-hour
television debate on legalization. Radio talk-show hosts such as Tom
Leykis and Dr. Dean Edell have frequently discussed the subject. Even
William Bennett did his share to publicize the cause by calling it
"morally scandalous."[55]

Concrete Planning

Professor Steven Wisotsky of Nova University outlines a proposal
which many drug reformers would endorse as part of the planning
step. He suggests "appointment of a national study commission of
experts, politicians and lay leaders to make findings of fact, canvass
a full range of policy options, and recommend further research where
needed."[56] Wisotsky explains that the work of the National Commission on Marijuana and Drug Abuse performed useful educational
functions by publicizing options in marijuana policy. He believes the
goals of the commission should be to suggest policies that would
(1) reduce drug abuse and (2) reduce "black market pathologies."[57]

Wisotsky would like to see such a commission

- define the drug problem, separating its different components;
- state national goals clearly;

- set realistic and principled priorities based on truth, with protecting children as the highest priority;
- protect public health;
- respect the value of individual liberty and responsibility.

Incremental Steps

Implementation of drug legalization should move through several stages. We should immediately adopt a more pragmatic policy concerning AIDS contagion among intravenous drug users. Needle exchange, a commonsense public-health measure, would do more than help halt the spread of AIDS. Legalizing needle exchange might help to convince the public that the drug abuser is a person who needs to be treated with compassion. Legalizing needle exchange can be done state by state.[58]

The government also should immediately "reschedule" the antiemetic marijuana. It is unconscionable that marijuana is a Schedule I drug, which physicians cannot even prescribe for purely medicinal purposes.

The next phase of implementation probably should include establishing programs to assist heroin addicts, most of whom could participate responsibly in society if they could get a clean, reliable and affordable supply of heroin. It also ought to be politically feasible to decriminalize marijuana for recreational use.

The ultimate goal of the implementation steps should be institution of a comprehensive drug-regulation scheme such as described earlier.

THE PROGNOSIS FOR CHANGE

Few critics of drug prohibition foresee substantial decriminalization or legalization happening soon. They are aware of the widespread support for present punitive enforcement policies. "We need to keep pointing out the problems with current laws, pointing out the costs of the criminalizing approach. We need to be patient, persistent and polite. It will take time, though I can't even guess how long," says Arnold Trebach, president of the Drug Policy Foundation.[59] "It would require a sociological equivalent of Hiroshima," said William F. Buckley, Jr., in a telephone interview. The same would have been said a few years ago about the collapse of Communism.

New York State Senator Joseph Galiber advocates legalization, and his press spokesperson, Tricia Doyle, says she can't imagine the New York legislature approving the bill he introduced to permit sale of narcotics or anything like it, for "a long time—decades." She notes, however, that the Senator got a lot of mail after he testified in the House, and that only about 5 percent of the letter-writers opposed Galiber's legislation. Little opposition has arisen in his district, but little active support has emerged either.

Marshall Fritz, president of the libertarian educational organization Advocates for Self-Government, is much more optimistic."[60] Fritz believes more intense enforcement—as during alcohol prohibition—will convince a rising number of people that drug laws not only don't work, they do harm. "More respected leaders will be going public in favor of legalization—changing their minds or getting the courage to speak out."[61] Once public opinion changes noticeably, "relegalization" will happen fairly quickly.

A remarkable development has occurred since 1989: several of our most respected judges have publicly supported legalizing drugs. United States district judges Warren W. Eginton of Connecticut,[62] Robert W. Sweet of New York[63] and James C. Paine of Florida[64] have all taken that position. United States district judge Scott O. Wright of Missouri supports legalization of marijuana,[65] and United States District Judge Whitman Knapp favors repeal of federal drug prohibition, leaving the matter entirely to the states.[66] Orange County, California, Superior Court judge James P. Gray supports legalization of marijuana, cocaine and heroin,[67] as does a United States magistrate for Orange County, Ronald W. Rose.[68] The potential influence of such judicial opinion should not be underestimated.

The most troublesome obstacle to legalization is cognitive. Legalization is counterintuitive. When presented with undesirable behavior of others, the natural reaction of human beings is to try to suppress it. Sometimes that works, but sometimes, as in drug prohibition, it has the opposite effect. Drivers whose cars get in cornering skids have to be trained to reject their intuitions and steer into, rather than away from, the skid. Drivers whose brakes lock up and produce a braking skid have to be trained to ease up on the brake pedal rather than pressing even harder. These solutions, like drug legalization, are counterintuitive, but they work.

CHAPTER 14

A Harm Minimization
Approach

*"[T]he primary goal of our national drug policy . . .
should be to reduce and control the use of all the
recreational mood-altering drugs in order to provide
for their safe, pleasurable use, consistent with
centuries-old human experience, while minimizing
their harmful effects on individuals, in the family,
and society as a whole."*

DR. STEVEN JONAS, PROFESSOR OF PREVENTIVE
MEDICINE, SCHOOL OF MEDICINE, STATE
UNIVERSITY OF NEW YORK AT STONY BROOK[1]

WHETHER AMERICA legalizes and regulates the distribution of illicit
drugs or simply de-escalates the drug war, our basic objective must be
essentially the same: harm minimization. Neither the appetite for
psychoactive drugs nor their supply can be made to disappear. A
"drug-free" society is no more attainable than a "sex-free" society.
Pretending otherwise ignores at least eight thousand years of history
and guarantees failure.[2] We must accept reality and adopt policies and
programs designed to minimize the harm, to both users and the rest
of society, resulting from the use of psychoactive drugs.

One way to minimize the harm from drugs is to reduce the number of people who use them. Strategies designed to curtail or reduce the numbers of drug consumers are a legitimate part of a rational drug-control program, but they cannot be the only, or even the primary strategies, as they are today. The reasons are at least twofold: (1) apart from tobacco use, serious drug abuse—drug use that is dangerous to health, obsessive, destructive of the user's values, incapacitating, or criminogenic—occurs in only a small fraction of drug users.[3] Treating all drug users as needing conversion to abstention is a monumental waste of resources; (2) abstention from all psychoactive drugs is usually unobtainable; nonabusers do not want to quit in most cases and are poor prospects for abstention programs.

We must also approach the drug problem as a unity, not a duality or a trinity. The major differences between alcohol and tobacco, prescription psychoactives, and illicit drugs reflect their legal status, not their pharmacological properties. All such drugs are mood-altering chemicals that cannot rationally be regulated independent of the regulation of others. The dangers of using such drugs differ, as do their addictive properties, but the basic needs that they respond to and their psychosocial and physiological functions overlap considerably. A contradictory regulatory approach to these drugs undermines harm reduction.

A rational program, consistent with American traditions of individual liberty and responsibility, should include governmental sponsorship of a panoply of noncoercive methods of discouraging nonmedical drug use. One of these methods is education in the narrow sense of imparting truthful information about drugs to those who lack it. Another is education in the broader sense of assisting people in processing information and in understanding the role of drug use in their own lives; even attempting to alter values that predispose toward drug use. Other ways to discourage drug consumption would include many methods that we sketched when we discussed the forms of legalization. These methods include taxing the drugs sufficiently to discourage consumption but not so high as to create rivers of illegality, and prohibiting drug use in public places.

Equally important, government should support educational programs aimed at teaching drug users how to reduce the risks—to themselves and others—of deaths by overdose, of transmitting infectious diseases through sharing of drug paraphernalia and of accidents caused by operating machinery while under the influence. Educational efforts should also include imparting understanding of the causes of addiction and dependency, how to avoid these syndromes and how to recognize them when they are present, in ourselves and others. Drug policy must treat drug abuse as primarily a health problem. If it is also a moral problem, it is not one that the state can or should try to solve by punitive measures. Approaching drug abuse as a health matter should not, however, cause us to treat drug dependency or intoxication as an excuse for criminal conduct. The law should and must punish those who seriously harm others, whether or not the harmdoer was under the influence of drugs.

Until controlled legalization is fully accomplished, we should, as an interim measure, permit physicians to prescribe any psychoactive drug to those who are seriously dependent upon it or a related drug, just as we now permit methadone maintenance of heroin addicts. Such maintenance programs should be integrated with treatment programs, but their availability should not be conditioned upon simultaneous submission to treatment.

We should abandon all efforts to bribe or coerce producer countries into trying to eliminate the growing of the raw materials for psychoactive drugs. We should simply set an example for them by terminating our own governmental support of the tobacco industry. We should also dissociate our government from any efforts to promote the consumption of American tobacco products abroad.

Treatment should be available, at nominal or no cost, to anyone who needs help with substance abuse, whether the substance is tobacco, alcohol, heroin, caffeine, sleeping pills, aspirin or any other. Few more cost-effective investments in people can be imagined.

We should continue to fund research on psychoactive drugs, but broaden its scope. We should not only emphasize a search for new drugs to be used in both prevention and treatment of drug abuse but also encourage the discovery and development of safer and less addictive drugs. We should also fund honest, objective research on the effects of our present drugs on both mental and physical health.

PREVENTION PROGRAMS

Drugs and the American Culture

In no major country in the world are drugs and their kin more pervasive a part of daily life than in the United States. Americans not only consume a disproportionate share of cocaine and marijuana, they are guzzlers of alcohol, major smokers of tobacco, users of tens of billions of dollars' worth of vitamins, minerals, pills and nostrums. Our mental and physical health delivery systems increasingly rely upon pills and potions both to cure and to prevent illness. Advertisers annually spend billions of dollars trying to persuade us that tobacco and alcohol will not only make us sexy and happy but that over-the-counter medication will free us from pain and discomfort, even make us more agreeable and productive. Drugs available only on prescription are heavily promoted to health professionals and even commonly advertised to the general public. We are told to ask our doctors to prescribe all sorts of medication, including drugs to remove wrinkles and to grow hair. The news media announce almost daily the development of miracle drugs or the discovery of mysterious but beneficial effects of older, common chemicals or of foods or vitamins. It is as though we believe in the fountain of youth and eagerly await discovery of the correct combination of vitamins, minerals, herbs and drugs that are its constituents. Even discounting for fads and fantasies, American pharmacology is an awesome enterprise.

It is a formidable if not impossible task for government to achieve major reductions in the demand for psychoactive drugs in a society peppered with propaganda that reinforces the drug culture. Since there are chemicals that will cure, prevent or ameliorate most major illnesses, and will remove many symptoms of previously incapacitating mental illnesses, why can't there be one that will make us happy? The truth, of course, is that there are such drugs, hundreds of them. The happiness they impart is transitory, and there are risks attached to their use, but the euphoria that accompanies the use of many drugs is real, and it is virtually the only euphoria experienced by many of their users.

Weakening the drug culture would create a better climate for preventive efforts, but that is a task that the government has not undertaken. Part of the explanation of this hands-off approach to the drug culture is in the realm of economics. Tobacco and alcohol are major American industries, providing employment to millions of Americans. The pharmaceutical companies are one of the few American industries that remain major national and international growth industries. American companies lead in the development and distribution of legitimate drugs in the same way their predecessors led in automobiles half a century ago. Sales of vitamins, minerals, herbs, aspirin, cough syrup, cold medicine and other over-the-counter medications are also huge national and international industries. All these enterprises are free to advertise their wares and they do so, dramatically and effectively. No major industry has a financial interest in counteradvertising to overcome the ethos of the drug culture.

Even if economic factors didn't keep the government from combatting the drug culture, health factors might. Much of what ordinary people learn about health and sickness, about symptoms and treatment, they learn from the same advertising and news sources that created and nourish the drug culture. The drug culture is here to stay.

The Tobacco Model

Despite the drug culture; the popularity and addictiveness of tobacco; the ubiquity of tobacco advertising; the willingness of the American tobacco industry to spend billions supporting friendly legislators, researchers and propagandists,[4] and centuries of lawful use of the drug in the United States, preventive efforts have worked as well with tobacco as with any other drug.

From 1965 to 1987, the number of adults who smoke tobacco dropped from 40 percent to 29 percent.[5] The numbers have now dropped to about 25 percent of the adult population. Half the living adults who smoked have now quit.

A major source of this impressive reduction in smoking is the educational efforts led by the Surgeon General, the Health and Human Services Agency, the American Cancer Society and many other organizations. The major thrust of the preventive effort regarding tobacco is informational: imparting truth about the devastating effects of smoking on the human body. The average smoker lives several years less than the nonsmoker, and the differences in general health are even more pronounced.[6] Americans have responded rationally to truthful data about a drug.

Other important factors are at work. Because smoking is harmful and offensive to nonsmokers, the past decade has seen an outpouring of regulations prohibiting or regulating smoking in schools, medical facilities, restaurants and public and semipublic buildings—even private offices. Smoking on domestic airlines flights has been eliminated. Even the White House became smoke-free when Hillary Rodham Clinton became First Lady, an edict that was preceded in millions of American homes and will be emulated across the nation in millions of others. Such restrictions have not only forced smokers to moderate their use, thus improving their health, but have provided strong motivation to quit entirely. Since smokers experience withdrawal discomfort when they can't satisfy an urge to smoke (every thirty minutes or so), the only way to avoid much discomfort—given the pervasiveness of the restrictions—is to quit smoking. Antismoking campaigns have been much more effective among college-educated and upper-class Americans than among less-educated and blue-collar workers. Not smoking is therefore becoming a status symbol, providing further impetus to quit.

Prevention programs have not been very successful with youngsters. About 20 percent of high school seniors smoke cigarettes, and this number has remained fairly constant since 1980. High school females are smoking at an even greater rate than they did a decade ago. The common explanation is that they have become more weight-conscious and that smoking is an effective weight control device.[7] A study by the National Center for Health Statistics also suggests that teenagers who take up smoking do not understand the addictive power of cigarettes. Virtually all who start smoking expect to quit in a short time, and almost none are able to do so. Commenting on the study, based upon interviews of 9,965 teenagers, former Health and Human Services Secretary Louis Sullivan opined that "Teen-agers greatly underestimate the addictiveness of tobacco and greatly overestimate their ability to control it."[8]

Since at least nine out of ten smokers are addicted, and become addicted quickly, the emphasis in smoking control programs should be upon achieving total abstinence. "Responsible smoking" is not a concept taken seriously even by the tobacco companies. Tobacco manufacturers try to retain their addicts, and recruit new ones, however, by suggesting that the use of "low-tar," filtered, mentholated or other smoke-delivery systems may be less damaging than higher-tar, non- or less-filtered cigarettes. As a fallback, tobacco companies also peddle "smokeless tobacco," i.e., snuff and chewing tobacco, falsely implying that there may be little or no health risk with such alternatives.[9]

Preventive programs aimed at other drugs have aligned themselves with antismoking campaigns, but with much less success. Scare tactics are commonly used with marijuana, cocaine, heroin and other illicit drugs that have little grounding in fact. Such exaggeration is unnecessary in discussing the dangers of tobacco. Smoking not only presents risks to health, it is harmful to health, not only to the health of susceptible persons but to the health of every smoker, regardless of gender, race, age or physical characteristics;—indeed, harmful to the health of nonsmokers as well. Since tobacco is universally harmful and almost universally addictive, abstinence programs make eminent sense and are often, ultimately, effective. A "drug-free society" is a pipe dream, but a smoke-free society may be within the bounds of possibility.

School Prevention Programs

Early drug-prevention efforts were mainly aimed at wholly illicit drugs and were based primarily upon instilling fear. The classic example is *Reefer Madness,* a drug "education" film produced by the Federal Bureau of Narcotics. The film depicts a young man who goes berserk on a puff of marijuana, becomes violent, abusive and sexually aggressive and destroys his promising career. Released in 1937, *Reefer Madness* became a cult film in the 1960s, causing millions of belly laughs and strongly supporting the belief among youngsters that the government either didn't know the truth about marijuana or was prepared to lie about it to make young people conform.

Prevention programs in high schools then turned largely to providing information about the hazards of drugs, in the expectation that high school students who understood those hazards would eschew drugs. The programs appeared to fail. Efforts to elevate students' self-esteem were added. The programs still seemed to fail. There is even some evidence that they aroused the curiosity of high schoolers without also providing a deterrent, and thus encouraged drug experimentation.[10]

Most current prevention programs are aimed at younger students, those in junior high school or even elementary school. The reasons for targeting younger children are several. Our most vulnerable youngsters—the ones most likely to become abusers of alcohol or other drugs—drop out of school before reaching high school or soon thereafter. School programs that reach these children must start early. We must also face the reality that many American children, a majority in some areas, begin to experiment with tobacco and alcohol by the age of ten or eleven, and move on to other drugs in their early teens. The earlier children experiment with drugs, the more likely they are to become drug dependent in later years. Seventy-five percent of all smokers, for example, started smoking before they were twenty-one.[11] The way to prevent people from using a drug is to reach them before they begin.

Virtually all modern prevention programs used in elementary or junior high schools emphasize the teaching of skills in decision making about drugs. A major goal is to help students understand the pressures they feel to use drugs and how to resist those pressures. They study advertising to understand how it seeks to manipulate them (especially cigarette and alcohol advertising). They examine data about the extent of drug use and thus discover that it is not true that "everybody does it." Information is also provided about the health risks of drugs, as in predecessor programs, but with less emphasis and, hopefully, greater fidelity to truth.[12]

The most popular program in American schools is DARE (Drug Abuse Resistance Education), the brainchild of former Los Angeles chief of police Daryl Gates. It is taught to more than 5 million children in three thousand communities and fifty states. The popularity of the program rests in part on some early studies suggesting that DARE works[13] and also on the fact that it is taught by a uniformed police officer. No teacher need be trained in drug education if DARE is adopted. Rigorous follow-up studies, however, fail to show that DARE reduces the use of tobacco, alcohol or illicit drugs.[14] It has some such effect for the first two years after the program, but that effect wholly disappears by the third year, so that students exposed to DARE are just as likely to use drugs as those who were not exposed to it.[15] The reason for DARE's apparent failure is unclear.[16] The curriculum is similar to that of programs that do seem to work. However, the program lasts for only seventeen weeks. Reinforcement may be needed for several years. The training of the police officer–teachers may be inadequate and some may (in disregard of the curriculum) emphasize scare tactics, as of old. Nor is there any integration of DARE into the regular school curriculum and thus no reinforcement from teachers in other courses.

A more promising program is STAR (Students Taught Awareness and Resistance) begun, as was DARE, in the early 1980s. Like DARE and other programs, STAR has classroom exercises designed to help students understand and cope with peer pressure, advertising and other external influences, but it also involves parents and the community. Students are given assignments to take home and work through with their parents. This often causes parents to realize that their own drug usage has a powerful effect on their children, and causes them to change those habits. Community organizations are also involved in STAR, as are media campaigns. Coalitions work together to reduce the availability of drugs to children, especially by monitoring local stores that sell tobacco and alcohol to minors, and pressuring them to stop. Children are often involved in the monitoring programs. A five-session booster program is taught the following year to reinforce resistance skills and attitudes.

STAR is widely taught in middle and junior high schools in Kansas, Missouri and Indiana. It has also been introduced in fifteen schools in Washington, D.C. Five-year follow-up studies involving 5,065 students show rates of tobacco, marijuana and alcohol use to be 20 to 40 percent below those of students who did not have the STAR program.[17] By ninth and tenth grades, STAR students used cocaine at half the rate of other students.[18]

No school programs seem to be very effective in preventing the use of alcohol among teenagers.[19] Forty percent of youngsters between twelve and seventeen used alcohol in 1991,[20] and 75 percent by the time they are high school seniors.[21] This is about the same as the percentage of adults who use alcohol. It is very difficult to persuade anyone not to use alcohol when their parents use it, their churches and synagogues use it, when it is served in virtually every restaurant and in most households, is sold in grocery and convenience stores and is among the most heavily advertised products on television.

For high-risk children, such as residents of communities where drug use is prevalent, the mentally ill, school dropouts, children without parents, children of drug abusers, students who perform poorly in school, an even more comprehensive program is needed.[22] Programs like STAR need to be integrated into organizations having access to such children: churches, athletic and recreational clubs, Scouts and so forth. Efforts, both in and outside of school, to increase the general skill levels of such children and their access to educational and employment opportunities are also necessary. Parents, too, should be involved in the drug-prevention efforts on behalf of their children.

HARM MINIMIZATION AND DRUG EDUCATION

The Alcohol Model

Current educational efforts aimed at preventing the use of alcohol are largely confined to children in their pre-teens and to self-labeled alcoholics. Although alcohol is included in the list of substances that children and high schoolers are advised to avoid, drinking by teenagers is simply too pervasive for that advice to be the centerpiece of prevention efforts. The emphasis in most high school programs, and even some junior high schools, is similar to that for adults: responsible use. Even though it is illegal in every state for high schoolers (and most college students) to drink, students are commonly taught the difference between "social" and "problem" drinking, how to recognize the signs and symptoms of alcoholism, how to get help for alcohol abuse and the immorality and recklessness involved in driving cars while under the influence of alcohol. "Designated driver" programs are common in high school social functions, and are often applauded by parents who are less worried about their children getting drunk than about their getting killed.

The alcohol model is also largely applied to problems of teenage pregnancy and sexually transmitted diseases. Sex among children and teenagers is unlawful, but they are still taught "safe sex" in school. Some schools even distribute condoms. Most educators and parents would prefer that their children refrain from sexual intercourse, but their stronger concern is with teenage pregnancy, AIDS and other diseases. A "Just say no" approach to sex is a denial of reality that exposes children to premature pregnancy and even death.

A Comprehensive Approach to All Drugs

A rational drug-control program would provide reliable information about the major effects of all common drugs: effects on cognition, on mood, on ability to operate machinery; addictive properties; adverse side effects; effects of combining the drug with other drugs (such as alcohol and cocaine); risks to fetuses. Some progress has been made in requiring such information on tobacco and alcohol labels, but much more remains to be done in that regard. The same should be required with other drugs in a legalized system. But whether or not labeling disclosure requirements are implemented or strengthened, a responsible educational program would teach these subjects in far richer detail than is possible on a packaging label.

An agency that is independent of law enforcement and other political pressures should be charged with making findings concerning the important health and other risks of all psychoactive drugs. A new classification system would be advisable. Drugs could be separately classified according to several characteristics, such as addictive potential, overdose risks, adverse effects on the ability to operate machinery and so forth.[23] The new system should replace the controlled-drug classification system now in effect, a system largely politically determined, one that idiotically ranks marijuana as more dangerous than crack.[24] When illicit drugs are legalized, the Food and Drug Administration may be the appropriate agency to make these findings. A separate agency should probably be created in the interim to classify illicit drugs. Classifications should be based upon the best available scientific evidence, not the rantings of turf-protecting law enforcers.

There is understandable opposition to safe sex programs for teenagers because such programs may undermine abstinence programs if they are interpreted by some children as condoning teenage sexual experimentation. But, particularly in inner cities, the prevalence of teenage pregnancy and sexually transmitted diseases is increasingly producing a willingness to compromise. Exclusively focusing educational efforts on abstinence is an irresponsible betrayal of our youth, whether the education involves alcohol or sex.

When the subject is illicit drugs, however, the pragmatism prominent in many schools cannot be found. In virtually no schools, even colleges, do courses include drug-consumption safety practices. Nor is there discussion of possible benefits of drug use. Although marijuana is far less damaging to health than tobacco[25] or alcohol, if there are any school health programs that acknowledge that possibility, we have not heard of them. Nor is there any teaching about "responsible use" of illicit drugs or how to recognize drug "abuse" or "dependency." *Any* use of illicit drugs is treated as "abuse," and moralizing takes the place of teaching about different symptoms and severities of drug abuse or dependency. Education about illicit drugs is dominated by the tobacco model, where abstinence is the only goal. A rational program should include the alcohol model as well.

REESTABLISHING CULTURAL CONTROLS

As we noted in the chapter on drug history, most of the world, throughout most of its history, has relied upon nonlegal, cultural controls to deal with drug abuse. That worked fairly well in America until prohibition was instituted in this century. There is no reason cultural controls cannot make a major contribution today. Indeed, many such controls are already in effect, and they probably account for much of the reduction in the numbers of drug users that has taken place in the past decade.

The consumption of both tobacco and alcohol has been reduced substantially over the past decade or two, despite their lawfulness. The numbers of users of illicit drugs has also declined since about 1980, nearly a decade before the drug war was intensified by President George Bush. There are many explanations for these trends, all of them probably true in part.

America has become more health-conscious and aware that drugs, legal as well as illegal, can be and often are harmful to health. The carnage on the highways and the connection of alcohol to that carnage has finally begun to be appreciated, in large part due to organizations like Mothers Against Drunk Driving (MADD). These organizations not only engage in campaigns to persuade drinkers not to drive, they changed the way the laws against drunk driving are enforced. Moral sensitivity to drunk driving was greatly heightened in the process. We are also an aging society. The estimated median age of Americans rose from twenty-eight years in 1970 to almost thirty-three years in 1989. Older people tend to use psychoactive drugs, including alcohol, less than do younger adults. Dr. David Musto, a Yale Medical School drug historian, has a pendulum theory about drugs: our tolerance and intolerance for drug use (and drug abuse) is cyclical, and we are now in the early stages of a temperance cycle.[26]

Our intolerances are capable of producing great swings in drug-consumption patterns. Owners of or workers in bars and liquor stores can lose status as can patrons of them; inebriates can cease to be amusing and become disgusting to those who interact with them. It can become more difficult to engage in the liquor business in numerous ways. Zoning restrictions can be interpreted strictly as can licensing qualifications. Liquor stores, like crack markets, can be pushed farther away from schools and other potential customers. Cultural influences move government institutions far more powerfully than government can move them. They are likely to pick up strength, moreover, as less control is expected *of* government. Now, as during alcohol prohibition, many Americans seemingly believe that the government can end the "scourge" of drugs as George Bush promised he would. When we rid ourselves of such superstitions, we can then bring our cultural influences into fuller play.[27]

What the broad culture of a society can accomplish, smaller, more homogeneous subcultures can also accomplish within their ranks. An example is the drastic alteration of attitudes among Marines about getting drunk.

For more than two hundred years, Marines have had an image as hard-fighting, two-fisted drinkers. Soon after the Continental Congress authorized their formation in 1775, the first Marines were recruited and sworn in at Tun Tavern, in Philadelphia. Marines learn this in boot camp, and taverns and hard drinking have long been part of Marine folklore. In the past, a Marine who did not carouse with his comrades received severe social sanctions, and career advancement for someone who did not drink with the boys was often retarded. On anniversaries of the organization's formation, alcohol has flowed liberally. In sum, there was pervasive pressure in that military brotherhood to participate lustily in off-duty social events in which a drug—alcohol—was abused.

During the past decade, however, Marine Corps leaders have made a substantial effort to change the norms of behavior regarding the use of alcohol and other drugs.[28] These changes coincided with efforts to transmute the United States military into an all-volunteer force, whose members are professionals of both genders. The Corps' reputation—as a good-ol'-boy's club of brawling, rambunctious alcoholics—was inconsistent with professionalization. In an age of technological warfare, drinking severely impairs the ability to wage war. Thus, Marine Corps commands encouraged their officers to promote after-work athletic events and entertainment for young Marines which do not involve drinking. Happy hours at Marine Corps clubs have been curtailed, and the practice of announcing closing time so that the patrons can "load up" has been eliminated. Low-price drinks no longer are served, nor are extra-potent cocktails (that mix more than one type of alcohol but include no other liquid) served at the clubs. Alcoholics no longer are protected and coddled by the command structure, and a drunk-driving conviction is very detrimental, if not fatal, to a Marine Corps career.

The self-reported use of alcohol among Marines declined 29 percent between 1980 and 1988.[29] Even more impressive: despite increased enforcement of drunk-driving laws, the arrests of Marines for driving while intoxicated dropped 45 percent from 1982 to 1991.[30]

The Marine Corps' alteration of a dysfunctional standard of behavior, which was deeply rooted in Corps history and closely identified with the central norms of the organization, is an example of what can be done in many organizations. Redefinitions of appropriate or desirable behavior and conformity to the new definitions can be generated within the organization itself.

TREATMENT

Treatment objectives in a harm minimization program should be the reduction of harm, to the user and to others. Accordingly, our definition of treatment includes any sustained, supportive, professional intervention in the drug-use practices of another that is designed to help the user reduce the harm of such drug use. Abstinence should be the central objective where, as in tobacco smoking, controlled, relatively safe use is virtually impossible, due to the addictive nature of the drug use and the quick onset of withdrawal symptoms. Abstinence should be the main goal with respect to other drugs only if the client agrees with that objective and it seems clear to the clinician that responsible use is unlikely.

The problems (and definitions) of drug abuse vary with different drugs. Tobacco use is primarily a long-term physical health problem. Alcohol abuse may consist of frequent, almost daily intoxication that is bad for health, job satisfaction and personal relationships; or occasional binges accompanied by high-risk or clearly antisocial behavior (such as assaults). Abstinence may not be the only conceivable solution to either type of alcohol abuse. If problem drinkers can be helped to reduce the number or occasions when they drink to excess, or even to improve the nature of their behavior when they do drink to excess (e.g., avoiding unsafe sexual encounters), a harm minimization approach suggests that such an outcome is not a "failure" of treatment.

The same may be said of treatment for any other substance abuse. Even if the use of the substance cannot be terminated, or even curtailed by treatment, harm can be reduced if unsafe practices (such as use of contaminated needles) can be reduced or eliminated. No treatment is a failure that has reduced the harmfulness of a user's relationship with drugs.

All of which is not to say that the prospect of *any* success, in any form, should be sufficient to warrant admission of an applicant into a treatment program. Unless clients pay the entire cost of their treatment programs, the treatment objectives they accept and the likely beneficial effects must be considered in allocating the public's scarce treatment resources.

KINDS OF TREATMENT PROGRAMS

Methadone Maintenance

A common form of treatment for opiate dependents is methadone maintenance. Methadone is a synthetic opiate that satisfies opiate cravings without producing either a rush or a significant high. It is addictive, however, and transferring a morphine or heroin addict to methadone is thought by some to be not really treatment but a mere substitution of addictions. But methadone maintenance has several advantages over street-level heroin. It is uncontaminated and therefore unlikely to transmit disease or to poison the user. It is also administered orally, in liquid or tablet form, and a single dose can produce a stable metabolic level that lasts for an entire day. This permits the user to engage in employment and otherwise to lead a normal life. Heroin, on the other hand, must be replenished every three or four hours. Heroin maintenance is difficult to reconcile with normal employment and other activities. It is also expensive to administer.*

What methadone does, therefore, is stabilize addicts, removing them from the criminal subculture so that they can seek and maintain employment and, hopefully, reorient their lives free of heroin. The motivation to commit crimes to buy heroin is also eliminated by methadone maintenance programs.

Since both addicts and society are better off if the addicts are on methadone than if they are on street heroin, treatment is effective if the addicts remain in the program, whether or not they are ever weaned from opiate dependence. By that measure—retention rates—methadone maintenance programs are extremely successful. The retention rates are higher in such programs than in any other programs for opiate addicts.[31]

Methadone programs have been severely constrained in recent years because they are of no value in the treatment of cocaine dependency, which has mushroomed while opiate dependency has remained fairly constant. Since many heroin addicts are HIV positive before entering the methadone program, they often need a broad range of

---

*Heroin maintenance, now illegal in the United States, will become a feasible alternative to methadone when the technology is developed to deliver it in a "patch" or in subcutaneous timed-release capsules. It is an alternative in Europe, especially when methadone doesn't eliminate opiate craving or for some other reason is not effective in displacing heroin or morphine.

medical services that further strain the resources of methadone clinics. Plainly, methadone maintenance programs should be expanded.[32]

Therapeutic Communities

The most expensive treatment programs are therapeutic communities, where drug abusers commonly are expected to live for nine to fifteen months. Except for tobacco, the use of all other psychoactive drugs is usually strictly prohibited by the community. Smuggling is controlled and drug testing is routine. The use of any but approved drugs is ground for termination of treatment. The underlying strategy of these programs is to create a new culture for the drug abuser where resocialization, behavioral modification and training in self-discipline and self-awareness can take place. Occupational therapy is sometimes included, as is psychotherapy. Clients in these programs are commonly polydrug abusers and the therapies are virtually the same, after detoxification, regardless of the drugs formerly used by the clients. Those in such programs often voluntarily drop out or are terminated for infraction of rules.[33] The longer they remain, however, the more effective the treatment is.[34] Since these facilities are also scarce—and expensive—they are largely devoted to drug users with serious criminal behavioral problems or major adaptational impairments. Often, probation of a person convicted of a serious crime and facing prison is granted on condition of treatment in such a facility for a specified time.[35]

The fact that treatment is in a sense involuntary seems to have little or no adverse effect on treatment outcomes when compared to patients who enter "voluntarily."[36] The reason that there is little difference, apparently, is that all entrants into the program are pushed there by something or somebody, or a combination of circumstances.[37] Whether they are dysfunctional because of the way they relate to their families or the way they relate to society generally, or to the criminal law, they go into these programs because they cannot live their lives as they want to live them. What the programs need in order to work is motivation and exposure. It doesn't matter where the source of that motivation comes from, as long as it is related to drug abuse.

Outpatient Programs

By far the most common treatment modality for drug abuse is the outpatient treatment program. As a group, the clients of these programs tend to be less seriously maladapted or dysfunctional than those in either of the other two basic programs. The motivations for entering such programs vary enormously and this shows up in the attrition rates, which are high. Opiate addicts offered the opportunity to "detox" may accept primarily to begin a new cycle of drug use, wherein they can get more enjoyment on lesser quantities of the drug they are dependent upon—usually heroin. Others frequently enter such programs to satisfy their family members or courts and to limit or avoid criminal punishment or other adverse consequences, but not really to get off drugs.

The methods or theories of nonresidential programs are extremely varied, and none seem to work appreciably better or worse than most others. Here, as in residential programs, favorable outcomes are most positively correlated with length of time in the program.[38]

In all these programs, dropping out or being terminated before graduation is not an unqualified failure, for dropping out of a program may be itself therapeutic. Relapses are common in all efforts to combat drug dependency, whatever the drug. Relapses are as great in tobacco addiction treatment as with any other kind of substance abuse. Each time clients drop out or relapse, they learn something about their problems and their weaknesses and are often better able to cope with them on subsequent treatment attempts. Moreover, according to Dr. Douglas Anglin, director of the Drug Abuse Research Center at U.C.L.A., although most addicts go into and out of treatment several times, "Each time they do, their drug abuse goes down, along with their criminal activity. Even if they never achieve abstinence, they may be able to reduce the size of their habits, or shift to less harmful drugs. These are positive gains, both for the addict and society."[39]

Hybrid Programs

Drug treatment is a phase or aspect, but not the sole objective, of institutions in which thousands of persons with drug problems are confined. Prisons and mental health hospitals are the major institutions of this kind. In many prisons, 60 to 80 percent of inmates were abusers before they went into prison and many are able to remain so while behind bars.[40] Every prison should have drug treatment available to every inmate who wants it. Unfortunately, many prisons have no such programs, and many of those that do provide treatment have far more applicants than available space. In some

respects, institutional programs resemble those in drug-treatment centers and in some respects outpatient programs, hence their separate
description here as hybrids.

Are Treatment Programs Successful?

Many studies have been conducted of treatment programs. All concur
that, contrary to common assumptions, treatment for drug abuse
"works." Two major longitudinal studies did follow-ups on participants in all major treatment modalities: methadone maintenance, residential therapeutic or therapeutic community and outpatient
drug-free. No significant differences were seen based upon the modality of treatment.[41] Considering the unscientific methods of most treatment programs, and the primacy of the profit motive in many of them
as well, the similarity in their outcomes is puzzling. What the
similarity suggests is that effective treatment is distinctly humanistic.
Persons who participate in drug therapy are depressed and poorly
adjusted; they are in pain, vulnerable and confused. They need nurturing and support. They receive it in any decent program. The results
may reflect the "Hawthorne Effect": any human-to-human intervention is likely to produce beneficial changes in behavior if it conveys
respect, concern and the desire to make things better.* Treatment
counselors expect substantial success and they get it. Many treatment
programs include group meetings in "Twelve-Step" structures, patterned after Alcoholics Anonymous. These programs offer support
and friendship from an entire group of people with similar problems,
support that persists after formal treatment is completed.

One of the studies, called TOPS (Treatment Outcome Perspective
Study), found that 40 to 50 percent of the participants were abstinent
three to five years after entering treatment and another 30 percent
reduced their drug consumption significantly. Fewer than 20 percent
were still regular users three to five years later.[42]

Another major study called DARP (Drug Abuse Reporting Program) found similar abstinence and improvement rates. Seventy-four

---

*The Hawthorne Effect is named after its place of discovery. Researchers at the Western Electric
Company in Hawthorne, Illinois, discovered, when trying to find out how changes in working
conditions affected productivity, that *everything* they tried increased productivity, even things
that were supposed to decrease it. The reason: workers who were part of the experiment felt that
the company cared about their working conditions. The resulting esprit de corps made them
more productive. See Elton Mayo, *The Human Problems of an Industrial Civilization* (New York:
Macmillan Company, 1933).

percent of the daily heroin users in the study had stopped completely or substantially reduced their usage twelve years after entering treatment.[43] Numerous other studies are confirmatory. They converge in suggesting that virtually any treatment works, the treatment works better the longer the subject remains in the program and the results endure over time.[44]

Reducing demand for illegal drugs produces much lower crime rates among treatment subjects, more stable employment, more productivity and better physical health.[45]

A cautionary note: There are rarely any control groups in these studies. Drug abuse is a self-limiting problem. Most serious drug abusers either die or get their problems under control, with or without treatment. Treatment is not a prerequisite to controlling drug consumption, or even to abstinence. Most drug users who quit, including heroin addicts and tobacco addicts, do so without treatment.[46] Hence the impressive improvements found in treatment studies are somewhat misleading. *All* the improvement cannot be attributed to treatment; some of it would have occurred anyway. But that does not destroy the basic premise: treatment does work; it just is not the only thing that works.

Are Treatment Programs Cost-Effective?

Every study that seems to have been done on cost-effectiveness of treatment programs has made positive findings. A 1990 study by the Institute of Medicine of the National Academy of Science found that even the most expensive programs saved more than their price in reducing the costs of crime, health care and lost productivity.[47] A comprehensive study of drug-abuse treatment in California found a cost-benefit ratio of 1:12. For every dollar spent on effective treatment, twelve dollars of social costs were saved.[48] These studies did not substantially take AIDS into account. Treatment costs for the average AIDS patient are at least $50,000, compared to less than one tenth of that for a year's outpatient methadone maintenance, and perhaps $15,000 for inpatient treatment community therapy.[49] If treatment more than pays for itself in avoiding AIDS health costs, imagine the cost-benefit ratio that would result if we could attach a dollar value to a human life!

Treatment is also much less costly than jail or prison. A Miami program that offers drug offenders a treatment alternative to jail or prison costs $500 to $700 per person per year, which is roughly the cost of jailing a person for nine days. Of the 4,500 people routed to the program since it began in 1989, 40 percent have completed it, avoiding drugs and other run-ins with the criminal justice system. Fewer than 10 percent have returned to the system as offenders.[50]

NEW DIRECTIONS

Therapeutic Drugs

A number of drugs have been found useful in various aspects of drug-dependency treatment. Some of those discoveries are recent.

Disulfiram (Antabuse) is useful in treatment of alcohol abuse, because it nauseates alcohol users when they drink, and thus provides an extra motivation to remain alcohol-free.[51] It is not by itself treatment, but it can be a helpful adjunct to treatment, especially in early stages, where the force of previous habits is strongest and the ability of the client to resist temptation is most in need of support.

Two categories of drugs that are useful in treating drug dependency are agonists and antagonists. Drugs that act as agonists satisfy the craving for the abused drug, and those that act as antagonists block the effects of the abused drug, so that taking the drug provides no euphoria or other psychoactive effects. Several such drugs exist for treatment of opiate dependency.

As noted, a common treatment for opiate addicts is methadone maintenance. Methadone is an opiate agonist; it satisfies the craving for all opiates. Methadone maintains the addiction, and may even intensify it, but because a twenty-four-hour dose can be administered, those who are maintained on methadone can work and otherwise carry on fairly normal lives. Other synthetic opiates may be superior. One, called LAAM, resembles methadone but is even more long-lasting, a single dose lasting forty-eight to seventy-two hours. For this reason, and possibly others, LAAM may eventually replace methadone. It has not yet been approved by the FDA.[52] Detoxification from opiate dependency can be severely unpleasant for the addict, sufficiently painful to be a strong deterrent to entering or remaining in a treatment program. Clonidine is a drug that greatly reduces the symptoms of opiate withdrawal, but it does not suppress the craving for opiates. Relapse rates during withdrawal have therefore been quite high in the past. Researchers have discovered, however, that by combining the administration of clonidine with the opiate antagonist naltrexone, the symptoms of withdrawal can be suppressed while the craving for opiates is eliminated.[53] Patients can then be maintained and treated on naltrexone alone while psychotherapy and group therapy provide the necessary reorientation. These drugs are therefore extremely helpful in converting persons on methadone maintenance into an opiate-free state.

Getting the right balance of clonidine and naltrexone is difficult, and if there is too much naltrexone, withdrawal symptoms can be intense. If there is an excess of clonidine, opiate craving persists. Another drug, buprenorphine, is also useful because it is an agonist-antagonist. It both alleviates withdrawal symptoms and reduces craving. When withdrawal is completed, the patient can be introduced to naltrexone and should be free of craving thereafter.[54]

A major problem remaining is to provide sufficient motivation for the clients to take their naltrexone faithfully. That problem may soon be solved, however, by the development, by Biotek, Inc., of a subcutaneous patch containing time-release capsules of naltrexone, administered similarly to the contraceptive Norplant.[55] There would then be no purpose for the addict to take opiates, since they would have no effect. The client would be immune to their power and therefore, in most cases, free of craving as well.[56]

Combined with aggressive outreach programs to identify opiate addicts and persuade them to accept treatment, opiate addiction could be brought under control, if not virtually eliminated, with the help of agonistic and antagonistic drugs. Cocaine, however, may be a more difficult problem. A central nervous system stimulant, cocaine seems not to have any antagonists. For reasons that are unclear, however, buprenorphine seems to suppress the appetite for cocaine as well as for opiates.

Several studies of monkeys provided access to unlimited supplies of cocaine show that monkeys will eventually kill themselves by cocaine overdose. But in a recent test on four monkeys supplied with cocaine in unlimited quantities but first administered buprenorphine, cocaine self-administration was reduced by 90 percent in one to two days. Cocaine self-administration remained suppressed by up to 92 percent during four months of buprenorphine administration.[57] Thus, buprenorphine may be a partial agonist to cocaine as well as to heroin.[58]

Researchers at Columbia University also recently developed an enzyme that not only blunts the effects of cocaine but breaks it down into inert constituents. The enzyme should greatly reduce any euphoric effects of cocaine and thus facilitate treatment of those who are cocaine-dependent.[59]

It has also recently been discovered that naltrexone, the drug that blocks opiate effects, has similar effects with alcohol. Unlike Antabuse, which makes one who takes a swallow of alcohol seriously sick, naltrexone seems largely to block the effects of alcohol and greatly reduces the appetite for it, without serious side effects.[60]

Other promising therapeutic approaches involve the use of psychotropic drugs. These approaches are based on the belief that drug addiction is often a manifestation of mental illness which itself often reflects chemical disorder in the brain. Drugs are sometimes abused in an effort to self-medicate an underlying natural chemical imbalance.[61] Tobacco addicts aside, only about 5 percent of the population are seriously drug-dependent, but the rate is nearly six times that among the mentally ill. Of the 14 percent or so of the population that have mental disorders, about 27 percent also have drug disorders. Conversely, about 37 percent of the population with alcohol disorders and about 53 percent with drug disorders other than alcohol also have a mental disorder.[62] The overlap is sufficient to complicate but eventually, perhaps, to simplify both psychotherapy and drug treatment in the areas of overlap.

Cocaine dependency is believed by many mental health professionals to be the result—in many instances—of inadequately treated depression. Antidepression drugs can help to eliminate or reduce the craving for cocaine and can help the patient to live a cocaine-free life. Administration of alternative stimulants, such as Ritalin, has also been effective in weaning patients from cocaine dependency.[63]

Heavy users of opiates or alcohol are often trying to control rage, aggression or hyperexcitability, which themselves are often symptoms of brain-chemical imbalances. Extremely aggressive persons, for example, may have low levels of serotonin, for which they compensate by consuming opiates or alcohol. Serotonin, tranquilizers or other drugs may be more effective mood-control agents and reduce the craving for drugs of abuse.[64]

As in the case of drugs that block the effects of drugs of abuse, the use of psychotropic drugs is not treatment itself, but is an adjunct or component of treatment. Almost any course of drug-abuse treatment requires reordering and rehabituation of the abuser's life patterns, enhancement of self-esteem, development of support networks and training in work and people skills. Strong cravings can be suspended, but the extensive conditioning or imprinting of reward mechanisms associated with drug dependency must be attended to on a daily basis, sometimes for decades.

Other promising nonchemical therapeutic techniques that have not been thoroughly tested include acupuncture, hypnosis, meditation and biofeedback. Many who receive acupuncture treatments claim that they reduce the craving for drugs.[65] Nobody knows why. It may be a placebo or a Hawthorne effect or it may be that the needles release chemicals in the body that perform functions similar to drugs of abuse. Acupuncture may be a method of squeezing a slight high from our own bodies, sort of a lazy person's jog. Meditation may also alter brain chemistry temporarily, producing a natural high.[66] Hypnosis has been quite successful in treating smoking addiction, when used not to create aversions but to leverage the subject's motivation. Dr. Herbert Spiegel of Columbia College of Physicians and Surgeons developed a simple, one-hour hypnosis treatment for smoking that results in the patient's quitting at least 20 to 25 percent of the time. Lengthier treatments produce claimed success rates of 80 to 90 percent.[67] If it works for tobacco, it might work for any drug. Biofeedback is also promising,[68] but the methods of harnessing biofeedback principles to the service of drug treatment are still being explored.

Recent discoveries in brain chemistry also hold promise for new drugs and new treatments for drug abuse. A few decades ago, neuroscientists discovered that there are specific proteins, called receptors, located on the surface of certain brain cells.[69] Some drugs attach themselves to the receptors, much like a key fits into a lock. This attachment, or "binding," then triggers activity within the brain cell itself. This led to the conclusion that there must be an original "key," a naturally produced brain chemical, for which the receptor was built. Fifteen years ago, keys to the opiate receptors, the endorphins, were discovered. Four years ago, a team at the National Institute of Mental Health discovered the marijuana receptor and soon thereafter researchers identified the natural brain molecule that binds to the marijuana receptor.[70]

It seems reasonable to hope that the natural molecules that bind to the receptors can be broken down into their constituents so that in the case of opiates, the portion of the chemical that produces euphoria or deadens pain can be separated from that which produces addiction.

The latter would then be a powerful drug for treatment or prevention of opiate addiction. Similarly, the portion of the molecule in marijuana that prevents nausea may be isolated and used as an antiemetic without producing a high, as might the components of marijuana that stimulate hunger, reduce blood pressure or reduce eye pressure in glaucoma sufferers. The portions that produce a high might even be separable from those that produce hallucinations.

Also of interest are some psychedelic drugs that some assert are of great benefit in helping the user kick drugs of abuse. One of these is ibogaine, a psychedelic obtained from the roots of an African rain forest shrub. A small industry has grown up outside the United States involving the use of ibogaine to help cut cravings for cocaine and heroin. The FDA is considering approval of research involving ibogaine, LSD and other psychedelics, in the hope that they can—among other benefits—help treat drug abuse.[71]

PUBLIC HEALTH PROGRAMS

Reducing Death and Disease from Drug Use

As we have argued throughout this book, far more death and disease are caused by drug prohibition than by the use of illicit drugs itself. Most deaths by "overdose" would not occur if drugs were legalized and regulated. Some may not be moved by that argument, even if they believe it to be true, because they feel that illicit-drug users are entitled to little sympathy. But drug prohibition also does great damage to the entire society, not only in crime and social deterioration and money out of our pockets, but in its adverse effects on our own health. Drug prohibition, especially as it is administered in America, kills thousands of innocent people by infectious disease.

The Drug Enforcement Administration persuaded state after state to criminalize the possession of hypodermic needles and other drug paraphernalia, as an adjunct of the drug war.[72] Drug users caught possessing "works" can be punished even if no drugs can be found on them; sellers of works can be punished even if they sell no drugs; and the risk of using drugs intravenously can be escalated by making needles scarce and thus encouraging users to share them. The results of these policies are devastating.

One in five inmates in Washington, D.C.'s prison system is HIV positive. Most of them got that way by intravenous injections of contaminated needles.[73] "Unsafe sex" is almost the only kind of sex that takes place in prisons, and rape is commonplace. Anyone sentenced to prison stands a good chance of having that sentence elevated to a death sentence through acquisition of AIDS. If they don't die from AIDS in prison, most prisoners will eventually be released into the community, regardless of the diseases they carry. If they are HIV positive, they will then begin to spread the virus to the society at large. HIV can be spread through sexual intercourse and to unborn children through the mother's infected blood. Unless a vaccine or a cure is found for AIDS we may all eventually perish from the plague.

In July 1991, the National Commission on AIDS, after a two-year study, found that 1 in 3 adult/adolescent AIDS cases are related to intravenous drug use;[74] 71 percent of female AIDS cases are linked to IV drug use or sex with an IV drug user; 26 percent of AIDS cases in men are linked to IV drug use or sex with infected persons. Half of New York City's 200,000 IV drug users are HIV positive.

The Commission also found that HIV is transmitted by unsafe sexual practices associated with the crack trade. Women commonly exchange sex for crack and are rarely in a position to insist on safe sex. One crack dealer reported having unprotected sex with thirty women in a single month in trade for crack.[75]

The AIDS Commission recommended drug treatment on demand and termination of the appalling practice of denying drug treatment to the HIV infected that it found in many programs. The Commission also urged the lifting of any and all prohibitions against sale or possession of injection equipment, and the expansion of clean needle exchange programs. The latter recommendation was opposed by the Bush administration and the rest were ignored.[76]

Europeans are more pragmatic. Among the earliest Western Europeans to respond rationally to the increases in hard-drug use among their populace were the Dutch. In the early eighties, the Dutch government adopted a harm-reduction approach to drug regulation.[77] Marijuana use was effectively decriminalized, and a comprehensive set of programs was adopted to integrate hard-drug users into society rather than making them outcasts. Treatment on demand is available and encouraged. Methadone is easily available to heroin addicts and sterile needles are accessible. Efforts are made to identify and monitor the health of hard-drug users. Although about 30 percent of Dutch addicts still take their drugs intravenously, the levels of HIV infection and AIDS are among the lowest in Europe, and only about 8 percent of AIDS patients are IV drug users (compared to about 23 percent in Europe as a whole and 26 percent in America). Despite this "user-friendly" approach to drugs, marijuana use is quite low and hard-drug use has stabilized. Drug-related death rates are also among the lowest in Europe.[78]

Even more radical reforms have recently taken place in parts of England and Scotland.

In 1985, doctors in Edinburgh discovered that more than 50 percent of their heroin addicts were infected with HIV, about the same as New York's rates.[79] In eight years, the numbers of addicts who inject has been reduced from thousands to only a few hundred, and the spread of HIV via contaminated needles has virtually stopped. The reason for the Scotch success: doctors are authorized to prescribe virtually any drug, in oral form, to addicts. Treatment programs are available and addicts are encouraged to become drug-free, but the major focus is on harm reduction. Only 22 percent of new patients entering treatment programs are IV users compared to 87 percent only five years ago. Local crime rates have also declined. The number of new HIV cases linked to contaminated needles in Scotland dropped from 120 per year to only 8 in 1992.[80]

A program in Liverpool has had equally dramatic results. In Liverpool, as in Edinburgh, prescription of oral drugs, even smokable cocaine, is permitted and sterile-needle exchanges function effectively. Police rarely arrest a first-time possessor or user of any illicit drug. Instead, they provide information about health and treatment services. Violent crime rates are down and many addicts are able to lead useful, productive lives.[81]

British drug policy has undergone dramatic changes. In the 1960s, Britain permitted the prescription of any drug for maintenance purposes, even heroin and cocaine.[82] This was changed in the late 1970s, in response to an increase of heroin availability in the black market. The privilege of physicians to prescribe drugs to addicts was curtailed and the emphasis shifted to criminalization. Not only dealers but users were criminally prosecuted. In the late 1980s, however, the pendulum swung back, largely in response to the AIDS crisis and partly in response to the failure of the drug-war approach. The older approach has been resurrected, with considerable success.[83] Throughout Britain where harm reduction has been revived, the police are supportive. Crime rates associated with drugs are down.

Clean needle programs have also been instituted in pockets of the United States, usually with great political difficulty, sometimes in defiance of law, by anti-AIDS activists or others concerned with health.[84] One of the objections to needle exchange programs, apart from the claim that they condone drug use, is the notion that needle sharing is a valued part of the illicit-drug culture and that making clean needles available would not reduce the transmission of disease because it would not diminish needle sharing. A program developed at Yale and tested in New Haven establishes otherwise.[85] Under the New Haven program, addicts who visit the needle exchange van select a code name. They are then given new needles in exchange for old, and the needles are coded, so that records can be kept of who receives and who exchanges the needles. The old needles are then routinely tested for HIV. On the assumption that needles that are turned in by the person who received them were not shared and that those returned by someone other than the person who received them were shared, the program supports the inferences that sharing dropped dramatically. Moreover, since needles returned by the person to whom they were issued tested positive for HIV at a much lower rate than those returned by someone else, an inference of reduced HIV transmission seems warranted. Ninety-four out of ninety-eight needles recovered from a shooting gallery which was not part of the program tested positive for HIV. When the exchange program began, two thirds of the exchanged needles tested positive. A bit more than a year later, the rate was less than 50 percent.[86]

As to the claim that clean needle programs will encourage heroin use, the New Haven program, like those in Amsterdam, Edinburgh and Liverpool, demonstrate otherwise. In New Haven the average age of the participants in the needle exchange program remained the same over a period of nearly two years. Moreover, the average length of addiction of the participants did not decline. Yale University professor Edward Kaplan interprets these results as evidence that the program has not increased heroin addiction.[87] Both phenomena provide a basis for concluding that the recruitment of younger addicts has been quite limited.

A Long-Term Solution

It is a liberal bromide that poverty, racism, family disintegration, poor education; inadequate employment, housing or health care are the root causes of whatever social problem is under discussion. In the case of drug abuse, however, the bromide captures considerable truth.

That drug abuse is more common among the impoverished, the unemployed; among the homeless and the mentally ill is not mere coincidence. Those who are deprived of the essentials of a decent life are in pain. People in pain look for relief wherever they can get it. Often the only succor they see is sold in small packets on the streets of their neighborhoods. If they succumb to the lure of drugs and then need help to control their cravings, the help is rarely there. Even those who are fortunate enough to get into treatment programs find it almost impossible to stay in them, or to get on top of their drug dependencies. People without jobs, skills, intact families and money, or with untreated mental illness, are much less likely to succeed in treatment programs than others who are not so burdened.[88] These are the root causes of the most intractable drug abuse in this nation. Unless these causes are ameliorated, many of our neediest people will remain enslaved by drugs.

In a recent book,[89] Elliott Currie, a sociologist at the University of California, Berkeley, makes the case that there are two distinct drug problems in America. One is drug abuse by the upper classes, those who have jobs, money, opportunity. The other is among the poor. The upper-class problem is self-limiting. People with much to gain from quitting or cutting down on drugs are usually able to do so, albeit with difficulty. The poor, who perceive no real alternative to drugs, are different. Their drug problems have been worsened by escalations in the drug war. If we are to have any hope of reversing the devastating effects of drug abuse among those most enslaved by it, we must declare drug peace and return to our ideals of social justice.

NOTES

Preface

1. Televised address of President George Bush, 5 September 1989. See *Los Angeles Times,* 6 September 1989, A1.   2. See John Hart Ely, "The American War in Indochina, Part 1: The (Troubled) Constitutionality of the War They Told Us About," *Stanford Law Review,* 42–2, 1990, 877, 884–91.

Chapter 1   An Overview: The Greater Evil

1. *Town & Country,* May 1979.   2. Ronald K. Siegel, *Intoxication: Life in Pursuit of Artificial Paradise* (New York: E. P. Dutton, 1989), 266–76.   3. Ibid., 260.   4. Ibid., 262–65.   5. Edward Brecher and the Editors of *Consumer Reports, Licit and Illicit Drugs* (Boston: Little Brown and Company, 1972) 7, 42.   6. See Douglas Husak, *Drugs and Rights* (New York: Cambridge University Press, 1992), 124–25.   7. Stephen J. Hedges and Gordon Witkin with Anne Moncreiff Arrarte, "Kidnapping Drug Lords: The U.S. Has Done It for Decades, But It Rarely Causes Trouble," *U.S. News & World Report,* 14 May 1990, 28–30. 8. Steven Wisotsky, "Crackdown: The Emerging 'Drug Exception' to the Bill of Rights," *Hastings Law Journal,* 38 (1987) 889–926, at 895, estimates that ". . . a $2–$3 gram of pure pharmaceutical cocaine becomes an $80–$100 gram of 35 percent street cocaine." From this it is possible to project that pure (100 percent) cocaine would have to cost between $228 and $285 per gram, or almost three times as much as does 35-percent cocaine. Dividing the range of street prices by the pharmaceutical prices, we can deduce that street cocaine costs somewhere between 70 and 140 times as much as pharmaceutical cocaine.   9. See Daniel Seligman and Patty de Llose, "The Case of the Crooked Bench," *Fortune,* 25 March 1991, 139.   10. "Judge Nixon says he 'Has Nothing to Hide,'" *National Law Journal,* 2 October 1989, 5.

Chapter 2   Identifying the Enemy: "Drugs," "Drug Abuse" and Other Concepts

1. President's Commission on Law Enforcement and Administration of Justice, *Task Force Report: Narcotics and Drug Abuse* (Washington, D.C.: Government Printing Office, 1967), 23. 2. Erich Goode, *Drugs in American Society,* 2d ed. (New York: Alfred A. Knopf, 1984), 15. 3. The United States Code (21 U.S.C. §321(1)) defines "drug" as "an article intended for use in diagnosis, cure, mitigation, treatment or prevention of disease . . ." or an article "other than food" that is "intended to affect the structure or any function of the body of man or other animals. . . ." Intended *by whom* is undefined. For a detailed discussion of definitional problems,

see Franklin Zimring and Gordon Hawkins, *The Search for Rational Drug Control* (New York: Cambridge University Press, 1992), 22–44.   4. Ronald K. Siegel, *Intoxication: Life in Pursuit of Artificial Paradise* (New York: E. P. Dutton, 1989), 36.   5. Despite common reports of the resurgence of LSD, survey data suggest that the use of hallucinogens remains fairly constant, and rare, in recent years. See Substance Abuse and Mental Health Services Administration, Office of Applied Studies, *Preliminary Estimates from the 1992 National Household Survey on Drug Abuse: Selected Excerpts,* 1993, 1–5.   6. Lester Grinspoon and James B. Bakalar, *Cocaine: A Drug and Its Social Evolution* (New York: Basic Books, 1971), 184–85, citing World Health Organization, *Technical Report Service,* 407 (1969), 61.   7. Thomas Szasz, *Ceremonial Chemistry: The Ritual Persecution of Drugs, Addicts, and Pushers* (Garden City: Anchor Press/Doubleday, 1974), 170–74; Herbert Fingarette, "Alcoholism: The Mythical Disease," *The Public Interest,* 91 (Spring 1988), 3.   8. John Kaplan, *The Hardest Drug: Heroin and Public Policy* (Chicago: The University of Chicago Press, 1983), 14.   9. Ibid., 15.   10. Ibid., 19.

Chapter 3   Our Most Harmful Legal Drugs

1. Douglas N. Husak, *Drugs and Rights* (New York: Cambridge University Press, 1992), 95. 2. Edward Brecher and the Editors of *Consumer Reports, Licit and Illicit Drugs* (Boston: Little, Brown and Company, 1972), 208–09.   3. Jerome Brooks, *The Mighty Leaf: Tobacco Through the Centuries* (Boston: Little, Brown and Company, 1952), 40.   4. Ibid., 41. 5. Count Egon Caesar Corti, *A History of Smoking,* translated by Paul England (New York: Harcourt Press, 1932), 137.   6. Ibid., 145.   7. Ibid., 141.   8. Ibid. 9. Ibid., 146.   10. Brecher et al., *Licit and Illicit Drugs,* 212–13.   11. Corti, *History of Smoking,* 139.   12. Brecher, 229.   13. Brooks, *Mighty Leaf,* 275.   14. Ibid., 281.   15. Erich Goode, *Drugs in American Society,* 2nd ed. (New York: Alfred A. Knopf, 1984), 194.   16. Brecher, 225.   17. See generally Thomas C. Schelling, "Addictive Drugs: The Cigarette Experience," *Science,* 24 January 1992, 430.   18. See Leon G. Hunt and Carl D. Chambers, *The Heroin Epidemics: A Study of Heroin Use in the U.S., 1965–1975* (New York: Spectrum Publications, 1976); Mark A. Kleiman, *Against Excess: Drug Policy for Results* (New York: Basic Books, 1992), 364; John Kaplan, *The Hardest Drug: Heroin and Public Policy* (Chicago: The University of Chicago Press, 1983), 34.   19. "Treatment for Crack Addicts: Drug Experts Report Finding Clues to a Cure," *New York Times,* 24 August 1989. See also, Henry Brownstein, "Demilitarization of the War on Drugs: Toward an Alternative Drug Strategy," in Arnold Trebach and Kevin Zeese, eds., *Great Issues of Drug Policy* (Washington, D.C.: Drug Policy Foundation, 1990), 114; Kleiman, *Against Excess,* 42.   20. Only about 10 percent of smokers smoke five or fewer cigarettes a day. United States Surgeon General, *The Health Consequences of Smoking: Nicotine Addiction* (Rockville, MD: Department of Health and Human Services, 1988), 253.   21. Smokeless tobacco is still very damaging to health. See Abram Katz, "Chewing Tobacco Just as Bad as Smoking It," *New Haven Register,* 19 November 1992.   22. Surgeon General, *Health Consequences,* iv–v.   23. Ibid., 314. 24. Brecher, 217.   25. Ibid., 226.   26. Ibid., 226–27.   27. James H. Barron, "Smoke Signals in Eastern Europe," *Christian Science Monitor,* 23 October 1990; and Editorial, "Marlboros Instead of Manna," *Chicago Tribune,* 18 September 1990.   28. "Ill Effects Force Easing of Ban on Prison Smoking," *New York Times,* National, 26 November 1992. 29. "Tobacco Strike Has Italy's Smokers Burning," *USA Today,* International edition, 25 November 1992; "No Buts About It; Tobacco Strike Enrages Italians," *Chicago Tribune,* 26 November 1992; Alan Cowell, "A Tobacco Strike Is Driving Italians to Desperate Ends," *New York Times,* 26 November 1992.   30. William D. Montalbano, "For Smokers in Italy, Strike Stubs Out Dolce Vita," *Los Angeles Times,* 25 November 1992.   31. Ethan Nadelmann, "The Case for Legalization," in James A. Inciardi, ed., *The Drug Legalization Debate* (Newbury Park, CA: Sage Publications, 1991), 25–26.   32. Mary Williams Walsh,

"Smokes Schemes: Some Would Rather Risk Arrest Than Pay Canada's Super Tax on Cigarettes. They Smuggle in Cheaper U.S. Tobacco in Kayaks, Frozen Turkeys, Car Seats . . . ,'"' *Los Angeles Times,* 9 September 1991.   33. Joseph R. Di Franza, Thomas H. Winters, Robert J. Goldberg, Leonard Cirillo, Timothy Biliouris, "The Relationship of Smoking to Motor Vehicle Accidents and Traffic Violations," *New York State Journal of Medicine,* 86 (September 1986), 464.   34. Kenneth E. Warner, "The Tobacco Subsidy: Does It Matter?" *Journal of the National Cancer Institute,* 80, no. 2 (16 March 1988), 81.   35. "Smoking Tied to Leukemia Risk," *New York Times,* 23 February, 1993.   36. "Smoking Found to Accelerate AIDS," *Los Angeles Times,* 13 May 1993, A24.   37. United States Surgeon General, *Reducing the Health Consequences of Smoking: 25 Years of Progress* (Rockville, MD: Department of Health and Human Services, 1989), 197.   38. Ibid.   39. United States Surgeon General, *The Health Consequences of Involuntary Smoking* (Rockville, MD: Department of Health and Human Services, 1986).   40. "Study Shows How Secondhand Smoke Hurts Heart," *New York Times,* 22 November 1992.   41. Surgeon General, *Reducing Health Consequences,* 160.   42. Centers for Disease Control, "Smoking-Attributable Mortality and Years of Potential Life Lost—United States, 1988," *Morbidity and Mortality Weekly Report,* 40, no. 4 (1 February 1991), 63, report 434,175 deaths in 1989 in the U.S. from smoking-attributable diseases and burns; included in this figure are also deaths from passive/involuntary smoking.   43. Surgeon General, *Reducing Health Consequences,* 121. 44. Morton Mintz, "Tobacco Decimating World, Says WHO Epidemiologist," *Washington Post,* 5 April 1990.   45. Department of Health and Human Services, *Smoking and Health, A National Status Report,* 2d ed. (Rockville, MD: Department of Health and Human Services, Office of Smoking and Health, 1990).   46. Ibid., 8.   47. Michael Barry, "The Influence of the U.S. Tobacco Industry on the Health, Economy and Environment of Developing Countries," *New England Journal of Medicine,* 324, no. 13 (28 March 1991), 917.   48. Surgeon General, *Reducing Health Consequences,* vii.   49. Seth Shulman, "Global Smokeout; Promoting Tobacco Control," 94 *Technology Review* (MIT Alumni Assn., May 1991), 20. 50. "China Executes 62 in One Day for Drug Crimes," *Reuters Library Report,* 1 July 1992. 51. Charles P. Wallace, "Clearing the Air in Singapore," *Los Angeles Times,* 2 July 1992, A1. 52. David Holley, "New 'Opium War' Cuts Across the Third World," 5 June 1990, *World Report,* H1.   53. Masayoshi Kanabayashi, "In 'Tobacco Smoker's Paradise' of Japan, U.S. Cigarettes Are Epitome of High Style," *Wall Street Journal,* 23 September 1991. 54. Ibid.   55. Surgeon General, *Health Consequences of Smoking: Nicotine Addiction,* 567. 56. Ronald K. Siegel, *Intoxication: Life in Pursuit of Artificial Paradise* (New York: E. P. Dutton, 1989), 102.   57. Ibid., 104.   58. Ibid.   59. Ibid., 104–5.   60. Department of Health and Human Services, *National Medical Expenditure Survey: Household Survey 1991* (Ann Arbor, MI: Inter-University Consortium for Political and Social Research, 1991), 83.   61. Secretary of Health and Human Services, *Seventh Special Report to the U.S. Congress on Alcohol and Health* (Rockville, MD: Department of Health and Human Services, 1990), 107.   62. Ibid., xxiii.   63. Ibid., xxiv.   64. Ibid.   65. Ibid., 124.   66. Ibid.   67. Ibid., 20.   68. Centers for Disease Control, "Alcohol and Related Mortality and Years of Potential Life Lost—United States, 1987," *Morbidity and Mortality Weekly Report,* 39, no. 11 (23 March 1990), 175.   69. Of the drug-related deaths reported by NIDA for 1990, 66% were attributed to drug overdoses. About 85% of those overdose deaths were attributed to a combination of drugs (only 15% to a single drug). National Institute on Drug Abuse, "Annual Medical Examiner Data-1990" from DAWN, 1, no. 10-B, 13. By far the most common of all drug combinations found in drug-abuse deaths is cocaine and alcohol. Ibid. 32.   70. Arnold Trebach, *The Great Drug War: And Radical Proposals That Could Make America Safe Again* (New York: Macmillan Publishing Company, 1987), 12.   71. Secretary of Health and Human Services, *Seventh Special Report,* 174. 72. Ibid., 172–74.   73. Diane Colaranto and John Zeglarski, "Alcohol Consumption at Lowest Level in 30 Years," *Gallup Report,* 288 (September 1989), 168–70.   74. Secretary of Health and Human Services, *Seventh Special Report*, 168–70.   75. E. B. Rimm, E. L. Giovannucci, W. C. Willett, G. A. Colditz, A. Ascherio, B. Rosner, M. J. Stampfer, "Prospective Study of Alcohol Consumption and Risk of Coronary Disease in Men," *Lancet*, 338 (24 August 1991), 464–68.   76. Ibid., 467.   77. Ibid.   78. R. D. Moore and T. A. Pearson, "Moderate Alcohol Consumption and Coronary Artery Disease," *Medicine*, 65 (1986), 242–67.   79. Siegel, *Intoxication*, 113–14.   80. M. Friedman and R. H. Rosenman, *Type A Behavior and Your Heart* (New York: Alfred A. Knopf, 1974).   81. Katherine Jamieson and Timothy Flanagan, eds., *Sourcebook of Criminal Justice Statistics—1989* (Washington, D.C.: Department of Justice, Bureau of Justice Statistics, Government Printing Office, 1990), 481.   82. Secretary of Health and Human Services, *Seventh Special Report*, 163.   83. Ibid.   84. Centers for Disease Control, "Alcohol-Related Traffic Fatalities—United States, 1982–1989," *Morbidity and Mortality Weekly Report*, 39, no. 49 (14 December 1990), 889.   85. David Reed, "Reducing the Costs of Drinking and Driving," in Mark Moore and Dean Gerstein, eds., *Alcohol and Public Policy: Beyond the Shadow of Prohibition* (Washington, D.C.: National Academy Press, 1981), 340.   86. Centers for Disease Control, "Alcohol-Related Mortality," 174.   87. Leif Lenke, "Alcohol and Crimes of Violence: a Causal Analysis," *Contemporary Drug Problems* (Fall 1982), 357.   88. Ibid., 357–58.   89. Ibid., 361.   90. Tracy Wilkinson, "In Alcohol-Free Gulf, GIs Stayed Out of Hot Water," *Los Angeles Times*, 29 March 1991, reporting on court-martial statistics and analyses released by Judge Advocate General, United States Central Command, Riyadh, Saudi Arabia.   91. Craig MacAndrew and Robert B. Edgerton, *Drunken Comportment: A Social Explanation* (Chicago: Aldine Publishing Company, 1969).   92. Ibid., 17.   93. Ibid., 87–88.   94. Siegel, *Intoxication*, 122–23.

Chapter 4   Our Most Popular Illegal Drugs

1. Quoted in Thomas Szasz, *Our Right to Drugs* (New York: Praeger Publishers, 1992), 145.   2. Roger A. Roffman, *Marijuana as Medicine* (Seattle: Madrona Publishers, 1982), 33.   3. Ibid.   4. Ibid., 34.   5. Edward Brecher and the Editors of *Consumer Reports, Licit and Illicit Drugs* (Boston: Little Brown and Company), 1972, 398.   6. Roffman, 36.   7. Robert Cooke, "Scientists Find Evidence of Ancient Marijuana Use," *Houston Chronicle*, 20 May 1993, A23; "Morning Edition," National Public Radio, 20 May 1993.   8. Winifred Black, *Dope: The Story of the Living Dead* (New York: Star Company, 1928), 42.   9. Jerome L. Himmelstein, *The Strange Career of Marijuana* (Westport: Greenwood Press, 1983), 60.   10. "Marihuana More Dangerous Than Heroin or Cocaine," *Scientific American*, May 1938, 293.   11. "The History of Marijuana," *Newsweek*, 28 November 1938, 29.   12. Richard J. Bonnie and Charles H. Whitebread, II, *The Marihuana Conviction: A History of Marihuana Prohibition in the United States* (Charlottesville: University of Virginia Press, 1974), 145.   13. National Institute on Drug Abuse, National Household Survey on Drug Abuse: Population Estimates—1991 (Rockville, MD: Department of Health and Human Services, Public Health Service, 1991), 25.   14. Erich Goode, *Drugs in American Society*, 2nd ed. (New York: Alfred A. Knopf, 1984), 99.   15. Ibid.   16. Ibid., 100–05.   17. National Institute on Drug Abuse, *National Household Survey on Drug Abuse: Population Estimates 1991*, 25.   18. Goode, 105.   19. Joel Hochman and Norman Brill, "Marijuana Usage and Psychosocial Adaptation," unpublished manuscript (1971), cited by Goode, *Drugs in American Society*, 91.   20. Goode, 91–92.   21. Jonathan Shedler and Jack Block, "Adolescent Drug Use and Psychological Health," *American Psychologist*, 45, no. 5 (1990), 612.   22. John Kaplan, *Marijuana—The New Prohibition* (New York: World Publishing Company, 1970), 84.   23. Ibid., 285.   24. See, for instance, Alfred Crancer et al., "A Comparison of the Effects of Marijuana and Alcohol on Simulated Driving Performance," *Science*, 164 (1969), 851–54, and a discussion of this study in Kaplan, *Marijuana*, 281–84.   25. Kaplan, 284–86.   26. In a study of 100 drivers killed in single-vehicle crashes, 62 had

blood alcohol levels in excess of .09, and therefore were legally intoxicated, while only 9 tested positive for marijuana, including 3 who tested positive for marijuana only. Since a positive test for marijuana in the blood merely indicates marijuana use during the preceding two weeks or so, there is no evidence of marijuana intoxication in these findings. In any event, marijuana's contribution to highway deaths is extremely modest. See Mark Kleiman, *Marijuana: Costs of Abuse, Costs of Control* (New York: Greenwood Press, 1989), 11.   **27.** Ibid. **28.** *The People v. Block* (1971), 103 Cal. Rptr. 281, 499 P.2d 961.   **29.** Kaplan, 61–62. **30.** Mark Kleiman, *Against Excess.*   **31.** Brecher et al., *Licit and Illicit Drugs,* 451. **32.** Although they acknowledge that smoking marijuana can harm the pulmonary system, Dr. Lester Grinspoon and James Bakalar note in a recent book that "so far, not a single case of lung cancer, emphysema, or other significant pulmonary pathology attributable to cannabis use has been reported in this country." Lester Grinspoon, M.D., and James B. Bakalar, *Marihuana, the Forbidden Medicine* (New Haven: Yale University Press, 1993), 152.   **33.** Mikuriya "Physical, Mental and Moral Effects of Marijuana," 77. See also Brecher et al., 460.   **34.** *Technical Papers of the First Report of the National Commission on Marijuana and Drug Abuse,* Vol. 1 (Washington, D.C.: Government Printing Office, 1972), 58.   **35.** Drug Abuse Council, *The Facts About "Drug Abuse"* (New York: Free Press, 1980).   **36.** Ibid., 165. **37.** "In the Matter of Marijuana Rescheduling Petition," Dkt. No. 86-22, in R. C. Randall, ed., *Marijuana, Medicine and the Law,* Vol. 2 (Washington, D.C.: Galen Press, 1989), 440. **38.** Bob Martinez, letter to Paul Reynolds, 19 June 1991.   **39.** Peter T. White, "The Poppy," *National Geographic,* February 1985, 143, 144.   **40.** It is also of great value in treating acute cases of congestive heart failure. It dilates the blood vessels and thus prevents fluid from backing up and flooding the lungs. Ibid., 148.   **41.** John Kaplan, *The Hardest Drug: Heroin and Public Policy* (Chicago: The University of Chicago Press, 1983), 7.   **42.** White, 157.   **43.** Brecher et al., *Licit and Illicit Drugs,* 3–4.   **44.** Ibid., 5.   **45.** Ibid., 6. **46.** Kaplan, *Hardest Drug,* 5.   **47.** Brecher et al., 17.   **48.** Ibid.   **49.** National Institute on Drug Abuse, *Population Estimates—1991,* 104.   **50.** Kaplan, 23. **51.** Ibid., 24.   **52.** Brecher et al., 40.   **53.** Ibid.   **54.** Dr. William Halsted (1852–1922) was a morphine addict his entire adult life. (Brecher et al., *Licit and Illicit Drugs,* 35). McCarthy did not publicly acknowledge his morphine addiction. However, his friend Harry Aslinger, the head of the Federal Bureau of Narcotics, mentions in his book *The Murderers: The Story of the Narcotics Gangs* (New York: Farrar, Straus and Cudahy, 1961), 181–82, that he arranged to supply a powerful member of Congress who was hooked on morphine and had no desire to quit. The Congressman was later identified by others as Senator Joseph McCarthy. See Maxine Cheshire, "Drugs and Washington, D.C.," *Ladies' Home Journal,* December 1978, 180–82; John C. McWilliams, *The Protectors* (Newark: University of Delaware Press, 1990), 99. **55.** Brecher et al., 39.   **56.** Jerome H. Jaffe, "Drug Addiction and Drug Abuse," in Louis Goodman and Alfred Gilman, *The Pharmacological Basis of Therapeutics,* 4th ed. (New York: Macmillan Publishing Company, 1970), 286.   **57.** See discussion of Samuel Gompers and his 1902 pamphlet "Some Reasons for Chinese Exclusion: Meat vs. Rice, American Manhood Against Asiatic Coolieism—Which Shall Survive?" in Szasz, *Ceremonial Chemistry,* 78–79. **58.** Kaplan, *Hardest Drug,* 12–13.   **59.** See Herbert Spiegel and David Spiegel, *Trance and Treatment* (New York: Basic Books, 1978), 252–58.   **60.** Ibid., 35.   **61.** Kaplan, 32.   **62.** Ibid., 33–34.   **63.** Surgeon General, *Nicotine Addiction,* v.   **64.** Lee Robins, Darlene Davis, Donald Goodwin, "Drug Use by U.S. Army Enlisted Men in Vietnam: A Follow-up on Their Return Home," *American Journal of Epidemiology,* 99, no. 4 (April 1974), 235.   **65.** Kaplan, 105.   **66.** Brecher et al., *Licit and Illicit Drugs,* 27.   **67.** Edward Preble, "El Barrio Revisited," Annual Meeting, Society for Applied Anthropology (1980), cited in Paul J. Goldstein, "Homicide Related Drug to Drug Traffic," *Bulletin New York Academy of Medicine,* 62 (June 1986), 509–16.   **68.** Brecher et al., 104.   **69.** Ibid., 108.   **70.** Ibid.   **71.** Lester Adelson, *The Pathology of Homicide* (Springfield, IL: Charles C. Thomas, Publishers, 1974), 797.   **72.** Brecher et al., 106.   **73.** David

Musto, *The American Disease: Origins of Narcotic Control* (New Haven: Yale University Press, 1973), 190–91.   74. Kaplan, *Hardest Drug,* 56.   75. Ibid., 57.   76. Ibid. 77. Siegel, *Intoxication,* 169.   78. Timothy Plowman, "Coca Chewing and the Botanical Origins of Coca (Erythroxylum SPP) in South America," in Deborah Pacini & Christine Franquemont, eds., *Coca and Cocaine: Effects on People and Policy in Latin America* (Cambridge, MA: Cultural Survival, 1986), 8.   79. Ibid.   80. E. M. Thornton, *Freud and Cocaine: The Freudian Fallacy* (London: Blond and Briggs, 1983), 39–46.   81. Ibid., 46. 82. Musto, *American Disease,* 160.   83. Lloyd Johnston, Patrick O'Malley, Jereld Bachman, *Drug Use Among American High School Seniors, College Students and Young Adults, 1975–1990, Vol. 1* (Rockville, MD: Department of Health and Human Services, National Institute on Drug Abuse, 1991), 52.   84. Goode, *Drugs in American Society,* 108. 85. National Institute on Drug Abuse, *Population Estimates—1991,* 31.   86. Robert Byck, "Cocaine, Marijuana, and the Meanings of Addiction," in Ronald Hamowy, ed., *Dealing with Drugs* (Lexington: Lexington Books, 1987), 228.   87. R. W. Foltin and M. W. Fishman, "Ethanol and Cocaine Interactions in Humans, Cardiovascular Consequences," *Pharmacol. Biochem. Behav.* 31 (1989), 877–83.   88. R. W. Foltin, W. M. Fishman, J. J. Pedroso, G. D. Pearlson, "Marijuana and Cocaine Interactions in Humans: Cardiovascular Consequences," *Pharmacol. Biochem. Behav.* 28 (1987) 459–64.   89. Goode, *Drugs in American Society,* 189.   90. Ronald K. Siegel, "New Patterns of Cocaine Use: Changing Doses and Routes," in N. J. Kozel and E. H. Adams, eds., "Cocaine Use in America: Epidemiologic and Clinical Perspectives," *NIDA Research Monograph No. 61* (Washington, D.C., Government Printing Office) 204–20.   91. Ibid., 12; NIDA, "Cocaine: Pharmacology, Effects and Treatment of Abuse" (*Research Monograph No. 50* (1984)) 46; Terrence Cox, Michael Jacobs et al., *Drugs and Drug Abuse: A Reference Text* (Toronto: Addiction Research Foundation, 1983), 229–30.   92. NIDA, "Cocaine: Pharmacology, Effects and Treatment of Abuse," 100–01; Dean Gerstein and Henrich Harwood, eds., *Treating Drug Problems* (Washington, D.C.,: National Academy Press, 1990) 175; Ronald K. Siegel, "Changing Patterns of Cocaine Use: Longitudinal Observations, Consequences and Treatment," in *NIDA Research Monograph No. 50,* 100.   93. See Husak, *Drugs and Rights,* 124–25.   94. "Cocaine, Pharmacology, Effects and Treatment of Abuse," 40–41, 44–45, 74–75; Siegel, "Changing Patterns of Cocaine Use," 96.   95. See Husak, *Drugs and Rights,* 124–25.   96. Secretary of Health and Human Services, *Drug Abuse and Drug Abuse Research: The Third Triennial Report to Congress* (Rockville, MD: Department of Health and Human Services, 1991), 113. 97. Andrew M. Gill and Robert J. Michaels, "Does Drug Use Lower Wages?" *Industrial and Labor Relations Review,* 45 (April 1992), 419.   98. See Dorothy E. Roberts, "Punishing Drug Addicts Who Have Babies: Women of Color, Equality, and the Right of Privacy," *Harvard Law Review,* 104, no. 7 (1991), 1419.   99. Charles V. Wetli, "Fatal Reactions to Cocaine," in Washton and Gold, *Cocaine,* 33, 38.   100. Secretary of Health, Education and Welfare, *Drug Abuse Research,* 115. See also Jeffrey M. Isner et al., "Acute Cardiac Events Temporarily Related to Cocaine Abuse," *New England Journal of Medicine,* 4 December 1986, 1433. 101. Arnold M. Washton and Mark S. Gold, "Recent Trends in Cocaine Abuse as Seen from the '800-Cocaine' Hotline," in Washton and Gold, eds., *Cocaine: A Clinician's Handbook* (New York: Guilford Press, 1987), 10.   102. See Albert J. Reiss, Jr., and Jeffrey A. Roth, eds., *Understanding and Preventing Violence* (Washington, D.C.: National Academy Press, 1993), 194; Goldstien, P. J., et al., "Crack and Homicide in New York City, 1988: A Conceptually Based Event Analysis," *Contemporary Drug Problems* 16 (Winter, 1989), 651–87.   103. National Institute on Drug Abuse, Division of Epidemiology and Prevention Research, "Annual Emergency Room Data—1990," in *The Drug Abuse Warning Network,* series 1, no. 10-A (Rockville, MD: Department of Health and Human Services, 1991), 4.   104. Ibid., viii.   105. Ibid., 11.   106. Ibid., 8.   107. Ibid., 33.   108. Ibid., 11.   109. National Institute on Drug Abuse, Division of Epidemiology and Prevention Research, "Annual Medical Examiner Data—1990" from *The Drug Abuse Warning Network,* series 1, no. 10-B (Rockville,

MD: United States Department of Health and Human Services, 1991), 1.   110. The World Almanac, 1993 (New York: ScrippsHoward, 1993), 938.   111. Ibid., 16.   112. Ibid. 113. United States Surgeon General, *The Health Benefits of Smoking Cessation* (Rockville, MD: Department of Health and Human Services, 1990), 75.   114. National Institute on Drug Abuse, "Annual Medical Examiner Data—1990," from *DAWN*, 1, no. 10-B, 2. 115. Ibid., 4.   116. Ibid., 7.   117. Telephone interviews with Janie Dargan, DAWN Project Officer, public health analyst, National Institute on Drug Abuse, Division of Epidemiology and Prevention Research (5 April 1990) and Patrice Roth, also from the Division of Epidemiology and Prevention Research (17 September 1991).   118. James Ostrowski, "The Moral and Practical Case for Drug Legalization," *Hofstra Law Review*, 18, no. 3 (Spring 1990), 607–702.   119. Ibid.   120. Ibid., 697.   121. See Husak, *Drugs and Rights*, 92–97.

Chapter 5   Lessons from the Past

1. *Homage to Daniel Shays: Collected Essays 1952–1972* (New York: Random House, 1972), 374.   2. Virginia Berridge and Griffith Edwards, *Opium and the People: Opiate Use in Nineteenth Century England* (New Haven: Yale University Press, 1987), xxv.   3. Ibid. 4. Ibid., 9.   5. Leonard P. Adams, II, "China: The Historical Setting of Asia's Profitable Plague," in Alfred W. McCoy with Cathleen B. Reed and Leonard P. Adams, II, *The Politics of Heroin in Southeast Asia* (New York: Harper & Row, 1972), 366.   6. Ibid. 7. Berridge and Edwards, *Opium*, 34.   8. Ibid., 260.   9. Ibid., 66.   10. Ibid., 22. 11. Ibid., 252.   12. David J. Bellis, *Heroin and Politicians: The Failure of Public Policy to Control Addiction in America* (Westport, CT: Greenwood Press, 1981), 5.   13. David Musto, *The American Disease: Origins of Narcotic Control,* expanded edition (New York: Oxford University Press, 1987), 2.   14. Joseph R. Gusfield, *Symbolic Crusade* (Urbana, IL: University of Illinois Press, 1963). For a brief discussion of Gusfield's thesis see John Kaplan, *Marijuana—The New Prohibition* (New York: World Publishing Company, 1970), 4. 15. Testimony of the San Francisco Police Department recorded in California State Senate Committee, "Chinese Immigration, Its Social, Moral and Political Effects" (Sacramento, CA: State Publishing Office, 1878), 152. See also Patricia Morgan, "The Legislation of Drug Law: Economic Crisis and Social Control," *Journal of Drug Issues*, 8, no. 1 (Winter 1978), 171–92. 16. Musto, *American Disease*, 24–69.   17. Ibid., 65.   18. Ibid., 24.   19. Edward Brecher and the Editors of *Consumer Reports, Licit and Illicit Drugs* (Boston: Little, Brown and Company, 1972), 8–11.   20. Musto, 77–85.   21. Brecher, et al., 49. 22. Ibid.   23. 241 U.S. 394 (1915).   24. 249 U.S. 96 (1918).   25. Musto, 133. 26. Ibid., 134.   27. Sean Dennis Cashman, *Prohibition: The Lie of the Land* (New York: Free Press, 1981), 44.   28. Ibid., 219.   29. James Ostrowski, "The Moral and Practical Case for Drug Legislation," *Hofstra Law Review*, 18, no. 3 (Spring 1990), 646.   30. Cashman, 40.   31. Ibid., 36.   32. Ibid., 37.   33. Ibid., 39.   34. Ibid., 43. 35. Ibid., 44.   36. Ibid., 47.   37. Ibid., 86.   38. Ostrowski, "Moral and Practical,"   641.   39. Ibid.,   645–46.   40. Ibid.,   646.   41. Ibid. 42. Musto, *American Disease*, 33.   43. Ibid., 146–47.   44. Ibid., 184.   45. Ibid., 204–06.   46. Mark H. Moore, "Actually, Prohibition Was a Success," *New York Times*, 16 October 1989.   47. Ethan Nadelmann, "Nadelmann's Response," *Notre Dame Journal of Law, Ethics and Public Policy: Symposium on Drugs and Society,* 5, no. 3 (1991), 817–18. 48. Ibid., 819. See also John P. Morgan, "Prohibition Is a Perverse Policy: What Was True in 1933 Is True Now," in Kraus and Lazar, *Searching for Alternatives: Drug Control Policy in the United States* (Stanford: Hoover Institution Press, 1991) 405, 415–17.   49. Cashman, *Prohibition*, 3.   50. Ibid., 212.   51. Jerome L. Himmelstein, *The Strange Career of Marihuana: Politics and Ideology of Drug Control in America* (Westport, CT: Greenwood Press,

1983).   52. Howard S. Becker, *Outsiders: Studies in the Sociology of Deviance* (New York: Free Press, 1963).   53. Musto, *American Disease,* 219–21.   54. Himmelstein, 39–40.   55. Donald T. Dickson, "Bureaucracy and Morality: An Organizational Perspective on a Moral Crusade," *Social Problems* 16, no. 2 (Fall 1968), 143–56; John F. Galliher and Allyn Walker, "The Puzzle of the Social Origins of the Marihuana Tax Act of 1937," *Social Problems,* 24, no. 3 (February 1977), 367–76, cited in Himmelstein, *Strange Career,* 42.   56. After the act passed, writers had a tough time getting any magazines to buy articles about marijuana for roughly the next three decades; that is, until interest in the topic blossomed in the late 1960s. Between 1939 and 1967, America's major magazines published an average of one article per year about marijuana. In the next decade (1967–1977) the average jumped to nearly twenty-nine marijuana articles each year, or roughly the same number of articles per year as were written about alcohol.   57. Himmelstein, 77.   58. Ibid., 69.   59. Ibid., 77.   60. Ibid., 141.   61. Ibid., 142.   62. McCoy, *Politics of Heroin.*   63. John Kaplan, *The Hardest Drug: Heroin and Public Policy* (Chicago: The University of Chicago Press, 1983), 113, writes: ". . . some 24 percent of American ground troops [in Vietnam] became addicted to the drug and considerably more were nonaddicted users."   64. See McCoy's own account of the weeks just prior to the book's publication and the attempted CIA ban of it in Alfred W. McCoy, *The Politics of Heroin: CIA Complicity in the Global Drug Trade* (Brooklyn: Lawrence Hill Books, 1991), xvii–xviii; Seymour Hersh, "CIA Aides Assail Asia Drug Charge," *New York Times,* 22 July 1972; WGBH-Boston, "Guns, Drugs and the CIA," *Frontline,* television program episode first aired 17 May 1988.   65. See, for example, Jonathan Marshall, *Drug Wars: Corruption, Counterinsurgency and Covert Operations in the Third World* (Berkeley: Cohan and Cohen, 1991); Peter Dale Scott, "Introduction," in Henrick Kruger, *The Great Heroin Coup: Drugs, Intelligence and International Fascism* (Boston: South End Press, 1980).   66. McCoy, *Politics of Heroin,* 5–6. See also United Nations Economic and Social Council, *World Trends of the Illicit Traffic During the War 1939–1945,* E/CS 7/9 (23 November 1946), 10–14; United States Treasury Department, Bureau of Narcotics, "History of Narcotic Addiction in the United States," in Senate Committee on Government Operations, *Organized Crime and Illicit Traffic in Narcotics* (Washington, D.C.: Government Printing Office, 1964), pt. 3, 771.   67. McCoy, *Politics of Heroin,* 15.   68. Ibid., 16.   69. Ibid., 20; William B. Herlands, "Report," in *University of Rochester: Thomas E. Dewey Papers,* 17 September 1954, 66–67, 93; Alan A. Block, "A Modern Marriage of Convenience: A Collaboration Between Organized Crime and U.S. Intelligence," in Robert J. Kelly, ed., *Organized Crime: A Global Perspective* (Totowa, NJ: Ronman and Littlefield, 1986), 62–65.   70. McCoy, *Politics of Heroin,* 21; Michele Pantaleone, *The Mafia and Politics* (London, U.K.: Chatto and Windus, Ltd., 1966), 58–59.   71. McCoy, 24–25; Pantaleone, 59.   72. McCoy, 24.   73. Ibid.   74. Melinda Liu, "Burma's 'Money Tree,'" *Newsweek,* 15 May 1989, 42.   75. National Institute on Drug Abuse, *National Household Survey on Drug Abuse: Main Findings 1985* (Rockville, MD: United States Department of Health and Human Services, 1989), 19.   76. Adam P. Weisman, "I Was a Drug-hype Junkie: 48 Hours on Crack Street," *New Republic,* 6 October 1986, 14.

Chapter 6   The Crime Caused by Prohibition

1. Franklin P. Adams, "The Wickersham Report," *New York World,* 1931, quoted in Harry G. Levine, "The Birth of American Alcohol Control: Prohibition, the Power Elite and the Problem of Lawlessness," *Contemporary Drug Problems,* 12, no. 1 (Spring 1985), 75, also quoted in Andrew Sinclair, *Era of Excess: A Social History of the Prohibition Movement* (New York: Harper & Row, 1964), 336.   2. Caroline Wolf Harlow, "Drugs and Jail Inmates, 1989," United States Bureau of Justice Statistics Special Report (August 1991).   3. Chapman, "Naming Reagan and the Real Villains in the Drug War," *Chicago Tribune,* 6 March 1988.

4. Bruce Benson and David Rasmussen, "Relationship Between Illicit Drug Enforcement Policy and Property Crimes," *Contemporary Policy Issues,* 9, no. 4 (October 1991), 106–13. These University of Florida economists, studying data in South Florida, conclude there exists a "causal" connection between drug crackdowns and increased levels of property crimes. 5. David Burnham, *A Law unto Itself: Power, Politics and the IRS* (New York: Random House, 1989), 102.   6. Mark Kleiman, *Against Excess: Drug Policy for Results* (New York: Basic Books, 1992), 370.   7. David N. Nurco, T. Hanlon, T. Kinlock, "Recent Research on the Relationship Between Illicit Drug Use and Crime," *Behavioral Sciences & The Law,* 9, no. 3 (Summer 1991), 223.   8. James A. Inciardi, "Heroin Use and Street Crime," *Crime and Delinquency,* 25 (July 1979), 335–46.   9. John C. Ball, Lawrence Rosen, John A. Flueck, David Nurco, "The Criminality of Heroin Addicts: When Addicted and When off Opiates," in James A. Inciardi, ed., *The Drugs-Crime Connection* (Beverly Hills: Sage Publications, 1981), 60. 10. James A. Inciardi, *The War on Drugs: Heroin, Cocaine, and Public Policy* (Palo Alto: Mayfield, 1986), 126–27.   11. Arnold Washton and Mark Gold, "Recent Trends in Cocaine Abuse as Seen from the '800-Cocaine' Hotline," in Arnold Washton and Mark Gold, eds., *Cocaine: A Clinician's Handbook* (New York: Guilford, 1987), 10–14.   12. B. Johnson, E. Wish, C. Huizinga, "The concentration of delinquent offending: The contribution of serious drug involvement to high rate delinquency," *Report prepared for the National Institute of Justice and the New York State Division of Substance Abuse Services* (Boulder: Behavioral Research Institute, 1983).   13. J. Collins, R. Hubbard, J. Rachal, "Expensive Drug Use and Illegal Income: A Test of Explanatory Hypotheses," *Criminology,* 23, no. 4 (August 1985), 743–64. 14. Inciardi, *War on Drugs,* 129.   15. Studies cited in David N. Nurco et al., "Illicit Drug Use and Crime," 229.   16. According to the National Institute on Drug Abuse, *National Household Survey on Drug Abuse—Population Estimates 1991* (Rockville, MD: Department of Health and Human Services, Public Health Service, 1990), 19, less than 18 percent of the male population between the ages of eighteen and twenty-five used *any* illicit drug within the previous month.   17. Bureau of Justice Statistics, *Special Report, Drugs and Jail Inmates,* 1989 (Department of Justice, August 1991).   18. Federal Bureau of Investigation, *Uniform Crime Reports: Crime in the United States—1991* (Washington, D.C.: Department of Justice, 1991), 36.   19. Ibid.   20. Ibid., 27.   21. In 1989 there were 438 murders in Washington, D.C., and 62 deaths attributed to the religious animosities of Northern Ireland. (Sources for Washington, D.C., fatality data: legislative finding in 1990 D.C. Act 8-289; *Los Angeles Times,* 6 April 1990. Source for Northern Ireland fatality data: Department of State, *Notice to the Press,* Federal News Service, 7 March 1990.   22. Isabel Wilkerson, "Crack Hits Chicago, Along with a Wave of Killing," *New York Times,* 24 September 1991.   23. See for example Dennis Hevesi, "9 Men Posing as Police Are Indicted in Three Murders," *New York Times,* 30 September 1992.   24. James Brady, "Straight Talk About Children and Guns," *New York Times,* 30 March 1992.   25. Joseph Treaster, "Teen-Age Murderers, Plentiful Guns, Easy Power," *New York Times,* 8 March 1992.   26. William Finnegan, "A Reporter at Large: Out There," *The New Yorker,* 10 September 1990, 68.   27. See Erik Larson, "Paxton Quigley Shows Her Women Students How to Shoot a Man," *Wall Street Journal,* 4 February 1993.   28. See for example Alex Freedman, "The NRA Mounts a Militant Campaign Taking Aim at Criminal Justice System," *Wall Street Journal,* 28 April 1992. 29. Erick Eckholm, "Ailing Gun Industry Confronts Outrage Over Glut of Violence," *New York Times,* 11 March 1992.   30. Don Terry, "How Guns Fall into the Hands of Criminals: Many Ways and All Too Easily," *New York Times,* 11 March 1992.   31. Katherine M. Jamieson and Timothy J. Flanagan, eds., *Sourcebook of Criminal Justice Statistics—1990* (Washington, D.C.: Department of Justice, 1990), 287, 366.   32. Daryl Kelley and Victor Merina, "Cases Reviewed in L.A. in Wake of Suspension," *Los Angeles Times,* 3 September 1989. See also Daryl Kelley and Victor Merina, "Number of L.A. Deputies in Drug Scandal Grows," *Los Angeles Times,* 5 October 1989.   33. Mark Swain, "Hillbillies in Dope," *High Times,* January 1985.   34. "A DEA Hero Is Busted," *Newsweek,* 28 August 1989, 32.

35. "Ex-Agent Is Guilty on 5 Drug Charges," *New York Times,* 17 April 1991.
36. Joseph Treaster, "Officers in Drug Case Formed Tightly Knit Group," *New York Times,* 9 May 1992; Joseph Treaster, "More Drug Allegations Against Accused Officer Emerge," *New York Times,* 30 May 1992.   37. Sandra Torry, "Lawyers on Drugs Create Problem Fraught With Legal, Moral Questions," *Washington Post,* 5 October 1988.   38. "Judge Nixon Says He 'Has Nothing to Hide,'" *National Law Journal,* 2 October 1989, 5.   39. See for example John Kaplan, "Taking Drugs Seriously," *Public Interest,* no. 92 (Summer 1988), 32.
40. Knapp Commission, *Report on Police Corruption* (New York: George Braziller, 1973).
41. Paul Lieberman, "Raid Rules Being Tightened: Rising Tide of Drug Cash Testing Honesty of Police," *Los Angeles Times,* 11 September 1989.   42. Department of Justice Office of Justice Programs, Bureau of Justice Statistics, "Fact Sheet: Drug Data Summary," November 1991, 1.   43. Joseph D. Pistone with Richard Woodley, *Donnie Brasco, My Undercover Life in the Mafia* (New York: New American Library, 1988).   44. Michel Girodo, "Drug Corruption in Undercover Agents: Measuring the Risk," *Behavioral Sciences & The Law,* 9, no. 3 (Summer 1991), 362.   45. Steven Duke, "Making *Leon* Worse," *Yale Law Journal,* 95, no. 7 (1986), 1406.   46. Alan Dershowitz, *The Best Defense* (New York: Random House, 1982), xxi–xxii.   47. United Press International distribution in Michigan, "Burnmovie," 28 April 1989.   48. Howard Kurtz, "Across the Nation, Rising Outrage: Authorities Often Overwhelmed by Increase in Drug-Driven Crime," *Washington Post,* 4 April 1989.
49. "Crime, Drugs, and the Official Threat to Civil Liberties." Speech by Justice Richard Neely to West Virginia Boys' States, 11 June 1989.   50. See George Kelling, "The Contagion of Public Disorder," *NY: The City Journal,* Spring 1991, 57.   51. For a general discussion see Wesley G. Skogan, *Disorder and Decline: Crime and the Spiral of Decay in American Neighborhoods* (New York: Free Press, 1990).   52. United States President's Commission on Law Enforcement and Administration of Justice, *The Challenge of Crime in a Free Society* (Washington, D.C.: Government Printing Office, 1967), 222.   53. William Finnegan, "A Reporter at Large," 66.

Chapter 7   Freedom Costs

1. *Olmstead v. United States,* 277 U.S. 438, 479 (1928).   2. "Violent Police Searches Often Yield Fear, Anger; LAPD Department Defends Its Tactics. But Hostility Lingers Among Residents Subjected to Nighttime Raids," *Los Angeles Times,* 18 December 1991.
3. Kathy Scruggs, "Surprise Is Key, Police Nationwide Say; Officers Defend Drug-Raid Tactics After Boy's Death," *Atlanta Constitution* 19 December 1991.   4. *Illinois v. Gates,* 462 U.S. 313 (1983).   5. See Stephen A. Saltzburg, "Another Victim of Illegal Narcotics: The Fourth Amendment, As Illustrated by the Open Fields Doctrine," *University of Pittsburgh Law Review* 48, 1 (1986).   6. *United States v. Leon,* 468 U.S. 897 (1984).   7. See *Florida v. Bostwick,* 111 S. Ct. 2382 (1991); *United States v. Place,* 462 U.S. 696 (1983).   8. *Oliver v. United States,* 466 U.S. 170 (1984).   9. George Orwell, *Nineteen Eighty-Four* (New York: Harcourt, Brace & World, 1949), 4.   10. *Florida v. Riley,* 488 U.S. 455 (1989).
11. *California v. Greenwood,* 486 U.S. 35 (1988).   12. *California v. Acevedo,* 111 S. Ct. 1982 (1991).   13. *United States v. Montoya De Hernandez,* 473 U.S. 531, 538 (1985).
14. Ibid.   15. Alan Abrahamson, "Tactics at Border Checkpoint Under Fire. Law: Civil Libertarians Contend That Zeal Over War on Drugs Is Eroding Privacy Rights of Innocent People at San Onofre Stop," *Los Angeles Times,* 26 January 1992.   16. Joseph F. Sullivan, "New Jersey Police Are Accused of Minority Arrest Campaigns," *New York Times,* 19 February 1990.   17. Andrew Schneider and Mary Pat Flaherty, *Presumed Guilty: The Law's Victims in the War on Drugs* (reprinted from the *Pittsburgh Press,* 11–16 August 1991).   18. Ibid., 12.   19. *United States v. Sokolow,* 831 F.2d 1413, 1418 (9th Cir. 1987).   20. *United States v. Moore,* 675 F.2d 802 (6th Cir. 1982).   21. *United States v. Mendenhall,* 446 U.S. 544, 564 (1980).   22. *United States v. Buenaventura-Ariza,* 615 F.2d 29, 32 (2d Cir. 1980).

23. *United States v. Sullivan,* 625 F.2d 9, 12 (4th Cir. 1980).   24. *United States v. Craemer,* 555 F.2d 594, 595 (6th Cir. 1977).   25. *United States v. McCaleb,* 552 F.2d 717, 720 (6th Cir. 1977).   26. *United States v. Sokolow,* 808 F.2d 1366, 1370 (9th Cir. 1987). 27. *United States v. Smith,* 574 F.2d 882, 883 (6th Cir. 1978).   28. *United States v. Fry,* 622 F.2d 1218, 1219 (5th Cir. 1980).   29. *United States v. Andrews,* 600 F.2d 563, 565 (6th Cir. 1979).   30. *United States v. Himmelwright,* 551 F.2d 991, 992 (5th Cir. 1977). 31. See Judge George Pratt, dissenting, in *United States v. Hooper,* 935 F.2d 484, 499 (2d Cir. 1991).   32. Schneider and Flaherty, *Presumed Guilty,* 14.   33. Tom Morganthau, "Uncivil Liberties," *Newsweek,* 23 April 1990, 18.   34. Schneider and Flaherty, *Presumed Guilty,* 14.   35. Pratt, J. dissenting in *United States v. Hooper,* 500.   36. 18 U.S.C. §2516.   37. "Big Brother Is Napping," *National Law Journal,* 17 (16 May 1992), 119. 38. Ibid.   39. Ibid.   40. Steven Duke, "Making *Leon* Worse," 95 *Yale Law Journal,* 95, no. 7 (1986), 1414.   41. *United States v. Havens,* 445 U.S. 620 (1980).   42. *New Jersey v. T.L.O.,* 469 U.S. 325 (1985).   43. Wayne LaFave & Jerold Israel, *Criminal Procedure,* 2d ed. (St. Paul, MN: West Publishing Co., 1992), 232.   44. Williams by *Williams v. Ellington,* 936 F.2d 881 (6th Cir. 1991).   45. "Camera in School Bathroom Curbs Vandalism But Sets Off Debate," *New York Times,* 25 March 1992.   46. Tom Morganthau, "Uncivil Liberties," *Newsweek,* 23 April 1990, 18.   47. *Cornfield v. Consolidated High School District 230,* 1992 U.S. Dist. LEXIS 2913 (N.D. Ill. 12, March 1992); Jerry Shnay, "Stripsearch Student Is Ruled OK by Judge," *Chicago Tribune,* 25 March 1992. 48. Donald Baker and John Harris, "Wilder Eyes Drug Tests on Campus," *Washington Post,* 3 April 1991.   49. *United States v. Verdugo-Urquidez,* 494 U.S. 259 (1990). 50. *United States v. Alvarez-Machain,* 112 S. Ct. 2188 (15 June 1992).   51. *Ker v. Illinois,* 119 U.S. 436 (1886).   52. "Mexican Officers Reportedly Cross Border to Nab Fugitives," *San Francisco Chronicle,* 19 June 1992.   53. William Genego, "The New Adversary," *Brooklyn Law Review,* 54 (1988), 781.   54. Fred Zacharias, "A Critical Look at Rules Governing Grand Jury Subpoenas of Attorneys," *Minnesota Law Review,* 76 (April 1992), 917. 55. A federal Circuit Court has even held that a state ethics rule that requires prosecutors to get court approval before subpoenaing attorneys to snitch on their clients is unenforceable against federal prosecutors. *Baylson v. Penn.* S. Ct. Disciplinary Board, CA 3, No. 91-1425, 16 September 1992.   56. Caplin & Drysdale, *Chartered v. United States,* 109 S. Ct. 2646 (1989). 57. *United States v. Noriega,* 764 F. Supp. 1480 (SD Fla. 1991). See also, *United States v. Morris,* 451 F.2d 969 (8th Cir. 1971).   58. See *In re Grand Jury Investigation (Shroeder),* 842 F.2d 1223 (11th Cir. 1987).   59. *United States v. Zolin,* 109 S. Ct. 2619 (1989). 60. See Geoffrey C. Hazard, Jr. and W. William Hodes, *The Law of Lawyering: A Handbook on the Model Rules of Professional Conduct,* 2d ed. (Englewood, NJ: Prentice-Hall Law & Business, 1990), ¶1.6:306; Charles W. Wolfram, *Modern Legal Ethics* (St. Paul, MN: West Publishing Co., 1986), 309–10.   61. *United States v. Ofshe,* 817 F.2d 1508 (11th Cir. 1987). 62. *United States v. Marshank,* 777 F.Supp. 1507 (N.D. Calif. 1991).   63. *United States v. Morrison,* 449 U.S. 361 (1981).   64. *Weatherford v. Bursey,* 429 U.S. 545, 557 (1977). 65. Richard Fricher, "Doing Time," *American Bar Association Journal,* 76 (February 1990), 24. 66. 18 U.S.C. §1957.   67. 18 U.S.C. §1957 (c).   68. No attorney seems to have yet been charged under this statute, merely for receiving a tainted fee. In *United States v. Campbell,* 777 F.Supp. 1259 (W.D.N.C. 1991), however, the government prosecuted a real estate agent for helping to sell a house to one who later admitted he was a drug dealer. The court indicated that his flashy lifestyle and reputation as a drug dealer, while evidence of the defendant's knowledge or "wilful blindness" of the illegal source of the purchase price, were themselves insufficient to prove that she knew that the money was acquired from the sale of drugs. In the hypothetical attorney's case, however, there would be more than a "reputation" as a drug dealer; the client would stand formally accused as such. A mere indictment for a drug transaction has been held for many purposes to constitute "probable cause" to believe the accused is guilty.   69. As we noted in Chapter 6, defense lawyers, like police, prosecutors and judges, are sometimes

corrupted by drug money and engage in clearly criminal activities with their clients. It is because defense lawyers are occasionally guilty of such crimes that the threat of indictment remains a serious risk to all who practice, guilty and innocent alike. If all indictments turned out to be baseless, they would soon cease to exist.   70. H. Richard Uviller, "Presumed Guilty: The Court of Appeals Versus Scott Turow," *University of Pennsylvania Law Review,* 136 (1988), 1883–84.   71. Steven Wisotsky, "Crackdown: The Emerging 'Drug Exception' to the Bill of Rights," *Hastings Law Journal,* 38 (1987), 889.   72. Steven Duke, "Civil Procedure," *Brooklyn Law Review,* 45 (1979), 847–50. On various ways that appellate courts and others are trying to curtail appeals, see Marc Arkin, "Rethinking the Constitutional Right to a Criminal Appeal," *UCLA Law Review,* 39 (1992), 508–10.   73. Donna Haupt and John Neary, "Justice Revealed," *Life,* September 1987, 105.   74. The Act presumes that anyone *charged* with a serious drug crime is a flight risk and should be detained without bail in any amount. 18 U.S.C. §3142(e).   75. See Steven Duke, "Bail Reform for the Eighties: A Reply to Senator Kennedy," *Fordham Law Review,* 49 (October 1980), 47.   76. Steven Wisotsky, *Beyond the War on Drugs* (Buffalo, NY: Prometheus Books, 1990) 130–31. Steven Daig, "Judge Calls Agents' Tactics Outrageous," *Miami Herald,* 20 September 1984.   77. Wisotsky, 131.   78. Ibid., 137–38; Karen Payne, "Upset with Court Trends, Top-Rated Nimkoff to Quit," *Miami News,* 4 January 1986.   79. James W. Ely, *The Guardian of Every Other Right* (New York: Oxford University Press, 1992).   80. 21 U.S.C. §881(a). 81. Schneider and Flaherty, *Presumed Guilty,* 3.   82. 21 U.S.C. §881(h).   83. 21 U.S.C. §881(b)(4).   84. *Fuentes v. Shevin,* 407 U.S. 67 (1972).   85. *Bell v. Burson,* 402 U.S. 535 (1971).   86. *Goldberg v. Kelly,* 397 U.S. 254 (1970).   87. *Cleveland Board of Education v. Laudermill,* 470 U.S. 532 (1985).   88. *Calero-Toledo v. Pearson Yacht Leasing Company,* 416 U.S. 663 (1974).   89. *United States v. $37,780 in U.S. Currency,* 920 F.2d 159 (2d Cir. 1990).   90. *United States v. 141st Street Corporation by Hersh,* 911 F.2d 870 (2d Cir. 1990).   91. *United States v. RD1, Box 1, Thompsontown, Delaware Township, Juniata County, Pennsylvania,* 952 F.2d 53 (3d Cir. 1991).   92. See David B. Smith, *Prosecution and Defense of Forfeiture Cases* (New York: Matthew Bender, 1992), §4.02. 93. *United States v. Property At 4492 S. Livonia Road, Livonia, New York,* 889 F.2d 1258 (2d Cir. 1989).   94. *United States v. Tax Lot 1500 Township 38 South, Range 2 East, Section 127, Further Identified as 300 Cone Road, Ashland, Jackson County, Oregon,* 861 F.2d 232 (9th Cir. 1988); *United States v. One 107.9 Acre Parcel of Land Located in Warren Township, Bradford County, Pennsylvania,* 989 F.2d 396 (3d Cir. 1990).   95. *United States v. All Monies ($477,048.62) in account 90-3217-3,* 754 F.Supp. 1467 (D. Hawaii 1991).   96. *United States v. Rivera,* 884 F.2d 544 (11th Cir. 1989).   97. Dave Altimari, "Property Seized in Drug Arrests Boon to Suburbs," *New Haven Register,* 3 May 1992.   98. *United States v. 141st Street Corporation.*   99. One of the students, who sold a half ounce of marijuana and one-third ounce of hallucinogenic mushrooms to an undercover agent later received thirteen months in prison for having done so. See "Student Arrested in Virginia Raid Given Prison for Selling Drugs," *New York Times,* 5 June 1991. Each of the three seized fraternity houses was eventually returned to the owners on payment of undisclosed sums of money. See "U.S. Is Returning a Third Fraternity House," *New York Times,* 15 September 1991.   100. Schneider and Flaherty, *Presumed Guilty,* 9.   101. Seth Mydans, "Powerful Crimes of Drug War Arousing Concern for Rights," *New York Times,* 17 October 1989.   102. Lynne Touhy, "Tables May Turn Against Attorney," *Hartford Courant,* 22 March 1991; Dennis Horgan, "Let Innocent People Keep Assets; Toss Out Unjust Rules," *Hartford Courant,* 25 March 1992.   103. Stephanie Saul, "High Cost of Breaking the Law," *Newsday,* 12 April 1990, 4.   104. Schneider and Flaherty, 15.   105. *Calero-Toledo v. Pearson Yacht Leasing Company,* 416 U.S. 663 (1974).   106. Smith, *Prosecution and Defense,* §4.02, n. 10.   107. *United States v. 141st Street Corporation.*   108. Schneider and Flaherty, 18.   109. A similar point is made in George C. Pratt and William B. Peterson, "Civil Forfeiture in the Second Circuit," *St. John's Law Review,* 65 (1991), 667.   110. See Smith,

Prosecution and Defense, ¶4.02(d), arguing that such is the correct interpretation of the statute. **111.** *United States v. 60 Acres in Etoway County,* 930 F.2d 857 (11th Cir. 1991). **112.** *United States v. 92 Buena Vista Ave., Rumson,* 1993 U.S. LEXIS 1782 (24 February 1993). **113.** 21 U.S.C. §§853, 882 (drugs), 18 U.S.C. §§981, 982 (money laundering), 18 U.S.C. §1955 (gambling), 18 U.S.C. §§2253, 2254 (obscenity), 18 U.S.C. §981 (savings and loan offenses), 26 U.S.C. §7302 (tax offenses).   **114.** *In re Forfeiture of 1978 Ford Fiesta,* 436 S.2d 373 (Fla. App. 4 Dist. 1983).   **115.** George Judson, "Price of Prostitution: Your Car," *New York Times,* 4 December 1992.   **116.** 26 U.S.C. §7203. See N.C. Gen. Stat. sec. 20-28.2 (1992). **117.** 26 U.S.C. §7302.   **118.** *United States v. One Pontiac Coupe,* 298 F.2d 421 (7th Cir. 1962).   **119.** *Tumey v. Ohio,* 273 U.S. 510 (1927).   **120.** *Williamson v. United States,* 311 F.2d 441 (5th Cir. 1962).   **121.** Mark Curriden, "Making Crime Pay: What's the Cost of Using Paid Informers?" *American Bar Association Journal,* 77 (June 1991), 43. **122.** See Cynthia Cotts, "Year of the Rat," *Reason* (May 1992), 41.   **123.** Mark Curriden, "Snitches Score Big in Noriega Case. Defense May Assail 'Bought' Testimony," *Atlanta Constitution* 2 February 1992.   **124.** Mark Curriden, "Making Crime Pay," 44. **125.** *United States v. Cervantes-Pacheco,* 826 F.2d 310 (5th Cir. 1987).   **126.** *United States v. Gonzales,* 927 F.2d 139 (3d Cir. 1991).   **127.** John McQuiston, "Asset Seizure Is Questioned in Suffolk," *New York Times,* 2 October 1992.   **128.** "The Case of the Prosecutor's BMW," *New York Times,* 8 October 1992.   **129.** See Gideon Kanner, "Never Mind, 'Only' Property Rights Were Violated," *Wall Street Journal,* 25 August 1993; "D.A. Releases New Evidence on Fatal Drug Raid," *Los Angeles Times,* 1 April 1993. **130.** Celestine Bohler, "Citizens of Russia to Be Given Share of State's Wealth," *New York Times,* 1 October 1992.

Chapter 8   Autonomy Costs

1. Thomas Szasz, *Our Right to Drugs: The Case for a Free Market* (New York: Praeger, 1992), 96.   **2.** John Stuart Mill, *On Liberty* (London, UK: John W. Parker & Son, 1859), 22. **3.** Ibid., 158.   **4.** Ibid., 161.   **5.** *The 1992 Information Please Almanac* (New York: Houghton Mifflin, 1991), 818.   **6.** National Highway Traffic Safety Administration Fact Sheet, *Traffic Safety Issues.*   **7.** Yale Health Plan, *Preventive Medicine Newsletter,* 1 (September 1992), 3.   **8.** Gina Kolata, "The Burdens of Being Overweight: Mistreatment and Misconceptions," *New York Times,* 22 November 1992.   **9.** Ibid.   **10.** Elizabeth Rosenthal, "Commercial Diets Lack Proof of Their Long Term Success," *New York Times,* 24 November 1992.   **11.** Jane Brody, "For Most Trying to Lose Weight, Dieting Only Makes Things Worse," *New York Times,* 23 November 1992.   **12.** Kolata, "The Burdens of Being Overweight."   **13.** Based upon National Institute of Drug Abuse, *National Household Survey on Drug Abuse: Population Estimates 1990* (Rockville, MD: Department of Health and Human Services, Public Health Service, 1990), an estimated 27 million people used illicit drugs at least once during the previous year, yet only about 662,000 were estimated to have used cocaine once a week or more and only 704,000 were estimated to have used needles for drug delivery at least once during the previous year. This suggests that the numbers of seriously drug-dependent people in America are in the range of 1 million or less, about 4 percent of the users. For other data and estimates, see Peter Reuter, "Hawks Ascendant: The Punitive Trend of American Drug Policy," *Daedalus,* 121, no. 3 (Summer 1992), 30–31.   **14.** Jennifer N. Toth, "In the Quest for Thin, the Badly Misguided Have Resorted to Crack and Cocaine. Drugs are Increasingly Being Linked to Eating Disorders," *Los Angeles Times,* 31 July 1990, E1. **15.** Dixie Farley, "Eating disorders require medical attention; teen health includes related information on definitions," *Consumer* (Washington, D.C.: Government Printing Office, 1992); Kerry O'Neil, " 'The Famine Within' Probes Women's Pursuit of Thinness," *Christian Science Monitor,* 31 August 1992, Arts, 11.   **16.** Terence McKenna, *Food of the Gods* (New York: Bantam, 1992), 218–20.   **17.** *1992 Information Please,* 742.   **18.** John P. Robinson,

"I Love My TV," *American Demographics* (September 1990), 24.   19. John Kaplan, *The Hardest Drug: Heroin and Public Policy* (Chicago: The University of Chicago Press, 1983), 106–08; Robert Bartels, "Legislative Control of Mind-Altering Drugs," *University of Kansas Law Review,* 21, no. 3 (Spring 1973), 461.   20. National Highway Traffic Safety Administration Fact Sheet, *Traffic Safety Issues.*   21. Ibid.   22. James Q. Wilson, "Against the Legalization of Drugs," *Commentary* (February 1990), 26.   23. Perhaps the all-time record "runaholic" was Tina Marin Stone of Irvine, California, who ran 15,472 miles in 1983, an average of 42.39 miles per day. See Albert C. Gross, *Endurance: The Events, The Athletes, The Attitude* (New York: Dodd, Mead & Company, 1986), 3–4. On exercise "addiction," see Ibid. at 188–91. One authority estimates that there are 2.5 million exercise "addicts" in America. Richard Benyo, "The Perils of Exercise Addiction," *San Francisco Chronicle,* 21 January 1991. 24. See Patrick Carnes, *The Sexual Addiction* (Minneapolis: CompCare Pubs., 1983). 25. See Michel Marriott, "Fervid Debate on Gambling: Disease or Moral Weakness?" *New York Times,* 21 November 1992; "Problem Gambling Masks Severe Depression," *New York Times,* 8 December 1992; "The Addiction of the '90s: Compulsive Gambling Comes into Its Own in Recessionary Times," *Washington Post,* 30 November 1992.   26. See Stanton Peele with Archie Brodsky, *Love and Addiction* (Chicago: New American Library, Signet edition, 1976), 68–80.   27. See *Roe v. Wade,* 410 U.S. 113 (1973); *Eisenstadt v. Baird,* 405 U.S. 438 (1972); *Griswold v. Connecticut,* 381 U.S. 479 (1965).   28. See *Riggins v. Nevada,* 112 S. Ct. 1810 (1992); *Washington v. Harper,* 494 U.S. 210 (1990). On the right generally to refuse unwanted medical treatment, see *Cruzan v. Director, Missouri Department of Health,* 110 S.Ct. 2841 (1990). 29. In *Stanley v. Georgia,* 394 U.S. 557, 656–66 (1969), the Court held that a person has a constitutional right to possess and read obscenity in the privacy of the home. "Our whole constitutional heritage rebels at the thought of giving government the power to control men's minds." Ibid. at 565. The state has no power to "premise legislation on the desirability of controlling a person's private thoughts." Ibid., 566.   30. See Steven Wisotsky, "Exposing the War on Cocaine: The Futility and Destructiveness of Prohibition," *Wisconsin Law Review,* 1983, no. 6 (1983), 1425; Laurence Tribe, *American Constitutional Law,* 2d ed. (Mineola, NY: Foundation Press, 1988), 1326.   31. Some of the assumptions in the text are beginning to be questioned—and tested. It appears that teenagers are about as good as their parents in assessing risk. What adults do not understand well is the immense personal, emotional significance to the teenager of certain behavior, such as drug usage. See Daniel Goleman, "Teenagers Called Shrewd Judges of Risk," *New York Times,* 2 March 1993, C1.   32. Charles A. Reich, "The Individual Sector," *Yale Law Journal,* 100, no. 5 (March 1991), 1409.   33. See, for example, Aldous Huxley, *The Doors of Perception* and *Heaven and Hell* (New York: Harper & Row, Perennial Library, 1990).   34. Lester Grinspoon, "Marijuana Enhances the Lives of Some People," in Arnold Trebach and Kevin Zeese, eds., *Drug Prohibition and the Conscience of Nations* (Washington, D.C.: The Drug Policy Foundation, 1990), 157. 35. Ibid.   36. Rachel Ehrenfeld, *Narco-Terrorism* (New York: Basic Books, 1990), 173. 37. See, for example, Huxley, *Doors of Perception;* Aldous Huxley, "Exploring the Borderlands of the Mind," in Michael Horowitz and Cynthia Palmer, *Aldous Huxley: Moksha, Writings on Psychedelics and Visionary Experience (1931–1963)* (New York: Stonehill Publishing Co., 1977), 210–16.   38. Douglas N. Husak, *Drugs and Rights* (New York: Cambridge University Press, 1992).   39. Szasz, *Our Right to Drugs.* Another excellent, more balanced analysis is James B. Bakalar and Lester Grinspoon, *Drug Control in a Free Society* (New York: Cambridge University Press, 1984).   40. See Jane Weaver, "In Manhattan, 'Smart' Bars Within Bars," *New York Times,* 10 June 1992; Andrew Purvis, "Ultra Think Fast; Smart Drugs and Think Drinks Promise to Brighten Your Personality, Boost Your Brain and Jump Start Your Sex Drive, But Truly Smart Consumers Will Be Wary," *Time,* 8 June 1992; Patricia Bibby, "The Rise of 'Smart Drugs'—Cerebral Stimulation or Brainless Pursuit?" *Los Angeles Times,* 10 May 1992.   41. See Roger Weiss and Steven Mirin, "Substance Abuse as an Attempt at Self-Medication," *Psychiatric Medicine,* 3, no. 2, (1987), 357.   42. See Alan Watts, "Psychedelics and Religious Experience," *California Law Review,* 56 (1968) 75; Walter Houston Clark, "Religious Aspects of Psychedelic Drugs," *California Law Review,* 56 (1968), 86. See also Terence McKenna, *Food of the Gods.*   43. Thomas Szasz, *Ceremonial Chemistry* (Garden City, NY: Anchor Press, 1974).   44. Erwin Chemerinsky, "State Now Has Free Reign to Meddle," *Los Angeles Daily Journal,* 11 May 1990, 6.   45. 110 S. Ct. 1595 (1990). 46. Ibid., 1604.   47. Ibid., 1606.   48. Chemerinsky, 6.   49. See "When the Faithful Tempt the Serpent," *New York Times,* 11 September 1992; "Snake Bites Indiana Man," ibid.   50. Ehrenfeld, *Narco-Terrorism,* 154–62.   51. See Tribe, *American Constitutional Law,* 1326.   52. William J. Bennett, "Drug Policy and the Intellectuals," speech at Kennedy School of Government, Harvard University, 11 December 1989, reprinted in Trebach and Zeese, eds., *Drug Prohibition and the Conscience of Nations,* 14. See also Bennett, "A Response to Milton Friedman," *Wall Street Journal,* 19 September 1989.   53. Wisotsky, "Exposing the War on Cocaine," 1425.

Chapter 9   Social Costs

1. Ron Harris, "Blacks Feel Brunt of Drug War," *Los Angeles Times,* 22 April 1990. 2. National Institute on Drug Abuse, *National Household Survey on Drug Abuse: Population Estimates 1991* (Rockville, MD: Department of Health and Human Services, Public Health Service, 1991), 20–21.   3. Ibid., 32.   4. Ibid., 32–33.   5. "No. 105. Expectation of Life at Birth, 1960 to 1988, and Projections, 1990 to 2010," U.S. Bureau of the Census, *Statistical Abstract of the United States: 1990,* 111th ed. (Washington, D.C.: Department of Commerce, 1991), 73.   6. "No. 120. Acquired Immunodeficiency Syndrome (AIDS) Deaths, By Selected Characteristics: 1982 to 1989," Bureau of the Census, *Statistical Abstract: 1991,* 83.   7. "No. 110. Infant, Maternal, and Neonatal Mortality Rates, and Fetal Mortality Ratios, by Race: 1960 to 1988," Bureau of the Census, *Statistical Abstract: 1991,* 77. 8. "No. 123. Death Rates from Accidents and Violence: 1970 to 1988," Bureau of the Census, *Statistical Abstract: 1991,* 85.   9. "No. 196. Persons with Activity Limitation, by Selected Chronic Conditions: 1985," Bureau of the Census, *Statistical Abstract: 1991,* 121. 10. Howard Kurtz, "Conspiracy or Paranoia?—Some Think Drugs Are Allowed to Hurt Black Communities," *Seattle Times,* 7 January 1990.   11. Ibid.   12. Jason DeParle, "Talk of Government Being Out to Get Blacks Falls on More Attentive Ears," *New York Times,* 29 October 1990.   13. Ibid.   14. Ibid.   15. Ibid.   16. Ibid.   17. Stephen Carter, *Reflections of an Affirmative Action Baby* (New York: Basic Books, 1991), 215–25. 18. William Raspberry, "Black Creativity, Black Solutions," *Washington Post,* 10 March 1990; William Raspberry, "Putting the Family First," *Washington Post,* 25 September 1991. 19. Clarence Page, "Talk of 'the Plan' is a Paranoid View of Black Problems," *Chicago Tribune,* 24 January 1990.   20. Harlon Dalton, "AIDS in Blackface," *Daedalus,* 118 (Summer 1989), 217.   21. Michael Z. Letwin, "Report from the Front Line: The Bennett Plan, Street-Level Drug Enforcement in New York City and the Legalization Debate," *Hofstra Law Review* 18 (Spring 1990), 795.   22. Ibid. at 805–07. See also Michele Sviridoff, Susan Sadd, Richard Curtis and Randolf Grinc, *The Neighborhood Effects of Street Level Drug Enforcement-Tactical Narcotics Teams in New York* (New York: Vera Institute of Justice, August 1992). 23. DeParle, "Talk of Government."   24. Loren Siegel, "A War on Drugs or on People?" *Civil Liberties,* Fall/Winter 1989, 1.   25. Bruce Schreiner, "Pro-marijuana Candidates Begin Cropping Up," *Los Angeles Times,* 29 July 1991.   26. "The State Legislature: Voter's Guide Section, Bronx Voter's Guide 90," *Newsday,* 4 November 1990, 17. 27. *Report of 21st Century Commission on African American Males, to Senate Banking, Housing and Urban Affairs Committee, 19 March 1991,* cited in Nicole Weisensee, "Youth," *States News Service,* 19 March 1991. Committee chairs: Virginia governor Douglas Wilder and North Carolina senator Terry Sanford. Honorary Board Member: Pennsylvania senator Arlen Specter. 28. See Michael Z. Letwin, "Wrong Way to Fight Crime," *New York Times,* 6 October 1990.

29. Harris, "Blacks Feel Brunt of Drug War."   30. Thomas Moore, Ted Gest, Gordon Witkin, Jeffrey C. Sheler, Peter Carey, Stephen J. Hedges, Joseph Shapiro, Scott Minerbrook, Pamela Ellis-Simmons, Patrick Barry, "Dead Zones," *U.S. News & World Report*, 10 April 1989, 20.   31. Tracey Wood and Sheryl Stolberg, "Patrol Car Log in Beating Released," *Los Angeles Times*, 19 March 1991. See also Claire Spiegel, "PCP's Effects: Separating Myth from Reality," *Los Angeles Times*, 17 June 1991.   32. Wayne LaFave and Austin Scott, Jr., *Criminal Law*, 2d ed. (Minneapolis: West Publishing Company, 2d ed. 1986) 423–24.   33. Philippe Bourgeois, "Just Another Night on Crack Street," *New York Times Magazine*, 12 November 1989, 53.   34. William Glaberson, "One in 4 Young Black Men Are in Custody, Study Says," *New York Times*, 4 October 1990.   35. Bill MacAllister, "Study: 1 in 4 Young Black Men Is in Jail or Court Supervised; Author Warns of Risk of Losing 'Entire Generation,'" *Washington Post*, 27 February 1990.   36. Jason DeParle, "42% of Young Black Males Go Through Capital's Courts," *New York Times*, 18 April 1992.   37. "Double Standard in Justice," *USA Today*, 4 September 1992.   38. DeParle, "42% of Young Black Males."   39. DeWayne Wickham, "Drug War Is a Failure; Let's Call a Truce Now," *USA Today*, 8 September 1992.   40. Department of Justice, *Sourcebook of Criminal Justice Statistics—1990* (Washington, D.C.: Government Printing Office, 1990), 424.   41. Aaron Epstein, "Stiff Sentences for First-Time Drug Offenders Decried," *The Orange County Register*, 11 May 1991.   42. Ibid.   43. 21 United States Code §848.   44. CNN Transcripts, No. 93-4, 17 June 1992. The Supreme Court of the United States held, in *Harmelin v. Michigan*, 111 S.Ct. 2680 (1991), that mandatory life without possibility of parole for mere possession of cocaine did not violate the United States Constitution. The Michigan Supreme Court, however, held that it did violate the state constitution and therefore invalidated the "no parole" feature of the life sentence for mere possession. *People v. Bullock*, 440 Mich. 15, 485 N.W.2d 866 (1992). Whether the no parole feature can stand in cases of sales of cocaine, or possession of much larger amounts or other variables, is uncertain. See "Sentencing—Cocaine Delivery," *Michigan Lawyers Weekly*, 11 January 1993.   45. John Powell and Eileen Hershenov, "Hostage to the Drug War: the National Purse, the Constitution and the Black Community," *U.C. Davis Law Review*, 24, no. 3 (Spring 1991), 569–70.   46. Carter, *Reflections of an Affirmative Action Baby*, 218–19.   47. Ibid., 213–25.   48. See also Clarence Lusanne, *Pipe Dream Blues: Racism and the War on Drugs* (Boston: South End Press, 1991).   49. Dewayne Wickham, "Drug War Field Commander Suffering Shell Shock," *Gannett News Service*, 10 September 1990.   50. National Drug Policy Network, *Newsbriefs*, 1, no. 2 (15 February 1990), 3.   51. Evan Thomas, "Crack Down: Reagan Declares a War on Drugs and Proposes Tests for Key Officials," *Time*, 18 August 1986.   52. Naomi Freunlich, ed., "Drug Tests That Require Neither Needle Nor Cup," *Business Week*, 23 October 1989.   53. See Jonathan Alter with Eleanor Clift, "Pot and Politics: After Ginsburg Admits Using Marijuana His Supreme Court Nomination Goes Up in Smoke," *Newsweek*, 16 November 1987, 46.   54. "Our Manifold Sins and Wickedness," *Economist*, 21 April 1990; New York Times News Service, "Richards Survives Brawl, Is Nominated for Texas Governor," *San Diego Union*, 11 April 1990.   55. John J. Goldman, "Attacks Mark N.Y. GOP Mayoral Primary: Giuliani Trades Blows as Campaign Winding Down," *Los Angeles Times*, 8 September 1989.   56. Garry Trudeau, "Doonesbury," *Los Angeles Times*, intermittently 11 November 1991 to 13 December 1991. Although the charges that Quayle had used cocaine and marijuana were never substantiated, there was a cover-up nonetheless. See Mark Singer, "The Prisoner and the Politician," *The New Yorker*, 5 October 1992, 108.   57. "Drug-Tough School Suspends Students for Sharing Tylenol," *New York Times*, 1 March 1992, 16.   58. See Jonathan Marshall, "Keep the Troops in the Barracks," in Arnold S. Trebach and Kevin B. Zeese, eds., *Drug Prohibition and the Conscience of Nations* (Washington, D.C.: The Drug Policy Foundation, 1990), 187; Vincent Bugliosi, *Drugs in America: The Case for Victory* (New York: Knightsbridge, 1991), 49–123.   59. David Malpas, "All Things Considered," National Public Radio, 10 April 1990.   60. "Glamour: Survey Says Majority

of Women Anti-Drug," *PR Newswire,* 9 February 1987.   61. Times Wire Services, "Drug Czar Urges Pupils to Turn in Parents, Says It's Not 'Snitching,' " *Los Angeles Times,* 18 May 1989.   62. Joseph Pereira, "The Informants, In a Drug Program, Some Kids Turn in Their Own Parents," *Wall Street Journal,* 20 April 1992.   63. Ibid.   64. "The Gallup Organization–Newsweek Poll," *Newsweek,* 16 November 1987, 52.   65. Jonathan Alter with Eleanor Clift, "Pot & Politics: After Ginsburg Admits Using Marijuana His Supreme Court Nominations Goes Up in Smoke," *Newsweek,* 16 November 1987, 46.   66. Anna Quindlen, "Just Say Yes," *New York Times,* 1 April 1992.   67. Jefferson Morley, "Crossfire in the Drug War: Aftermath of a Crack Article," *Nation,* 20 November 1989, 592.   68. Lester Grinspoon, "Marijuana Enhances the Lives of Some People," in Arnold S. Trebach and Kevin B. Zeese, eds., *Drug Prohibition and the Conscience of Nations* (Washington, D.C.: The Drug Policy Foundation, 1990), 157.   69. Jonathan Shedler and Jack Block, "Adolescent Drug Use and Psychological Health," *American Psychologist,* 45, no. 5 (1990), 612.   70. John Diaz, "Furor Over Report on Teenage Drug Use, Researchers Said Those Who Experimented Were Healthier Than Those Who Didn't," *San Francisco Chronicle,* 14 May 1990.   71. *Pride Quarterly* (Atlanta), Summer 1990, 1, 8. See generally, Lester Grinspoon, M.D., and James B. Bakalar, *Marihuana: The Forbidden Medicine* (New Haven: Yale University Press, 1993), ix–xiii.   72. Grinspoon, 159.   73. Joseph Berger, "Chancellor Finds Support Eroding on School Board, Memoir Angers Members," *New York Times,* 8 December 1992.   74. Fernandez was later fired, by a 4/3 decision of the school board, despite the strong support of New York City's mayor. Ironically, among the reasons for the firing was Fernandez's insistence on condom distribution and AIDS education in the high schools. Sam Dillon, "Board Removes Fernandez as New York Schools Chief After Stormy 3-Year Term," *New York Times,* 11 February 1993. The *Times,* which had also ardently supported Fernandez, called for a firing of the school board. Ibid., A30.   75. Jonathan Rabinovitz, "Former Addict to Head Drug Abuse Office," *New York Times,* 27 December 1992.   76. 18 U.S.C. §1001.   77. See comments of Georgetown University law professor Samuel Dash, as reported by Associated Press, "War on Drugs Held Burdening Justice," *New York Times,* 5 December 1988.   78. See comments of California chief justice Lucas, as reported by Philip Hager, "Drug-Related Cases Clog Courts, Lucas Warns," *Los Angeles Times,* 18 September 1989.   79. See comments of Chief Justice of the United States Supreme Court William Rehnquist, as reported by David Savage, "Federal Drug Cases More Than Triple in Last 10 Years," *Los Angeles Times,* 1 January 1990.   80. See Michael Tackett, "Drug War Chokes Federal Courts, Assembly-Line Justice Perils Legal System," *Chicago Tribune,* 14 October 1990.   81. Edna McConnell Clark Foundation, *Americans Behind Bars* (March 1992), 14.   82. Interview, Statistics Division, Administrative Office of United States Courts, July 14, 1993.   83. Chief Justice of the United States Supreme Court, *1989 Year-end Report on the Federal Judiciary* (1 January 1990), 9.   84. Scott Pelley, "Crack Trials," "CBS Evening News with Dan Rather," aired 9 December 1991.   85. Ibid.   86. Ibid.   87. Philip Hager, "Drug-Related Cases Clog Courts, Lucas Warns," *Los Angeles Times,* 18 September 1989.   88. Ibid.   89. Ibid, and interview, Statistics Research Office, Los Angeles Municipal Court, July 14, 1993.   90. Ibid.   91. "Bar Group Sees Overemphasis on Drug Cases," *New York Times,* 14 February 1993.   92. Lawrence Greenfield, *Prisoners in 1989* (Washington, D.C.: Department of Justice, Bureau of Justice Statistics, 1990); Allen Beck, *Profile of Jail Inmates, 1989* (Washington, D.C.: Department of Justice, Bureau of Justice Statistics, 1991).   93. Mar Mauer, *Americans Behind Bars: A Comparison of International Rates of Incarceration,* The Sentencing Project (1991).   94. George M. Camp and Camille Graham-Camp, *1989 Corrections Yearbook* (South Salem, NY: Criminal Justice Institute, 1989).   95. American Correctional Association, Directory—Juvenile and Adult Correctional Departments, Institutions, Agencies and Paroling Authorities of the United States and Canada (College Park, MD: American Correctional Association, 1990).   96. Bureau of Justice Statistics, *Bureau of Justice Statistics Bulletin, Census of Local Jails 1988* (Washington, D.C.: Department of Justice,

February 1990).   97. Source for prison-population data: Patrick Lagan et al., *Historical Statistics on Prisoners in State and Federal Institutions, Year End 1925–1986* (Washington, D.C.: Department of Justice, Bureau of Justice Statistics, 1988). Source for average-daily-jail-population data: Margaret Werner Cahalan with assistance of Lee Anne Parsons, *Historical Corrections Statistics in the United States, 1850–1984* (Washington, D.C.: Department of Justice, Bureau of Justice Statistics, 1986).   98. See Greenfeld, *Prisoners in 1989;* Beck, *Profile of Jail Inmates, 1989.* See also Tom Wicker, "Czar Vs. Intellectuals," *New York Times,* 26 December 1989.   99. Edna McConnell Clark Foundation, *Americans Behind Bars* (1993). 100. Ibid.   101. Caroline Wolf Harlow, "Drugs and Jail Inmates, 1989," *Bureau of Justice Statistics Special Report* (Washington, DC: Department of Justice, Office of Justice Programs, Bureau of Justice Statistics, 1991).   102. Source for cumulative state and federal prison data: Greenfeld, *Prisoners in 1989.* Separate federal-prison data are available: In 1989 there were 54,864 inmates in federal prisons, of whom 17,336 were drug offenders. Thus, 31.6 percent of the inmates of federal prisons were serving time for drug crimes. Source for federal-prison data: Office of Research, Federal Bureau of Prisons, telephone interview, 27 June 1990. 103. Peter Reuter, "Hawks Ascendant: The Punitive Trend of American Drug Policy," *Daedalus,* 121 (Summer 1992), 24.   104. Ibid.   105. Ibid., 25.   106. Ibid. 107. Alan Abrahamson, "Irving Heard Flurry of Sentence Appeals as He Left Bench," *Los Angeles Times,* 7 January 1991.   108. Douglas N. Husak, *Drugs and Rights* (New York: Cambridge University Press, 1992), 58.   109. Joseph B. Treaster, "2 Federal Judges, in Protest, Refuse to Accept Drug Cases," *New York Times,* 17 April 1992, 1.   110. See M. Fellner, "Judges Debate Drug Decriminalization," *Los Angeles Daily Journal,* 23 February 1990.   111. *Americans Behind Bars.*   112. Telephone interview of Charla Jefferson, Undergraduate Admissions Office, Harvard University, 3 February 1993.   113. "Five Correctional Systems Seek One Billion Dollars," *The Correction Compendium,* December 1988, 11.   114. "Criminal Justice Needs Reform," *ACLYou in Action,* November 1988, 4. 115. Ibid.   116. Wicker, "Czar vs. Intellectuals."

Chapter 10   Health and Safety Costs

1. Kurt L. Schmoke, "Back to the Future," *Humanist,* 50 (September/October 1990), 28. 2. National Institute on Drug Abuse, Division of Epidemiology and Prevention Research, "Annual Medical Examiner Data—1990," from *The Drug Abuse Warning Network,* Series 1, no. 10-B (Rockville, MD: Department of Health and Human Services, 1991), 17.   3. Ibid., 26. 4. See *State of Florida v. Jenks,* 582 S.2d 676 (1991); J. P. Morgan and L. Zimmer, "U.S. Needs a Dose of Compassion; We Should Loosen the Rules for Medical Use of Marijuana," *Newsday,* 28 August 1991, 103; L. Grinspoon and J. Bakalar, "Medical Users of Pot Are Drug War Victims," *San Francisco Chronicle,* 6 October 1990.   5. *State of Florida v. Jenks,* 582 S.2d 676 (1991).   6. Ibid.   7. Robert C. Randall, ed., *Marijuana, Medicine and the Law,* Vol. 1 (Washington, D.C.: Galen Press, 1988), 278–80.   8. 21 U.S.C. §801, et seq. 9. Morley Safer, "Smoking to Live," CBS "60 Minutes," 1 December 1991.   10. Ibid. 11. Ibid., 269.   12. "Affidavit of Robert C. Randall," *Alliance for Cannabis Therapeutics et al. v. Drug Enforcement Administration,* 930 F.2d 936 (1991), reproduced in Randall, *Marijuana, Medicine and the Law,* Vol. 1, 40.   13. Ibid., 39.   14. Ibid.   15. Department of Justice, Drug Enforcement Administration, "Marijuana Rescheduling," in Randall, Vol. 2, 445.   16. "DEA Rejects Petition to Allow Doctors to Prescribe Marijuana," *Los Angeles Times,* 30 December 1989. See also 54 Federal Register 537 67.   17. Department of Justice, Drug Enforcement Administration, "In the Matter of Marijuana Rescheduling Petition: Opinion and Recommended Ruling, Findings of Fact, Conclusion of Law and Decision of Administrative Law Judge," reproduced in Randall, Vol. 2, 439.   18. National Institute on Drug Abuse, Division of Epidemiology and Prevention Research, "Annual Medical Examiner Data—1990," from *DAWN,* 1, 10-B, 17.   19. Department of Justice, Drug

Enforcement Administration, "Marijuana Rescheduling," in Randall, Vol. 2, 440.
20. Ibid., 339.   **21.** See Stephen E. Sallan, Norman E. Zinberg, Emil Frei, III, "Antiemetic Effect of Delta-9-Tetrahydrocannabinol in Patients Receiving Cancer Chemotherapy," *New England Journal of Medicine*, 293, no. 16 (16 October 1975), 785–97; AMA Council on Scientific Affairs, "Marijuana: Its Health Hazards and Therapeutic Potentials," *Journal of the American Medical Association*, 246, no. 16 (16 October 1981), 1823–1827; Roger A. Roffman, *Marijuana as Medicine* (Seattle: Madrona Publishers, 1982); Randall, Vols. 1 and 2.   **22.** Sallan, Zinberg, Frei, "Antiemetic Effect," 795–96.   **23.** A. E. Chang, D. J. Shiling, R. C. Stillman, N. H. Goldberg, C. A. Seipp, I. Barofsky, R. M. Simon, S. A. Rosenberg, "Delta-9-Tetrahydrocannabinol as an Antiemetic in Cancer Patients Receiving High-dose Methotrexate: A Prospective, Randomized Evaluation," *Annals of Internal Medicine*, 91, no. 6 (December 1979), 819–24.   **24.** See "Affidavits" from *Alliance for Cannabis Therapeutics et al. v. Drug Enforcement Administration*, reproduced in Randall, Vol. 1.   **25.** John Laszlo, "Tetrahydrocannabinol: From Pot to Prescription?" *Annals of Internal Medicine*, 91, no. 6 (December 1979), 916–18.   **26.** Dan Rather, Bernard Goldberg, Victoria Corderi, Gary Reaves, Doug Tunnell, "Home Grown High," "48 Hours," CBS News, 12 October 1989.   **27.** Richard Doblin and Mark A. R. Kleiman, "Marijuana as Antiemetic Medicine: A Survey of Oncologists' Experiences and Attitudes," *Journal of Clinical Oncology*, 9 (July 1991), 1314–19; see also "Medical Marijuana: Cross-eyed and Painless," *Economist*, 6 July 1991, 89.   **28.** Physician's Desk Reference (Oradell, NJ: Medical Economics Company), 1925–26.   **29.** "Medical Marijuana," *Economist*, 89.   **30.** Doblin and Kleiman, "Marijuana as Antiemetic," 1316.   **31.** Vincent Vinciguerra, T. Moore, E. Brennan, "Inhalation Marijuana as an Antiemetic for Cancer Chemotherapy," *New York State Journal of Medicine*, 86 (October 1988), 525–27.   **32.** Robert S. Hepler and Ira R. Frank, "Marijuana and Intraocular Pressure," *Journal of the American Medical Association*, 217, no. 10 (September 1971), 1392; Robert S. Hepler, Ira R. Frank, R. Petrus, "Ocular Effects of Marijuana Smoking," in Monique Braude and Stephen Szara, eds., *Pharmacology of Marihuana* (New York: Raven Press, 1976), 815–24; "Affidavits of Robert S. Hepler, M.D.," *Alliance for Cannabis Therapeutics et al. v. Drug Enforcement Administration*, reproduced in Randall, ed., *Marijuana, Medicine and the Law*, Vol. 1, 355–57.   **33.** "Affidavit of Robert C. Randall," ibid., 27–51.   **34.** *United States v. Randall*, 104 Daily Wash. L. Rep. 2249 (Super. Ct. D.C. 1976).   **35.** "Glaucoma Victim Gets Marijuana Use Rights," *Washington Post*, 19 May 1978.   **36.** "Affidavit of Robert C. Randall," in Randall, Vol. 1, 27–51.   **37.** Ibid.   **38.** Ibid.   **39.** "Affidavit of Robert S. Hepler, M.D.," in Randall, Vol. 1, 356; see also American Academy of Ophthalmology, "Information Statement: The Use of Marijuana in the Treatment of Glaucoma," Hepler Exhibit no. 2, in Randall, Vol. 1, 359.   **40.** See Lester Grinspoon, *Marijuana Reconsidered* (Cambridge, MA: Harvard University Press, 1971); T. H. Mikuriya, "Historical Aspects of Cannabis Sativa in Western Medicine," *New Physician* 18 (1969), 902; Solomon Snyder, *Uses of Marihuana* (New York: Oxford University Press, 1971); "Affidavit of Lester Grinspoon, M.D.," in Randall, Vol. 1, 421; Roffman, *Marijuana as Medicine*, 114–16.   **41.** Hobart Amory Hare, assisted by Walter Chrystie, *A System of Practical Therapeutics* (Philadelphia: Lee Brothers and Company, 1891–1897); Hobart Amory Hare, "Clinical and Physiological Notes on the Action of Cannabis Indica," *The Therapeutic Gazette*, 11 (1887), 225–28, cited in Roffman, *Marijuana as Medicine*, 114–15.   **42.** See W.W., "Toxic Effects of Cannabis Indica" (Letter to the Editor), *Lancet*, 1 (15 March 1890); J. R. Reynolds, "Therapeutical Uses and Toxic Effects of Cannabis Indica," *Lancet*, 1 (22 March 1890), 637–38, cited in Roffman, 115–16.   **43.** "Affidavit of Lester Grinspoon, M.D.," in Randall, Vol. 1, 421.   **44.** Ibid.   **45.** R. Noyes, S. F. Brunk, D. Baram, A. Canter, "Analgesic Effect of Delta-9-Tetrahydrocannabinol," *Journal of Clinical Pharmacology*, 15 (February/March, 1975), 139.   **46.** R. Noyes and D. Baram, "Cannabis Analgesia," *Comprehensive Psychiatry*, 15 (November/December 1974), 531–35, cited in Roffman, 114; S. L. Milstein, K. MacCannell, G. Karr, S. Clark, "Marihuana-Produced Changes in Pain Tolerance: Experienced and Nonexperienced Subjects,"

International Pharmacopsychiatry 10 (1975), 177–82; and R. Noyes, S. F. Brunk, D.A. Baram, A. Canter, "Analgesic Effect of Delta-9-Tetrahydrocannabinol," *Journal of Clinical Pharmacology* 15 (1975), 134–43; cited in Roffman, 119.   47. Department of Justice, Drug Enforcement Administration, "Marijuana Rescheduling," in Randall, Vol. 2, 431. 48. Harry Greenbar, J. E. Pugh, D. J. Anderson, S. A. S. Werness, R. O. Andres, E. F. Domino, "Marijuana and Its Effect on Postural Stability in Spastic Multiple Sclerosis Patients and Controls, (531p)," *Neurology,* 40, no. 4 (Supplement 1) (April 1990), 259.   49. Carl Ellenberger, Jr., and Denis J. Petro, "Treatment of Human Spasticity with Delta-9-Tetrahydrocannabinol," *Journal of Clinical Pharmacology,* 21, no. 5 (Supplement) (August/September 1981), 415S-416S.   50. David B. Clifford, "Tetrahydrocannabinol for Tremors in Multiple Sclerosis," *Annals of Neurology,* 13, no. 6 (June 1983), 669–71.   51. "Affidavit of Denis Petro, M.D.," *Alliance for Cannabis Therapeutics et al. v. Drug Enforcement Administration,* reproduced in Randall, Vol. 1, 464.   52. Ellenberger and Petro, "Treatment of Human Spasticity," 415S-416S.   53. "Affidavit of Denis Petro, M.D.," in Randall, Vol. 1, 464. 54. E. A. Carlini and J. M. Cunha, "Hypnotic and Antiepileptic Effects of Cannabadiol," *Journal of Clinical Pharmacology,* 21 (1981), 424S, cited in Roffman, *Marijuana as Medicine,* 108. 55. R. Karler and S. A. Turkanis, "The Cannabinoids as Potential Antiepileptics," *Journal of Clinical Pharmacology,* 21 (1981), 426S, cited in Roffman, *Marijuana as Medicine,* 109. 56. See Roffman, 109–28.   57. Ibid., 109.   58. Ibid., 126. There is substantial evidence that marijuana may even be of unique benefit in the relief of depression and other mood disorders. See Lester Grinspoon, M.D., and James B. Bakalar, *Marijuana, The Forbidden Medicine* (New Haven: Yale University Press, 1993), 115–26.   59. Sidney Cohen, Foreword, in Roffman, *Marijuana as Medicine,* x.   60. J. P. Morgan and L. Zimmer, "U.S. Needs a Dose of Compassion: We Should Loosen the Rules for Medical Use of Marijuana," *Newsday,* 28 August 1991, 91.   61. Ibid.   62. Paul Cotton, "Government Extinguishes Marijuana Access, Advocates Smell Politics," *Journal of the American Medical Association,* 267 (May 20, 1992), 2573–74.   63. Ibid.   64. Melzack, "Needless Pain," 27. 65. Ibid.   66. *Harrison Act of 1914,* ch. 1, 38 Stat. 785 (amended 1918).   67. *United States v. Jin Fuey Moy,* 241 U.S. 394 (1916).   68. *United States v. Doremus* 249 U.S. 86 (1919); *Webb et al. v. United States,* 249 U.S. 96 (1919).   69. Melzack, "Needless Pain," 25.   70. Matt Clark with Karen Springen, Mary Hager, Lisa Drew and Jeanne Gordon, "Cancer Hurts Before It Kills, Doctors Can Ease the Suffering with Drugs," *Newsweek,* 19 December 1988, 58.   71. Melzack, "Needless Pain," 25.   72. Arnold S. Trebach, *The Heroin Solution* (New Haven: Yale University Press, 1982), 59–84.   73. Barry Siegel, "Reaching for the Dying: How Far Should Nurses Go to Help Those in Pain, Even If They May Hasten Death? A Montana Hospice Case Ignites a Debate About the Risks of Compassion," *Los Angeles Times,* 23 June 1991.   74. "ABC Nightline," 5 January 1990. 75. Gayle Shirley, "Hospice Six," *Chicago Tribune,* 28 July 1991.   76. Richard Schlesinger, "Aids Needle Exchange," "CBS Evening News with Dan Rather," 5 January 1990. 77. Ibid.   78. Nicholas D. Kristof, "Hong Kong Program: Addicts Without Aids," *New York Times,* 17 June 1987.   79. S. H. Rowley and P. Weingarten, "Mexico an 'Open Door' for Cocaine," *Chicago Tribune,* 11 September 1989.   80. Michael Isikoff, "DEA Find Herbicides in Marijuana Samples," *Washington Post,* 26 July 1989.   81. See "The Nation," *Los Angeles Times,* 26 July 1989; Isikoff, "DEA Finds Herbicides."   82. See Gordon Witkin with Maudi Mukenge, Monika Guttman, Anne M. Arrarte, Kukula Glastris, Barbara Burgower, Aimee L. Stern, "The Men Who Created Crack," *U.S. News & World Report,* 19 August 1991, 44–53.   83. James Ostrowski, "The Moral and Practical Case for Drug Legalization," *Hofstra Law Review,* 18, no. 3 (Spring 1990), 695.   84. Ibid., 696.   85. Ibid. 86. Dean Gerstein, *Alcohol Use and Consequences,* in Mark Moore and Dean Gerstein, eds., *Alcohol and Public Policy: Beyond the Shadow of Prohibition* (Washington, D.C.: National Academy Press, 1981).   87. Virginia Ellis, "Lungren Wants Users Targeted in War on Drugs," *Los Angeles Times,* 28 November 1989.   88. See Steve Crane and Janet Naylor,

"Schaefer's State Speech: Filled with Warm Praise, a Hot Potato," *Washington Times,* 12 January, 1990, B1; "Drug User Laws Overstep Justice," *Christian Science Monitor,* 24 January, 1990, 18.   89. Testimony of Daryl Gates, Chief of Los Angeles Police Department, on "National Drug Strategy," to United States Senate Judiciary Committee, 5 September 1990. 90. See Arnold S. Trebach, *The Great Drug War* (New York: Macmillan, 1987); Diane R. Gordon, "Drug Wars Over There: Europe's Kinder, Gentler Approach," *Nation,* 252, no. 4, 4 February 1991, 128–36; Steven Jonas, "Solving the Drug Problem: A Public Health Approach to the Reduction of the Use and Abuse of Both Legal and Illegal Recreational Drugs," *Hofstra Law Review,* 18, no. 3 (Spring 1990), 751.   91. See Ministry of Welfare, Health, and Cultural Affairs, Rijswijk, the Netherlands, *Policy on Drug Users* (1985); and Govert van de Wijnhaart, "Heroin Use in the Netherlands," *American Journal of Drug and Alcohol Abuse,* 14, no. 1 (1988), 125.   92. Rone Tempest, "Bold Experiment: Drugs: Dutch Gain with a Tolerant Tack," *Los Angeles Times,* 22 September 1989.   93. United States Embassy, The Hague, "Annual Narcotics Status Report," 26 May 1989; see also Tempest, "Bold Experiment." 94. Kurt L. Schmoke, "Back to the Future," 28.

Chapter 11   The Drug War Cannot Succeed

1. Mathea Falco, *The Making of a Drug-Free America: Programs That Work* (New York: Times Books, 1992), 9.   2. White House Fact Sheets on President's Commitment to National Crusade Against Drugs, 16 September 1986; Gerald Boyd, "Reagan Signs Anti-Drug Measure; Hopes for 'Drug-Free' Generation," *New York Times,* 28 October 1986, B19.   3. The White House, *National Drug Control Strategy: A Nation Responds to Drug Use, January 1992* (Washington, D.C.: Government Printing Office, 1992), 167–69.   4. Ibid., 99–111. 5. Ibid., 113–27.   6. Ibid., 79–97.   7. National Narcotics Intelligence Consumers Committee, *The NNICC Report 1990: The Supply of Illicit Drugs to the United States* (Washington, D.C.: NNICC, June 1991).   8. Janine DeFao, "Andean Anti-Drug Plan Called a Failure," *Los Angeles Times,* 24 October 1991.   9. Perwe Andreas, Eva Bertram, Morris Blackman, Kenneth Sharpe, "Dead End Drug Wars," *Foreign Policy,* 85, no. 2 (Winter 1991– 1992), 113.   10. David Morrison, "Police Action," *National Journal,* 24, no. 5 (1 February 1992), 267.   11. Kenneth Freed, "Anti-Drug Effort Sows Bad Blood," *Los Angeles Times,* 15 October 1989.   12. Scott Pelley, "Cocaine," "CBS Evening News with Dan Rather," 23 November 1989.   13. Joseph Treaster, "Bush Sees Progress, But U.S. Report Sees Surge in Drug Production," *New York Times,* 1 March 1992.   14. Paul Richter and Ronald J. Ostrow, "Drug War Looks Like a Long One: As Cocaine Use Declines, New Problems Cloud the Horizon—Increased Violence Among Traffickers and a Rising Tide of Heroin," *Los Angeles Times,* 5 August 1991.   15. See, for example, Drug Enforcement Administration, Cannabis Investigations Section, *1989 Domestic Cannabis Eradication/Suppression Program* (Washington, D.C.: Department of Justice, 1989).   16. Treaster, "Bush Sees Progress."   17. John Kaplan, *The Hardest Drug: Heroin and Public Policy* (Chicago: The University of Chicago Press, 1983), 71.   18. Telephone interview of Duke Austin, public affairs officer, Immigration and Naturalization Service, 13 March 1992.   19. Ibid. In fiscal year 1990 there were 456 million legal entries into the United States. Another 889,000 people were denied entry to the country on such grounds as previous deportation.   20. Source: United States Border Patrol.   21. In fiscal year 1991, 57,163 commercial vessels, 85,076 private vessels and 4,516 military ships cleared United States Customs, direct from a foreign port. United States Customs Service, *U.S. Customs Update, 1991* (Washington, D.C.: Public Services Staff of the Office of Public Affairs, 1992).   22. Ibid. In fiscal year 1991, 112,305 private, 340,951 commercial and 36,679 military aircraft cleared United States Customs direct from foreign airports.   23. NNICC, *The NNICC Report, 1990,* 16.   24. Ibid., 15. 25. Peter Reuter, "Can the Borders Be Sealed?" *Public Interest,* 92 (Summer 1988), 53. 26. Vincent Del Giudice, "Federal Agents Raid Cross-border Drug Tunnel," *United Press*

International, 19 May 1990; Douglas Jehl, "$1-Million Drug Tunnel Found at Mexican Border: Narcotics: The Passageway Ends at a Warehouse in Arizona. It Was Used to Bring Cocaine into the U.S.," *Los Angeles Times,* 19 May 1990.　　27. Ibid.　　28. Elaine Washington, "New Kings of Coke," *Time,* 1 July 1991, 28.　　29. United Press International, "Cocaine Found in Fiberglass Doghouses," *Los Angeles Times,* 27 October 1992, B8.　　30. Richter and Ostrow, "Drug War Looks Like a Long One."　　31. *United States v. Contento-Pachon,* 723 F.2d 691 (9th Cir. 1984), in which the drug courier was allegedly recruited in Bogotá, Colombia, under the duress of threats to his family.　　32. NNICC, *The NNICC Report, 1990,* 2 and 15.　　33. Ibid., 15.　　34. Ibid.　　35. Ibid., 17.　　36. Reuter, "Can the Borders Be Sealed?" 55.　　37. Ibid.　　38. Ibid., 53–54.　　39. 18 U.S.-C.A. § 1961 et seq.　　40. The White House, *National Drug Control Strategy, January 1992,* 93–96.　　41. Vincent Bugliosi, *Drugs in America: The Case for Victory: A Citizen's Call to Action* (New York: Knightsbridge, 1991), 146.　　42. Ibid., 148.　　43. Michael Gordon, "U.S. Troops Move in Panama in Effort to Seize Noriega; Gunfire Is Heard in Capital," *New York Times,* 20 December 1989; "Transcript of Bush's Address on the Decision to Use Force in Panama," *New York Times,* 21 December 1989.　　44. Lindsey Gruson, "G.I.'s in Panama Report Gains in Restoring Order," *New York Times,* 24 December 1989.　　45. Paul Lewis, "U.S. Finding Scant Support for Action in Panama," *New York Times,* 22 December 1989; "American Nations Assail U.S. Action: Washington Sole Dissenter in 20-1 Vote Deploring Strike," *New York Times,* 23 December 1989.　　46. Neil Lewis, "U.S. to Start Noriega Case with Miami Indictment," *New York Times,* 17 January 1990. Majority Staff Report, *The Noriega Prosecution: What Price the General?* Subcommittee on Crime and Criminal Justice, House Judiciary Committee, April 1992.　　47. United States General Accounting Office, Report to the Chairman, Select Committee on Narcotics Abuse and Control, House of Representatives, *The War on Drugs: Narcotics Control Efforts in Panama* (July 1991), 1. See also Mark Uhlig, "Panama Drug Smugglers Prosper as Dictator's Exit Opens the Doors," *New York Times,* 21 August 1990.　　48. Robert Green, "Report Says Panama Still a Haven for Drug Money," Reuters release, 22 July 1991.　　49. "Eight Hanged for Drug Smuggling in Iran," Agence France Presse, 23 May 1991.　　50. "China Condemns 58 in One Day for Drugs," *Reuters Library Report,* 27 June 1992.　　51. David Henderson, "A Humane Economist's Case for Drug Legalization," *U.C. Davis Law Review,* 24, no. 3 (Spring 1991), 655.　　52. The White House, *National Drug Control Strategy, January 1992,* 118–19.　　53. New York Times Service, "Threats Are Nothing New for Colombia's Judiciary," *San Diego Union,* 27 August 1989.　　54. Elaine Shannon, "New Kings of Coke," *Time,* 1 July 1991, 29.　　55. James Brooke, "Cali, The 'Quiet' Drug Cartel, Profits by Accommodation," *New York Times,* 14 July 1991.　　56. United States Customs Service, *Annual Report for Fiscal Year 1980, Customs U.S.A.,* 33 (1980); United States Customs Service, *U.S. Customs Update 1991.* For an earlier study of these trends, see Steven Wisotsky, "Exposing the War on Cocaine: The Futility and Destructiveness of Prohibition," *Wisconsin Law Review,* no. 5 (1983), 1310–25.　　57. NIDA's Household Survey estimated that 1,640,000 people used cocaine in the past month during 1977, while 5,750,000 people used it in the past month during 1985. 1977 *Survey,* 31; 1985 *Survey,* 14.　　58. Richard Berke, "Bagging Noriega Is Not the Same as Winning the Drug War," *New York Times,* 7 January 1990.　　59. The White House, *National Drug Control Strategy, January 1992,* 26.　　60. Ibid.　　61. For a persuasive exploration of this theme, see Michael Massing, "Don't Just Throw Money at the Drug Problem," *Christian Science Monitor,* 6 November 1989.　　62. NNICC, The NNICC Report, 1990, 3; Jim Yardley, "Pot Harvest Hits a High Point Outlaw Crop." *Atlanta Constitution,* 1 November 1992.　　63. Henderson, "Humane Economist's Case," 659.　　64. Ibid., 658.　　65. See studies cited in A. Morgan Cloud, III, "Cocaine, Demand, and Addiction: A Study of the Possible Convergence of Rational Theory and National Policy," *Vanderbilt Law Review,* Vol. 42, no. 3 (April 1989) 725, 752–53, and in Jerome H. Skolnick, "Rethinking the Drug Problem," in "Political Pharmacology: Thinking About Drugs," *Daedalus* (Summer 1992) 133, 136.

66. M. A. Lerner, "The Fire of 'Ice,'" *Newsweek,* 27 November 1989, 37–38.   67. Joseph B. Treaster, "Smuggling and Use of Illegal Drugs Are Growing, U.N. Study Finds," *New York Times,* 13 January 1992, A11.   68. Peter Archer, "Crack Epidemic Fears Fade," Press Association Limited Newsfield, 28 July 1991.   69. Kaplan, *Hardest Drug,* 71–72. 70. Ibid., 72.   71. Malcolm Browne, "Problems Loom in Effort to Control Use of Chemicals for Illicit Drugs," *New York Times,* 24 October 1989.   72. See Ronald Clarke, "Eve Replaces Ecstasy as the Latest 'Designer Drug' Hit," Reuters North European Service, Los Angeles, 3 December 1985; Scott Armstrong, " 'Designer' Drugs Threaten to Open a New Era in Drug Abuse," *Christian Science Monitor,* 19 June 1985, 1.   73. Letter from H. Wayne Carver, M.D., to Steven Duke, 25 February 1992.   74. NIDA, *National Household Survey on Drug Abuse: Population Estimates 1991,* 31.   75. Shari Roan, "Cheap Thrill Can Become a Deadly High: Drugs: More and More Kids Are Inhaling the Vapors of Everything from Butane in Cigarette Lighters to Nail Polish Remover. The Use of Inhalants—the Kids Call it 'Huffing'—Worries Some Drug Abuse Experts," *Los Angeles Times,* 27 April 1993, E1.   76. Ibid.   77. In 1991 it was reported that the 3M Company had identified more than twenty teenagers who had died in the previous two years from sniffing Scotchgard. Eric Zorn, "Household Helper Can Be a Killer," *Chicago Tribune,* 18 April 1991, C1.   78. ABC News, "20/20," 21 May 1993.   79. Ethan Nadelmann, "The Case for Legalization," *Public Interest,* 92 (Summer 1988), 10.   80. Michael Massing, "Don't Just Throw Money at the Drug Problem."   81. Ibid.   82. Nadelmann, "Case for Legalization," 10.   83. "Many in Colombia Resisting Use of a Strong Herbicide on Poppies," *New York Times,* 17 January 1992.   84. Ronald Siegel, *Intoxication: Life in Pursuit of Artificial Paradise* (New York: E. P. Dutton, 1989), 283.   85. Vansun, "More Buzz for Your Buck," *Vancouver Sun,* 11 January 1992, A8; Katherine Bishop, "New Front in Marijuana War: Business Records," *New York Times,* 24 May 1991, B6; Jack Anderson, "Pot Growers Go High-Tech, Out of Sight," *Newsday,* 5 December 1988, 54.   86. The White House, *National Drug Control Strategy, February 1991* (Washington, D.C.: Government Printing Office), 102.   87. The White House, *National Drug Control Strategy: January 1992,* 33–55.   88. Ibid., 57–76.   89. The White House, *National Drug Control Strategy, January 1992,* 115.   90. National Institute on Drug Abuse, *National Household Survey on Drug Abuse: Population Estimates 1991* (Rockville, MD: Department of Health and Human Services, Public Health Service, 1991), 79.   91. Kaplan, *Hardest Drug,* 198. 92. NIDA, *National Household Survey,* 20.   93. Bureau of Justice Statistics, *Sourcebook of Criminal Justice Statistics 1991* (Washington, D.C.: Government Printing Office, 1992), 444. 94. The White House, *National Drug Control Strategy, January 1992,* 36.   95. Ibid. 96. Ibid., 38.   97. Ibid., 44–47.   98. Ibid., 48–52.   99. Ibid., 126. 100. Ibid., 153–54.   101. Ibid., 58.   102. Ibid.   103. The White House, *National Drug Control Strategy, February 1991,* 45.   104. Ibid., 46.   105. Kaplan, *Hardest Drug,* 197.   106. Peter Arnett, Associated Press, "Major Describes Move," *New York Times,* 8 February 1968.

Chapter 12   The Legalization Option

1. Gwen Ifill, "Clinton Resists Being Labeled Liberal," *New York Times,* 28 July 1992. 2. Gore Vidal, *Homage to Daniel Shays: Collected Essays, 1952–1972* (New York: Random House, 1972), 375.   3. Richard Schlesinger, "CBS Evening News with Dan Rather," 29 March 1990.   4. Ibid.   5. Ralph F. Salerno, "The Anger of a Retired Chief Detective," in Arnold S. Trebach and Kevin B. Zeese, eds., *Drug Prohibition and the Conscience of Nations* (Washington, D.C.: The Drug Police Foundation, 1990), 208, 209.   6. Ibid. 7. Jose deCordoba, "Carriage Trade, Big City Drug Dealers Draw Lots of Business from Suburban Buyers," *Wall Street Journal,* 19 November 1992.   8. United States Bureau of Justice Statistics, "Fact Sheet: Drug Data Summary," in *Drugs & Crime Data Center & Clearing-*

house (Washington, D.C.: Department of Justice, Office of Justice Programs, Bureau of Justice Statistics, November 1991), 1.   **9.** Ibid.   **10.** Statement of Richard L. Fogel, Assistant Comptroller General for General Government Programs, "Profitability of Customs Forfeiture Program Can Be Enhanced," *United States General Accounting Office Testimony,* 10 October 1989, 5, 9. Also see Robert A. Rosenblatt, "Seized Property Costs U.S., Panel Told," *Los Angeles Times,* 11 October 1989.   **11.** Fogel, "Profitability of Customs Forfeiture Program," 15.   **12.** Ibid., 18.   **13.** Rosenblatt, "Seized Property Costs U.S."   **14.** Fogel, 14.   **15.** Ibid., 9.   **16.** See Herbert Packer, *The Limits of the Criminal Sanction,* (Stanford: Stanford University Press, 1968).   **17.** See Tamara Lytle, "Feds Blast City's Needle Exchange," *New Haven Register,* 10 July 1992.   **18.** Peter Passell, "Economic Scene: Less Marijuana, More Alcohol?" *New York Times,* 17 June 1992; John DiNardo and Thomas Lemieux, "Alcohol, Marijuana, and American Youth: The Unintended Consequences of Government Regulation" (Working Draft for RAND's Drug Policy Research Center, March 1992).   **19.** Edward Brecher and the editors of *Consumer Reports, Licit and Illicit Drugs* (Boston: Little, Brown, and Company, 1972), 85–89; Mark Kleiman, *Against Excess: Drug Policy for Results* (New York: Basic Books, 1992) 260.   **20.** For more on drug switching, see James Ostrowski, "Thinking About Drug Legalization," in David Boaz, *The Crises in Drug Prohibition* (Washington, D.C.: Cato Institute, 1990), 45, 63–64.   **21.** See Guido Calabresi, "Views and Overviews," *University of Illinois Law Forum,* 1967, 606.   **22.** *The Harmfulness Tax: A Proposal for Regulation and Taxation of Drugs: Hearings on Legalization of Drugs Before the Select Committee on Narcotics Abuse and Control,* 100th Congress, 1st Session (1988) (statement of Lester Grinspoon, M.D.).   **23.** California Health & Safety Code § 424.10 (Deering 1991). See also further implementing legislation at California Health & Safety Code §24164 (Deering 1991).   **24.** Bureau of International Narcotics Matters, *International Narcotics Control Strategy Report, March 1991* (Washington, D.C.: Department of State, 1991), 156.   **25.** Rone Tempest, "Bold Experiment: Drugs: Dutch Gain with a Tolerant Tack." *Los Angeles Times,* 22 September 1989.   **26.** Ibid.   **27.** "Policy on Drug Users," (Rijswijk, the Netherlands: Ministry of Welfare, Health, and Cultural Affairs, 1985).   **28.** In Alaska, a court decision, *Ravin v. State,* 537 P.2d 494 (1975), allowed possession for individual use. In 1991, after fifteen years of lobbying by federal government drug warriors, Alaska voters, by a narrow margin, recriminalized the use of marijuana.   **29.** Lloyd D. Johnston, Jerald G. Bachman, Patrick M. O'Malley, "Marijuana Decriminalization: The Impact on Youth 1975–1980" (Ann Arbor: Monitoring the Future, Occasional Paper 13, 1981). See also Mark Kleiman, *Marijuana: Costs of Abuse, Costs of Control* (New York: Greenwood Press, 1989), 176; Eric W. Single, "Impact of Marijuana Decriminalization: An Update," *Journal of Public Health Policy,* 10, no. 4 (Winter 1989).   **30.** Richard Dennis, "The American People Are Starting to Question the Drug War," in Arnold Trebach and Kevin Zeese, eds., *Drug Prohibition and the Conscience of Nations* (Washington, D.C.: Drug Policy Foundation, 1990), 217, 218.   **31.** Joseph Treaster, "Hospital Visits by Drug Users Rise Sharply," *New York Times,* 9 July 1992.   **32.** United States Surgeon General, *Reducing the Health Consequences of Smoking: 25 Years of Progress, A Report of the Surgeon General* (Rockville, MD: Department of Health and Human Services, 1989), 536–39.   **33.** Even thoughtful analysts who oppose legalization agree on this point. See John Kaplan, *The Hardest Drug: Heroin and Public Policy* (The University of Chicago Press, 1983); Mark Kleiman, *Against Excess: Drug Policy for Results* (New York: Basic Books, 1992), 260, 362.   **34.** See Brecher et al., *Licit and Illicit Drugs,* 111–14; Linda W. Wong and Bruce K. Alexander, "Cocaine Related Deaths. Who Are the Victims? What Is the Cause?" in Arnold Trebach and Kevin Zeese, eds., *Drug Policy 1989–1990: A Reformers Catalogue* (Washington, D.C.: The Drug Policy Foundation, 1989), 177.   **35.** Stephen Labaton, "Federal Judge Urges Legalization of Crack, Heroin, and Other Drugs," *New York Times,* 13 December 1989.   **36.** "Opium of the People: The Federal Drugstore," *National Review,* 5 February 1990, 34.   **37.** See A. M. Rosenthal, "On My

Mind, Captive Neighborhood," *New York Times*, 10 July 1992. **38**. Gina Kolata, "Bias Seen Against Pregnant Addicts," *New York Times*, 20 July 1990. **39**. Jean Seligman with Lucy Howard, "Easing the Pot Laws," *Newsweek*, 28 March 1977, 76.

Chapter 13   Forms of Legalization

1. ABC News, "The Koppel Report: A National Town Meeting on the Legalization of Drugs," 13 September 1988, Transcript, 6.   **2**. Ibid., 15.   **3**. See Charles B. Rangel, "Arguments Against Legalization," *Drug Abuse Update*, September 1988.   **4**. See for example: Drug Enforcement Administration, *A Position Against Legalization of Illicit Drugs* (Washington, D.C.: Department of Justice, June 1990).   **5**. James B. Jacobs, "Imagining Drug Legalization," *Public Interest*, 101 (Fall 1990), 28.   **6**. See Kurt L. Schmoke, "An Argument in Favor of Legalization," *Hofstra Law Review*, 18, no. 3 (Spring 1990), 523–25.   **7**. "America After Prohibition," *Reason*, October 1988, 22–29.   **8**. "A Symposium on Drug Decriminalization," *Hofstra Law Review*, 18, no. 3 (Spring 1990).   **9**. "Symposium on Legalization of Drugs," *U.C. Davis Law Review*, 24, no. 3 (Spring 1991).   **10**. Introduced, as New York State Senate Bill S-1918, 6 February 1989. Reintroduced, as New York State Senate Bill 4094-A, 21 March 1991.   **11**. Jacobs, "Imagining Drug Legalization," 29.   **12**. "America After Prohibition," 22–29.   **13**. Milton Friedman, "Prohibition and Drugs," *Newsweek*, 1 May 1972, 104.   **14**. See for example Uncle Fester, *Secrets of Methamphetamine Manufacture*, 2d ed. (Port Townsend, WA: Loompanics Unlimited, 1989 and 1991); Michael V. Smith, *Psychedelic Chemistry* (Port Townsend, WA: Loompanics Unlimited, 1981).   **15**. Michael S. Gazzaniga, "Opium of the People," *National Review*, 5 February 1990, 34.   **16**. Roger Cohen, "Amid Growing Crime, Zurich Closes a Park It Reserved for Drug Addicts, *New York Times*, 11 February 1991.   **17**. Michele L. Norris, "D.C. The Most Lax on Issue, Study Says: Washington Called One of the Few Places Where Youths Can Legally Buy Alcohol," *Washington Post*, 3 March 1993, A14; Don Phillips, "Board Urges Curfew for Teen Drivers; National Crackdown on Youth Drinking Sought to Cut Deaths," *Washington Post*, 3 March 1993, A1.   **18**. "Minnesota Is Talking . . ." *Newsweek*, 6 November 1989, 7; Associated Press, "Town Delivers Health Kick to Cigarette Vending Machines," *Los Angeles Times*, 12 October 1989.   **19**. Myron Levin, "Fighting Laws on Smoking with Proxies: Retailing: Tobacco Companies Quietly Fund the Battle Against Restrictions, Opponents Say," *Los Angeles Times*, 5 August 1991.   **20**. "The Nation," *USA Today*, 1 April 1992.   **21**. Kevin Duchschere, "Chanhassen Orders Cigarettes Be Sold from Behind Counter," *Star Tribune*, 17 October 1991.   **22**. See Joseph R. DiFranza, John W. Richards, Jr., Paul M. Paulman, Nancy Wolf-Gillespie, Christopher Fletcher, Robert D. Jaffe, David Murray, "RJR Nabisco's Cartoon Camel Promotes Cigarettes to Children," *Journal of the American Medical Association*, 266 (11 December 1991), 3149–53; citing John P. Pierce, Michael C. Fiore, Thomas E. Novotny et al., "Trends in Cigarette Smoking in the United States—Projections to the Year 2000," *JAMA*, 261, no. 1 (6 January 1989), 61–65.   **23**. DiFranza, Richards, Jr., Paulman et al., "RJR Nabisco's Cartoon Camel," 3149–53.   **24**. Ibid., 3151.   **25**. Ibid., 3149–53; Geoffrey Cowley, "I'd Toddle a Mile for a Camel: New Studies Suggest Cigarette Ads Target Children," *Newsweek*, 23 December 1991, 70.   **26**. Paul M. Fisher, Myer P. Schwartz, John W. Richards, Jr., Adam O. Goldstein, Tina H. Rojas, "Brand Logo Recognition by Children Aged 3 to 6 Years; Mickey Mouse and Old Joe the Camel," *Journal of the American Medical Association*, 266 (11 December 1991), 3145–48; DiFranza, Richards, Jr., Paulman et al., "RJR Nabisco's Cartoon Camel," 3149–53; and John P. Pierce, Elizabeth Gilpin, David M. Burns, Elizabeth Whalen, Bradley Rosbrook, Donald Shopland, Michael Johnson, "Does Tobacco Advertising Target Young People to Start Smoking?: Evidence from California," *JAMA*, 266 (11 December 1991), 3154–58. See also Henry Waxman, "Tobacco Marketing; Profiteering from Children," *JAMA*, 266 (11 December 1991), 3185–86.

27. Fisher et al., "Brand Logo Recognition," 3145–48.   28. Daniel K. Benjamin and Roger Leroy Miller, *Undoing Drugs: Beyond Legalization* (New York: Basic Books, 1991). 29. Whitman Knapp, "Dethrone the Drug Czar," *New York Times*, 9 May 1993, E15. 30. See Jonathan Karl, "Lotto Baloney: The Great State Lottery Swindle," *New Republic*, 4 March 1991, 13.   31. Introduced, as New York State Senate Bill S-1918, 6 February 1989. Reintroduced, as New York State Senate Bill 4094-A, 21 March 1991.   32. They may, of course, be liable for fraudulent advertising. See *Cipollone v. Liggett Group, Inc.*, 60 U.S.L.W. 4703 (24 June 1992).   33. Milton Friedman, in *Reason*, October 1988.   34. "Media Advertising for Tobacco Products," *Board of Trustees Report, Journal of the American Medical Association*, 255 (28 February 1986), 1033.   35. See Peter Grier, "Coalition Asks FTC to Prohibit Liquor Ads Aimed at Young People," *Christian Science Monitor*, 23 November 1983. 36. *Valentine v. Chrestensen*, 316 U.S. 52 (1942).   37. *Posadas de Puerto Rico Associates v. Tourism Company*, 478 U.S. 328 52 (1986).   38. Ibid., 346.   39. Ibid. 40. 425 U.S. 748 (1976).   41. *Bates v. State Bar of Arizona*, 429 U.S. 813 (1976). 42. *Linmark Associates, Inc. v. Willingboro*, 431 U.S. 85 (1977).   43. Cynthia Cotts, "Condoning the Legal Stuff: Hard Sell in the Drug War," *Nation*, 9 March 1992, 300. 44. See *Capital Broadcasting Co. v. Mitchell*, 333 F. Supp. 582 (D.C. 1971), affd. sub nom. *Capital Broadcasting Co. v. Acting Attorney General Kleindienst*, 405 U.S. 1000 (1972).   45. PR Newswire Association, "U.S. Small Business Administration Named as Member of Federal Drug-Fighting Team," *PR Newswire*, 29 January 1992.   46. The United States Chamber of Commerce claims that drugs cost American business $160 billion per year (Eric Reguly, "Drug Abuse Still a Problem for U.S. Firms," *Financial Post*, 25 October 1991). A University of California San Francisco study, commissioned by National Institute on Drug Abuse, estimates that in 1988 drug and alcohol abuse cost the United States economy a total of $144.1 billion, including medical expenses and other costs in addition to business-productivity losses. (Dorothy P. Rice, Sander Kelman, Leonard S. Miller, Sarah Dunmeyer, *The Economic Costs of Alcohol and Drug Abuse and Mental Illness, 1985*. Report submitted to the Office of Financing and Coverage Policy of the Alcohol, Drug Abuse, and Mental Health Administration, Department of Health and Human Services (San Francisco: Institute for Health & Aging, University of California, 1990), 2.   47. Dale A. Masi, Testimony before the House Select Committee on Narcotics and Drug Control, 29 September, 1988.   48. See Ann Landers, "Debate Rages Over Legalizing Drugs," *Los Angeles Times*, 1 April 1990; Ann Landers, "Legalizing Drugs Called Dopey Idea," *Los Angeles Times*, 2 April 1990.   49. Ibid.   50. Telephone interview with Eric E. Sterling (6 April 1990).   51. See, for example, "Bring Drugs Within the Law," *Economist*, 15 May 1993, 13.   52. Ethan Nadelmann, "Drug Prohibition in the United States: Costs, Consequences, and Alternatives," *Science*, 1 September 1989, 939–47.   53. Steven Wisotsky, *Beyond the War on Drugs* (Buffalo: Prometheus Books, 1990).   54. Randy E. Barnett, "Curing the Drug-Law Addiction: The Harmful Side Effects of Legal Prohibition," in Ronald Hamowy, ed., *Dealing with Drugs* (Lexington, MA: Lexington Books, 1987).   55. Michael Isikoff, "Bennett Rebuts Drug Legalization Ideas: Harvard Speech Scorns Liberal Intellectuals for Betraying Poor," *Washington Post*, 12 December 1983.   56. Steven Wisotsky, *Prepared Statement Before the Select Committee on Narcotics Abuse and Control, House of Representatives, Concerning a New Beginning in U.S. Drug Policy*, 29 September 1989, 2.   57. Ibid., 3.   58. 21 United States Codes § 863(f)(1). 59. Arnold Trebach, "Accepting the Presence of Drugs," *New Perspectives Quarterly* (Summer 1989), 42.   60. Marshall Fritz, editorial, *Fresno Bee*, 25 September 1988.   61. Ibid. 62. Joyce Price, "Nobel Winner, 2 Judges Want Drugs Made Legal," *Washington Times*, 17 November 1991.   63. Ibid.   64. Peter J. Howe, "Meeting endorses legalized drug use; Advocates vary on means, extent," *Boston Globe*, 10 May 1992.   65. PR Newswire Association, "Marijuana Makes the News in Triplicate," *PR Newswire*, 4 March 1991. 66. Whitman Knapp, "Dethrone the Drug Czar," *New York Times*, 9 May 1993. 67. "Judge Besieged After Call for Legalized Drugs," *Los Angeles Times*, 10 April 1992. 68. Matt Lait, "Make Drugs Legal, U.S. Judge Urges," *LA Times*, 25 April 1992.

Chapter 14   A Harm Minimization Approach

1. Steven Jonas, "Solving the Drug Problem: A Public Health Approach to the Reduction of the Use and Abuse of Both Legal and Illegal Recreational Drugs," *Hofstra Law Review*, 18, no. 3, 751 (Spring 1990).   2. See Jerome H. Jaffe, "Drug Addiction and Drug Abuse," in *Goodman and Gilman's The Pharmacological Basis of Therapeutics*, 7th ed. (New York: Macmillan Publishing Company, 1985), 532: "As far back as recorded history, every society has used drugs that produce effects on mood, thought and feeling. . . . Both the nonmedical use of drugs and the problem of drug abuse are as old as civilization itself"; Ronald K. Siegel, *Intoxication: Life in the Pursuit of Artificial Paradise* (New York: E. P. Dutton, 1989), 1–56.   3. Hardly any marijuana users are serious drug abusers and about 10 percent of alcohol users and 5 to 20 percent of cocaine users are such. Perhaps 50 percent of heroin users fall into this category, but heroin users make up only about 5 percent of illegal-drug users, so that the total number of heroin abusers is a small fraction of the relevant universe.   4. See A. Lee Fritschler, *Smoking and Politics*, 3d ed. (Englewood Cliffs, NJ: Prentice-Hall, 1983); Alex M. Freedman and Laurie Cohen, "Smoke and Mirrors, How Cigarette Makers Keep Health Question 'Open' Year After Year," *Wall Street Journal*, 11 February 1993.   5. United States Surgeon General, *25 Years of Progress: Reducing the Health Consequences of Smoking, A Report of the Surgeon General* (Rockville, MD: Department of Health and Human Services, 1989), 269.   6. See Department of Health and Human Services, *Smoking and Health, A National Status Report*, 2d ed. (Rockville, MD: Department of Health and Human Services, Office of Smoking and Health, 1990).   7. See David Krogh, *Smoking: The Artificial Passion* (New York: W. H. Freeman & Co., 1991), 7, 65–69.   8. "Teens Underestimate Nicotine's Hold," *New Haven Register*, 3 December 1992.   9. See Abram Katz, "Chewing Tobacco Just as Bad as Smoking It," *New Haven Register*, 19 November 1992.   10. William B. Hansen, C. Anderson Johnson, Brian R. Flay, John W. Graham, Judith Sobel, "Affective and Social Influences Approaches to Prevention of Multiple Substance Abuse Among Seventh Grade Students: Results from Project SMART," *Preventive Medicine*, 17 (1988), 135.   11. Department of Health and Human Services, *Smoking and Health*, 2d ed., 35.   12. See Mathea Falco, *The Making of a Drug-Free America: Programs That Work* (New York: Times Books, 1992), 49.   13. PR Newswire Association, "Study Confirms That D.A.R.E. Program Significantly Impacts Our Nation's Youth," *PR Newswire*, 14 August 1990.   14. Falco, *Drug Free America*, 43.   15. Dennis P. Rosenbaum, Robert L. Flewelling, Susan Bailey, Donald Faggiani, Chris Ringwalt, *Third-Year Evaluation of D.A.R.E. in Illinois* (Chicago: Center for Research in Law and Justice, University of Illinois at Chicago, 1992).   16. The failure of research to support a claim that DARE, or any other educational program, works is not proof that the program has no preventive influences. Research into educational programs involving drugs is hampered by the fact that the control groups, with whom the program is compared, are themselves subjected to many of the same influences in their school drug programs, their churches, their families, television and newspapers. The same basic messages are conveyed to both control and test groups, through many sources. Thus, if no differences in drug use are observed, the most that is suggested is that the program being studied is no more effective than the unknown influences at work in control groups.   17. Mary A. Pentz, James H. Dwyer, David P. MacKinnon, Brian R. Flay, William B. Hansen, Eric Yu Wang, Anderson Johnson, "A Multicommunity Trial for Primary Prevention of Adolescent Drug Abuse: Effects on Drug Use Prevalence," *Journal of the American Medical Association*, 261, no. 22 (9 June 1989), 3259–66.   18. Falco, *Drug Free America*, 41. For a detailed survey of research findings regarding drug use prevention programs, see Gilbert J. Botvin, "Substance Abuse Prevention: Theory, Practice and Effectiveness," in Michael Tonry and James Q. Wilson eds., *Drugs and Crime* (Chicago: The University of Chicago Press, 1990), 461.   19. Joel M. Moskowitz, "The Primary Prevention of Alcohol Problems: A Critical Review of the Research Literature," *Journal of Studies on Alcohol*, 50, no. 1 (1989), 54.   20. NIDA, *National Household Survey on Drug Abuse: Population Estimates 1990*, 85.   21. Lloyd D. Johnson, Patrick M. O'Malley, Jerald G.

Bachman, *Drug Use Among American High School Seniors, College Students, and Young Adults, 1975–1990* (Rockville, MD: National Institute on Drug Abuse, 1991), 12.   22. For a summary of studies correlating drug abuse with other psychological, social, and biological factors, see Diana H. Fishbein, "Medicalizing the Drug War," in *Behavioral Sciences and the Law*, 9 (Summer 1991), 328–32. See also Jonathan Shedler and Jack Block, "Adolescent Drug Use and Psychological Health," *American Psychologist* (May 1990) 612.   23. See Robert S. Gable, "Risk Management Strategies for Abusable Substances," in Arnold S. Trebach and Kevin B. Zeese, eds., *Drug Policy 1989–1990, A Reformer's Catalogue* (Washington, D.C., The Drug Policy Foundation, 1990), 152–56.   24. For a critique of the present classification system, see Douglas N. Husak, *Drugs and Rights* (New York: Cambridge University Press, 1992), 27–37.   25. Smoking a single marijuana cigarette *may* cause as much or more *lung* damage than smoking a tobacco cigarette, but virtually no one smokes 10 percent as much marijuana as the average cigarette smoker smokes of tobacco, nor do more than a minuscule fraction of marijuana users smoke marijuana throughout most of their lives.   26. David Musto, "Opium, Cocaine and Marijuana in American History," *Scientific American*, 265 (1991), 40.   27. See generally on this subject, Norman E. Zinberg, "The Use and Misuse of Intoxicants: Factors in the Development of Controlled Use," in Ronald Hamowy, ed., *Dealing with Drugs* (Lexington, MA: Lexington Books, 1987), 247.   28. Eric Bailey, "The Few, The Proud, The Sober: The Day of the Two Fisted Leatherneck Carouser Is Fading as the Marine Corps Wages a Determined Assault on Its Lusty Tradition of Drinking to Excess," *Los Angeles Times*, 15 October 1989.   29. Ibid.   30. Commandant of the Marine Corps, Headquarters United States Marine Corps, *U.S. Marine Corps Crime Statistics Annual Report, 1991* (Washington, D.C.: Department of the Navy, 1991).   31. Dean Gerstein and Henrick Harwood, eds., *Treating Drug Problems* (Washington, D.C.: National Academy Press, 1990), 13.   32. There are between 300,000 and 800,000 heroin addicts in the United States (depending on, among other things, how one defines "addicts"). Fewer than 100,000 participate in methadone maintenance programs. See Department of Health and Human Services, *Highlights from the 1989 National Drug and Alcoholism Treatment United Survey* (Rockville, MD: Department of Health and Human Services, 1990).   33. Gerstein and Harwood, *Treating Drug Problems*, 15. Phoenix House, the nation's largest therapeutic community program, loses about a third of its clients within the first six weeks. Falco, *Drug-Free America*, 110.   34. Ibid.   35. M. Douglas Anglin and Yih-Ing Hser, "Criminal Justice and the Drug-Abusing Offender: Policy Issues of Coerced Treatment," *Behavioral Sciences and the Law*, 9 (Summer 1991), 243.   36. Ibid.   37. Richard Schottenfeld, "Involuntary Treatment of Substance Abuse Disorders: Impediments to Success," *Psychiatry*, 52 (1989), 164.   38. See Benjamin Kissin, "Theory and Practice in Treatment of Alcoholism," in Benjamin Kissin and Henry Begleiter, eds., *Treatment and Rehabilitation of the Chronic Alcoholic* (New York: Plenum Press); Gerstein and Harwood, *Treating Drug Problems*, 15.   39. Falco, *Drug-Free America*, 111.   40. Larry Gostin, "An Alternative Public Health Vision for a National Drug Strategy: 'Treatment Works,'" *Houston Law Review*, 28, no. 1 (1991), 300. The overall similarity in favorable outcomes among all treatment modalities also suggests that there is pretty good matching of the needs of particular clients with particular modalities, the most disturbed drug abusers ending up in treatment communities, the least needy in outpatient therapy and so forth. It is also clear, moreover, that there are substantial differences in the effectiveness of particular programs *within* modalities. See Gerstein and Harwood, *Treating Drug Problems*, 134, 147, 163–64, 169, 173.   41. Gostin, "Alternative Public Health Vision," 300; M. Douglas Anglin and Yih-Ing Hser, "Treatment of Drug Abuse," in Michael Tonry and James Q. Wilson, eds., *Drugs and Crime* (Chicago: The University of Chicago Press, 1990), 393, 395, 430–31.   42. Gostin, "Alternative Public Health Vision," 300, and works cited therein.   43. Ibid.   44. Ibid.   45. Ibid. 301–02.   46. Mark A. Kleiman, *Against Excess: Drug Policy for Results* (New York: Basic Books, 1992) 179; Bruce Johnson, "Once an Addict, Seldom an Addict," *Contemporary Drug Problems*, 7 (Spring 1978), 48–49.   47. Gerstein and Harwood, *Treat-*

ing Drug Problems, 152, 165–66, 170.   48. V. Tabbush, *The Effectiveness and Efficiency of Publicly Funded Drug Abuse Treatment and Prevention Programs in California: A Benefit Cost Analysis* (UCLA, March 1986).   49. Gostin, "Alternative Public Health Vision," 303.
50. Ronald Smothers, "Miami Tries Treatment, Not Jail, in Drug Cases," *New York Times,* 19 February 1993.   51. Secretary of Health and Human Services, *Seventh Special Report to the U.S. Congress on Alcohol and Health* (Rockville, MD: Department of Health and Human Services), 267.   52. See generally, Staff Report, *Pharmacotherapy: A Strategy for the 1990's* (Committee on the Judiciary, United States Senate, 1989).   53. Robert Senft, "Experience with Clonidine-Naltrexone for Rapid Detoxification," *Journal of Substance Abuse Treatment,* 8 (1991), 257.   54. Thomas R. Kosten, Charles Morgan, Herbert Kleber, "Treatment of Heroin Addicts Using Buprenorphine," *American Journal of Drug Abuse,* 17, no. 2 (1991), 119.   55. E. S. Nuwayser, D. J. DeRoo, P. D. Balskovich, A. G. Tsuk, "Sustained Release Injectable Naltrexone Capsules," National Institute of Drug Abuse, *Research Monograph 105,* 532.   56. Craving for a drug requires a sense of the drug's availability. The strength of a craving may also reflect the apparent ease of availability. Thus, if a heroin addict returns to the neighborhood where he used to buy drugs and encounters people selling drugs on the street corner, his craving is likely to be intense. If he is confined in an isolation cell in jail, however, his craving will quickly disappear or be suspended until the sensation of availability returns. See Meyer and Mirin, "A Psychology of Craving: Implications of Behavioral Research," in Joyce Lowenstein and Pedro Ruiz, eds., *Substance Abuse Clinical Problems and Perspectives* (Baltimore: Williams & Wilkins, 1981), 57–62.   57. Jonathan B. Kamien, Nancy K. Mello, Jack H. Mendelson, Scott E. Lukas, "Buprenorphine Suppresses Cocaine Self-Administration by Rhesus Monkeys Over 1 to 4 Months of Daily Treatment," National Institute of Drug Abuse, *Research Monograph 105,* 619.   58. Buprenorphine also protects against lethal effects of large doses of cocaine administered to mice, suggesting that it acts similarly to a cocaine agonist. It also has a low liability for producing buprenorphine dependence. J. M. Witkin, R. E. Johnson, J. A. Jaffe, S. R. Goldberg, N. A. Grayson, K. C. Rice, J. L. Katz, "The Partial Opiod Agonist buprenorphine protects against lethal effects of cocaine," *Drug and Alcohol Dependence,* 27 (1991), 177.   59. Warren Leary, "Scientists Find Enzyme That May Ease Cocaine's Addictive Effects," *New York Times,* 26 March 1993, A18.
60. Abram Katz, "Drug Offers Hope for Drinkers," *New Haven Register,* 11 November 1992; Roger Highfield, "Drug Stops 'Pleasure' of Drinking," *Daily Telegraph,* 11 July 1991.
61. Daniel Goleman, "Scientists Pinpoint Brain Irregularities in Drug Addicts," *New York Times,* 26 June 1990.   62. See Darrel A. Regier, Mary E. Farmer, Conald S. Rae, Ben Z. Locke, Samuel J. Keith, Lewis L. Judd, Frederick K. Goodwin, "Comorbidity of Mental Disorders with Alcohol and Other Drug Abuse Results from the Epidemiologic Catchment Area (ECA) Study," *Journal of the American Medical Association,* 264, no. 19 (21 November 1990), 2511–18.
63. Goleman, "Scientists Pinpoint Brain Irregularities in Drug Addicts." Other drugs such as desipramine and bromocriptine have also been helpful with cocaine-dependent persons who are depressed when off cocaine. Charles A. Dakis and Mark S. Gold, "Bromocriptine as a Treatment of Cocaine Abuse," *Lancet,* 1, no. 8438 (18 May 1985), 1151–52.   64. Ibid. See also Marguerite Holloway, "RX for Addiction: Include the Courting of the Pharmaceutical Industry, Trends in Pharmacology," *Scientific American,* 264, no. 36 (1991), 94.   65. Elizabeth Folberth, "A Last-Ditch Effort; Needles Are New Therapy for Addicts," *Newsday,* 7 October 1992, 27; Paul W. Valentine, "Baltimore Shifts Drug War to Human Front; Controversial Mayor Trying to Focus on Addiction as Health Issue," *Washington Post,* 8 May 1990.
66. See Andrew Weil, *The Natural Mind: A New Way of Looking at Drugs and Their Higher Consciousness* (Boston: Houghton Mifflin, 1972), 69–72; Kristi Nelson, "Program Helps Addicts Regain Control; Oak Cliff–Based Comeback House Planning to Expand Its Services," *Dallas Morning News,* 5 January 1993.   67. Herbert Spiegel and David Spiegel, *Trance and Treatment: Clinical Uses of Hypnosis* (New York: Basic Books, 1978), 211–19; Chris Henning, "Breaking an Addiction Through Hypnosis; World-Renowned Hypnotherapist Speaks on

Treating Addictive Disorders," *Michigan Lawyers Weekly*, 23 November 1992, 21.   **68.** See Barbara Brown, *New Mind, New Body: Bio-Feedback: New Directions for the Mind* (New York: Harper & Row, 1974), 425–29.   **69.** Marguerite Holloway, "RX for Addiction: Include the Courting of the Pharmaceutical Industry, Trends in Pharmacology," *Scientific American*, 264, no. 36, March 1991, 94.   **70.** Thomas H. Maugh, II, "Keys to Body's Pain Control System Found," *Los Angeles Times*, 18 December 1992, A3.   **71.** Spencer Ramsey, "Howard Lotsof insists he has the cure for drug addiction. Some authorities are beginning to take him seriously," *Newsday*, Nassau and Suffolk Edition, 19 November 1992, Part II, 68; *Addiction and Obsession*, 68. For a theory linking psychedelics to treatment for alcohol addiction, see Lester Grinspoon and James Bakalar, "Medical Uses of Illicit Drugs," in Ronald Hamowy, ed., *Dealing with Drugs* (Lexington, MA: Lexington Books, 1987) 183, 204–07. See also, Harry Nelson, "LSD Still on Some Minds; Scientists Believe the Drug Could Be a Valuable Tool in Probing Mysteries of Brain Chemistry," *Los Angeles Times*, 25 March 1991.   **72.** See Larry Gostin, "The Needle-Borne HIV Epidemic: Causes and Public Health Responses," in *Behavioral Sciences and the Law*, 9 (Spring 1991), 287, 291.   **73.** Stephanie Mencimer, "D.C.'s New Death Row," *Washington Post, Outlook*, 31 January 1993.   **74.** United States National Commission on AIDS, *The Twin Epidemics of Substance Abuse and HIV: Report* (Washington, D.C.: The Commission, 1991), 4.   **75.** Ibid., 6.   **76.** George Bush's drug czar, Bob Martinez, opposed the clean needle recommendations on the ground there is insufficient "scientific evidence that such programs reduce risk-taking behavior." Marlene Cimons, "Federal Aids Commission Attacks Bush Drug Policy," *Los Angeles Times*, 7 August 1991.   **77.** Henk Jan van Vliet, "The Uneasy Decriminalization: A Perspective on Dutch Drug Policy," *Hofstra Law Review*, 18, no. 3 (Spring 1990), 726.   **78.** Ibid., 728. See also John Shad, "The United States Ambassador Tells the Truth About Holland," in Arnold S. Trebach and Kevin B. Zeese, eds., *Drug Prohibition and the Conscience of Nations* (Washington, D.C., The Drug Policy Foundation, 1990), 46; Eddy L. Engelsman, "The Pragmatic Strategies of the Dutch 'Drug Czar,' " Ibid., 49; Arnold S. Trebach, "Their Spirit of Moderation and Experimentation Is Unmatched," Ibid., 55.   **79.** William E. Schmidt, "To Battle AIDS, Scots Offer Oral Drugs to Addicts," *New York Times*, 8 February 1993.   **80.** Ibid. **81.** Pat O'Hare, "Compassion and Success in Liverpool—The Mersey Harm Reduction Model Today," in Trebach and Zeese, *Drug Prohibition and the Conscience of Nations*, 141; Arnold Trebach, "When They Visit New York They Say They Want to Cry," Ibid., 146. **82.** Schmidt, "To Battle AIDS."   **83.** See Virginia Berridge, "AIDS and British Drug Policy: History Repeats Itself," in David K. Whynes and Philip T. Bean, eds., *Policing and Prescribing: The British System of Drug Control* (London, U.K.: Macmillan Academic and Professorial, Ltd., 1991), 176.   **84.** See *State of New Jersey v. Rode Sorge et al.*, 249 N.J. Super. 144; 591 A.2d 1382 (New Jersey Superior Court, 1991); Gostin, "The Needle-Borne HIV Epidemic: Causes and Public Health Responses."   **85.** National Public Radio, "New Haven Needle Exchange: Tracking Needles," *Morning Edition*, 24 June 1992; Dick Thompson, "Getting the Point in New Haven," *Time*, 25 May 1992. Preliminary reports on a needle exchange program in New York City are consistent: needle sharing is down and IV drug use is not increasing. Mireya Navarro, "New York Needle Exchange Called Surprisingly Effective," *New York Times*, 18 February 1993.   **86.** Ibid.   **87.** Amy Pyle, "Clean Needles Put into War on AIDS," *Los Angeles Times*, 9 September 1992. For similar findings elsewhere, see Gerald S. Cohen, "Anti-AIDS Lobbyists Urge Needle Swaps," *San Francisco Chronicle*, 7 November 1990.   **88.** Richard A. Rawson, "Cut the Crack: The Policymaker's Guide to Cocaine Treatment," *Policy Review* (Winter 1990), 10.   **89.** Elliott Currie, *Reckoning: Drugs, the Cities, and the American Future* (New York: Hill and Wang, 1993).

Name Index

SUBJECT INDEX